W9-DEU-042

"Tennis is not all about gentility—a fact amply illustrated on the following pages. Here, some of the giants of the mystery genre have brought their murderous intentions to center court.

"There's murder, of course, some of it not terribly genteel at all. You'll encounter blackmail, voodoo, insanity, and clever scams. You'll see that human behavior doesn't vary that much, whether it's on the pro tour, at the country club, or on a public court.

"Whether the action is centered on a top-ranked player, a hopeless pitty-pat struggler, or a ball boy, there are always secrets to keep and mysteries to unravel. And who better to create these mysteries (and solve them) than a gathering of some of the world's top-ranked crime writers?"

—Otto Penzler, from the Introduction

MURDER
IS
MY RACQUET

EDITED BY

OTTO PENZLER

NEW YORK   BOSTON

This book is a work of fiction. Certain real locations and public figures are mentioned to make the stories more vivid, but all other names, characters, places, and incidents are the product of the authors' imaginations or are used fictitiously.

Compilation copyright © 2005 by Otto Penzler • Introduction copyright © 2005 by Otto Penzler • "Terrible Tommy Terhune" copyright © 2005 by Lawrence Block • "Tennis, Anyone?" copyright © 2005 by Kinky Friedman • "Six Love" copyright © 2005 by James W. Hall • "Promise" copyright © 2005 by John Harvey • "A Debt to the Devil" copyright © 2005 by Jeremiah Healy • "Stephen Longacre's Greatest Match" copyright © 2005 by Stephen Hunter • "No Strings" copyright © 2005 by Judith Kelman • "A Killer Overhead" copyright © 2005 by Robert Leuci • "Needle Match" copyright © 2005 by Peter Lovesey • "The Rematch" copyright © 2005 by Mike Lupica • "Continental Grip" copyright © 2005 by David Morrell • "Close Shave" copyright © 2005 by Ridley Pearson • "Love Match" copyright © 2005 by Lisa Scottoline • "A Peach of a Shot" copyright © 2005 by Daniel Stashower

All rights reserved.

Mysterious Press
Warner Books

Time Warner Book Group
1271 Avenue of the Americas, New York, NY 10020
Visit our Web site at www.twbookmark.com.

The Mysterious Press name and logo are registered trademarks of Warner Books.

Printed in the United States of America
Published simultaneously in hardcover by Mysterious Press

FIRST TRADE EDITION JUNE 2005

10 9 8 7 6 5 4 3 2 1

The Library of Congress has cataloged the hardcover edition as follows:

Murder is my racquet / edited by Otto Penzler.
p. cm.
Contents: Terrible Tommy Terhune / Lawrence Block—Tennis, anyone? / Kinky Friedman—Six love / James W. Hall—Promise / John Harvey—A debt to the devil / Jeremiah Healy—Stephen Longacre's greatest match / Stephen Hunter—No strings / Judith Kelman—A killer overhead / Robert Leuci—Needle match / Peter Lovesey—The rematch / Mike Lupica—Continental grip / David Morrell—Close shave / Ridley Pearson—Love match / Lisa Scottoline—A peach of a shot / Daniel Stashower.
ISBN 0-89296-015-9
1. Detective and mystery stories, America. 2. Tennis players—Fiction. 3. Tennis stories.
I. Penzler, Otto.

PS648.D4M8594 2005
813'.087208357—dc22   2004058773

ISBN 978-0-446-69588-6

Cover design by Bradford Foltz

For Thomas H. Cook
A truly wonderful writer—
and an even better friend

Contents

INTRODUCTION

T ennis. Now there's a word that conjures the height of genteel sportsmanship. Fresh white clothes, lemonade, polite tapping of hands together, the occasional "well played" acknowledgment.

Look a little closer, however, and the nasty underside of tennis, with its many connections to crime and violence, readily rises to the surface. The very name itself, tennis, is probably derived from the French word "tenez," which means "take it." No niceties here of accept it, or earn it, or try for it. No, the flat out felonious "take it" is unambiguous in its directive. And the criminal and murderous connections do not end there. The implicit violence of terms like "overhead smash" and "killer serve" are far removed from the gentle lawn game of softer imaginations.

The violence of the game is not limited to its terminology. Players are coached to rebuff a charge to the net by smashing the ball directly at the opponent, resulting in more than one black-and-blue mark, if not worse.

And check out old tapes of John McEnroe and his blood

rage, directed mainly at umpires and linesmen but also at opponents. Yet those actions, when seen from the perspective of today, seem modulated compared with some of the younger thugs who had the door opened for them by the boorish McEnroe (who, admittedly, now seems to be somewhat embarrassed by his out-of-control actions).

Also recall Jennifer Capriati being busted on drug charges, and the parental abuse of Mary Pierce's father, who needed a court order to stop him from terrorizing his daughter. And let's not forget the fanatic who rooted so enthusiastically for Steffi Graf that he attacked her greatest rival, Monica Seles, stabbing her in the back during a match.

No, tennis is not all about gentility—a fact amply illustrated on the following pages. Here, some of the giants of the mystery genre have brought their murderous intentions to center court.

There's murder, of course, some of it not terribly genteel at all. You'll encounter blackmail, voodoo, insanity, and clever scams. You'll see that human behavior doesn't vary that much, whether it's on the pro tour, at the country club, or on a public court.

Whether the action is centered on a top-ranked player, a hopeless pitty-pat struggler, or a ball boy, there are always secrets to keep and mysteries to unravel. And who better to create these mysteries (and solve them) than a gathering of some of the world's top-ranked crime writers?

Lawrence Block has received the highest honor bestowed by the Mystery Writers of America: the Grand Master Award for lifetime achievement. He is also a multiple award winner in both the best novel and best short story categories. The versatile and prolific Block has produced more than fifty novels and short story collections, most notably about his tough private eye, Matt Scudder, his comedic bookseller/burglar, Bernie Rhodenbarr, and his amoral hit man, Keller.

Kinky Friedman has had more than one career. He began as an outrageous country and western singer, leading a group called Kinky Friedman and the Texas Jewboys. Although the group remained successful, he turned his hand to writing hilarious novels of crime and murder starring no less formidable a light than Kinky himself. He also once ran for a local office in Texas as a Republican in a district that was, he reports, 98 percent Democratic. He lost.

James W. Hall began his writing career as a poet but switched to the mystery genre, creating one of Florida's most memorable characters in Thorn, the hero of most of his best-selling novels. Hall has been hailed by the *San Francisco Chronicle* as "brilliant" and by *Newsweek* as "a poet." His most recent short story, "Crack," was nominated for an Edgar Allan Poe Award.

John Harvey is one of the best of England's new breed of gritty noir writers whose ten Charlie Resnick novels have been lavishly (and justly) praised. Elmore Leonard has compared him to Graham Greene; Jim Harrison has likened him to James Lee Burke and Elmore Leonard; the *London Times* has called him "The King of Crime," and the *Denver Post* stated unequivocally that "Harvey writes better crime novels than anybody else in the world."

Jeremiah Healy, creator of the Boston-based private eye John Francis Cuddy, has been nominated for six Shamus Awards by the Private Eye Writers of America, winning the Best Novel Award for *The Staked Goat.* Two of his short stories have been selected for the prestigious *Best American Mystery Stories of the Year.*

Stephen Hunter has become a perennial name on the best-seller list with such gritty thrillers as *Hot Springs*, *Time to Hunt*, *Point of Impact*, and *Dirty White Boys*. His sometimes shocking adventures of "Bob the Nailer" (and if you haven't already, read the books so you can learn how he got the name!) have been applauded by Robert Ludlum ("breathtaking, fascinating"), John Sandford ("Stephen Hunter is Elmore Leonard on steroids"), and Nelson DeMille ("Stephen Hunter is in a class by himself").

Judith Kelman is the best-selling author of thirteen novels of psychological suspense, including *Summer of Storms*, *After the Fall*, *Fly Away Home*, and *More Than You Know*, which have been praised by such masters of the genre as Mary Higgins Clark ("Judith Kelman gets better all the time!"), Dean Koontz ("swift, suspenseful, highly entertaining"), and Susan Isaacs ("riveting . . . loaded with suspense, smart characters, and wonderfully acute observations").

Robert Leuci was a detective with the New York City Police Department for more than twenty years and served as the subject of Robert Daley's best-selling *Prince of the City* and the motion picture made from it. He is the author of terrifically realistic police novels, including *The Snitch* and *The Blaze*, of whom Nicholas Pileggi, author of *Wiseguys*, has said, "In the writings of the world of cops and the mob, there is no more authentic voice than Bob Leuci's."

Peter Lovesey capped a brilliant career by winning the British Crime Writers Association's highest honor, the Cartier Diamond Dagger Award for lifetime achievement. He began writing in 1970 with *Wobble to Death*, introducing Sergeant Cribb, who appeared in seven more novels and two television series (seen in the U.S. on PBS's *Mystery!*).

Mike Lupica is one of the most talented and honored sportswriters in America. His controversial columns and articles in the *New York Daily News*, *Esquire*, and other publications have helped make him a household name. His weekly appearance on the television series *The Sports Reporters* has further enhanced his reputation at the top of his field. He has written several mystery novels about Peter Finley, the first of which, *Dead Air*, was nominated for an Edgar and then filmed for CBS as *Money, Power and Murder*.

David Morrell, although a consistent best-seller for nearly twenty years with such novels as *The League of Night and Fog*, *The Brotherhood of the Rose*, *Desperate Measures*, and *Extreme Denial*, will always be remembered for having created an American icon, Rambo, in his novel *First Blood*. More than 12 million copies of his novels are in print in the United States.

Ridley Pearson won the American Library Association's Best Fiction Award in 1994 for *No Witnesses*. He has been a best-seller ever since with such books as *Beyond Recognition*, *The Pied Piper*, *Middle of Nowhere*, and *The First Victim*. He has been translated into more than twenty languages, and his Lou Boldt series is being produced as an A&E original movie.

Lisa Scottoline, called "the female John Grisham" by *People* magazine, has had numerous *New York Times* best-sellers, including *Mistaken Identity*, *Moment of Truth*, and *The Vendetta Defense*. She won an Edgar Allan Poe Award for her second legal thriller, *Final Appeal*. Her books are regularly used by bar associations to illustrate issues of legal ethics.

Daniel Stashower was nominated for an Edgar Allan Poe Award for his first novel, *The Adventure of the Ectoplasmic Man*, and won the coveted award for *Teller of Tales: The Life of Arthur Conan Doyle*. In between, he won the Raymond Chandler Fulbright Fellowship in Detective and Crime Writing and spent much of his time in Oxford researching his definitive biography.

So these are the players—not seeded, as each of them has a game worth watching. There are hard hitters here, as well as devious ones. Enjoy the smashes and the lobs, but beware these killer writers because *Murder Is Their Racquet.*

—Otto Penzler

MURDER
IS
MY RACQUET

TERRIBLE TOMMY TERHUNE

LAWRENCE BLOCK

A s every high school chemistry student knows," wrote sportswriter Garland Hewes, "the initials TNT stand for tri-nitro-toluene, and the compound so designated is an explosive one indeed. And, as every tennis fan is by now aware, the same initials stand as well for Thomas Norton Terhune, supremely gifted, immensely personable, and, as he showed us once again yesterday on the clay courts of Roland Garros, an unstable and violently explosive mixture if ever there was one, and a grave danger to himself and others."

The incident to which the venerable Hewes referred was one of many in Tommy Terhune's career in world-class tennis. In the French Open's early rounds, he dazzled players and spectators alike with the brilliance of his play. His serve was powerful and on-target, but it was his inspired all-around play that lifted him above the competition. He was quick as a cat, covering the whole court, making impossible returns look easy. His drop shots dropped, his lobs landed just out of his opponent's reach but just inside the white line.

But when the ball was out, or, more to the point, when the umpire declared it to be out, Tommy exploded.

In his quarterfinal match at Roland Garros, a shot of Terhune's, just eluding the outstretched racquet of his Montenegrin opponent, landed just inside the baseline.

The umpire called it out.

As the television replay would demonstrate, time and time again, the call was an error on the official's part. The ball did in fact land inside the line, by two or three inches. Thus Tommy Terhune was correct in believing that the point should be his, and he was understandably dismayed at the call.

His behavior was less understandable. He froze at the call, his racquet at shoulder height, his mouth open. While the crowd watched in anticipatory silence, he approached the umpire's raised platform. "Are you out of your mind?" he shouted. "Are you blind as a bat? What the hell is the matter with you, you pop-eyed frog?"

The umpire's response was inaudible, but was evidently uttered in support of his decision. Tommy paced to and fro at the foot of the platform, ranting, raving, and drawing whistles of disapproval from the fans. Then, after a tense moment, he returned to the baseline and prepared to serve.

Two games later in the same set, he let a desperate return of his opponent's drop. It was long, landing a full six inches beyond the white line. The umpire declared it in, and Tommy went berserk. He screamed, he shouted, he commented critically on the umpire's lineage and sexual predilections, and he underscored his remarks by gripping his racquet in both hands, then swinging it like an axe as if to chop down the wooden platform, perhaps as a first step to chopping down the official himself. He managed to land three ringing blows, the third of which shattered his graphite racquet, before another official stepped in to declare the match a forfeit, while security personnel took the American in hand and led him off the court.

The French had never seen the like and, characteristically, their reaction combined distaste for Terhune's lack of savoir-faire with grudging respect for his spirit. Phrases like *enfant terrible* and *monstre sacre* turned up in their press coverage. Elsewhere in the world, fans and journalists said essentially the same thing. Terrible Tommy Terhune, the tennis world's most gifted and most temperamentally challenged player, had proven to be his own worst enemy, and had succeeded in ousting himself from a tournament he'd been favored to win. He had done it again.

· · ·

The racquet Tommy shattered at the French Open was not the first one to go to pieces in his hands. His racquets had the life expectancy of a rock star's guitar, and he consequently had learned to travel with not one but two spares. Even so, he'd been forced to withdraw from one tournament in the semifinal round, when, after a second double fault, he held his racquet high overhead, then brought it down full-force upon the hardened playing surface. He had already sacrificed his other two racquets in earlier rounds, one destroyed in similar fashion to protest an official's decision, the other snapped over his knee in fury at himself for a missed opportunity at the net. He was now out of racquets, and unable to continue. His double fault had cost him a point; his ungovernable rage had cost him the tournament.

Such episodes notwithstanding, Tommy won his share of tournaments. He did not always blow up, and not every episode led to disqualification. In England, one confrontation with an official provoked a clamor in the press that he be refused future entry, not merely to Wimbledon, but to the entire United Kingdom; in response, Tommy somehow held himself in check long enough to breeze through the semifinals, and, in the final round, treated the fans to an exhibition of play unlike anything they'd seen before.

Playing against Roger MacReady, the rangy Australian who was the crowd's clear favorite, Tommy played Centre Court at Wimbledon as Joe DiMaggio had once played center field at Yankee Stadium. He anticipated every move MacReady made, moving in response not at the impact of ball and racquet but somehow before it, as if he knew where MacReady was going to send the ball before the Australian knew it himself. He won the first two sets, lost the third in a tiebreaker, and soared to an easy victory in the fourth set, winning 6–1, and winning over the crowd in the process. By the time his last impossible backhand return had landed where MacReady couldn't get to it, the English fans were on their feet cheering for him.

A month later, the laurels of Wimbledon still figuratively draped around his shoulders, Terrible Tommy Terhune diagnosed an official as suffering severely from myopia, astigmatism, and tunnel vision, and recommended an unorthodox course of ophthalmological treatment consisting of the performance of two sexual acts, one incestuous, the other physically impossible. He then threw his racquet on the ground, stepped on its face, and pulled up on its handle until the thing snapped. He picked up the two pieces, sailed them into the crowd, and stalked off the court.

· · ·

Morley Safer leaned forward. "If you were watching a tennis match," he began, "and saw someone behave as you yourself have so often behaved—"

"I'd be disgusted," Tommy told him. "I get sick to my stomach when I see myself on videotape. I can't watch. I have to turn off the set. Or leave the room."

"Or pick up a racquet and smash the set?"

Tommy laughed along with the TV newsman, then assured him that his displays of temper were confined to the tennis court. "That's the only place they happen," he said. "As to why they happen, well, I know what provokes them. I get mad at myself when I play poorly, of course, and that's led me to smash a racquet now and then. It's stupid and self-destructive, sure, but it's nothing compared to what happens when an official makes a bad call. That drives me out of my mind."

"And out of control?"

"I'm afraid so."

"And yet there are skeptics who think you're crazy like a fox," Safer said. "Look at the publicity you get. After all, you're the subject of this *60 Minutes* profile, not Vasco Barxi, not Roger MacReady. All over the world, people know your name."

"They know me as a maniac who can't control himself. That's not how I want to be known."

"And there are others who say you gain by intimidating officials," Safer went on. "You get them so they're afraid to call a close point against you."

"They seem to be dealing with their fears," Tommy said. "And wouldn't that be brilliant strategy on my part? Get tossed out of a Grand Slam tournament in order to unnerve an official?"

"So it's not calculated? In fact it's not something subject to your control?"

"Of course not."

"Well, what are you going to do about it? Are you getting help?"

"I'm working on it," he said grimly. "It's not that easy."

•   •   •

"It's rage," he told Diane Sawyer. "I don't know where it comes from. I know what triggers it, but that's not necessarily the same thing."

"A bad call."

"That's right."

"Or a good call," Sawyer said, "that you *think* is a bad call."

Tommy shook his head ruefully. "It's embarrassing enough to explode when the guy gets it wrong," he said. "The incident I think you're referring to, where the replay clearly showed he'd made the right call, well, I felt more ashamed of myself than ever. But even when I'm clearly right and the official's clearly wrong, there's no excuse for my behavior."

"You realize that."

"Of course I do. I may be crazy, but I'm not stupid."

"And if you *are* crazy, it's temporary insanity. As I think our viewers can see, you're perfectly sane when you don't have a tennis racquet in your hand."

"Well, they haven't asked me to pose for any Mental Health posters," he said with a grin. "But it's true I don't have to struggle to keep a lid on it. That only happens when I'm playing tennis."

"The court's where the struggle takes place."

"Yes."

"And when you honestly think a call has gone against you, that it's a bad call . . ."

"Sometimes I can keep myself in check. But other times I just lose it. I go into a zone and, well, everybody knows what happens then."

"And there's nothing you can do about it."

"Not really."

"You've had professional help?"

"I've tried a few things," he said. "Different kinds of therapy to help me develop more insight into myself. I think it's been useful, I think I know myself a little better than I used to, but when some clown says one of my shots was out when I just plain know it was in—"

"You're helpless."

"Utterly," he said. "Everything goes out the window, all the insight, all the coping techniques. The only thing that's left is the rage."

· · ·

"You have a life most women would envy," Barbara Walters told Jennifer Terhune. "You're young, you're beautiful, you've had success as a model and as an actress. And you're the wife of an enormously talented and successful athlete."

"I've been very fortunate."

"What's it like being married to a man like Tommy Terhune?"

"It's wonderful."

"The clothes, the travel, the VIP treatment . . ."

"That's all nice," Jennifer acknowledged, "but it's, like, the least of it. Just being with Tommy, sharing his life, that's what's truly wonderful."

"You love your husband."

"Of course I do."

"But I'm sure there are women in my audience," Walters said, "who wonder if you might not be the least bit afraid of your husband."

"Afraid of Tommy?"

Walters raised her eyebrows. "Mr. TNT? Terrible Tommy Terhune?"

"Oh, that."

" 'Oh, that.' You're married to a man with the most famously explosive temper in the world. Don't tell me you're never afraid that something you might do or say will set him off."

"Not really."

"What makes you so confident, Jennifer?"

"Tommy has a problem with rage," Jennifer said, "and I recognize it, and *he* recognizes it. He's been working on it, trying a lot of different things, like, to help him cope with it. I just know he'll be able to get a handle on it."

"And I'm sure our hopes are with him," Walters said, "but that doesn't address the question, does it? What about you, Jennifer? How do you know that terrible temper, that legendary rage, won't one day be aimed at you?"

"I'm not an umpire."

"In other words . . ."

"In other words, the only time Tommy loses it, the only time his temper is the least bit of a problem, is when an official makes a bad call against him on the tennis court. He never gets mad at an opponent. He doesn't go into the stands after fans who make insulting remarks, and I've heard some of them say some pretty outrageous things. But he

takes that sort of thing in stride. It's only bad calls that set
him off."

"And after an explosion?"

"He's contrite. And ashamed of himself."

"And angry?"

"Only during a match. Not afterward."

"So it's never directed at you?"

"Never."

"He's a perfect gentleman?"

"He's thoughtful and gentle and funny and smart," Jennifer
said, "in addition to being the best tennis player in the world.
I'm a lucky girl."

Later, watching herself on television, Jennifer thought the
interview had gone rather well. She sounded a little ditsy, saying *like* often enough to sound like a Valley Girl, but outside of
that she'd done fine. Her hair, which had caused her some concern, wound up looking great on camera, and the dress she'd
worn had proved a good choice.

And her comments seemed okay, too. The *likes* notwithstanding, she came across not as an airhead but as a concerned
and supportive life partner and helpmate. And, she told herself,
that was fair enough. Everything she'd said had been the truth.

Though not, she had to admit, the whole truth. Because
how could she have sat there and told Barbara Walters that
Tommy's temper was one of the things that had attracted her
to him in the first place? All of that intensity, when he served
and volleyed and made impossible shots look easy, well, it was
exciting enough. But all of that passion, when he roared and
ranted and just plain lost it, was even more exciting. It stirred
her up, it got her juices flowing. It made her, well, *hot*—and
how could she say all that to Barbara Walters?

In fact, when you came right down to it, she was a little disappointed that Tommy never lost it except on the tennis court. It was a pity, in a way, that he never brought that famous temper home with him, that he never lost it in the bedroom.

Sometimes—and she would never admit this to anyone, on or off camera—sometimes she tried to provoke him. Sometimes she tried to make him mad. Even if he were to get physical, even if he were to slap her around a little, well, maybe it was kinky of her, but she thought she might like that.

But it was hopeless. On the court, with a racquet in his hand and an official to argue with, he was Mr. TNT, the notorious Terrible Tommy Terhune. At home, even in the bedchamber, he was what she'd said he was, the perfect gentleman.

Darn it . . .

• • •

"So we begin to make progress," the psychoanalyst said. "The need to win your father's approval. The approval sometimes granted, other times withheld, for reasons having nothing to do with your own behavior."

"It wasn't fair," Tommy said.

"And that is what so infuriates you about a bad call on the tennis court, is it not so? The unfairness of it all. You have done everything you were supposed to do, everything within your power, and still the approval of the man in authority is denied to you. Instead he sits high above you, remote and unreachable, and punishes you."

"That's exactly what happens."

"And it is unfair."

"Damn right it is."

"And you explode in rage, the rage you never let yourself

feel as a child. But now you know its source. It's not the official, who of course cannot be expected to be right every time."

"They're only human."

"Exactly. It's your father you're truly enraged at, and he's dead, and out of reach of your anger, no longer available to approve or disapprove, to applaud or punish."

"That's it, all right."

"And now, armed with the insight you've developed here, you'll be able to master your rage, to dispel it, to rise above it."

"You know something?" Tommy said. "I feel better already."

• • •

In a first-round match two weeks later, an unreturnable passing shot by his unseeded opponent fell just outside the sideline marker. The umpire called it in.

"You blind bastard!" Tommy screamed. "How much are they paying you to steal the match from me?"

• • •

"With every breath," the little man in the loincloth intoned, "you draw the anger up from the third chakra. Up up up, past the heart chakra, past the throat chakra, to the third eye. Then, as you breathe out, you let the anger flow in a stream out through the third eye, transformed into peaceful energizing white light. Breathe in and the anger is drawn upward from the solar plexus where it is stored. Breathe out and you release it as white light. With every breath, your reserve of rage grows less and less."

"Om," Tommy said.

• • •

In his next tournament, the Virginia Slims Equal Opportunity Challenge (dubbed Men Deserve Cancer Too by one commentator), Tommy waltzed through the early rounds, breathing in and breathing out. Then, in the quarterfinals, he smashed his racquet after a service double fault.

He had a replacement racquet, and it wasn't until midway through the next game that he snapped it over his knee.

• • •

"Why put you on the couch for ten or twelve years," the doctor said, "when I can give you a little pill that'll fix what's wrong with you? If you had high blood pressure, you wouldn't probe your psyche to uncover the underlying reasons for it, would you? You might stroke out while you were still trying to remember your childhood. No, you'd take your medication. If you had diabetes, you'd watch your diet and take your insulin. I'm going to write you a prescription for a new tranquilizer, and I want you to take one first thing every morning. And you won't have to master your anger, or figure out where it comes from. Because it'll be gone."

"Neat," said Tommy.

• • •

"There's something curiously listless about Terhune's play," the television announcer reported. "He's performing well enough to win his early matches, but we're used to seeing him rush the net more often, and his reflexes seem the tiniest bit less sharp. We've heard rumors that he's been taking medication to help him with his emotional difficulties, and it looks to me as though whatever he's taking is slowing him down."

"But his temper's in check, Jim. When that call went against him in the first set, he barely noticed it."

"Oh, he noticed it. He stared over at the official, and he looked puzzled. But he didn't seem to care very much, and he lifted his racquet and played the next point without incident."

"If he's on something, it does seem to be working. . . . Oh, what's this?"

"He thought Beckheim's return was out."

"But it was clearly in, Jim."

"Not the way Terhune saw it. Oh, there he goes. Oh, my."

.   .   .

"Your eyelids are very heavy," the hypnotist said. "You cannot keep them open. You are sleeping, you are in a deep sleep. From now on, you will be completely calm and unruffled on the tennis court. Nothing will disturb your composure. If anything upsetting occurs, you will stop what you are doing and count slowly to ten. When you reach the count of ten, all tension and anger will vanish, and you will once again be calm and unruffled. Now how will you be when you play tennis?"

"Calm," Tommy mumbled. "Calm and unruffled."

"And what will you do if something upsetting occurs?"

"Count to ten."

"And how will you feel when you reach the count of ten?"

"Calm and unruffled."

"Very good. When I reach the count of five, you will wake up feeling curiously refreshed, with no conscious recollection of this experience. One. Two. Three. Four. Five. How do you feel, Tommy?"

"Calm and unruffled," he said. "And curiously refreshed."

• • •

Looking neither calm nor unruffled, Tommy stalked over to where the official was perched. "One," he said, and swung his racquet at the platform. "Two," he said, and he continued his count, punctuating each number with a hammer blow to the base of the platform. The racquet shattered on the count of six, but he continued counting all the way to ten as he marched off the court.

• • •

"You have the chicken?" Atuele said. "Perfect white chicken. No dark feather, no blemish. Very good." He placed the chicken on the little altar, placed his hands gently on the bird, and gazed thoughtfully at it. After a long moment the chicken fell over and lay on its side.

"What happened to the chicken?" Tommy asked.

"It is dead."

"But, uh, how did it die?"

"As it was supposed to," Atuele said.

Tommy looked around. He was in a compound about a third the size of a football field, just a batch of mud huts strung around an open area that faced the altar, where the chicken was apparently still dead. He'd flown Air Afrique from New York to Dakar, then transferred to Air Gabon, whatever that was, for a harrowing flight to Lomé, the capital of Togo, wherever *that* was. He'd been granted an audience with this Sorbonne-educated witch doctor, who'd sent him off to buy a chicken. And now the chicken was dead, and he felt like an idiot. What did any of this have to do with tennis? What could it possibly have to do with Thomas Norton Terhune?

"I don't know what this guy does," a friend had told him, "and you feel like the world's prize jackass while he's doing it, but it's magic. And it works."

"Maybe if you believe in it . . ."

"Hell, I didn't believe in it. I thought it was pure-Dee ooga-booga horseshit. But it worked anyway. You want to know something? I *still* think it was ooga-booga horseshit. But now I believe in it."

How, he wondered, could you believe in something while still believing it to be horseshit? And how could it possibly work? And—

"You need a spirit," Atuele told him. "A spirit who will live within you, and who will have the job of keeping you serene while you are playing tennis."

"A spirit," Tommy said hollowly.

"A spirit. In order to give you this spirit, you require a ceremony. Go to your hotel. Return at sunset. And you must bring something."

"Another chicken?"

"No, not another chicken. A bottle of scotch whiskey and a box of cigars."

"That's easy enough. What are we going to do, get drunk and smoke cigars together?"

"No, they are for me. And bring five thousand dollars."

"Five thousand dollars?"

"For the ceremony," Atuele explained.

The ceremony turned out to be ridiculous. Six half-naked men pounded on drums, while two dozen young women danced around, heads thrown back, eyes rolling. Atuele broke an egg in a bowl, poured it onto Tommy's head, rubbed it into his scalp. He gave him a ball of ground-up grass and told him to eat it, then left him to sit in the circle, and eventually to shuffle around on the dance floor. After an hour or so of this Tommy got a taxi back to his hotel and went to bed.

In the morning he showered, packed, and went to the airport, knowing he'd wasted his money, hoping only that nothing had leaked to the press, that the world would never know the lengths to which he'd been driven or how utterly he'd been made a fool of. He flew to Dakar and on to JFK, then caught another flight to Phoenix for the Scottsdale Open.

Jennifer met him at the airport. "Waste of time," he told her. She knew only that he'd heard about a secret treatment, not where you went for it or what it consisted of, and he didn't feel like filling her in. "Lots of mumbo jumbo," he said. "It won't work."

But it did.

• • •

At Scottsdale, Tommy Terhune reached the final round of the tournament, losing to Roger MacReady in four sets. He used the same racquet for the entire tournament, and never used it to hit anything but the ball. He didn't raise his voice, didn't once curse himself, his opponents, the largely hostile audience, or the officials, who made their share of inaccurate calls. He was, that is to say, a perfect gentleman.

And he managed all this with no effort whatsoever. He didn't take a pill, didn't count to ten, didn't clamp a lid on his anger, didn't chant or meditate. All he did was play tennis, and the moment he stepped onto the court each day, a curious calm settled over him. He still took notice when a call went unfairly against him, but he didn't mind, didn't take it personally. He stayed focused on his game, and his game had never been better.

Of course, he told himself, one tournament didn't necessarily prove anything. He'd gone through whole tournaments before without treating the crowd to a display of the famous Terhune temper, only to lose it a week or a month down the line. How could he be sure that wouldn't happen?

Somehow, though, he knew it wouldn't. Somehow he could tell that something had happened within that circle of mud huts in Togo. According to Atuele, he now had a spirit invested inside of him, a spirit who took control of his temper the moment he picked up a racquet and stepped onto a court. And that's just how it felt. One way or another, he'd morphed into a person who didn't have to control himself because he didn't experience any anger to begin with. He played his matches, won or lost, and went home feeling fine either way.

Calm and unruffled, you might say.

· · ·

Tommy played brilliantly in his next tournament. He sailed serenely through the early rounds, fell behind in his quarterfinal match, then rallied to salvage a victory over his unseeded opponent. Then, in the third set of the semis, the audience fell silent when Tommy served, came to the net, and leaped high into the air to slam his opponent's return. The ball struck near the baseline, but everyone present could see it was clearly in.

Except the official, who declared it out.

Tommy took a step toward the platform. The official cowered, but Tommy didn't seem to notice. He said, "Was that ball out?"

The official nodded.

"Oh," Tommy said, and shrugged. "From here it looked good, but I guess you can see better from where you're sitting."

He went back to the baseline and served the next point. He went on to win the match and advance to the finals, in which he played brilliantly, beating Roger MacReady in straight sets.

•   •   •

"And here's Mrs. Tommy Terhune, the lovely Jennifer," said the TV reporter, sticking a mike in her face. "Your husband was really commanding out there, wasn't he?"

"He was," she agreed.

"He played brilliant tennis, and he seems to have triumphed in the inner game as well, wouldn't you say?"

"The inner game?"

"He didn't lose his temper at all."

"Oh, that," she said. "No, he didn't."

"I'll bet you're proud of him."

"Very proud."

"You've been quoted as saying he's always been a perfect gentleman off the court. Now he seems to be every bit the perfect gentleman on the court as well. That must be extremely gratifying to you."

"Yes," she said, smiling furiously. "Extremely gratifying."

•   •   •

It was in the U.S. Open that the extent of the change in Terrible Tommy Terhune became unmistakably evident. Earlier, before his still-secret visit to West Africa, some commentators had theorized that the brilliance of his play might be of a piece with the ungovernability of his temper. Passion, after all, was the common denominator. Put the one on a leash, they suggested, and the other might wind up hobbled in the bargain.

But this was clearly not the case. Tommy had an easy time of it in the early rounds at Flushing Meadows, winning every match in straight sets. In the quarterfinals, his Croatian opponent won a single game in the first set and none at all in the second and third, but the fellow's play was not as pathetic as the score suggested. Tommy was simply everywhere, getting to every ball, his returns always on target and, more often than not, unreturnable.

The calls, of course, did not always go his way. But his reaction was never greater than a shrug or a raised eyebrow. Spectators looked for him to be struggling with his emotions, but what was becoming clear was that there was no struggle, and no emotions.

In the semifinals, Tommy's opponent was the young Chinese-American, Scott Chin, but most fans were looking past the semis to a final round that would see Tommy pitted once again against his Australian rival, Roger MacReady. But this was not to be—while Tommy moved easily past Chin, MacReady lost the fifth set to a previously unknown Belgian player named Claude Macquereau.

Two days later, after a women's final in which one player grunted while the other wept, Terhune and Macquereau met for the men's championship. If the fans had been disappointed by MacReady's absence, the young Belgian soon showed himself as a worthy opponent for Tommy. His serve was strong and accurate, his game at net and at the baseline a near mirror-image of Tommy's. Macquereau won the first set 7–6, lost the second 7–5. Most games went to deuce, and most individual points consisted of long, wearying volleys marked by one impossible return after another.

By the third set, which Tommy won in a tiebreaker, the fans knew they were watching tennis history being made. Midway through the fourth set, won by Macquereau in an even more attenuated tiebreaker, the television commentators had run out of superlatives and the crowd had shouted itself hoarse. Both players, run ragged in the late-summer heat and humidity, looked exhausted, but both played as though they were fresh as daisies.

In the third game of the final set, a perfectly placed passing shot of Tommy's was called out. The audience drew its collective breath—they knew the ball was in—and Tommy approached the platform.

"Ball was out?" he said conversationally.

The official managed a nod. The man must have known he'd missed the call, and must have been tempted to reverse himself. But all he did was nod.

"Okay," Tommy said, and played the next point, while the audience released its collective breath in a great sigh that mingled relief with disappointment.

After ten games in the final set, they had taken turns breaking each other's service, and were tied 5–5. In the eleventh game, Tommy served and went to the net, and Macquereau's return flew past Tommy's outstretched racquet and landed just inside the sideline.

The official called it out.

It was close, certainly closer than the call that had gone against Tommy earlier in the set, but the ball was definitely in and, more to the point, Tommy Terhune knew it was in. The game had been tied at 15–all, and this point put Tommy ahead, 30–15.

His response was immediate. He went to the service line, hit two serves into the net to tie the score at 30–all, then deliberately double-faulted a second time, putting Macquereau a point ahead, as he would have been had the call been correct.

The act was uncommonly gracious, and all the more so for coming when it did. It is, as one reporter pointed out, easier to give back a questionable point when you're winning or losing by a considerable margin, but Tommy's unprecedented act of chivalry might well cost him the championship.

Not so. Trailing 30–40, he won the next point with a service ace, then won the game by playing brilliantly for the next two points. The final game was almost anticlimactic; Macquereau, serving, seemed to know how it was going to end, and scored only a single point while Tommy broke his service to take the game, the set, the match, and the United States Open championship.

All of which made the aftermath just that much more tragic.

·   ·   ·

The whole world knows the rest. How Tommy Terhune, flushed with triumph, accompanied by his curiously unemotional wife, returned to his hotel, racquet in hand. How Roger MacReady was waiting for them in the lobby, and accompanied them upstairs to their suite. How Jennifer explained haltingly that she and MacReady had fallen in love, that they had been, like, having an affair, and that she wanted Tommy to give her a divorce so that she and MacReady could be married.

She said all this calmly, expecting Tommy to take it every bit as calmly. Perhaps she thought it was a good time to tell him— riding high after his victory, he could presumably take a lost love in stride. In any event, Tommy had never shown much emotion off the court, and now was equally cool on it, so she knew she could count on him to be a gentleman about this. If he could be gallant enough to hand two points to Claude Macquereau through purposeful double faults, wouldn't he be equally gallant and self-sacrificing now?

As it happened, he would not.

He was clutching his tennis racquet when she told him all this. It was the racquet he had been using ever since his return from Togo, and it had lasted longer than any racquet he had previously owned, because he had not once swung it at anything harder than a tennis ball.

By the time he let go of it now, it was in pieces, and his wife and his rival were both dead. He smashed the edge of the racquet into Roger MacReady's head, striking him five times in all, fracturing his skull even as he smashed the racquet, and he went on swinging until all he had left in his hand was the jagged handle.

Which he continued to hold as he backed the terrified Jennifer into a corner, where he pinned her against the wall and drove the racquet handle into the hollow of her throat.

Then he picked up the phone and told the desk clerk to summon the police.

•   •   •

Everyone had a theory, of course, and one that got a lot of play held that Tommy's temper, no longer released periodically on the tennis court, didn't just disappear. Instead it got tamped down, compressed, so that the eventual inevitable explosion was that much greater and more disastrous.

One enterprising newsman found his way to Togo, where

the enigmatic Atuele told him essentially the same thing. "I gave the man a spirit," he said, between puffs on a cheroot. "To help him when he played tennis. And it helped him, is it not so?"

"But off the court—"

"Off the court," Atuele said, "the man had no problem. So, when he was not playing tennis, the spirit's work was done. And the anger had to go somewhere, didn't it?"

Tennis, Anyone?

Kinky Friedman

Haven't played tennis since high school. Haven't touched a racquet since Christ got aced but I was pretty hot way back when. Got to the state finals in my senior year. My coach, Woodrow Sledge, always emphasized basic skills and groundstrokes, a dominant serve, strong forehand and backhand, and a confident, yet conservative approach to the net. Therefore, he was never completely happy with what I will call the peculiar morality of my game. As long as I was winning, however, he'd just pat me on the back and shake his head.

They say sports does not build character, it just reveals it. Maybe this is true but I think I learned important life lessons from the way I was able to win at tennis. To put the best face on it you could say I played like a high-stakes poker player or a riverboat gambler. There was nothing *wrong* with my game. It was just that I'd allowed my basic tennis fundamentals to be corrupted and seduced by weaving a web of artifice and delusion. Playing me was, for most good church-going Americans, like playing tennis with a sentient wall of carnival mirrors. And that has been my style ever since. Maybe even before I ever picked up a racquet.

You see, I was a chess prodigy when I was very young. At the tender age of seven I played the world grandmaster, Samuel Reschevsky, in Houston, Texas. He was there to play a simultaneous match with fifty people, all of whom, except for me, were adults. He beat all of us, of course, but afterward he told my dad he was sorry to have had to beat his son. He just had to be very careful with seven-year-olds. If he ever lost to one of them it'd be headlines.

The way you play a game, especially as a child, does more than reveal your character. I believe, after some grudging reflection, it provides a psychological peephole into the kind of person you will someday be. The way you play the game becomes an ingrained, living thing, a succubus that eventually determines how you play the game of life.

As far as chess was concerned, however, you could say I peaked at the age of seven. But by then, I now realize, I'd internalized the nature of the game. Very possibly, I'd unconsciously brought a sidecar of chess to my game of tennis. After all, tennis is not a team sport; the way you play tends to reveal who you really are. As long as you're winning, of course, nobody ever notices.

The game I played, the one that mildly irritated Coach Sledge, was an extremely duplicitous, downright deceitful at times, fabric of cat-and-mouse conceit. Yes, I'd begin with a strong, left-handed serve. But after that, things tended to degenerate. My stock-in-trade became a willful charade of evil fakes, feints, and last-moment viciously undercut backhands. In other words, I was playing physical chess. There is no morality in chess or tennis, or course; morality, I suppose, is considered to be confined only to the game of life. Again, when you're winning, nobody notices.

Opposing players, many of whom were superior to me in basic tennis skills, were often left shaking their heads in what looked to me like a slightly more demonstrative impersonation of Coach Sledge. I would smile and graciously accept whatever accolades were thrown my way by any lookers-on. Sometimes there were stands full of people and sometimes there was only the sound of one hand clapping. It didn't matter. I knew. Deceiving the opponent was just as good as, indeed, it almost seemed preferable to, beating him with sound groundstrokes and solid play. When you beat a highly skilled player in such a fashion, you almost have to struggle to contain your glee. I got pretty good at that, too.

When I graduated high school I left the sport of tennis far behind me, much as I'd done with chess back in my childhood. I could still play either of them, of course, but life was moving too fast for chess, and tennis seemed to require too high a degree of tedium in finding appropriate courts, lining up appropriate opponents, and constantly changing into appropriate clothing. It just didn't seem appropriate. Besides, I had college to deal with. My tennis racquet remained in the closet; the only webs of deceit associated with it were now woven exclusively by highly industrious spiders.

But, to be sure, I was quite busy myself. College was a whole new ballgame, as they say. Many of the kids who were the stars of my high school senior class went directly to pumping gasoline. New facts emerged in college and I discovered to my personal delight that I flourished in this new environment. A deft talent for obfuscation works wonders with any seemingly sophisticated social set. "What you do in this world," the

great Sherlock Holmes once said, "is a matter of no conse-
quence. The question is what you can make people think you
have done." Like Sherlock, I somehow instinctively knew
never to reveal my methods.

No matter what anybody tells you, relationships between
men and women on this particular planet are anything but
straightforward and forthright. A successful relationship is
usually governed by forces ingrained from childhood that one
or both parties often remain totally unaware of. One may be a
born gold-digger looking forever for a free ride. One may be a
caregiver, always looking for a bird with a broken wing. It's not
so important who the two people are: timing and *what* they are
is usually what counts. That's how the game is played and won.
Sometimes, however, the bird with the broken wing heals up
and beats you to death with it.

I met my future ex-wife, Leila Marie, in anthropology class,
on one of the rare occasions I attended. I cut a lot of classes
and (I hope you won't be disappointed) I also cribbed an exam
now and then in the manner of Ted Kennedy at Harvard.
After all, I was enrolled in a highly advanced liberal arts program at the time that was mainly distinguished by the fact that
every student had some form or other of facial tic. Every student, that was, except Leila Marie.

Leila Marie was a perky brunette with flashing green eyes
who helped me write my monograph for anthropology: *The Flathead Indians of Montana.* Even with Leila Marie's talented and efficient help, it soon became apparent that liberal arts was never
intended to be my long suit. I didn't want to become some stuffy
professor helping students learn about the Flathead Indians of
Montana. If they were burning with intellectual desire to find out
about the Flathead Indians, they could damn well go to Montana

and study campfire shards. I needed a field that was more applicable to today's world. A field in which I could help others, but also help myself. Meanwhile, the only field of study I seemed to be identifying with was Leila Marie.

Not only did Leila Marie appear to have an infinite amount of income, but she was also very easy on the eyes and lips. On top of that, no pun intended, she seemed to be willing to do anything it took to see that I succeeded. As things transpired, it was going to take quite a bit. I had decided that I wanted to go to medical school. It was not going to be easy and it was not going to be cheap. That was where Leila Marie came in.

I was always pretty strong when it came to the old gray matter department but I must confess I was not prepared for organic chemistry. Leila Marie had to practically walk me through that one. But somehow we managed. I came to rely upon her judgment, her hard work ethic, and, yes, her financial resources. But I worked hard, too. Leila just worked a little harder. She even took a waitress job on the side when medical school tuition loomed near. That meant a lot to me. Besides, I've always been a sucker for attractive waitresses.

I didn't get into the best medical school, but I did get into medical school and that's what counts. In medical school, the guy who comes in last in his class is still called Doctor. We had to move to the island of Grenada and Leila Marie was beginning to appear a bit shopworn from working two jobs, but we looked to the future and somehow kept moving forward. I believed in myself and Leila Marie believed in me and sometimes that's all that keeps you going. Fortunately, I could stand the sight of blood. Otherwise, I would've had to go to law school.

Leila Marie and I got married about the time I realized I wasn't going to be a brain surgeon. As long as I finished medical school and got my internship I didn't really care what kind of doctor I'd become. Just as long as I didn't have to make house calls. You had to be sort of ruthless about the whole thing or otherwise you wouldn't get through. What was the point of saving the world if you couldn't save yourself? So I became a proctologist. It's nothing to be ashamed of, I figured. Besides, you have to work with so many assholes every day you might as well get paid for it.

After medical school we moved to a new town where I took my internship at the local hospital. If you've never gone through an internship you probably have no idea how much of your personal life it consumes. Every night in the emergency room I'd witness the flotsam and jetsam of humanity walk, crawl, wheel themselves, or be carried past my increasingly jaded irises. People with limbs missing. People with gunshot wounds. People stuck together fucking. It was a real mess but I think I can truly say that it made a doctor out of me. All those hours at the hospital, of course, had a rather debilitating effect on my marriage. But it was at about that time that I took a turn for the nurse.

She was a gorgeous, young, blue-eyed blonde from the Great Northwest and she had a real way with people and one of them was me. When you work with somebody in life-and-death situations, you really get to know them. Her name was Lana Lee and I credit her with bringing the fun and excitement back into my life. Somehow, I had grown past Leila Marie, who'd continued working her dreary jobs and complaining about the long hours the internship was causing me to keep. It was kind of sad but increasingly Leila Marie seemed to be living in the past and I seemed to be living for the future. And Lana Lee seemed inexorably to be a part of that future.

If there's one thing I know about destiny it is that you can't count on it forever. I knew things couldn't go on like this and sure enough they didn't. Tragically, in the first year of my private practice, Leila Marie died rather suddenly of a fairly arcane illness that is faintly related in the literature to toxic shock syndrome. The malady was impossible to treat, diagnose, or detect and it caused me no little grief to realize the irony that I was a doctor and there was nothing I could do for her. The subsequent autopsy revealed no clue as to the cause of her death.

Lana Lee was there to support me, however, and one thing led to another. When the Lord closes the door He opens a little window, they say. In my case, at least, it certainly seems that way. There was, indeed, a nasty little hint of suspicion surrounding me after Leila Marie's death but it comes with the territory. Doctors have become as used to this sort of mean-minded gossip as we are to scribbling prescriptions or working with HMOs. I didn't let it get me down.

Today I'm happily married to Lana Lee and I have a thriving practice. If you're patient and you see a lot of patients, the medical profession can provide a very lucrative lifestyle. Not only that, but it's a good way to help serve your fellow man. And speaking of serving, guess what? I've taken up tennis again.

SIX LOVE

JAMES W. HALL

In the delicate crosshairs of Roger's telescopic sight, Gigi Janeway stood at her open window, only the thin mesh of window screen and a hundred yards of humid, bug-dense summer air separating them. With the golden lights of her room blazing behind her, her body seemed to glow.

Gigi still wore her white tennis dress with the blue bows on the sleeves and she was brushing her long auburn hair. For years Roger had observed her close-up each afternoon when he came to retrieve his daughter, Julie, from tennis practice. Since the age of six, Gigi had been Julie's nemesis, and Roger had made a careful study of this girl who caused his daughter such torment.

By now he was intimately familiar with the scent of sour peppermint that Gigi's clammy flesh gave off. And he could picture exactly the glint of long blonde hairs coating her forearms and lately he noticed the razor line at midthigh, just above the hem of her pleated tennis skirt, the rigidly precise border where she stopped shaving her legs. He knew her half-dozen habitual facial expressions, from the subtle smirk she made when one of her inferiors blew an easy shot, to the hawkish squirt that furrowed her forehead when she fell behind and had to summon an extra quotient of concentration.

Gigi looked out at the dark and for a half-second seemed to stare directly at Roger Shelton where he stood, tense and uncertain, the coarse bark of the pine pressed hard against his left cheek, the smooth stock of his deer rifle flat against the other. He was five yards beyond the halo of the neighborhood security lights, in the shadows of the dense stand of pines that bordered Deepwood Estates, the exclusive community where Arthur Janeway, owner of the largest Cadillac dealership in Florida, resided. Arthur was a corpulent man who held a cold disdain for second-raters of every type, which most certainly included Roger Shelton, a common salesman on one of Janeway's used car lots.

Arthur's wife, Bettina, was from Dusseldorf. Gaunt and thin-lipped, with the cigarette-roughened voice, the white-blonde hair, and the pale icy detachment of Greta Garbo in her prime. Ages ago, while still a bachelor, Roger had stumbled into Bettina during her first week in Sand Hills. New to America and deeply disoriented, she had briefly mistaken Roger for someone with a promising future and had dallied with him for two nights at a motel on the fringe of town. On the third night when she failed to appear, Roger Shelton went searching and located her at the Hotel Flamingo's wood-paneled bar. On the stool next to her, Arthur Janeway was touching a flame to her cigarette. She turned and saw Roger in the doorway and the lungful of smoke that bloomed from her lips was directed at him with dismissive finality. When she turned back to Arthur, she gave a long, guttural laugh to some sly remark of his. In reply, Arthur reached up and touched a finger to one of her chiseled cheekbones. For several moments Roger stared from the doorway as Bettina pressed her baton, firmly and assuredly, into the hand of the swifter runner.

As he was turning to go, Molly Weatherstone appeared beside him in the doorway of the Hotel Flamingo bar. She wore a shimmering black cocktail dress and spiky heels. Roger managed a distracted hello but she didn't reply. Her furious gaze was fixed on the back of Arthur Janeway's head.

"You too, huh?" Roger said. "What'd he do, stand you up?"

After absorbing the scene for a moment more, Molly stalked across the room, bent to Arthur's ear and spoke a few short, sibilant words then swung around and marched out of the bar.

Less than a month later Bettina and Arthur Janeway eloped to Las Vegas. It was only days after that when Roger and Molly consummated their own hasty romance with a civil ceremony at the Sand Hills courthouse. And though over the years their marriage had proved sound enough, Roger always wondered if their bond had not been forged on the flimsy foundation of spite.

Gigi Janeway, the girl in Roger Shelton's wavering sights, was Arthur and Bettina's cherished princess. Fourteen years old. A bony girl with pale gray eyes and a world-class two-handed backhand, a good kick serve and a killer instinct around the net. As Roger watched through the telescopic sight, Gigi Janeway drew the brush through her coarse brown hair with the same mindlessly mechanical motion she employed on the court. Every stroke exactly like the last. Not a quiver of difference between the first backhand crosscourt of the afternoon and the five hundredth stroke that came two hours later. Her game was fearsomely robotic. She swung her racquet like a scythe through the golden wheat of other men's daughters. Harvesting their vulnerabilities, their mind-wandering lapses, their muscular frailties. Gigi moved forward and forward again in an ever-widening swath, mowing down girl after girl with pitiless perfection.

Roger could see the shelf of trophies on the wall behind her. Not the small runner-up plaques Julie had managed to collect. But the big, gaudy, golden vessels of the triumphant. It was not simply to amass these trophies that drove Roger's daughter Julie to dash herself over and over and over against the impervious wall of Gigi Janeway's tennis game. Roger's daughter was guided by an artistic temperament. Capricious and creative and capable of flights of giddy inspiration, Julie played the game with volatile abandon. She was a poet on those strict and unforgiving courts. Lithe and inventive, mesmerizing in her finest moments, she had a dazzling array of shots and angles and paces and spins that sent the balls skidding away from her opponent's racquet as if charmed.

On other days, however, when Julie's juices were not flowing, when the muse deserted her, she simply crumpled under the fractional weight of air. She could be sluggish and erratically self-destructive and painful to watch. Sometimes she fell into a daze of slow-motion awkwardness, eyes unlocked from the moment, stumbling about on the green clay as if she no longer cared about the game of tennis or about anything else on earth.

At her finest moments, Julie exposed Gigi for the mindless automaton that she was, yo-yoing her from side to side and up and back, twisting and turning the girl until she had to be dizzy, using her vast array of spins and speeds to search out the tiny chinks in Gigi's heavy armor. But those glorious moments came and went like fragile wisps of starlight. Julie had so far been unable to sustain her quicksilver magic for an entire match against Gigi's inexhaustible onslaught.

In the small town of Sand Hills, in the tennis crazy county of Palm Cove, Gigi was the unfailing winner and Julie was the eternal runner-up. A girl with more talent and flair than a hundred Gigis, though lacking in Gigi's single-minded focus, her stubborn, animal appetite for conquest.

If simply winning her matches against Julie had been enough for Gigi Janeway, Roger would not be standing in the woods at that moment, aiming his deer rifle at the girl. But like her rapacious father, Gigi seemed to hunger for more than victory. Nothing less than total domination appeared to satisfy her. Every match against Julie was a blood-letting so vicious and so total that their accumulated effect was to drain the reservoirs of Julie's very spirit. Between matches, each word Gigi spoke to Julie had a belittling purpose. Every act, each haughty look or whispered remark to a fellow player tormented Julie, mocked her, undermined her faith in her abilities and reminded her of her inferior station in Sand Hills, Florida, where her father was merely an unremarkable salesman.

On too many nights, Julie lay in her sleepless bed and stared into her father's eyes pleading for Roger to tell her what she might do to alter her fate.

Roger had no answer. But he knew that Gigi Janeway and she alone blocked the way of his daughter. Her talent thwarted, skills obstructed, her very personality was being permanently stunted. No matter how hard she worked, no matter the peaks of athletic grace she reached, her efforts were forever mocked by Gigi Janeway. Just as his own career had been arrested by men like Gigi's father who were willing to be more aggressive, more relentlessly ruthless and hardnosed than Roger.

Out on the glaring pavement of the used car lot Roger had known his own moments of artistic grace. Closing deals in half an hour with penny-pinching old fools from the beachfront condos. There were days when he'd summoned his silver tongue and not even the devil himself could have withstood his sales pitch. He held the single-day sales record of five used cars. However, he also held the record for the longest stretches without a sale. It was, Roger believed, all a function of the ebb and flow of the artistic temperament. But men like Arthur Janeway didn't appreciate transcendent qualities. Janeway, like his daughter, was unapologetically cold-blooded, relying on his superior focus and his boundless stamina to wear down and eventually crush his competition. He got what he wanted by wanting it more than anyone else.

Roger was certain all Julie needed was the smallest of boosts. What father could turn away from such need? Truly, all he wished to do was wing the girl in the golden window, a non-fatal wound that would keep her sidelined for a month or two, long enough for Julie to replenish her confidence and gather the momentum she needed.

Framed by honeyed light, Gigi stood in her window and dared Roger to shoot. Dared him to still the shudder in his arms and summon the courage that had eluded him for months.

He watched as Gigi took hold of a clump of her hair and brought it close to her face and inspected it. He watched her pluck a split end and flick it toward the screen. A casual gesture that was a perfect echo for the way she mercilessly brushed aside her flawed opponents. Then he watched with fascination as she released her hair and lifted the hairbrush to her mouth—turning it into a microphone, tipping her head to the side as if searching for a more flattering angle in the sunlight of Centre Court Wimbledon. Having completed the entire fortnight without the loss of a set, Gigi had dispatched her final opponent and now curtseyed before the duke and duchess, and explained to the enraptured crowd how she had managed this stunning victory at such a young age. Lucky sperm, Roger imagined her to say. Lucky sperm swam up my mother's thingy and infected her with me and gave me the endless stamina and the narrow focus and the ability to be unbored by hours of unvarying repetition. I am not worthy of this trophy, she would say. The deserving one is Julie Shelton back in Sand Hills, Florida, a girl who went farther than anyone would have expected given the fact she had such unlucky sperm. Julie Shelton, a beautiful loser. This is for you, unlucky Julie. This is for you, you pathetic girl, who never found the guts and gristle and monotonous meanness to succeed.

Through his sight Roger Shelton watched as Gigi dropped the hairbrush and came to sudden attention. Her smile went rigid as if someone had plucked the harp string that joined her cerebellum with the million unbearable nerves of her body. And then Gigi's mouth went slack and with one final puff of energy those ruthless blue eyes fixed on Roger's and all around his hiding place the woods glowed with Gigi Janeway's outrage. In her last moment of consciousness, a pout took control of her lips as if she were suffering an unaccustomed disappointment, some treasure withheld, some bauble snatched from her grasp.

Roger lowered the rifle and listened to the echo of the blast swallowed by the thick, damp air, the surf roar of traffic, the high keening of crickets and mosquitoes, and the muffled television laughter leaking from behind insulated walls and all that machine-driven air.

He was to learn later that no one had heard the shot. No witnesses came forward with descriptions of a man dressed in camouflage. Apparently Roger had moved back to his car with perfect anonymity. In the following days, police investigators searched the nearby woods but failed to locate his nest in the trees or any other sign of him. The Sand Hills police were utterly baffled. Their theory was that Gigi had been struck by a stray slug from someone taking target practice in the woods. Arthur and Bettina pleaded for help from state authorities or the FBI but they were denied. A month after the incident the furor had subsided.

What Roger learned of Gigi's condition came from the newspaper stories and the scuttlebutt around the used car lot. For seven weeks Gigi Janeway lay in a coma. When she woke, she remembered little of her previous life. The most mundane physical movements were now monumental challenges. For a while, every breath was a test, every eye blink an accomplishment. Her muscle memory had been totally erased. It would be a year before she could walk without crutches. Two before she might even grip a tennis racquet again.

Indeed, it was almost two years to the day of her shooting when Roger witnessed Gigi's return to the courts at the Sand Hills Racquet Club. Her spastic swing, her heavy trudge, her immediate weariness were a cruel parody of her former game. Roger took no pleasure in her misery. But the acid drip of guilt he felt was neutralized by the welling pleasure and satisfaction as he watched his own daughter thrive. With a single tighten-

ing of his finger, Roger had liberated Julie and had given a totally justifiable rebuke to the imperious Janeway family.

· · ·

The week before Christmas, on the clay courts of Flamingo
Park on Miami Beach, Julie was serving at 40–15 in the second
set. This was the final match of the most prestigious junior
tournament in the world. The best players from Europe and
South America and Australia had assembled, and Julie had
roared through her draw to the finals, knocking off two seeded
players in the process. After winning the first set, she was up a
service break in the second. As the match progressed her serve
seemed to be gaining strength. Now it was skittering into the
corners, and occasionally blasting directly at her dark-haired
opponent with such vicious pace that the poor Spanish girl's
heavy thighs were pocked with bruises.

Roger wanted to signal Julie to ease off. She was losing the
sympathy of the crowd. There were already a few whistles,
some murmuring around him about the tall, lean American's
lack of sportsmanship. But the referee sitting in the chair at the
net had already given Julie one warning for sneaking looks at
her father's hand signals. Another warning and she'd be penalized a game. Though she was well ahead, such a small inter-
ruption in her concentration might just be enough to tip the
momentum back to the Spaniard.

"She's killing her," Molly whispered. She beamed with
motherly delight.

Roger Shelton's wife, Molly, was as thin and jumpy as a
whippet. She kept her sandy hair chopped short and her skin
had been forever ruined by countless hours in the sun and now
was crisped to the hue and texture of the wrappings of a cheap

cigar. She was an indefatigable doubles player, a woman who thought nothing of playing ten grueling sets in a day.

"I know, I know," Roger said. "Two more games. Just two more."

Roger sat still and suffered the crowd's restlessness and loss of support for his daughter. Julie had begun to employ an ugly strategy, drawing the Spaniard to the net with vicious drop shots, and rather than lobbing over her to exploit her ponderous gait, again and again Julie drove the ball directly at the sluggish girl and more than once the ball found meat.

Finally Julie was a game from victory. The Orange Bowl trophy gleamed on a nearby table. Such a win would kick the door wide open for her tennis future. Endorsement requests would begin to tumble in the mail slot, media attention would escalate, all the best agents would be calling. Already in the last year she had been attracting ever-increasing attention. Tall and blonde with shockingly blue eyes and an easy smile, gorgeously muscled legs and a voluptuous figure so different from her mother's hipless, flat-chested anatomy and from Roger's rail-thin body. Known as "The Stick" for all his high school years, Roger found it amazing that he and Molly had produced such a plush beauty. In the last year a dozen websites had sprung up in cyberspace devoted to the worship of Julie Shelton. Fourteen-year-old boys posted photos of her lunging for net shots, her pleated skirt kicking up just enough to show a swatch of white panties. And it wasn't just an adolescent following, either. Throughout her matches, Roger had to endure the soft groans of yearning all about him, a grumble of lust for his little girl. At first he'd wanted to search out each lecher and wrench him from his seat and toss him over the edge of the bleachers. A satisfaction he could not grant himself, however, for, like it or not, Julie's sexual aura would count as much in her future success as her victories on the courts.

She was serving for the match, for the Orange Bowl title, a win that would bring her a giant step closer to the day when she could etch her name beside those of the great ones of the game, Billie Jean, Chrissie, Martina, Steffi. Roger shifted on the bleacher seat, about to rise to his feet and head down to give her a hug, when he saw from three rows away Arthur Janeway glaring at him. In a white warmup suit, Gigi Janeway sat serenely next to him, her gaze fixed on the final moments of the match. On the far side of her ravaged daughter, Bettina was hunched forward, hollow-eyed and ashen. As if she felt the touch of his anxious stare, she turned her head slowly and locked her bitter gaze on Roger.

Shocked and befuddled, Roger raised a hand and gave the Janeways a ludicrous wave. Neither of them acknowledged the gesture, but continued to observe him coldly.

"Where are you going?" Molly asked as Roger rose. "She's still serving. You're going to distract her."

But Roger was already in motion. Thudding down the bleacher aisle, leaving a murmur of displeasure in his wake, he pushed past two wolfish teenagers in red sweatsuits, the Hungarian contingent, excused himself and hurried into the shadows beneath the bleachers.

His breath was still hot in his throat when he felt the presence behind him.

"You can't get away from me."

Roger swung around and bumped his shoulder into the deep chest of Arthur Janeway.

Janeway was a few inches taller and outweighed Roger by fifty pounds. Since Gigi's injury, he'd virtually disappeared from the dealership. Indeed, this was the first time Roger had seen him in months. The man had lost his steak-and-martini paunch and his florid face, and the rigors of his grief had hardened his thickset body and turned his cheeks the color of frozen iron.

Roger tried to force some compassion into his smile.

"Hello, Arthur. It's good to see you. How is everything?"

Janeway eased his bulk close to Roger. He drew down a breath and blew it out so fiercely it was as if the very taste of air disgusted him.

"I know what you did, Shelton. I know everything."

Roger floundered for a half-second, then found a salesman's smile somewhere down in the hollow depths of his chest.

"You mean that Olds Ciera fiasco? Yeah, yeah. I low-balled it a little, but I had the wholesale numbers jumbled. Don't worry, Arthur, I'll get it back on the next deal."

"I'm not talking about a fucking Oldsmobile, Shelton. You know exactly what I'm talking about."

Roger watched as Bettina helped Gigi down the last steps of the bleachers then halted and surveyed the grounds until she caught sight of the two of them.

"Hey, Arthur, you know I'd love to talk shop a little more, but I really need to give Julie a big hug of celebration."

"You fucked my wife, Shelton," Janeway hissed.

"What?"

Roger drew a careful breath and eyed the big man, whose lips had begun to quiver with rage.

"She told me the whole story. Everything."

Bettina had her arm around Gigi's waist. The girl was leaning against her mother as the two of them plodded closer.

"What in God's name are you talking about?"

Janeway's eyes were slitted now, tipping close to Roger's face. He could smell Arthur's breath, taste the green peppers he'd eaten the night before, and the sour fumes of incompletely digested meat.

"She's yours, Shelton. She's your little girl."

"You really shouldn't joke about something like that, Arthur."

"No one's kidding."

Roger nodded stupidly, a ridiculous smile twisting his lips as he watched mother and daughter draw near.

"Hello, Bettina," he said. "Hello, Gigi. How're you doing?"

Gigi's mouth flickered. She stretched her neck as if something might be stuck in her throat. When she spoke, her voice was a raspy croak.

"I'm surviving."

"Good, good," Roger said, then turned to his employer. "Well, it's certainly nice to see you all. Nice that you're out and around again."

Roger turned to go but Janeway clapped a meaty paw on his shoulder and spun him around.

"Don't bother showing up on the lot again, Shelton. Not that anyone would notice you were missing."

Roger shrugged free of Janeway's grip and headed for the court where Julie was speaking to a writer for *Tennis* magazine. As he stood waiting for the interview to conclude, he could feel the sting of three pairs of eyes on the back of his neck.

A week later, Roger Shelton sat in the den surveying the bleak landscape of the want ads while Julie was in the living room knee to knee with a sales rep for Nike apparel. She was evaluating their latest offer sheet, and even from two rooms away Roger could hear her bargaining tone turn severe. The girl adamantly insisted on making all her own deals. Even with the avalanche of offers she received after winning the Orange Bowl, Julie hadn't so much as requested a hint of advice from Roger or Molly. So far she'd signed a half dozen contracts on her own, a shoe deal, a racquet contract, another agreement to wear a Rolex watch, another to drink only Gatorade on the court. Not even out of high school, and already well on her way to her first ten million.

Roger had been making the rounds of dealerships but had met nothing but cold smiles. He was certain Janeway had blacklisted him. Roger had not given Molly any details about the disquieting conversation with Janeway, only telling her that he'd been downsized from his job of twenty years, without warning or just cause. Molly made a sad face, gave him a buck-up pat on the shoulder and poured him a double martini, and the next morning she was back to her punishing tennis schedule as if nothing had changed, as if Roger was not languishing in his pajamas till noon with the classifieds open in his lap.

On the mantel across the living room, the round-faced clock ticked loudly. Roger stared at it, watching the second hand stutter around its face. He found himself ticking off the seconds as if counting down to some kind of blastoff, waiting, waiting, waiting for the great rocket to lift from its silos and carry him away, giddy and free of gravity. At last the terrible weight lifted from his chest, the earth's pressures relieved.

"Hey, Dad." It was Julie in the doorway. She was wearing a new outfit, a dark blue warmup with a silky sheen. Her name was embroidered in gold over the left breast. And beside her name was the company's logo. His daughter, a freshly minted trademark.

"Yes?"

"Mr. Martino wanted to meet you."

The young man with slicked-back hair and tight muscles and a dark tan marched across the room before Roger could rise from the chair. The salesman stuck out his hand and crushed Roger's meager grip.

"Julie's a damn hard bargainer, Mr. Shelton. Must've inherited that from you. I understand you're in the car business."

"Used cars," Julie said. "The junkers."

Martino nodded, fetching for a smile.

"And he couldn't even hack that," Julie said. "He got fired."

Roger looked at his daughter and then at Martino. Roger tried to smile but felt it wilt on his lips.

"A career transition," Roger said. He tapped the pile of newspapers in his lap, the pathetic red circles around job prospects.

"Well, I'm sure Julie owes a great deal to you, Mr. Shelton. You should be very proud."

"I am, I am."

"I owe something to Mom, maybe," Julie said. She was looking down at the breast of her new warmup, studying the golden twist of letters that spelled out her name. "But I can't think of what Dad did. What I think is, the two of them found me on the doorstep. I mean, come on, look at me. And look at him."

Julie tugged the bottom of her warmup to tighten the fabric against her swelling breasts.

"Sure, genes can be funny, but hey, you saw my mother. She's even skinnier than the old man. I think they found me under a cabbage somewhere."

Roger worked up the smile again and showed it to Martino.

"She's a spunky one," Roger said. "She's right, though. What she's accomplished is her own doing."

"Oh, sure, Dad picked me up after practice now and then. But he only did that so he could check out the other girls. He's a major lech."

"A lech?" Roger said. "Me?"

Martino backed up a step, looking between the two of them, trying to keep his smile in place as if this was a comedy routine still building to the punch line.

"I've earned it all myself," Julie said. "Just look at Gigi Janeway and her dad. He's got more money than the pope, so Gigi had all the best teaching pros. Lessons every day. A coach to work on her serve, one for her backhand, another one for her net game. I had like this one guy, he couldn't even speak English. All he did, he hit me balls from his basket. *Bueno, bueno.* An hour like that, him just hitting me forehands then backhands and yapping in Spanish, ninety-nine percent of which I couldn't understand. So yeah, I'd say I pretty much did it all on my own."

Martino left, chuckling and nodding like it was all an enormous joke. That uproariously witty Shelton family.

Julie went up to her room, shut the door and turned on her rap music and Roger sat in the living room and watched the clock on the mantelpiece tick away the rest of the afternoon.

At dawn the next morning, he rolled from his sleepless bed and went downstairs and paced back and forth across the deck, staring out at the open field behind the house. As the sun broke into view above the pines, he went inside and took down a photo of Julie from the mantelpiece and stared at it. He sat in the living room easy chair and held it up, tilting it back and forth, to catch the light. He put the photo back on the mantel and tiptoed upstairs and eased open the door to Julie's room. She was lying on her back, her head denting the pillow exactly in the center. She snored quietly. He stood there for several minutes watching the girl sleep.

At nine o'clock he roared into the used car lot, got out and stalked into the showroom. Gathered around the coffee machine, the other salesmen watched him but didn't so much as nod when he walked across the floor and went into his old office. Manny Mendoza was closing a deal with a black couple and their teenage daughter. He looked up at Roger and frowned.

"I'm looking for my stuff."

"Stuff?"

"My photos," Roger said. "The stuff I kept on my desk."

Manny nodded toward the far corner where a cardboard box was jammed behind the black couple and their daughter. He picked it up and took it out to the showroom and set it on the hood of a ten-year-old red pickup truck and dug through it till he found what he was looking for. He walked over to the large portrait of Arthur Janeway that hung on the back wall. He held his daughter's photo up to the portrait and cut his eyes back and forth between the two images.

The pouty lips, the heavy lids, the same crease in the earlobes, even an identical arch in the right eyebrow. When he was satisfied the likeness was unmistakable, he dropped the photo back in the box, left it on the hood of the pickup and went out to his nine-year-old Cadillac and drove straightaway to the Sand Hills Racquet Club where he found Molly and her regular doubles partner engaged in a furious exchange of volleys with two much younger women.

Roger walked onto the court in the midst of the point, the ball whacking him between the shoulder blades.

"Roger! We were about to go up a service break. What in the hell are you doing?"

"We need to talk," he said quietly, and pried the racquet from her hand and marched over to a bench in the shade of a royal palm.

Molly stormed over and stood looking down at him with her fists balled against her narrow hips.

"This better be good, Roger."

"It's not good," he said. "No, not good at all."

Molly stared into his eyes and whatever she saw melted the knot in her jaw, neutralized the acid in her eyes. She sat down beside him and together they looked out at the busy courts. The balls passing back and forth across the nets, the cries of exultation and disgust, the peals of laughter. Those neatly lined rectangles of green clay that had always seemed so tranquil to Roger, so calming. The orderliness of it all, a stage so neatly structured, while all around those courts the cosmos whirled haphazardly.

"She's not mine, is she?" Roger said. "Yours, but not mine."

"What are you talking about?"

"It's a wonder I never saw it before. It's so obvious, really. So damn plain when you look at it. Even her personality. That same elbow-your-way-to-the-front approach. I guess on some level I've always known she couldn't be mine."

Roger watched the balls traveling back and forth and back and forth again across the precisely measured nets. He listened to the thwock of cleanly hit serves, the machine gun exchanges with all four players at the net. Such an orderly game. So pure, so simple, so perfectly symmetrical.

•　•　•

Two days later Roger stood in the field of tall grass and looked at the back of his two-story house, aglow with lights on that moonless night. He could see Molly finishing her cleanup in the kitchen. The evening news was over now. She was watching the entertainment shows, learning about the latest tribulations of her Hollywood pals.

Earlier that afternoon Roger had an interview at a Buick dealership down in Miami, over a hundred miles south. Then a half-hour ago he had called Molly to let her know he'd been caught in a snarl of rush-hour traffic, so he'd pulled off I-95 and stopped at some bar in Ft. Lauderdale to pass an hour till the roadways cleared.

The truth was, after the interview, he'd driven back to Sand Hills and made the call from a bar on the edge of town and then he'd driven to the junior high school a half mile from their house and waited till it grew dark. He'd carried the deer rifle through the stand of pine trees that separated the ball fields of the junior high from the development where he lived. And now he stood in the meadow watching the windows of his own home and thinking about justice and lucky sperm and the difference between an artistic temperament and a plodding, methodical one, which was, he was starting to believe, the difference between arrogance and humility. What utter hubris to have ever believed that a few lucky days of salesmanship was the equivalent of artistic triumph. Roger Shelton was a hopeless plodder just as his daughter was. All she had inherited from him was an unfathomable mediocrity. She wasn't flashy, wasn't a slugger, had no killing shot. All she'd ever done was keep the ball in play one hit longer than her opponent. Hanging on, surviving.

When Julie appeared in her window, Roger raised the rifle and brought her closer to him. He lay the center of the X across her ample chest. Julie was on the phone. She was wearing one of her new monogrammed warmups and her hair was damp from the shower. The words came from her lips in a furious rush. Maybe it was her agent or one of her numerous boyfriends. He could see her lips moving, then he watched the clench of her jaw as she forced herself to be silent and listen. It was a gesture he had witnessed in Arthur Janeway a hundred times. Exasperated restraint. As if the two of them believed what they had to say was without question worth more than what any other man might want to say.

Roger did not possess such confidence. He had no idea how it felt to be absolutely certain of anything. Even now, as he stood aiming his rifle, a lonely marksman in a field, he had only the faintest hope that he could undo some small part of the harm he'd caused. Indeed, justice was the smallest part of what brought him to that dewy grass. Roger was acting out the logic of a dream. Like some tennis player driven deep into a corner of the court, left with only one unavoidable shot.

He watched Julie glare out her window into the dark field where he stood. He watched her talk. This girl who was neither his flesh nor his blood, this alien creature who for fifteen years had lived within his household and who was now prospering only because he had wounded the wrong daughter. His own girl, her will broken, her precise, predictable, tireless stroke forever ruined. While this cheap impostor flourished.

He watched Julie Shelton talk on the phone. He watched her shake her head in disdain and spit a few words into the receiver and jerk it away from her ear in a fit of disgust. Then he watched her pop to sudden attention, her face drained of all but a last flicker of contempt. He watched her drop stiffly out of sight. Then he shifted his gaze to his wife, as Molly lifted her head and stared up at the ceiling where she must have heard a crash against the bedroom floor. He watched her cup her hand to her mouth and call out her daughter's name. He watched her throw her dish towel down and hurry to the door, then halt abruptly and send one backward glance toward the window that looked out on the darkened field. Her eyes touching his for an icy instant.

Roger Shelton stepped backward into the shadows and lowered his rifle. He listened to the fading echo of his shot. That single blast rippling through the humid air, loud and final, but already dissipating, in just those few seconds the waves of sound spreading outward, breaking up and scattering, until finally the blast was lost in the endless racket of the night.

PROMISE

JOHN HARVEY

At Wimbledon, Kiley found himself sharing over-priced strawberries and champagne with Adrian Costain, a sports agent he'd brushed up against a few times in his soccer days, and when Costain rang him a week later with the offer of some private work, he thought, why not?

So here he was, ten years down the line from his twenty-five minutes of fame, a private investigator with an office, a computer, pager, fax and phone; a small but growing clientele, a backlog of successfully resolved, mostly sports-associated cases.

Jack Kiley, whatever happened to him?

Well, now you know.

.   .   .

Kiley was alone in his office, August 3. Two rooms above a bookshop in Belsize Park. A bathroom he shared with the financial consultant whose office was on the upper floor.

"So what d'you think?" Kate had asked him the first time they'd looked round. "Perfect, no?" Kate having been tipped off by her friend, Lauren, who managed the shop below.

"Perfect, maybe. But rents in this part of London . . . there's no way I could afford it."

"Jack!"

"It's all I can do to keep up with the payments on the flat."

"Then let it go."

"What?"

"The flat, let it go."

Kiley had stared around. "And live here?"

"No, fool. Move in with me."

So now Kiley's name was there in neat lettering, upper- and lowercase, on the glass of the outer door. The office chair behind the glass-topped desk was angled round, suggesting his secretary had just popped out and would be back. As she might, were she to exist. In her stead, there was Irena, a young Romanian who waited on tables across the street at Café Pasta, and two mornings a week did Kiley's filing for him, a little basic word processing, talked to him of the squares and avenues of Bucharest, excursions to the Black Sea, of storks that nested by the sides of country roads.

In Kiley's inner sanctum were a smaller desk, oak-faced, an easy chair, a couch on which he sometimes napped, a radio, a TV whose screen he could span with one outstretched hand. There was a plant, jasmine, tiny white flowers amongst a plethora of glossed green leaves; a barely troubled bottle of single malt; a framed print Kate had presented him with when he moved in: two broad bands of cream resting across a field of mottled gray, the lines between hand drawn and slightly wavering.

"It'll grow on you," she'd said.

He was still waiting.

The phone chirruped and he lifted it to his ear.

"Busy, Jack?" Costain's voice was two-thirds marketing, one third market stall.

"That depends."

"Victoria Clarke."

"What about her?"

"Get yourself down to Queen's. Forty-five minutes to an hour from now, she should be toweling down."

Kiley was enough of a Londoner to know car owning for a mug's game. Within three minutes, he'd picked up a cab traveling south down Haverstock Hill and they'd set off on the zigzag course that would shuttle them west, Kiley wondering how many billboards of Victoria Clarke they would pass on the way.

That damp June and July she had been a minor sensation at the Wimbledon Championships, the first British woman to reach the semifinals since Boadicea, or so it seemed, and ranked currently twenty-three in the world. And she had sprung from nowhere, or somewhere near the Essex end of the Central line at best; a council flat she had shared growing up with her sister, step-dad and mum. And like the Williams sisters, Serena and Venus, in the States, she had learned to play on public courts, enjoying none of the privilege that usually attended the luckless Amandas and Betinas of the English tennis world. Nor did it end there. Her face, which freckled slightly in the sun, was beautiful in a Kate Moss kind of a way, her legs slender and long; the quality of the sports photographer's long lens and of television video ensured that not one salted bead of sweat that languished on her back then slowly disappeared into the decolletage of the T-shirt tops she liked to wear was spared from public view.

Before the tournament was over, Costain had the contracts signed, the company's ad campaign agreed. Less than a fortnight later, the first of the advertisements appeared: Clarke crouching on the baseline, racquet in hand, lips slightly parted, waiting to receive. In another she was watching the high toss of the ball, back arched, about to serve, white cotton top stretched tight across her breasts. For these and others, the strap line was the same: *A Little Honest Sweat!* Just that and a discreet Union Jack, the deodorant pictured lower right, close by the product's name.

Unreconstructed feminists protested and sprayed slogans late at night; students tore them down as trophies for their rooms; Kate devoted her column in *The Independent* to the insistent eroticizing of the everyday. One giant billboard near an intersection on the AI North was removed after advice from the Department of Transport.

In *The Observer Sport Monthly*'s annual list of Britain's Top Twenty Sportswomen, Victoria Clarke was number seven with a bullet, the only tennis player to appear at all.

"Looks like you forgot your racquet," the cabbie joked, glancing at Kiley, empty-handed, waiting outside Queen's Club for his change and his receipt.

Kiley half-grinned and shook his head. "Different game."

· · ·

Costain was in the bar: tousled hair, rimless glasses, Paul Smith suit and large gin. He bought Kiley a small scotch and water and they moved to a pair of low leather chairs by the far wall. Good living, Kiley noticed, had brought Costain a considerable gut, which the loose cut of his suit just failed to disguise.

"So how is it really?" Costain asked with a smile.

"You know."

"Still with Kate?"

Kiley nodded.

"How long's that now?" And then, quickly, "I know, I know, who's counting?"

In a week's time it would be two years since they'd started seeing one another; nine months, almost to the day, since he'd moved into Kate's house in Highbury Fields. Kate, Kiley knew, had gone out with Costain a few times some few years back; kissing him, she said, was like being force-fed marinated eel.

"Victoria Clarke," Kiley said, "what's the problem? There is a problem, I suppose."

Costain drank a little more gin. "She's being blackmailed."

"Don't tell me she was a Page Three Girl for *The Sun*."

For an answer, Costain took an envelope from the inside pocket of his suit coat and passed it across. Inside, a black-and-white copy of a photograph had been pasted to a single sheet of paper: a young woman in a park, holding a small girl, a toddler, high above her head; in the background, another woman, beside an empty buggy, looked on. The first woman, and the girl, were smiling, more than smiling, laughing; the second woman was not. The quality of the copy was such that it took a keen eye to identify the former as Victoria Clarke. Even then, there was room for doubt.

"Is this all there is?" Kiley asked.

"It arrived this morning, first post. A phone call some forty minutes later, man's voice, disguised." He nodded toward the paper in Kiley's hand. "I imagine the original's a lot clearer, wouldn't you?"

"And the child?"

"Hers. Victoria's."

Kiley looked at the picture again: The relationship between the two women was there, but it wasn't yet defined. "Whoever sent this, what do they want?"

"A quarter of a million."

"For what?"

"The negative, all originals, copies. We've got two days before they sell it to the highest bidder. The tabloids'd go apeshit."

Kiley tasted his scotch. "Why now?" he asked.

"We're in the middle of renegotiating Victoria's advertising contract. Very hush-hush. Big, big money involved. If nothing slips out of sync, everything should be finalized by the end of the week."

"Then, hush-hush or not, somebody knows."

"What?" Costain said, mouth twisting in a wry grin. "You don't believe in blind luck?" And, because Victoria Clarke was now walking through the bar toward them, he rose to his feet and smiled a reassuring smile.

She was tall, taller even than Kiley, who knew the stats, had thought, and wore a dark blue warmup suit, name monogrammed neatly along sleeve and leg, with something close to style. Sports bag slung over one shoulder, hair still damp from the shower and tied back, the only signs of distress were in the hollows of her eyes, the suggestion of a tremor when she shook Kiley's hand.

"You want something?" Costain asked. "Mineral water? Juice?"

She shook her head. Standing there devoid of makeup, she almost looked what she was: nineteen.

The envelope lay on the table between two unfinished drinks. "I don't want to talk about this here," Victoria said.

"I thought just . . ." Costain began.

"Not here." The voice wasn't petulant, but firm.

Costain shrugged and, with a glance at Kiley, downed his gin and led the way toward the door.

• • •

Costain owned a flat in a mansion block close to the Thames—in fact, he owned several between there and the Cromwell Road—and for the past several months it had been Victoria's home. Near enough to Queen's for her to hit every day.

"You'll have to excuse the mess," she said.

Kiley moved an armful of discarded clothing and a paperback copy of Navratilova's life story. The room resembled a cross between a Conran's window and the left luggage department at Euston Station.

Victoria left them to each other's company and reemerged some minutes later in a pale cotton top and faded jeans, hair brushed out and a little makeup around the eyes.

Sitting in an easy chair opposite Kiley, she tucked as much of her long legs beneath her as she could. "Can you help?" She had a way of looking directly at you when she spoke.

"It depends."

"On what?"

Kiley shook his head. "Timing. Luck. You. The truth."

Only for an instant did she lower her eyes, fingers of one hand sliding between those of the other then out again. "Adrian," she said over her shoulder. "Get me some water, would you? There's some in the fridge in . . ." But Costain had already gone to do her bidding.

"I had Alicia—Alicia, that's her name—when I was fifteen. Fifteen years and ten months. The year before I'd been runner-up in the National Under-Sixteens at Hove. I was on the fringes of the County team. I thought if I can get through to the last eight of the Junior Championships this next Wimbledon, I'm on my way. And then there was this lump that wouldn't go away."

She paused to judge the effect of what she'd just said.

Costain placed a tumbler of still mineral water in her hand and then retreated back across the room.

"Why didn't you have an abortion?" Kiley asked.

She looked back at him evenly. "I'd already made one bad mistake."

"So you asked your sister—that is your sister, isn't it? In the photo?" Victoria bobbed her head. "You asked your sister to look after her . . . No, more than that. To say that she was hers; bring her up as her own."

"Yes." In the wide, high-ceilinged room, Victoria's voice was suddenly very small.

"And she didn't mind?"

A shadow passed across Victoria's eyes. "You have to understand. Catherine, that's my sister, I mean, she's wonderful, she's lovely with Alicia, really, but she just isn't . . . Well, we're different, chalk and cheese, she isn't like me at all, she doesn't . . ." Victoria drank from her glass and went back to balancing it on her knee. "All she's ever wanted was to settle down, have kids, a place of her own. She didn't want to . . ." Victoria sighed. ". . . *do* anything. She and Trevor, they'd been going steady since she was fourteen; they were saving up to get married anyway. Mum chipped in, helped them get started. Trevor, he was bringing in good money by then, Fords at Dagenham. Of course, now I can I pay toward whatever Alicia needs; I do."

"A good percentage of her disposable income," Costain interrupted. "First-class holiday in Florida last year for the three of them, four weeks."

"Catherine and Trevor," Kiley said, "they haven't had children of their own?"

Victoria lifted her gaze from Kiley's face toward the window, where a fly was buzzing haphazardly against the glass. "She can't. I mean, I suppose she could try IVF. But, no, she can't have children of her own."

Kiley let the moment settle. "And Alicia?"

Victoria's lower lip slid over the upper and the water glass tipped from hand and knee onto the floor. "She thinks I'm her auntie, of course. What else?"

Adrian reached out for her as she ran but she swerved around him and slammed the bedroom door.

"What do you think?" he said.

"I think," said Kiley, "I need a drink."

•   •   •

Victoria had been seeing Paul Broughton ever since her fifteenth birthday. Broughton, twenty-three years old, a butcher boy in Leytonstone by day, by night the drummer in a band that might have been the Verve if the Verve hadn't already existed. A nice East London line on post-Industrial grime and angst. With heavily amplified guitars. After a gig at Walthamstow Assembly Rooms, he and Victoria got careless—either that, or Broughton's timing was off.

"For fuck's sake!" he said when Victoria told him. "What d'you think you're gonna do? Get rid of it, of course."

She didn't waste words on him again. She talked to her mum and her mum, who had some experience in these things, told her not to worry, they'd find a way. Which of them first had the idea about asking Catherine, they could never be sure. Nor how Catherine persuaded Trevor. But there was big sister, half-nine to half-five in the greetings card shop and hating every minute. Victoria wore looser clothes, avoided public showers; her sister padded herself out, chucked in her job, practiced walking with splayed legs and pain in the lower back. They chose the name together from a book. After the birth—like shelling peas, the midwife said—Victoria held the baby, kissed her close, and handed her across, a smear of blood and mucus on her cheek. Still, sometimes when she woke, she felt a baby's breath pass warm across her face.

As a Wimbledon junior, she reached the semifinals before dropping a set, strode out to take the final, as she thought, by right, and went down two and love to the LTA's new white hope in thirty minutes flat. Costain, who had been monitoring Victoria's progress, waited till the hurt had eased and offered her a contract, sole representation, which her mother, of course, had to sign on her behalf. Costain's play: retreat, lie low, for now leave domestic competition alone; he financed winters in Australia, the United States. Wait till they've forgotten who you are then hit them smack between the eyes.

So far it had worked.

·   ·   ·

"I assume you don't want to pay?" Kiley said. Victoria was still in the bedroom, door locked.

"Quarter of a million? No, thanks?"

"But you'd pay something?"

Costain shrugged and pursed his lips; of course he would. "Sooner or later, you know it'll come out."

"Of course. I just want to be able to manage it, that's all. And now . . . the timing . . . you can imagine what this company's going to be saying about their precious image. If they don't walk away completely, and I think they might, they'll strip what they're offering back down to what we're getting now. Or worse."

"You couldn't live with that?"

"I don't want to live with that."

"All right, all right. When are they getting in touch again?"

"Five this evening."

Kiley looked at his watch. One hour, fifteen to go. "Try and stall them, buy another twenty-four hours."

"They'll never wear it."

"Tell them if they want payment in full, they don't have any choice."

"And if they still say no?"

Kiley rose to his feet. "In the event the shit does hit the fan, I assume you've damage limitation planned."

"What do you think?"

"I think you should make sure your plan's in place."

●   ●   ●

"So what did you think of her?" Kate asked. "Ms. Teen Sensation."

"I liked her."

"Really?"

"Yes, really."

They were lying, half-undressed, across the bed, Kate picking her way through an article by Naomi Klein, seeking something with which to disagree in print. Kiley had been reading one of the Chandlers Kate had bought him for his birthday—Give you some idea of how a private eye's supposed to think—and liking it well enough. Although it was still a book. Before that, they had been making love.

"You fancied her, that's what you mean?"

"No. I liked her."

"You didn't fancy her?"

"Kate . . ."

"What?" But she was laughing and Kiley grinned back and shook his head and she shifted so that one of her legs rested high across his and he began to stroke her shoulder and her back.

"You got your extra twenty-four hours," Kate said.

"Apparently."

"Is that going to be enough?"

"If it's someone close, someone obvious, then, yes. But if it's somebody outside the loop, there's no real chance."

"And he knows that, Costain?"

Kiley nodded. "I'm sure he does."

"In which case, why not involve the police?"

"Because the minute he does, someone inside the Force will sell him out to the media before tomorrow's first edition. You should know that better than me."

"Jack," she said, smiling. "You'll do what you can." And rolled from her side onto her back.

· · ·

Victoria's mum, Leslie, was a dead ringer for Christine McVie. The singer from Fleetwood Mac. Remember? Not the skinny one with the Minnie Mouse voice, but the other one, older, more mature. Dyed blonde hair and lived-in face and a voice that spoke of sex and forty cigarettes a day; the kind of woman you might fancy rotten if you were fifteen, which was what Kiley had been at the time, and you spotted her or someone like her behind the counter in the local chemist or driving past in one of those white vans delivering auto parts, nicotine at her finger ends and oil on her overalls. *Rumours.* Kiley alone upstairs in his room, listening to the record again and again. Rolling from side to side on the bed, trying to keep his hands to himself.

"Won't you come in?" Leslie Clarke said. She was wearing a leisure suit in pale mauve, gold slippers with a small heel. Dark red fingernails. She didn't have a cigarette still in her hand, but had stubbed it out, Kiley thought, when the doorbell rang; the smell of it warm and acrid on her as he squeezed past into the small lobby and she closed the double-glazed Tudor-style external door and ushered him into the living room with its white leather-look chairs and neat little nest of tables and framed photographs of her granddaughter, Alicia, on the walls.

"I made coffee."

"Great."

Kiley sat and held out his cup while Leslie poured. Photographs he had expected, but of a triumphant Victoria holding trophies aloft. And there were photos of her, of course, a few, perched around the TV and along the redundant mantelpiece; Catherine, too, Catherine and Trevor on their wedding day. But little Alicia was everywhere and Leslie, following Kiley's gaze, smiled a smile of satisfaction. "Lovely, isn't she. A sweetheart. A real sweetheart. Bright, too. Like a button."

Either way, Kiley thought, Victoria or Catherine, Leslie had got what she wanted. Her first grandchild.

"Vicky bought me this house, did you know that? It's not a palace, of course, but it suits me fine. Cozy, I suppose that's what it is. And there's plenty of room for Alicia when she comes to stay." She smiled and leaned back against white vinyl. "I always did have a hankering after Buckhurst Hill." Unable to resist any longer, she reached for her Benson and Hedges, king size. "Coffee okay?"

"Lovely." The small lies, the little social ones, Kiley had found came easy.

They talked about Victoria then, Victoria and her sister, whatever jealousies had grown up between them, festered maybe, been smoothed away. Trevor, was he resentful, did he ever treat Alicia as if she weren't really his? But Trevor was the perfect dad and as far as money was concerned, since his move to Luton, to Vauxhall, some deal they'd done with the German owners, the unions that is, and Trevor had got himself off the shop floor—well, it wasn't as if they were actually throwing it around but, no, cash was something they weren't short of, Leslie was sure of that.

"What about Victoria's father?" Kiley asked.

Leslie threw back her head and laughed. "The bastard, as he's affectionately known."

"Is he still around? Is there any chance he might be involved?"

Leslie shook her head. "The bastard, bless him, would've

had difficulties getting the right stamp onto the envelope, never mind the rest. Fifteen years, the last time I laid eyes on him; working on the oil rigs he'd been, up around Aberdeen. Took a blow to the head from some piece of equipment in a storm and had to be stretchered off. Knocked the last bit of sense out of him. The drink had seen to the rest long since." She drew hard on her cigarette. "If he's still alive, which I doubt, it's in some hostel somewhere." And shivered. "I just hope the poor bastard isn't sleeping rough."

• • •

Paul Broughton was working for a record company in Camden, offices near the canal, more or less opposite the Engineer. Olive V-neck top and chocolate flat-front moleskin chinos, close-shaven head and stubbled chin, two silver rings in one ear, a stud, emerald green, at the center of his bottom lip. A&R, developing new talent, that was his thing. Little bands that gigged at the Dublin Castle or the Boston Dome, the Rocket on the Holloway Road. He was listening to a demo tape on headphones when Kiley walked toward him across a few hundred feet of open plan; Broughton's desk awash with takeaway mugs from Caffè Nero, unopened padded envelopes and hopeful fliers.

Kiley waited till Broughton had dispensed with the headphones, introduced himself and held out his hand.

"Look," Broughton said, ignoring the hand. "I told you on the phone . . ."

"Tell me again."

"I ain't seen Vicky in fuckin' years."

"How many years?"

"I dunno. Four, five?"

"Not since she told you she was carrying your child."

"Yeah, I s'pose."

"But you've been in touch."

"Who says?"

"Once you started seeing her picture in the paper, those ads out on the street. Read about all that money she was bringing in. And for what? It wouldn't have been difficult to get her number, you used your mobile, gave her a call."

Broughton glared back at him, defiant. "Bollocks!" And then, "So what if I did?"

"What did she tell you, Paul? The same as before? Get lost."

"Look, I ain't got time for this."

"Was that when you thought you'd put the bite on her, a little blackmail? Get something back for treating you like shit?"

Broughton clenched his fists. "Fuck off! Fuck off out of here before I have you thrown out. I wouldn't take money from that stuck-up tart if it was dripping out of her arse. I don't need it, right?"

"And you don't care she had your child against your will, kept her out of your sight?"

Broughton laughed, a sneer ugly across his face. "You don't get it, do you? She was just some cunt I fucked. End of fuckin' story."

"She was barely fifteen years old," Kiley said.

"I know," Broughton said, and winked.

Kiley was almost halfway toward the door before he turned around. Broughton was sitting on the edge of his desk, headphones back in place, watching him go. Kiley hit him twice in the face with his fist, hauled him back up onto his knees and hit him once more. Then left.

· · ·

They'd bought a nice house on the edge of Dunstable, with views across the Chiltern Hills. They'd done well. Alicia was in the back garden, on a swing. The apple trees were rich in fruit, the roses well into bloom. Catherine stood by the French windows, gazing out. Her expression when Kiley had arrived on the doorstep had told him pretty much all he needed to know.

Trevor was in the garage, tinkering. Tools clipped with precision to the walls, tools that shone with pride of ownership and use. Kiley didn't rush him, let him take his time. Watched as Trevor tightened this, loosened that.

"It's the job, isn't it?" Kiley eventually said.

Trevor straightened, surprised.

"You sold up, left friends, invested in this place. Not just for Catherine and yourself. For her, Alicia. A better place to grow up, country, almost. A big mortgage, but as long as the money's coming in . . ."

"They promised us," Trevor said, not looking at Kiley now, staring through the open door toward the trees. "The Germans, when we agreed the deal. Jobs for life, that's what they said. Jobs for sodding life. Now they're closing down the plant, shifting production to Portugal or Spain. No longer economic, that's us." When he did turn, there were tears in his eyes. "They bent us over and fucked us up the arse and all this bastard government did was stand by with the Vaseline."

Kiley put a hand on his shoulder and Trevor shrugged it off and they stood there for a while, not speaking, then went inside and sat around the kitchen table drinking tea. Alicia sat in

Catherine's lap, playing with her mother's hair. Her mother: That's what she was, what she had become.

"You could have asked," Kiley said. "Asked Victoria outright, explained."

"We've tried before," Catherine said bitterly. "It's hateful, like pulling teeth."

Trevor reached across and gave her lower arm a squeeze. "Vicky's not the problem," he said, "not really. It's him, the money man."

"Costain?"

Trevor nodded.

"Leave him to me," Kiley said. "I'll make sure he understands."

"Mum," Alicia said. "Let's read a book."

Trevor walked Kiley down the path toward his hired car, stood with one hand resting on the roof. The sun was just beginning to fade in the sky. "I'd go round to their house," he said. "Evenings, you know, when I was seeing Catherine, and she'd be there. Victoria. I doubt she was much more than fourteen then." He sighed and kicked the ground with his shoe. "She could've put a ring through my nose and had me crawling after her, all fours around the room." Slowly, he drew air down into his lungs. "You're right, it's nice out here. Quiet."

The two men shook hands.

"Thanks," Trevor said. "I mean it. Thanks a lot."

· · ·

Kiley didn't see Victoria Clarke until the spring, the French Open. He and Kate had traveled Eurostar to Paris for the weekend, stayed in their favorite hotel near the Jardins du Luxembourg. Kate had a French author to interview, a visit to the

Musée d'Art Moderne planned; Kiley thought lunch at the brasserie across from Gare du Nord, then a little tennis.

Costain, buoyant after marshaling Victoria's advertising contract safely through, had struck a favorable deal with Catherine and Trevor: 5 percent of Victoria's gross income to be paid into a trust fund for Alicia, an annual payment of six thousand pounds toward her everyday needs, this sum to be reviewed; as long as Trevor remained unemployed, the shortfall on the mortgage would be picked up. In exchange, a secrecy agreement was sworn and signed, valid until Alicia reached eighteen.

On court at Roland Garros, rain threatened, the sky a leaden gray. After taking the first set 6–2, Victoria was struggling against a hefty left-hander from Belarus. Concentration gone, suddenly she was double-faulting on her serve, overhitting her two-fisted backhand, muttering to herself along the baseline. Five–all and then the set had gone, unraveled, Victoria slump-shouldered and staring at the ground. The first four games of the final set went with serve and Kiley could feel the muscles across his shoulders knot as he willed Victoria to break clear of whatever was clouding her mind, shake free. It wasn't until she was 4–3 down that it happened, a skidding return of serve whipped low across the net and some instinct causing her to follow it in, her volley unplayable, an inch inside the line. After that, a baseline smash that tore her opponent's racquet from her hand, a topspin lob judged to perfection; finally, two aces, the first swinging away unplayably, the second hard down the center line, and she was running to the net, racquet raised to acknowledge the applause, a quick smile and touch of hands. On her way back to her chair, she glanced up to where Kiley was sitting in the stands, but if she saw him she gave no sign.

When he arrived back at the hotel, Kate was already there, damp from the shower, leaning back against the pillows with a book. The shutters out onto the balcony were partway open.

"So?" Kate said as Kiley shrugged off his coat, "how was it?"

"A struggle."

"Poor lamb."

"No call to be bitchy."

Kate poked out her tongue.

Stretched out on the bed beside her, Kiley bent his head. "Are you reading that in French?"

"Why else d'you think I'm moving my lips?"

The skin inside her arm was taut and sweet.

A DEBT TO THE DEVIL

JEREMIAH HEALY

D on Floyd led me into the memorial chapel as though he'd been there before, despite his mentioning on the drive over from the Lauderdale Tennis Club that he wasn't Jewish himself. Given the short time I'd lived in South Florida, much less at the Club, the building we entered looked more to me like a Spanish villa than a funeral parlor, what with exterior walls of yellow stucco and orange bumpy tiles on the roof. But around us a lot of grave markers dotted the flat, green meadow.

In a small vestibule, we signed a VISITORS log, Floyd—in the deliberate cadence of his native Georgia—introducing me to people as "Rory Calhoun." Back in the early sixties, my mom had developed a permanent crush on that B-movie star, so after she married his surname-sake and I came along, my given name was a forgone, if embarrassing, conclusion.

Floyd and I began to follow the flow into the chapel proper. It was a big, square room, with rows of oak benches like Catholic pews but upholstered on the seats, a Star of David carved into each end post. A seven-spiked candelabra stood centered at the front of the room, a large-lettered prayer entitled the "Mourner's Kaddish" to one side, a similar mural of the Twenty-third Psalm to the other, which kind of surprised me.

And, underneath the candelabra, a blonde-wood casket. Closed, which didn't surprise me.

Most of the benches were full already. I followed Floyd— eighty-plus and white of hair, but still as sharp as he was spry—into one of the back rows. As we sat, a woman moved with purpose toward a podium near the Kaddish mural. Identifying herself over the microphone as a rabbi, she announced she'd be reading the Twenty-third Psalm first in Hebrew, then in English. Tuning out the initial version, I began to wonder exactly why I was there.

You see, I'd gotten a college degree before going on the professional tennis circuit. After a few years of touring, however, a chronic knee problem and a mediocre first serve relegated me to satellite tournaments, especially those on clay, where stamina and strategy could carry a player past the first round. During the stretches I couldn't play, I'd apprenticed myself to private investigators for the day-labor money they paid. In fact, I'd just gotten my full Florida investigator's license, though I didn't understand—

Floyd nudged me in the ribs. "Rory?"

That's when I realized the rabbi was now reciting the psalm in English, most of the people in the chapel joining in. I mouthed the words, feeling strangely reassured by the chorus rising up in honor of Solomon Schiff, a man I'd seen on the courts at the club but only barely met.

After we all finished, the rabbi gave a short, thoughtful eulogy for "Sol," noting that he wasn't exactly a regular at "Shabbat" services, but still supported his faith in tangible ways. Then she invited any who wished to share a "remembrance" to succeed her at the podium.

A man who turned out to be the publisher of *Florida Tennis* magazine made his way there. He spoke with humor and grace about Sol Schiff's career as a college champion and solid amateur before the era of open tennis began with Rod Laver at the Longwood Cricket Club. Then he toted up Schiff's long history with the USTA—the United States Tennis Association—and Seniors' Sectional and National tournaments.

A few members of our club followed, including Don Floyd—its unofficial "mayor." All recounted different anecdotes about playing with Schiff or instances of kindness the decedent had shown to people over the years. The phrases most repeated were "fair opponent," "man of his word," and "tough negotiator."

I was kind of surprised no family spoke, then realized that a man in his seventies like Solomon Schiff might not have had any direct survivors. But as a woman in her forties moved to the podium, a hush fell over the room.

Floyd leaned into me a little. "She's the one who wanted you here today."

The woman identified herself as Naomi Schiff, Sol's niece. Her curly hair was black, only a few strands gray. When she began speaking, you could hear sniffling and outright sobbing for the first time during the service. Schiff herself kept swiping a hankie at her eyes, but the voice was strong and clear.

And more than a little angry.

"My uncle was known to all of you, but he was loved by

me. After my father died, Sol took me in as his own. He fed me, he educated me, he helped me finance a business of my own up in New Jersey, where we lived until Sol moved down here permanently twenty-two years ago. At every stage of my life, there was a step where I would have faltered if he hadn't taken my hand in his and led me the right way. Though he never married and had no children of his own, Sol was everything anyone could ever have asked for in a parent. Only now he's been taken from me. From all of us."

Schiff gripped the edges of the podium with both hands, bringing her lips very close to the microphone, although she spoke her next words most softly of all. "As some of you know, my father . . . committed suicide. I made my uncle promise then that he'd never do that to me. Well, I'm the one making a promise now." She turned to the casket. "Uncle Sol, I will not rest until the person who killed you is strapped into Florida's electric chair."

Don Floyd leaned into me again. "That's why she wants to hire you."

• • •

Naomi Schiff said, "You look more like Tom Selleck than William Conrad."

Stars of the television shows *Magnum, P.I.* and *Cannon.* "Is that a compliment?"

"Not really." She shrugged. "Selleck was good-looking, but Conrad gave the impression he was just good."

Schiff and I were walking back from the graveside toward the memorial chapel. The services over the coffin were mercifully brief, workers in tan jumpsuits and wrap-around shades lowering it into the ground via green straps attached to a perimeter frame of chrome. Some mourners, Don Floyd included, used a small shovel to take handfuls of pale-colored earth from a wheelbarrow and sprinkle it into the hole before the workers began disassembling the frame and straps for the next person needing them. Then Floyd went back to his car so Schiff and I could talk by ourselves.

We reached a little glade in the cemetery with half a dozen markers and a polished marble bench that read "Clarstein" on the edge of its seat. Schiff said, "Why don't we sit? I somehow don't think the Clarsteins would mind."

"All right."

Settling onto the stone, she smoothed the black dress down over her thighs almost to the knees. "I've never done this before."

"Talked with a private investigator?"

"Yes."

I didn't want to blow Don Floyd's cover. "I'm assuming it has something to do with your uncle's death?"

Schiff looked at me more closely. "Mr. Calhoun, how long have you been at the Lauderdale Tennis Club?"

"I've lived there about a month."

"So, you knew my uncle Sol."

"He was a nonresident member, so I more knew of him. Who he'd been, how people viewed him."

"Meaning, as an icon."

Give it to her. "My impression."

Schiff sighed, scuffing the soles of her shoes on the slate flagstones beneath her feet. "Tennis was everything to Sol, and he was everything to me—though once he moved down here, we lost track a little of each other's lives. You follow what I said in the chapel?"

I didn't want to tell her that Florida had switched from the electric chair to lethal injection, so I just said, "Yes."

"Well, my father—Sol's brother—suffered a series of . . . 'reversals,' he called them. 'Just business reversals, honey,' I remember him saying to my mother. Until one day when I was seven years old, and he blew his head off. Which sent my mother into a mental institution for the rest of her life."

"Ms. Schiff, I'm sorry."

A frustrated wave of the hand. "But my uncle got me through it, Mr. Calhoun, and through everything else, from dating boys to negotiating contracts. And now somebody's killed him."

"Word around the Club was he surprised a burglar."

Schiff ratcheted down a notch. "That's the theory the police fed me. But his place had been ransacked, and as I tried to clean up the mess, something else occurred to me."

"What?"

"That maybe the killer was searching for something. So many things got broken, it's hard to say if much is missing."

"I don't know exactly where your uncle lived."

"On the Intracoastal Waterway. Near 'Las Olas Boulevard,' I think you call it?"

Kind of Fort Lauderdale's Rodeo Drive, but toned down rather than tonier. Several engineered isles stuck out from Las Olas into the channel with canals cut between them to maximize the amount of "waterfront" property.

I said, "Are the Lauderdale police still investigating?"

"According to them, the case 'remains open.'"

Which could mean anything, but in my limited experience usually suggested there was no active suspect. "Why do you want to hire me?"

Schiff shrugged again. She seemed an "in-charge" kind of person, and I got the feeling "shrugging" wasn't something she did often or enjoyed doing at all.

Schiff said, "Sol was everything to—God, I'm repeating myself, aren't I?"

"Under the circumstances, I'd say you're entitled."

She passed her left palm over her face. "Thank you, Mr. Calhoun. To answer your question, though, I'd like you to approach this opposite to the way the police have."

"Meaning?"

"They're assuming it was a burglary gone wrong. If it was something else, I want to know that."

She fixed me with eyes I'd hate to negotiate against myself. Then I realized that, in a sense, I already was.

Schiff said, "And I want to know who killed the dearest man in my life."

I looked over her shoulder at a painfully blue sky, made the more so by a few clouds scudding past, pushed by the maybe-ten-mile-per-hour breeze that lifted the petals on the cut, graveside flowers all around us.

As though they were still living plants, reaching toward the sun.

Naomi Schiff said, "Mr. Calhoun?"

"I'll give it a try."

*   *   *

Don Floyd started his car, pulling out of the parking area of the chapel. "Did Naomi tell you there was a reception—the Jewish people call it 'sitting shivah,' I believe?"

"She told me." I shifted in the passenger seat. "Don, if what happened at Solomon Schiff's house wasn't a burglary, is there anyone I should talk to?"

Floyd frowned, then stopped for a traffic light. "Nobody who'd wish him harm, Rory. But there are some who knew him better than others."

"For instance?"

"Sol's business partner died—not like his brother, though. This was complications from a stroke, some five years or so back. The partner's name was Bourke, spelled B-O-U-R-K-E. Casey Bourke. His widow still lives at the Club. Karen?"

. "Haven't met her."

"Sweet lady. Then there's Sol's . . . girlfriend."

"You don't say it like you mean it."

The light changed, and we moved forward. "Well, she's quite a bit younger. Early thirties, I'd say. In my view, Karen—the widow—might have been a better choice, but Sol was kind of strongheaded that way."

"You sure that there *wasn't* anything between Schiff and this Karen Bourke?"

"Romantically? Hard to say for certain, Rory, but you know how the Club is."

I pictured it. Eight condominium buildings, four stories each, arrayed in a wide fishhook pattern around twenty clay—actually, Har-tru—tennis courts. Every building was a squared-off horseshoe with its own common-area patio, and the entrances to each unit were visible to pretty much anyone who bothered to look. Also, there was an "Olympic Village" atmosphere I'd sensed about the place within days of moving into my apartment there. Gossip would be hard to avoid.

I said, "What's the name of this girlfriend?"

"Shirlee—that's with two Es instead of E-Y. I don't remember her last name, but I can tell you which building she's in."

"Meaning, also at the Club?"

"Right."

"Anybody else, Don?"

"For you to talk to, now?"

"Yes."

Floyd seemed to mull it over. "Well, I don't know if they were real friends, but Luh-nell Kirby comes to mind."

"Can you spell that one for me, too?"

"Sure. L-Y-N-E-L-L. Big and black, with an even bigger serve."

"And this Kirby . . . ?"

Floyd seemed to stifle a laugh. "Sol was in his seventies, Lynell his sixties. They were pretty evenly matched, but Sol always beat him."

"Just as a regular opponent, or tournaments, too?"

"Tournaments only, I believe. You see, Sol was a real competitor. Nothing pleased him more than to play down and win."

In most tournaments, older entrants can "waive" age limits and "play down" in a lower, presumably tougher age bracket, but younger ones can't play up. Otherwise, so the thinking goes, they'd trounce their seniors.

"How did Kirby take that?"

"About as well as you'd expect a former colonel in the Army Rangers to accept defeat in anything."

I made simple, mental notes on all three people. "Don, thanks."

"You want, we can swing by the reception. I'm pretty sure Karen and Shirlee will be there, and maybe even Lynell as well."

"Not a comfortable time for interviewing people." I reached into my pocket. "Besides, Naomi Schiff gave me the key to her uncle's house, and I'd like to see it before talking with them about what happened there."

"Then you want to visit Sol's place?"

"No." I returned the key to my packet. "No, just drop me back at the Club so I can pick up my own car. There's a stop I ought to make even before the crime scene."

•   •   •

I'd used the prize money from my last satellite victory to buy a two-year-old Chrysler Sebring convertible at a rentacar fleet auction. It was candy-apple red, with a tan interior and top. Given the stalling of my tennis career, the flashy wheels soothed my ego.

I parked outside the Fort Lauderdale Police headquarters on West Broward Boulevard. The building is gray with blue piping detail, enough palm trees and flower beds around it to confuse you on its function.

Inside, I showed my investigator's license to the dour woman behind the first-floor INFORMATION counter, but she wouldn't buzz me upstairs to the Homicide Unit, telling me instead to have a seat on one of the gray plastic scoop chairs in the lobby.

A few minutes later, a different woman came through the security door to the left of the counter. She had a golden tan that I thought came more from gene pool than sunbathing, with slightly darker hair drawn up in a high ponytail that just reached the collar of her blouse. Slim and somewhere in her high thirties, she had the kind of cheekbones that would wear well.

"You are Rory Calhoun?"

A slight edge of Spanish on her words. Standing, I said, "Yes."

"Lourdes Pintana." She extended a hand, and we shook. "Can I also see your ID, please?"

I took it out again, remembering that a lawyer in town had told me Pintana was the sergeant in charge of the Homicide Unit.

She took her time studying the print on my license before giving it back. "And what does a private investigator want with us?"

"Just some time. And permission, maybe."

Pintana studied me harder than she had my ID. "It is a nice day. Let us walk a little."

I followed her outside, thinking she spoke precise, "no-contractions" English like the Castro refugees I'd met on the circuit. Pintana seemed to think the parking lot was safer than the sidewalk, because she simply began strolling between the rows of vehicles. I fell in beside the woman, shortening my strides to match hers.

Pintana said, "Your meter is running, no?"

I took the hint. "I've been asked to look into the murder of Solomon Schiff."

A sad smile. "Let me guess. The niece?"

"Her name's Naomi. She seems to feel you all may be looking in the wrong direction."

"It has been known to happen." Pintana kicked at a loose stone like a soccer player might a ball, sending it under one of the parked cars. "But this time, I think not."

"Because?"

She crossed her arms. "No motives among those he knew. Solomon Schiff seemed to live his life around a tennis court. He was retired from active business, had a young girlfriend with no other boyfriends, and a nice house on the Intracoastal that would tempt many who believe in the redistribution of wealth."

An academic way of putting it. "So, a burglary gone sour."

"*Sí*, and almost a refreshing change of pace." Pintana looked up at me. "We get so many domestics, so many 'senior suicides,' so many drug killings, that the occasional felony-murder invigorates us."

"But not quite to the level of solving this one."

"Solving it? What fingerprints and fibers we found one could have predicted: Mr. Schiff's, Shirlee Tucker—that's the girlfriend. There were marks on the victim's wrists, like somebody wearing gloves held him by both in a struggle, with traces of velvet left on his skin."

"A burglar who uses velvet gloves?"

A nod. "And the body was found face up on the floor at the foot of his bed. When the official cause of death came back 'heart failure,' it was not a surprise."

"Anything from the autopsy that was?"

Pintana crossed her arms. "I do not think it 'surprising' for a man in his seventies, but Mr. Schiff had cancer."

"Where?"

"Everywhere. Metastasis run wild."

I tried to match that up with the man I'd seen play tennis. "It didn't show."

"Some people are stronger than others."

"Schiff knew this about himself?"

"For about six months, according to his doctor. The victim declined the alternative treatments of chemotherapy and radiation, choosing instead to 'tough it out.'" Pintana shook her head. "In his situation, I might have felt the same."

We were almost at my car. "Okay if I visit the house?"

"Schiff's, you mean?"

"Yes."

"I do not see why not. We released it as a crime scene two days ago."

I stopped at the Sebring's rear bumper. "Thanks for the help."

Pintana continued for several steps before turning and looking at my convertible. "This is yours?"

"It is."

Sergeant Lourdes Pintana looked it over, then did the same for me. "Take my advice, Mr. Calhoun. You will not make a very good living by trying to follow subjects in secret."

•   •   •

Solomon Schiff's house was on the second isle south of Las Olas. The sprawling ranch looked like one of the older homes on the street, especially given the number of places being bought and then torn down for the construction of mansions, two of which were in progress. I parked in the driveway behind a jaunty, teal Toyota, which I assumed was Schiff's.

The key his niece had given me fit the top and bottom locks on the front door. When I swung it open and stepped into the foyer, the muzzle of a black semiautomatic was aimed about belly high on me from ten feet away.

The woman holding it said, "Sol always told me to aim at the fella's belt buckle and fire till he falls."

Slight southern lilt to the voice, hands shaking a little.

Keeping my own hands open and shoulder high, I managed to speak past a cottony tongue. "Even good advice isn't always right."

"Come any closer, and we'll both find out."

I decided to give her a moment. She was thirtyish, with dark, full hair cut just off her neck. The tank top showed about a third of the kind of breasts that make South Florida the true

"Silicon Valley," and her Capri pants looked to be painted on her butt and legs. I remembered Don Floyd saying Schiff's girlfriend was much younger.

She blinked first. "Well, aren't you going to tell me who you are?"

"A man given a key to this place," I said, wiggling it for her to see.

"Oh, hell," the woman said, lowering the gun. "Why didn't you say you were from the Realtor's?"

"I'm not, but if I can show you some identification . . . ?"

"Sure." She let the gun rest against her thigh as we moved together. Her eyes were hazel and just a little too far apart for smart.

"A private investigator? Like, really?"

"Really."

"Oh, wow. And you're even cute."

"And you're even Ms. Tucker?"

"Right, right. Shirlee Tucker. But with two Es. My mama couldn't spell real good. So, what are you doing here?"

"I've been hired to look into Solomon Schiff's death."

"Ugh. Tell me about it. I was the one found him."

"Where?"

"Just like on TV, huh?"

"Let's start there, anyway."

Tucker led me through a living room that seemed sparsely furnished except for shelving that held more tennis trophies than books, but then Naomi Schiff had told me there'd been a lot of breakage and that she'd cleaned up the house. By the time we reached the bedroom, Tucker's gait, enhanced by the fit of her Capris, had started to hypnotize me.

"In here."

I moved past her in the open doorway, something musky coming off Tucker that I didn't think originated in a bottle. The room was fifteen by twelve, a king-sized brass bed against one wall, a master bath through another. There were no sheets or pillows in sight, and just an overhead light fixture hung down from a ceiling fan.

"Where exactly was Mr. Schiff's body?"

Tucker now moved past me to the footboard of the bed, which had a pattern of sturdy, vertical pickets between lateral top and bottom pieces the diameter of bar rails. She grasped the top rail as support and lowered herself to the floor until she was faceup and lying flat, head toward the bed and feet toward the door.

Tucker said, "Sol was like this?" the lilt making her statement sound like a question.

"How about his arms?"

She moved hers to a more exaggerated version of my "Don't Shoot" in the foyer, her fingernails almost touching the base of the brass footboard.

"What else did you see?"

Tucker did a partial situp, now resting on her elbows, which pushed the doctored bust more aggressively forward. "His bed had been slept in," now a coy cocking of her head, "but not with me."

"Meaning with somebody else?"

"I didn't get any perfumy smell. Ugh, Sol's was bad enough."

When people die, their muscles relax and release a lot of unpleasantness. "You didn't see anybody else?"

"No. And Sol had pajama bottoms on."

"Bottoms, but no top?"

"Right, right. That's how he dressed for bed when I wasn't here."

"How do you know?"

"Because," the head now cocking the other way, though to the same effect, "when I was with him, he'd sleep naked."

Not exactly logical, but the last part struck me as pretty probable. And probably enjoyable.

Tucker said, "You're thinking about it, aren't you?"

I decided not to lie. "Yes."

Her tongue came out, moistened her lips. "Me, too. Minute I saw you in the foyer back there? I was hoping it wouldn't come to shooting you."

Reassuring. "Had you and Mr. Schiff been sleeping together much recently?"

A frown, like that wasn't my next line in her script. "No, truth to tell. Oh, Sol was no great shakes in the sack, but he was—Sol liked to call himself 'inventive.'"

"Inventive."

"Yeah. Loved going into the sex shops, buying me things like teddies or bikini thongs." Tucker stretched the top of her Capri pants to show me some red lace. "These, for instance."

My throat felt a little tight. "How about sex toys?"

"Oh, he had just a drawerful of those." Another frown, directed toward the bureau. "But I think his prudy niece must have gone and thrown them all away when she cleaned up the place, account of that's what I wanted to take back with me, and they aren't there now."

I couldn't see somebody ransacking the house for one of those. "Shirlee, did Mr. Schiff have anything in the house that somebody might have searched for?"

"Searched for? You mean like treasure or something?"

"Jewelry, cash, anything somebody else might want."

A third cocking of her head. "Just me."

Actually Tucker's answer gave me several ideas. "Did Mr. Schiff ever take any photos of you?"

"You mean, like, nudie shots?"

"Yes."

"No. No, Sol was into gadgets, not cameras." Yet another nice cocking of her head. "Of course, you don't look like you need any of those things to please, and this floor's getting awful hard."

The floor wasn't alone in that. "Maybe some other time."

"Oh, I get it." Full situp now. "Like when you're 'off-duty,' right?"

Clearing my throat, I agreed with Shirlee Tucker, who recited her phone number, including how easy it was to remember the last four digits because "you just have to keep subtracting by two for each?"

.   .   .

I had a resident decal pasted on my windshield, so the security guard at the Club just waved me through the main gate. As I drove around the fishhook road toward my building, Wingfield, I spotted the man I believed to be Lynell Kirby walking toward the clubhouse with a tennis bag slung over his shoulder and that purposeful stride that I've always associated with doctors on their way to major operations and players on their way to important matches. Instead of continuing all the way to Wingfield, I parked in a guest slot for Lenglen.

Every one of the Club's residential buildings is named for a historic tennis player, and there's a twenty-foot mosaic of each legend—in this case, Suzanne Lenglen of France—on a peach wall in the respective courtyard. Lends a nice air of tradition, a sense of permanence that I hadn't found anywhere else in the Lauderdale area.

Jogging, I caught up with Kirby as he reached the pool area, which, along with the tiki bar on the patio, overlooks the front five courts. "Colonel Kirby?"

The man turned. Six-three, great muscle definition in arms and legs, no gut. From fifty feet away, you'd be off thirty years on his age, but up close, his spring-coil hair was spritzed with gray, and his eyes had that faraway look of some older guys I'd known who'd fought in Vietnam.

"You look familiar," he said. "We serve together somewhere?"

"No," though I nearly added a "sir" to it. "I'd like to talk with you about Solomon Schiff."

"Police or reporter?"

"Neither." I took out my license.

Kirby barely glanced at it. "I've got a match in ten minutes, and that's all I'm thinking about right now. You've got the time to wait, I'll be happy to talk with you afterward."

"Seems reasonable."

• • •

You can tell a lot about people from the way they play tennis. What I could tell from watching Lynell Kirby was that Don Floyd's implication was dead-on: The man did not like to lose.

He was playing an athletic younger woman who had the kind of game you associate with Chris Evert: steady, deep, and enough pace to never let you rip at it. Even on Har-tru, which slows the ball down and causes it to sit up, I figured Kirby—a lefty with a powerful serve, but whose strokes were "by-the-numbers" mechanical—to have trouble staying with her.

I was wrong.

Kirby never quit on a point, and he had a sharply angled crosscourt forehand. His slice backhand showed good bite, and his topspin "approach" shots down the line were often winners in and of themselves. Plus Kirby was quick if not graceful, volleying the ball solidly.

After seventy-five minutes by my watch, he'd beaten a good player half his age by a break each set: 6–4, 6–3.

They shook hands, the woman leaving almost immediately by one of the fence doors. Kirby toweled off his face and neck, then beckoned me to come down under the awning separating his court from the next one, also empty.

When I reached him, Kirby said, "Sorry to be so curt with you up there," gesturing toward the elevated pool/patio area, "but I was trying to keep my mind on the game."

"No problem. I do the same thing."

Kirby yoked his towel around his neck, then sank into one white resin chair under the awning as I took another.

He said, "Didn't catch your name before."

"Rory Calhoun."

"Rory . . . you were on the tour."

"It's nice to be remembered."

"Saw you at the Lipton twice—called it the Ericsson later, and now the Nasdaq, but it's still held on Key Biscayne." Kirby grinned. "Of course, you'd know that."

"Probably won't be a difference for me anymore. Bad knee."

A judicious nod. "Comes from all that hard court you kids had to play on. Clay keeps the body young." Then Kirby straightened in his chair. "You said something about Sol, though, right?"

"His niece has asked me to look into his death."

The eyes grew shrewd, and he moved his head some, assessing me, I thought.

Finally, Kirby said, "Man was killed by a burglar, probably to feed a drug habit. What's there to look into?"

"She'd just like to put some concerns to rest."

"Like what?"

"I've heard you knew Mr. Schiff pretty well. Could he have had anything at his house somebody would be searching for?"

Kirby settled a little deeper into his chair. "You think somebody intentionally targeted Sol, and not just his place as a good candidate for loot?"

Loot. "That's what I'm trying to find out."

"Well, I guess I'd challenge your premise, then. Sol and I were more friendly opponents than friends."

I knew what he meant. "You didn't socialize off the courts?"

"Or really even on them." A faraway look in the eyes again. "You ever in the service, Rory?"

"No."

"I always was a scrapper, even scrambling to stay alive. And that's how I play tennis, because I never learned as a kid the way Sol did, with the right racquet and good coaching showing me the proper strokes. Sol was like a ballet dancer between the lines, always moving himself in balance to the ball, always under control. Like there was this overall . . . choreography for every match but he was the only one who got a peek at it in advance."

I knew what Kirby meant about that, too. The sense that you were playing the opponent's match instead of just the opponent. "And so?"

"And so it was damned frustrating to go up against him. I had ten years on the man, and he'd play down just so he could be the champion in his seventies *and* my sixties. The king of the geezers."

"You couldn't beat him."

"I never beat him. There's a difference."

"Meaning you were getting closer."

"That's right. Last tournament, I was up 4–2 in the third. Even had a match point at 5–4. I couldn't quite put him away, but next time out, I believe I would have. And I think he believed it, too."

What we all do, psyche out our opponents to psyche up ourselves. "Still, it must have galled you to lose all those—"

"Let me save you some time, my friend. Sol Schiff could be a prima donna and even a royal pain in the ass. But if I killed him in his bedroom, how would I ever have gotten the chance to beat him on a court?"

"How did you know that?"

"What?"

"That he was killed in his bedroom."

A grin, the fingers on his right hand flicking upward one at a time. "First, newspaper article. Second, Shirlee Tucker—his 'principal squeeze,' my grandson might call her—can't shut up about it. Third, the Tennis Club is like a primitive culture, and the drums tell us things."

At which point Lynell Kirby began to paddle his palms on his thighs like they were bongos.

• • •

Karen Bourke wasn't hard to find. She lived in a two-bedroom, townhouse apartment in the second building past the Club's security gate, diagonally across from the tennis center. Greeting me at her front door, Bourke listened to why I'd come to bother her and said it was no bother at all. By the time we sat down in the living room, it was "Karen" and "Rory."

Though she had to be in her sixties from what Don Floyd had told me, Bourke was another one whose appearance gave the lie to her age. Blonde and slim, with blue eyes and an eager smile, the only telltales that she was over forty were little crow's feet of lines around the corners of her eyes.

From laughing or crying, I thought, with no way to judge which.

"Rory, I'm really sorry about Sol."

I nodded. "Forgive me, but did I see you at the memorial chapel?"

"No." Bourke seemed to go inside herself for a moment. "The excuse I gave people is that I had committed to play doubles in a tournament near Palm Beach, but the real reason is . . ." She looked up to a shelf over my head. "I've become a little tired of funerals."

I twisted around to see a framed photo of two men, both in their fifties, dressed in business suits with lapels from the seventies. "Your husband and Mr. Schiff?"

"Yes. That's Casey on the left. I took that photo of them in their office, just after they'd closed the deal that made all of us functionally rich."

"Anything happen to change that, Karen?"

Bourke looked at me oddly. "To . . . change it?"

"I've visited Mr. Schiff's home. No palace, but—"

"—compared to this place, it looks as though I've come down in the world?"

Bourke's words came out sandwiched between smiling lips,

but I got a sense of strength and resolve buried deep within her. "Basically," I said.

The smile softened. "I don't blame you, Rory. No, I'm sure my condo here isn't worth a tenth of what Sol's house would bring as a tear-down, given that waterfront lot it's on. In fact, Casey and I owned a pretty similar place, but after my husband died, I sold ours to move here." Bourke looked back at the framed photo. "When you're alone as a woman, it's nice to have people around, and living here at the Club gives me a community to be part of. An . . . identity, if that makes any sense to you."

It did. I remembered back to my knee first failing me, and the pang of wondering whether I'd ever be part of the circuit—or any gregarious, sorority-fraternity experience—again. And, to be honest, I wondered if I hadn't moved into the Tennis Club for just the same reason Karen Bourke had.

She said, "But you're here about Sol, right?"

"Right." I tried to refocus. "I guess what I was getting at is whether you were on good terms with Mr. Schiff?"

"Good terms." Bourke looked down at her lap for a moment, then smiled, but very sadly. "Sol wasn't just Casey's partner: They were best friends as well. One was barely Jewish, the other never missed Mass. But they had tennis as well as business in common, and they played championship-level doubles for years until Casey's stroke. After that, Sol would visit every day, sitting at my husband's bedside, making conversation for both of them. And when Casey died, Sol made sure I had the kind of financial advice that let me—and still lets me—never worry about money." Bourke looked up now, the strength and resolve I'd heard in her words now shining through her eyes as well. "So, yes, I'd say Sol and I were on 'good terms.'"

Impressive speech. "Karen, anything in his home that somebody might have torn it apart to find?"

"To find? Like what?"

"That's why I'm asking."

"Sorry, Rory, but I can't help you there."

I decided to risk our first-name basis. "How did you feel about Shirlee Tucker?"

My question seemed to genuinely throw Bourke. "*Feel* about her?"

"Did you . . . approve of their relationship?"

A laugh, one that I thought would go on before I sensed Bourke realizing it already had lasted a little too long. "Sol never married, Rory. What he did romantically was hardly any of my business."

"I don't think you've answered my question."

"Well, then," said Karen Bourke, standing, "I guess that's the only one I haven't."

· · ·

After losing a professional tennis match, I practiced a little ritual whenever I had cash to spare. I'd rent a car and drive around to clear my head. I don't know why, but having to concentrate on steering, accelerating, and braking would help me analyze what had gone wrong as well as push myself toward improving next time out.

Now I just cruised some of the major streets around the Club, letting the Sebring kind of have its head as though it were a stable horse taking me for a slow, aimless ride. Maybe the last question I asked Karen Bourke is what let me notice something about the strip malls lining Oakland Park Boulevard as I headed east toward the beach.

Several of them sported sex shops.

I pulled into the parking lot of the second one. Shirlee Tucker had told me that Solomon Schiff was into kinky sex, but not recently. And Karen Bourke had dodged that issue entirely.

I thought about it, then drove back to my apartment to check the Yellow Pages and pick up my camera.

• • •

It was a single-lens reflex Canon, which is about all I understood of what the guy at a photography store in Chicago had explained to me years before. But I'd just reached the semis of a satellite near there, and I wanted my girlfriend of the weekend to have a decent camera to capture me winning the title. I lost both the finals and the girlfriend, but not the camera, and once I began doing daywork for private investigators, I'd invested in a telephoto lens as well.

Spending Naomi Schiff's retainer in what I hoped was a responsible way, I sat outside her uncle's house on the Intracoastal until I caught Shirlee Tucker arriving in her teal Toyota. I got three good head-and-shoulders portraits of her, one with the sunglasses off. A few hours later, I snapped two close-ups of Lynell Kirby as he picked up a pizza at the Big Louie's on Andrews Avenue. Finally, I caught Karen Bourke the next cloudy morning from the balcony of my unit as she walked onto Court Ten for a singles match wearing neither shades nor a baseball cap.

I drove to the Walgreen's and patiently waited for their one-hour photo service to prove itself, then I took the prints and began making the rounds of the sex shops I'd found in the phonebook.

• • •

"You're not a cop?"

I looked at the guy in the fifth place. He wore a palomino toupee, kept a dead cigar clamped between his teeth, and had breath foul enough to blister paint.

I said, "Cross my heart and hope to die."

"My loyal customers expect some privacy when they shop here, you know?"

I took in just the "impulse" items near his cash register. "I can see that."

"But you say this is about a killing?"

"That's right. And I'd rather not have the police drag you down for questioning, only to leave your loyal customers in the lurch."

His eyes told me I'd pressed the right button.

"Okay, let me see your photos."

As I'd done four times previously that day, I laid them face up in front of him on the counter as though I were dealing blackjack. He waited to see all three people before pointing with his cigar. "Her. Yeah, last week sometime."

"What did she buy?"

The dead end of the cigar went toward the "bondage" wall. "One of those sets there, on the left."

•   •   •

"Why," said Shirlee Tucker, the one-trick pony again cocking her head coyly from the bar stool, "you want to play with them?"

I'd called her, asking if she'd meet me at Lord Nelson's Pub on Southwest Second. Given the time of day, the bar was ours.

I centered my pint of Boddington's on its coaster. "Actually, what I'm wondering is why you were buying a pair of velvet handcuffs last week when you told me that lately Solomon Schiff hadn't been much into lovemaking, much less anything kinky?"

Tucker drew on the straw sticking in her Sex on the Beach, which made me shift a little uncomfortably on my own stool.

She said, "Do you like watching me . . . drink this?"

"More than we can go into now, but I'd still like to know—"

"Seemed funny to me, too," said Tucker, looking almost thoughtful. "But Sol asked it as a favor, and when I wanted to know why—if he wasn't going to use them with me?—all he said was, 'It's to repay a debt to the Devil.'"

"A what?"

"A debt to the Devil." Tucker waved with her drink. "Look, I didn't get it, either. Only, like I said, Sol asked me as a favor, so I went out and got the cuffs for him."

"What did he do with them?"

"Beats me. I know this: He'd never asked me to tie him up before, and he never asked me to cuff him last week after I gave the things to him." Then Shirlee Tucker drew on her straw again. "If you like the idea enough, though, we could always just . . . buy another pair?"

• • •

Exercising some willpower, I left Tucker at the bar and drove around some more, trying to sort through what I'd learned. Solomon Schiff dies of heart failure, apparently trying to defend himself against a burglar. Only his devoted niece Naomi doesn't completely buy that, and she hires me to find his killer. Shirlee Tucker seems almost detached from her lover's recent death, Lynell Kirby seems to regret only losing the opportunity to best an unbeaten opponent, and Karen Bourke seems to think her dead husband's partner was the salt of the earth. Besides, Sergeant Lourdes Pintana tells me the autopsy confirms a struggle but also found that cancer would have killed Schiff if his heart hadn't given out first. And the only thing I've discovered that somebody could have been ransacking his house to find—even assuming Naomi Schiff was right about that part—is a pair of velvet handcuffs that Shirlee Tucker says—

I stopped in the middle lane of Route 1, and the poor guy driving his family around on vacation behind me smacked into my rear bumper.

The damage to both cars was minimal, though it seemed to take forever to exchange licenses and registrations. I assured the tourist that I'd tell my insurance company I'd caused the accident.

Even if only indirectly.

• • •

"Karen?"

She turned toward me on the Club's patio, apparently on her way from a match back to her condo. I'd debated just following her there, but I figured to let her choose the ground.

"Rory. More questions?"

"Actually, more answers."

"I don't understand."

"I'm pretty sure what happened, Karen, but I'd like to talk with you about it first."

Bourke stared at me, then rolled her head on her shoulders, as though her neck was stiff and she wanted to relax before serving. Or, in this case, probably before returning serve.

Finally she said, "Can we walk?"

"Sure."

•   •   •

I'd guess the perimeter of the fishhook road around the Club's buildings is about half a mile. We hadn't gone more than a hundred feet, that sweet pong of female sweat wafting off her, before Karen Bourke said, "Why don't you start?"

Okay. "Your husband and Solomon Schiff were partners—both businesswise and tennis, but friends as well. They hit it big twenty-some years ago, big enough for both sides to be completely comfortable financially. But, as they say, if you don't have your health . . ."

Bourke nodded beside me, biting her lower lip. I waited a moment as a couple on their way to play greeted us cheerily.

When the couple had moved out of earshot, I continued. "The rabbi at Mr. Schiff's funeral said he wasn't terribly religious, and you confirmed that. On the other hand, a lot of people there felt Mr. Schiff had been a tough negotiator but a man of his word. And one of the promises he'd made—to his niece, after her own father had committed suicide—was that he'd never take his own life."

"Sol told us about that."

"Before you all reached . . . consensus?"

"Rory, I don't know what you're talking about."

"After your husband's stroke, he was bedridden."

"Yes." Bourke got quieter. "Casey couldn't walk, much less play tennis. Lying on his back every waking hour, the sores that . . ." She shook her head.

"Did you talk about . . . ending things?"

"Casey was very religious. Even if my husband could have

taken his own life, he wouldn't have. And I certainly couldn't do it for him."

"But Solomon Schiff could."

Karen Bourke looked at me, that strength back in her eyes. "Casey begged him, and Sol deflected it, tried everything to cheer my husband up. But the doctors told me there was no hope of improvement, and with that Kevorkian man being prosecuted up in Michigan, they were scared of acting themselves." She seemed to steady herself. "So Sol and I both did some . . . God, 'research,' I'd guess you'd call it, about how to 'simulate' heart failure, which is a pretty typical complication from a stroke. And one night, when we'd all come to peace about the decision," Bourke's pace of speaking accelerating, "Sol took a pillow and pressed it over Casey's face and smothered him."

After a few more strides, I said, "But Mr. Schiff first . . . negotiated a return promise, right?"

"Right." Bourke looked down at her tennis shoes now. "Sol told me about the promise to his niece. He made me agree that if he was ever like . . . in a situation like Casey's, that I'd do the same for him."

"Only Mr. Schiff wasn't—"

"—paralyzed?" She grunted, but not like a laugh. "Just by that promise. And by his pride, I suppose." Bourke looked at a court we were passing, two older men playing scrappy singles. "Sol was sick with cancer. He kept it from most people, and he still played well. But Sol himself told me that opponents he used to beat soundly were now creeping up on him, and he was afraid he couldn't maintain his game much longer."

I thought back to Lynell Kirby sensing the same thing. "And Mr. Schiff couldn't tolerate that."

"No. And I also think that, after seeing Casey the way . . . confined to his bed for so long." Another shake of the head. "I think Sol didn't want to wither away in a hospital somewhere with tubes sticking out of him."

"So to keep his promise to his niece, and to cover the mercy killing, you made it look like a burglary."

"He made it look that way. Slashed his furniture, smashed his things." A sad smile. "Except for the tennis trophies, of course. He couldn't bear to hurt those."

I'd registered that at his house. "But why stage it like a homicide at all? Why not have it look like just plain heart failure?"

"We talked about that, too. Sol had his pride, Rory, as I said before. And the man who could play three matches a day felt his overall level of conditioning would make it hard for people to believe that his heart would simply 'give out' in his sleep. Sol thought some kind of trauma—like 'struggling with a violent burglar'—was necessary."

"And the velvet handcuffs?"

"We actually tried it first the week before without anything. A 'practice session,' Sol called it. But each time I . . . pressed the pillow onto his face, even with me sitting on his chest, he'd flail away with his arms." A sadder smile. "The instinct to survive, I guess. He hadn't had that . . . problem with Casey, on account of the stroke."

"And so Mr. Schiff came up with the idea of the handcuffs, so he'd be restrained—"

"—we ran the cuffs through the brass rods at the foot of his bed—"

"—and it would look as though the 'burglar' had held his wrists while wearing gloves."

Just a nod now. "And he had me carry away all his . . . marital aids, so the police wouldn't think of anything 'velvet' *but* 'gloves.' "

Bourke's story was consistent with the facts.

Almost a laugh from her now. "You know what Sol called it?"

"Called what?"

"His agreement with me, that I'd do for him what he'd done for Casey."

I said, "A debt to the Devil?"

Bourke stopped cold in her tracks. "Who told you about—?"

"It's more what I'm going to tell everyone else."

She stared at me now. "Everyone."

"That Solomon Schiff died while trying to protect himself from a violent burglar."

I'd have walked Karen Bourke back to her condo, but after giving me a desperate hug, the woman excused herself, saying she really had to be alone for a while.

Stephen Longacre's Greatest Match

Stephen Hunter

Stephen Longacre picked things up quickly; that was his talent. He gave them up quickly as well; that was his curse. He just couldn't stay interested. He flunked out of Choate so resoundingly that neither Groton nor Essex would consider him, and finally ended up in a third-rate prep school in his mother's hometown in Baltimore, spending the cold Maryland winter well fortified with scotch, his drink as it was his father's.

When he came home to the largest cattle ranch in west Arkansas for the summer of 1948 as a semialcoholic with a three-pack-a-day habit, seventeen going on thirty-nine, his mission ostensibly was to prepare for the fall term at a somewhat better place, if his father could buy his way in, and, more generally, to think about some hideous destination called—how boring!—the future. Of course it was only a matter of a few days before the scandals started.

The state trooper Earl Swagger arrested him for speeding, driving under the influence, and providing alcohol to a minor, a Sally Mae Ford, fourteen, of Mount Ida, whom Stephen had spied riding a bicycle, stopped, and chatted up. He could be a charmer, when he wanted. Then he'd gotten the girl drunk. He was driving her home at four in the morning when Earl arrested him and he spent the night in the Blue Eye lockup until his mother called her great friend Sam Vincent, who was the Polk County prosecutor, and got Stephen let out.

"Connie," Sam explained, "I can talk to the judge here, but Earl caught him fair and square and I don't like to do the kind of favors for wealthy people that I don't do for poor ones."

"Sam, I wouldn't have it any other way. But he is such a mess, the poor boy. Any gentleness you can show him would be so appreciated."

Like most of the men who knew or saw her, Sam was already in love with Connie. He could no more defy her than he could defy the mandates of his own nature.

"Connie, I will do what I can. I think maybe the girl's parents could be persuaded not to press charges if—"

"I've already talked to them."

"How much?"

"Too much. Stephen is expensive to have around, but at least there's money if the girl has to go to St. Louis or something."

Stephen's father was less understanding.

"You had some fun," said Rance Longacre, leaning in close, faintly smelling of scotch. "But it stops there. I ketch you hanging with the trash, you gon' be a sorry customer. This here fine old life you live, you know, it can go away damn fast, pardner."

His father, who lived in a cusp of alcohol-induced rage, was always making absurd cowboy statements like that. Rance was another handsome idler, whose Navy career had not prospered and who was never the best man in the room. Stephen knew this; he accepted it; it had been a condition in his life since childhood. His father, however, was a handsome man. Rance had a big square head, thick black hair, a perpetual suntan (or, possibly, the complexion of someone permanently pickled), and gray highlights at the temples. He looked like a million dollars; he was worth a million dollars; he was a jerk.

Stephen was good for a few days. Then he went to his car, a new Buick coupe convertible, and drove across Polk County, through Blue Eye and on into Oklahoma, where he found the meanest, lowest Negro crib he could and proceeded to get wildly drunk on rotgut hooch until finally the club's owner called the Oklahoma State Police. But Stephen left before the police got there, and ended up in a ditch two miles down the road, with a sixteen-stitch gash in his forehead. The coupe was totaled. The officers who dug him out called Earl Swagger in Arkansas, rousing him out of a rare night of sleep at home.

Earl picked him up at the emergency ward and drove him home.

"You are a stupid one," said Earl. "I seen boys young as you blown to hell and gone in the Pacific. They'd have given anything to live one damn day of your life. Yet you act like buckra trash from morning till night and you will git yourself killed for nothing, and I am getting right sick of it."

"Yes, sir," said Stephen.

"Why? You're a smart boy. You been to a fancy school. You got money, looks, a nice car, a big future. Why? What's eating you?"

"Mr. Earl, I couldn't say."

"You going to kill yourself, your mama will be crushed, and

it will be a tragedy. She don't need no tragedy. She's a great lady and she should have a happy life."

"She chose what she chose. That's what she gets."

Earl could get no further with the youngster. It continued all summer: bouts of drunkenness, another two scrapes with an automobile in a ditch or among trees, and general lethargy.

The one change was that Stephen no longer loafed at the Longacre spread, though he loved the place, with its trees and horses and graciousness. He just could not stomach the way his mother looked at him, her face particularly tragic, her eyes bitter, her whole demeanor deflated. He could not stand his father, and all the sinewy, hard-working hands, some of them his own age, boys who had to work like hell for a lousy fifteen dollars a week and considered themselves lucky. Instead, he took up residence in the Polk County Country Club swimming pool, where he lounged the days away, growing tanner and handsomer, acquiring a taste for gin and tonics, and generally avoiding seriousness in all its forms.

It was there, in early August, that his father finally ran him to ground.

"So this is where you been hiding. Your mama wouldn't tell me."

"She is a grand woman," Stephen said.

"You are a little punk-ass weasel. That is the truth, Stephen. You been given every goddamn thing and you have turned into a wastrel and a monkey."

"Then you should disinherit me."

"I should. Mr. Earl could probably git you in the Marine Corps as a private. He has big connections. You would like that just fine."

That shut Stephen up. He had no interest in the military,

which, if he understood the concept, had to do with getting up very early.

"Yeah, I thought that'd dry you up. Well, here's the way it's going to be. I want you to *do something*. If I'm going to keep sending money off to these fancy schools and buying you cars to wreck and paying off doctors in St. Louis, I want to know it ain't being wasted. So, you have to do something this summer."

"Yes, sir. What would you suggest? I could cure polio, defeat the Reds, make a movie, write a song or a book."

"Damn you, Stephen, you are a wise guy to the end. I spent close to two thousand dollars the past three summers investing in your future as a tennis player."

"It wasn't my idea."

Stephen hated tennis, despite the fact that he actually had some talent at it.

"The club is having a tournament. I want you to enter it. I want you to start now, get in shape, work hard, and show me something."

Stephen's heart sank. Hitting that white puffy ball around those red clay courts for those Polk County doctors and lawyers and ranchers, all swell fellows, and their pathetic wives, who thought they'd made it into the gentry because they could afford to pay the pittance at the tennis club. He hated those people. They were so goddamned smug. And there was something even worse: His father was president of the club and chairman of the tennis committee. His father had played tennis at the Naval Academy in 1930, truly loved the game, and had taken it as his mission, his one accomplishment in life, to bring tennis to the children of Polk County.

"I hate tennis," said Stephen.

"I know. That's the point. I want you to do something you hate and do it well."

Stephen said nothing.

"That is it, Stephen. You play in that tennis tournament in two weeks or I won't be paying for your school, you won't go to a fine college, you'll break your mother's heart, and that will be that. I'm going to mend your wastrel ways, goddamnit, if it kills us both."

• • •

Possibly it worked. In any event, Stephen filled out his application, acquired a set of the tournament rules, studied them carefully, then studied the club rules carefully. Once he'd established them, he set to work.

His parents didn't see him except at night, when he returned, sweaty and weary. He showered, went quickly to bed, and got up early the next morning.

"Well, at last the boy is applyin' himself," his father said.

Yes, but at *what?* his mother wondered.

Finally she cornered him one night after Rance had passed out.

"What are you up to?"

"I am practicing at tennis, exactly as I was ordered. I go into the Fort Smith public courts every day and I hit against the backboard. Then I find games, anyone who'll play me. There are some pretty good players up there."

"Well, I'm impressed."

"I am making no guarantees, Mother. I am trying this hard, and will do my best and that is that. If he sends me to school or to the Marine Corps, that I have no control over."

"Stephen, why are you this way?"

"I am the way I am."

"We've discussed sending you to a psychiatrist."

"No, thank you. The tennis is therapy enough."

"It would help if you made some friends."

"I don't think so."

"You think these people are such rubes. But you found no friends in more elegant places, either."

"I was not cut out to be somebody's pal. It's something from the movies, but it doesn't exist in real life. Please, Mother, I have to get my sleep, if you don't mind."

"I should tell you that Jeff St. Sebastian is playing. Do you know who he is?"

"No."

"He is Bo Nickerson's cousin."

"The poultry people?"

"Yes, the Nickersons provide Ace Foods with their poultry. They seem to have a lot of money. Anyway, Jeff St. Sebastian is the number-two singles at LSU. They say he could play number one this year. He's quite good."

"Well, I will avoid him. I will play in doubles. I trust Rance won't go insane if I do that."

"You have a partner?"

"I do. As I read the rules, only one of us has to be a member of the club. Isn't that right?"

"I wouldn't know about that. Stephen, what is this all about?"

"It's all about nothing. I just want someone on my side, so if I get crushed, it's all right, I won't be completely humiliated."

"Stephen, I—"

"Mother. I promise you. I absolutely, absolutely promise you and Rance: I will obey the rules. I only ask that you do."

• • •

As expected, Jeff St. Sebastian ran through the rounds in singles, wiping out everybody he faced. He was tall and blonde and in his immaculate whites with his Jack Purcells grinding into the red clay, he was nimble, fleet, beautiful. He had been accepted at LSU law school and the world was his.

Rance sat under an umbrella in the third row, center, sipping a lemony Squirt, which he laced with gin, watching Jeff progress. Rance was clumsy at the game, and could never hit out, as he wanted to. Instead, he had to pitty-pat the ball to keep it in play, and knew he looked ridiculous. So he admired the way the slick Jeff St. Sebastian could really roll into the ball, some trick of spin, hit a stinging smash, and send it floating deep into the court until its own forward revolution overcame its velocity and pulled it down near the baseline. Jeff could do that all day long.

"He is a fine tennis player, no doubt about it," said Rance.

"Have you seen Stephen?" Connie asked.

"No," said Rance, "but the doubles don't get started till three, so he has plenty of time.

By two-thirty that day's singles were done. Jeff had played twice, triumphing love and three and two and two; he would meet an older man named Jerry Sieforth the next day in the finals.

After the singles matches, he wiped his handsome face with a towel and whispered something to his cousin Bo. Bo nodded, smiling, and went to the announcer.

"Well, folks," said that fellow, a retired radio star from Hot

Springs, "we are in for a treat. Seems Mr. St. Sebastian ain't done with his tennis. He's going to play in doubles with his cousin and his cousin's father will sit this one out."

A polite smattering of applause arose, and after a bit, the team took the court, and quickly enough mashed the Seahorn twins. The two sets, love and love, were over in a little less than half an hour.

Rance looked at his watch, took a little sip on his drink, looked about. He knew it was now his son's turn, but where was the boy?

"You see him?"

"No, no, I don't," said Connie. "Oh, look, there's Sam. Sam! Sam!"

Sam, in a straw fedora and sunglasses but as ever a dark suit off the rack that hung like a sack of grain, saw her, and advanced. Rance knew the rumors about Sam and his wife; he gritted his teeth but determined to give nobody the pleasure of seeing him uncomfortable. He took a fortifying shot of the ginned-up lemon Squirt, then rose magnanimously as if in command.

"Samuel. By God, sir, damned good to see you. Come on and join us. Sit next to Connie and keep her smiling. The fun is just beginning."

Sam edged in, but he wasn't particularly relaxed.

"Sam, what's wrong?" Connie asked with an intimacy to her voice that Rance hadn't heard in years.

"Well, I'm not much on tennis, but your boy called my office and requested my presence."

"What?"

"I don't know what this here's all about. And Earl, he's here, too. He's outside, sitting in his car, smoking a cigarette and listening to a ballgame. Earl isn't what you'd call your tennis fan either."

"I'd guess not," said Connie. "I wonder what—"

They felt it first as a buzz, unspecified, an unsettling loosened and set to marching through the small crowd. Rance looked about. His eyes scanned the clubhouse, which was actually the old Harry Etheridge country home, with seventy-five thousand dollars of his own money pumped into it, and the golf course beyond, somewhat raw and ungenteel as it was newly constructed and not yet fully grown in on what had once been cotton fields and hollows where the deer gathered, and beyond the blue rim of the Ouachitas. He had an image of a world he understood: It was so perfect. Here, the quality, people of distinction, who by their very distinction had claimed a rightful place in this little corner of paradise, where the games were formal if silly, in the fashion of the great eastern games, sat and enjoyed what was theirs. He had built the place out of love for his wife, whom he suspected no longer loved him, in hopes of offering her something of the tradition and distinction she had known in her moneyed enclave north of Baltimore, and in hopes of giving her son—his also—that same sense of an ordered world, where things were as they should be, and our tribe was up here, prosperous and pleased, and all the other tribes were invisible.

And then he saw his son and the Negro boy.

• • •

By the time Sam and Rance got down there, the thing was at full fever pitch.

"He brought a nigra!"

"Who that boy think he is, bringing a nigra in here!"

"Never heard of such a thing. It's a damned scandal."

"This ain't what we fought the war for."

"That's what it is, it's an insult to all our fighting boys."

Rance pushed bullishly through the crowd that had formed at the edge of the court, where his son stood with an oddly satisfied look on his face next to a tall, slender, almost impassive Negro youth who, Rance now saw, couldn't have been more than fifteen. Both were dressed immaculately in tennis whites, creased perfectly, unblemished. Both carried tennis racquets in presses, wore towels around their necks, and looked like the Harvard number-one doubles team, if Harvard permitted Negroes to attend, which, being a Yankee Communist conspiracy against America, it probably did.

"What the hell is going on here, boy!" Rance demanded.

Under his tan, his flesh had turned pinkish, as his blood pressure skyed. A Y of throbbing veins stood out on his temple, offsetting his gray highlights; two gobs of dried gunk had collected in the corners of his mouth.

Two men were yelling at Stephen, who appeared not to be noticing, but to be simply waiting for the ruckus to dry up and blow away.

"Mr. Longacre," said Jack Tyler, who was the tournament chairman, "we can't let a nigra boy play. Why, it's damned un-American."

"What are you up to, Stephen, goddamnit!" Rance bellowed.

"I'm simply trying to play in the match as I promised, and in accordance to the rules. If you look at the rules, you'll see that they specify that players must wear white but not that they *be* white."

He was right, of course, for the simple reason that the idea of a Negro youth coming to play at the Polk County Country Club was so utterly preposterous that no formal ruling had been necessary. It simply couldn't, wouldn't, ever, never happen. That was the way it was. Everybody understood.

Except Stephen.

"Stephen, this—"

"I'm sorry, but I'm absolutely correct. There is no formal law in the rules against someone of another race. The rules simply state that as a member in good standing of the club, I may enter the tournament and I may have as my partner any person I choose, as long as we both wear white and obey the etiquette of tennis."

"Rance, he can't do this! There's a unwritten rule everybody knows about."

"*I* don't know about it," said Stephen. "All I know is, I am here, I paid my fee, I found a partner, and here I am. Now, let's play."

"Sam! Mr. Sam, by God, help us out on this one. He can't bring no colored fellow in on this, can he? He can't just *do* it. There's such a thing as an *unwritten* law, isn't there?"

Sam was thinking: This little bastard! Oh, this little bastard. He has put me in a goddamn fix and a half.

Sam said, "Well, now, I don't know that the law would get involved here. I'm not one for the law poking its nose into everyone's business. This is the sort of thing best adjudicated by the board of directors of your club."

"Well, what about something on good order. Or disturbing the peace. Bringing this fellow in here sure disturbs our peace. Ain't that against the law?"

Sam struggled to find an even narrower line to walk along.

"Hmmm," he said, scrunching up his face as if in study,

"I'd have to think about that and research the statutes. Certainly, at this point there appears to be no civil law that's been breached and I don't know who would—"

But at that point two uniformed deputies from the town pushed their way through the crowd, and went immediately to the black youth.

"You under arrest, boy, you come with us," proclaimed the sergeant, a pugnacious fellow named Buddy Till.

"On what charge!" Stephen demanded. "You can't just *arrest* anybody without—"

"On a charge of the sheriff done been called and he is pure-D pissed off. Now, you git out of our way, goddamnit, while we take this fellow off."

"Sam—"

"Well, I—"

"Hold on!"

This last comment arrived in a low rumble that everybody understood was Earl Swagger of the Arkansas State Police.

Earl, carrying his little boy Bob Lee with him, pushed through the crowd. He was not in uniform today, wearing instead jeans and boots, a battered old Stetson and a white, pearl buttoned shirt open at the collar, which set off the mahogany of a skin turned to pottery by fifteen years of Marine duty, the last three in the Pacific.

"Mr. Earl," Stephen yelled, "they're going to arrest William for nothing."

"Earl, you stay out of this," Rance said. "This here's a town matter."

"Yeah, Earl," said Buddy Till.

"Well, technically, it ain't," said Earl. "Your boy Stephen showed me the town plat, and as a matter of fact, your club here is in the unincorporated area, which makes it my jurisdiction. We could go to court on it, sure, but I'd win. Stephen was right."

"Earl, I been called out here many a night when somebody had too much to drink at the clubhouse," said the deputy, Buddy Till.

"I know, Buddy, but that ain't the law, that's a courtesy for the richer people. If you're going to have a law, it's got to be fair and right."

"Damn." Buddy let William, the Negro boy, go. "Don't you git in no trouble up here," he warned. "And you better believe I'm going to be watching you. Say, where you from? You from around here?"

"No, suh," said the youth.

"It's nobody's business where he's from. He's my guest and he doesn't have to answer any questions at all."

"Stephen, I'm going to ask you one last time to see the common decency of it, and make every—"

"I am here to play tennis with my friend William. He has agreed to do so. Let's play the match."

Everyone looked at everyone. Then everyone looked at Sam, who as a county prosecutor, in the absence of a judge, appeared to be the convening legal authority.

"It's damned strange," Sam said. "But as I said, it doesn't appear to be against any written law."

Of course no one—except possibly Stephen—had thought of the effect of this ruling on the tournament. It quickly developed that the team of Winston and Morrison, Stephen and William's first opponents, refused to take the court against a Negro.

"You forfeit," Stephen said.

"We protest," they said.

"Same thing."

That taken care of, exactly the same happened to the team of Norton and O'Sullivan, next on the docket. So in the space of a few seconds, Stephen and his partner had reached the finals.

That left only the fabulous Jeff St. Sebastian of LSU and his cousin-partner Bo.

Suddenly St. Sebastian himself spoke up. He'd returned from a nice refreshing shower up at the clubhouse. He had a look of bemused pleasure on his face, as if this whole ruckus was absolutely smashing fun.

"Now, one second," he said. "I have no objection to playing anybody. But there's a bigger question here. Mr., ah—"

"His name's Longacre," said his cousin.

"Mr. Longacre, possibly you mean well. Possibly you believe in the cause of the Negro. Some folks do. I myself believe the Negro has made a valuable contribution to our nation. But I wonder about you: Why, if you profess to care, do you insist on your humiliating this poor young man? Surely he's done you no harm, yet you make a circus exhibit out of him and if you actually get him onto the court, you'll expose his weaknesses even more tragically. For what? For your own vanity? That's not the southern way."

"What makes you think he can't play tennis?" said Stephen.

"Why, simple facts. The Negro, typically, is not athletically gifted at the sports at which whites excel. They make excellent boxers, given the thickness of their skull, the lack of articulation in the brain, and the size of their hands. They also don't feel pain to the degree that other races do. You can't put a man like this poor young fellow in a sport that demands speed, reflexes, coordination, and powers of the intellect. Tennis isn't hammering other men with your hands. It's not violent, brute strength; it's finesse, practice, wisdom. You put a boy like this out there and you'll only produce another bitter Negro male who's found he can't fit into the white world, compete at the white level, and will therefore develop a whopping case of the shuffles and the stammers. You'll ruin him. What is the point of making him so unhappy? I am only thinking of him, which is what you should be doing."

"He can handle himself," was all Stephen could say.

"William," asked Jeff, "have you ever played tennis before?"

"No, suh."

"Have you ever held a tennis racquet in your hand?"

"No, suh."

"Do you understand the scoring?"

"Suh, it ain't one, two, three, fo'. It's love, five or fifteen, thirty, forty, game. You win six games fo' a set and two sets fo' a match."

"What's deuce?"

A look of panic flashed through William's eyes. He looked at Stephen, who said, "I didn't explain that to him yet. It's a tie, William. You don't say 'tied,' you say 'deuce,' that's all. You have to win two straight points after deuce to take the game. If you only win one, it goes back to deuce."

"Yes, suh."

"He doesn't even know what deuce is," said Bo, disgustedly.

"There you have it," said Jeff. "I say these two should be disqualified on humanitarian grounds, so as not to humiliate and destroy the ego of the Negro boy. He needs tender treatment and love, not immersion in humiliation. The poor guy doesn't even understand the mechanics of the game."

"See there," said Rance. "Young Mr. St. Sebastian said a mouthful. If you don't give a damn about your family, your town, your club, and your race, Stephen, and if you're so hell-fire intent on uplifting the Negro, why you doing this to poor William?"

"I already explained this to him," said Stephen. "I'll put it to him again. William, do you want to play? Some of these white people will laugh at you and it may hurt your feelings. Can you get through that?"

"Yes, suh," said William.

"Okay," said Stephen.

"I'll try and be merciful," said St. Sebastian.

•   •   •

The first set was over in a blinking of an eye. St. Sebastian hammered four hard first serves and only Stephen got a racquet on one of them, but not even enough to get it back in play. On his two chances, poor William whiffed entirely at one, doubling over the crowd in laughter.

It only got worse, until finally Stephen ran off three points on his second service game, two off Bo, but then Jeff nailed a stinger down the line and that game was lost, too. William, when he got to his first shot, hit the ball out of the park, again driving the crowd into hysterics. The second time he undercompensated and hit weakly into the net. He never really figured it out, spraying shots all over Arkansas. The first set went at love.

"All right," said Jeff, "do you want to quit now? It seems stupid to go on."

"Oh, let's play it out," said Stephen.

"Of course," said Jeff. "I'm not doing anything for the next ten minutes anyhow."

Stephen went up to William.

"Don't you see, you don't have to hit it so hard. To control the ball, you just meet it. Let the racquet strings supply the power. Try and hit it early with an upward arc, and follow through high. You've got to be relaxed, like basketball. If you tighten up, you don't have a chance."

"Yes, suh," said William.

"Okay," said Stephen, "we'll give it our all."

"By the way," said William, "that boy Jeff? If he gon' hit to your left, he bounces the ball three times. If he gon' hit to your right, he bounces it four times. And that fat boy, Bo? He got the willies. You pattycake it to him and he be too nervous and git all in a twist. He can't hit nothing."

"Ah, are you sure?"

"Sure as life. Been studyin'."

It was Jeff's serve and he bounced the ball three times. Stephen cocked his racquet a quarter-turn to get into his backhand and was already gliding to the left when Jeff's serve, flat, hard, and accurate, rocketed off the center line. Stephen turned a quarter-turn, dropped his shoulder, hit through, and felt the wonderful buzz of the sweet spot and he jacked a shot down the alley, a clean winner.

"Oh, nice shot, old man," called Jeff. "Well hit."

"Thank you," said Stephen.

He again bounced the ball three times on the serve to William, who was still awkward with the racquet. But, with his anticipation, he blocked it back into a dead zone between Jeff and Bo and neither could reach it.

"Good show!" called Jeff.

Four bounces: forehand side. The ball was a blur. Stephen's return was even more blurred as he teed off. The best part was he nailed the placid Bo in the middle of the forehead and the ball bounced off into the crowd.

"Oh, bad luck!" cried Jeff.

After some minutes of rubbing and stroking, the application of ice, and the ministrations of several junior leaguers oohing and ahhhing over him, though primarily to get Jeff's attention, Bo was manly enough to get up, but he had a red welt over the left eye.

"You'll be fine," said Jeff.

"I'm really sorry," said Stephen. "I couldn't have aimed it there in a hundred years."

Tight-lipped and in love with a heroic image of himself, Bo signaled that he could play on.

Jeff double-faulted to lose the opening game.

"Well, fellows," said Jeff, "nicely done. It won't be a love match after all. How sporting."

Who could say when, exactly, it started to happen. William never really seemed comfortable with the racquet in his hand, but it was amazing how quickly some other thing occurred, and that was that his imagination seized the center of the game. He had uncanny powers of anticipation when the ball was in play in his zone and he always seemed to be there to block it back. He looked like the crudest thing in the world of tennis, a big, spindly-awkward black teenager, all elbows and knees, without any strokes at all. He had no grace, no fluidity, no poetry. He took no backswing whatsoever, but more than anything simply placed the racquet in the way of the ball in a stiff-wristed thrust and kept the ball in play. He never hit winners. He just blocked the ball back, deep, to the open court, and though Jeff could get his shots back, he could not get any mustard or clever placement on them.

The court helped, too. The soft red clay seemed to suck the power from the ball, squirting it high and fat, giving William that extra second to get to it and punch it back. The Negro boy soon picked up the extra gift of the skid; he learned how to race for a shot, then jam his tennis shoe into the sandlike surface, brake himself against its friction, and come back under control to bop the ball back in play.

At the same time, the fraudulence of Bo was soon in evidence. That portly young man had never really come back mentally from his beaning, and the subtle brilliance of William, his awareness of this weakness, was such that he hit most of his shots Bo's way. Bo just deconstructed shamefully before everybody's eyes.

Meanwhile, Stephen got loose and fluid, and the shock on the faces of the audience propelled his adrenaline to even more powerful levels. A look at his father steaming like a piston engine about to blow thrilled him to no end. When the pathetic Bo popped an ineffectual lob his way at the net, he put it away with piledriver force, bouncing the white ball seven rows deep in the bleachers, and he caught a look at his father's incredible agony, as if the poor man were waiting for that final coronary thrombosis to send him earthward, led by the blue pulsing Y in his temple next to his gray highlights.

William and Stephen actually won the second set, 6–4, to the incredulity of the crowd.

"Lucky nigger!" someone yelled.

"He's too goddamn tall," someone else yelled.

"It ain't right, goddamnit," yelled a third.

Rance turned to Connie.

"That boy's going to start a riot," he said.

"Yes," said Connie, "but he is *doing* something. Have you

ever seen him so committed in his life. He's *trying,* and that's a first."

"Earl won't let there be any trouble," said Sam.

And indeed, Earl stood and fixed the dentist who'd yelled "nigger" with one of his hard stares, and that man immediately sat down.

But suddenly, as Earl looked up, someone ran out from the crowd. Earl saw him go too late and by the time he headed out there, he knew he'd never make it.

The man ran right past Stephen, who was stunned to see him go at poor William, who stood frozen as the fellow approached, all lathered up.

He ran as if he were on a killing frenzy, a berserker hellbent on mayhem and blood, a Confederate legend like the last man at Pickett's Charge, and when he reached William, he reached into his pocket and pulled out a gun and thrust it right at William.

Earl knew he wouldn't make it and heard the crowd gasp as the gun steadied for the shot. But then it continued upward and toward the mouth of the shooter, who bent and took a bite out of it.

It was chocolate.

Earl knocked it away and kicked it off the court and grabbed the shooter.

He hammerlocked him and bent him to his knees, to the rising torrent of boos and hisses.

He twisted him around and saw that it was not a man at all; it was that damned Jimmy Pye.

"You goddamned fool, Jimmy!" screamed Earl, but Jimmy, though not strong enough to resist Earl, was nevertheless laughing in operatic triumph. It seemed the town boys had heard what was going on out at the country club and had come on out to add their bit of intimidation to the ceremony, and Jimmy, as head miscreant and champion athlete of the county, had led the way.

"I ought to lock you up, boy! You have committed a crime now. You have made a public nuisance of yourself and you could do a month in jail."

"Mr. Earl, I'se just hoo-dooing the nigra. Boo! boy, them ha'ants a-gonna git you, you come back."

Stephen, for his part, looked at Jimmy as Earl led the boy off the court. Jimmy was his own age, a cracker hero of sorts, just the kind of boy who could have been his friend if he weren't so wild and stupid and vain and evil. He certainly had spirit.

As Jimmy was dragged by, he looked over at Stephen.

"Stephen, you'd best hope there's a early bus out of town tomorrow. The boys is cranked up something terrible!"

Stephen looked away, trying to deny the fear he felt.

But it came, nevertheless, dry and hot to his heart.

He walked over to William.

"You okay?"

"Like to died, seen that gun come up."

"He's an asshole. They're all assholes. You want to call it a day? We can get out of here. You get the same money, no problem. I won't short you."

"No, suh," said William. "Come to play. We can play it out now, if you want."

"Okay, William. You got some kind of nerve."

"You stay out here with me, *you* gots some kind of nerve."

Meanwhile, Earl took Jimmy to the two deputies and left him securely in their care. "If he tries anything, you bop his pretty curly head with that stick you're always carrying, Buddy."

"Can't b'lieve you're asking me to whap a white fellow in favor of a colored one."

"The law is the law and that's all it is," Earl said.

Then he turned and addressed the ugly townie contingent.

"Y'all settle down now. You let these fellows play their fool game, do you hear. I will call out a riot squad, by God, if I have to."

That was Earl. You couldn't scare him with an atom bomb. He'd face up to anybody anywhere anytime, over any issue. It would get him killed one of these days.

By the time some kind of order was restored, it was near twilight. The players now seemed almost bloody, not from their own plasma, but from the spray of red dust, which then clung to the sweat on their legs or the damp wool and canvas of their shoes. Where Bo had fallen, he wore a crown of red, like the red badge of courage; unfortunately, it was on his ass.

In the third set, St. Sebastian and Bo rallied, went up 2–0 on Jeff's serve and against William's, which remained the least impressive part of his game. But Stephen held, the rattled Bo double-faulted three times, and then everybody held through the next round, and it was 4–4, William's serve.

He nodded at Stephen, who came over.

"You okay?"

"Yes, suh," said William.

"What is it?"

"Do I have to hit it straightlike?"

"What do you mean?"

"I mean, do I have to hit it right in the center?"

"Well, if I understand you, you can hit it anyway you want to."

"I could hit it on an angle. Like, you know, I could sort of brush it and git it to spinning."

"Well, yes. You didn't know that? Gosh, I'm sorry, that's my fault. William, you can hit it any way you want to."

William nodded solemnly, taking all this in. His eyes were faraway and intent, as if he were figuring something out.

He went to the service line, showed the ball to signify the start of play, then stepped a good two yards back and tossed it high.

Too high.

He tossed it very high.

But as he tossed it, he himself leaped, and, airborne, he was a thing of majesty, as if suddenly having found his creativity, his place in the game and the universe, and he hit the ball at a sliced angle so that it rocketed downward but broke to the left radically, and poor Jeff couldn't get a racquet on it.

"Jesus Christ, you could do that all the time?" said Stephen.

"I guess," he said.

At any rate he did it three more times and each time, the other fellows struggled for it.

Suddenly the crowd was quiet.

A thunderhead rolled in from out of the mountains.

Nobody said a thing.

Jeff was serving at 4–5 to stay in the match.

William walked back to Stephen.

"You be cool, man. It ain't nothing. You just be there, man, cool and quiet and in control, you got me? We gon' take these motherfuckers, okay. Take they *asses*."

"You got that right."

Jeff double-faulted his first serve.

On his second serve he hit a nice shot that William blocked back, but he came up with a screamer.

Two more good serves and he was serving for the game at 40–15.

But he hit another double.

Stephen watched him. He bounced the ball three times. Backhand. Stephen began to cheat, but then it occurred to him that Jeff hadn't been bouncing the ball at all. He'd caught on! He cranked the racquet back to the forehand grip and at least got his momentum going, and when Jeff hit his best serve of the match, a bullet to the right, Stephen lunged and dinked a looper back that just hit on the line, which deflected its bounce just a bit, and Bo drove it into the net.

Deuce.

Jeff served to William, who blocked clumsily something like a Texas leaguer right at Bo at the net, but Jeff didn't trust him, screamed "NO" as he came in to take the ball on the hop, utterly confusing Bo, who didn't give way and hit it out.

Suddenly it was match point.

Jeff conferred ever so quickly with Bo.

He didn't bounce the ball.

He collected himself calmly, began the syncopation of the server, the orchestration of left to right, the shiver that liberated the strength to rise through his lean body, the delicacy of the toss, the ball, now red and shaggy, hanging at the equipoise as he craned his arm through, snapped shoulders and hips, the whole world, it seemed, resting on his brow.

•   •   •

His mother would always remember this moment. There were cruel days to come, when Connie didn't think she could live another second, and only the ministrations of good men like Sam kept her alive. But there was also her memory of this moment, her only son's, her doomed son's, her haunted, crazed, and self-destructive son's best moment on earth.

Jeff served, Stephen got it back, a nice return fated to go deep and extend the point, but Bo had been instructed to poach. So on the serve of the ball, he'd moved quickly to his left, and was set to volley Stephen's return into the alley, and for once his nerve and his coordination didn't fail him, and he got a good stiff-wristed volley onto the ball to tap it away.

What was not expected was that in the split second he left his position, William left his, too, and raced toward him along the net, and when Bo's volley crossed, there was William to volley it back, and it bounced in the alley, and Jeff ran full-goddamn-out to flick it back through the falling dusk, and did get it, too, hitting a nice clean shot into the open court, but alas, on the second bounce.

No cheer went up.

Rance didn't stay to congratulate his son.

Somehow the cup signifying victory was never presented.

The crowd filed out sullenly.

William and Stephen were too goddamned tired to embrace.

Jeff disappeared quickly; Bo seemed to fade from the surface of the planet in a split second.

The two boys stood there, heaving with oxygen debt.

"How'd you know he was going to poach?"

"Poach?"

"You know, come to my side of the court?"

"Oh, he up on his toes when the serve be tossed. He don't never do that before, so I figgered something was up. I just ran and as I ran I could see what he was trying to do and I just keep on running and got there."

"Wow," said Stephen, "you sure figured those boys out."

"Wasn't much," said William.

The one man who approached them was Earl.

"You know what, this ain't a place to be lingering. Let's git to my car and I'll get you boys out of here."

And that's the way it ended, the two tennis players, sweaty and smeared with red clay, climbing into Earl's State Police Ford. William sat in back, and held Earl's young son, Bob Lee, and Earl drove them straight up Route 71.

"Where to?"

"Can you cut over to Little Rock?"

They drove in silence the two long hours to Little Rock. William had nothing to say.

Finally, swallowed by the squalor of that city's black district, they drove by honky-tonks and fried chicken parlors and throbbing night crowds.

"Turn left up here," William finally said, guiding them down Kedzie to 154th, then right again, this time up Wilson.

They pulled up in front of a block of row houses, decrepit and mostly deserted.

"You live here?" Stephen said.

"Wif my mama. You got my money?"

"Of course."

He handed an envelope over.

"It's all there, plus something. Hey, you really did well."

"Yeah, we showed them boys, didn't we?"

"We sure did."

"William," said Earl, "is there someone we could talk to? A doctor, a priest, your dad, or someone? I'd like to tell them what a great young man you are and how well you did today. They should know. You were a real hero."

"No, suh," said William. "I am fine. Thank y'all fo' being so nice to me."

But then there was a moment of awkwardness. The child, Bob Lee, had fallen asleep in William's arms. William didn't want to wake him, but there was no other way. Gently, he laid the child down on the backseat of the car.

"So long, little man," he said, and with his envelope, left the car and was gone.

"That's an athlete," said Earl.

"That is an athlete. He's supposedly the best basketball player this city has ever seen. He's legend. He can do things with a basketball you can't believe."

"I hope he's all right. Is there a place for him to go?"

There seemed to be no answer to that question, so the trooper, the boy, and the child drove back in silence to Polk County and what lay ahead for them.

No Strings

Judith Kelman

Bobby Webber had Roy Duchamps down two sets to zip, five games to two, staring down the barrel of a possible triple match point. Duchamps was buckling under the strain, making desperate dumb tyro mistakes. All Webber had to do was hold steady, stay focused, and watch the lanky swamp rat self-destruct.

Duchamps poised at the baseline, muttering under his brackish breath. Vexation carved a ditch between his mud-brown eyes and pinched his crooked mouth. Sweat rained from his wild cayenne curls as he rocked forward and bounced the ball in short, fretful hops.

Webber shuffled deftly from side to side, keeping everything light and loose. Training his mind, he tuned out the heady magnolia scent and the sassy buzz of a flirting mosquito.

Ready . . . steady.

Duchamps reared back and flung the ball too high, so it was swallowed by the fierce midday glare. With an anguished grunt, he hammered down, trying to redeem the ruined toss.

Webber breezed toward the backcourt as the ball approached. His calculations were dead-on for a normal shot, but the swamp rat's aberration struck with a sickening thump and fell dangerously short.

Racing in, Webber lunged madly and scooped the ball before it hit ground. Somehow, he mustered enough force to send it dribbling back over the net. Duchamps watched gap-jawed from the baseline as the fuzzy orb died inches from the net post, raising red dust and explosive applause from the packed bleachers.

Flushed with pleasure, Webber dipped in a modest little bow. That was the kind of shot that had earned him the prized moniker *Bobby the Backboard*. That kind of shot would get him past Duchamps and all comers, on to the national tour and the big time.

"Love–forty. Match point, Mr. Webber," boomed the umpire.

As Webber turned back toward the baseline, his right shoe went slack. Peering down, he spotted a broken lace trailing from the cheek of his lucky Reebok. He caught the umpire's eye and signaled for a time-out.

Coach Deke Hardeman appeared at the bench with his axe jaw jutting, arms bulging force, and a new lace drooping from his ham-sized hand. Webber took the strand with a somber nod, striving to match the coach's fierce, muscular silence.

Propping his foot on the bench, he flicked out the broken lace. Quickly, he strung the replacement, yanked tight, and worked a double bow. He stepped on the foot, testing, and then tossed the ruined scraps aside.

Before he could make it back onto the court, a horrified shriek stalled Webber.

"You can't leave those lying around, Bobby. Jee-zuz."

Turning, Webber watched Earl Emerson dash onto the court, scoop up the broken lace strings and stuff them hard in the pocket of his grass-stained jeans.

Webber's ears went hot. "Are you nuts, Emerson? Get out of here. Can't you see I'm in the middle of a match?"

Emerson's eyes skittered nervously. "Hell with the match, Bobby. There's serious danger here. She's got her eye on you. I can see."

Webber tracked Earl's gaze to the dark, hulking woman in the first row. Large jet-lensed glasses masked her eyes, and a bright scarf bound her head like a giant wasp's nest. Sun sparks sprayed off the knitting needles that clicked with startling rapidity in her leathery hands. Blood-red yarn snaked up from the canvas tote bag beside her, and a beard of taut, even stitches stretched beneath the needle like a spreading wound.

"Take your crazy hokum nonsense and get the hell away, Earl. I've got a game to win."

Emerson touched his pocket, checking for the lace. Then he backed away, peering anxiously over his shoulder. "Sure, Bobby. You just go on ahead and play. I'll see she don't get a-hold of the strings. Don't you worry yourself one bit."

"Go, Earl."

Webber's heart was stammering. Damned Earl Emerson was forever hanging around, running at the mouth; and breaking his concentration. It had started as soon as Webber showed up at Beaumont Academy six weeks ago. Before he got his duffel bags unpacked, there was Earl, grinning and gawking, drawling his endless stream of irritating trash.

Webber still remembered Earl's first words, drooping off his lazy tongue like tar. "Stick with me, Bobby, and I'll show you what's what. Real soon, you'll be a genuine bayou-blooded southern boy, N'awlins to the bone."

Fat chance.

Webber had explained in picture-book terms that he was a bagel-blooded, Yanks-addicted Brooklyn boy to the bone, and glad of it. He had come to Beaumont for the tennis program, which regularly set its number-one player on a fast track to world-class prominence. His plan was to take the number-one seed from Roy Duchamps, then play ball and reap the juicy benefits. With any luck, by this time next year he would be back in civilization, enrolled at Columbia or NYU, armed with a Beaumont degree and the academy's powerful contacts.

But Emerson refused to listen. Kid was determined to convert Webber to Creole, jambalaya, and moonshine. Damned Earl was thick as gator hide and stubborn as a tick. And he was still standing at courtside, casting his slouchy shadow over Webber's shining moment in the sun.

"Go on, Earl! Get lost."

Stupid kid just stood there. "There's danger, Bobby. Real serious. You got to listen."

The umpire scowled. "Ready, Mr. Webber? This is a tennis court, not a chat room."

"Ready, sir." Webber took up his racquet and hurried onto the court. Earl's warnings echoed in his head. *She's got her eye on you. Serious danger.*

Waiting for Duchamps to serve, Webber's gaze drifted toward the woman on the bench. He imagined her staring at him behind those great black glasses, leaking lethal poison from her eyes.

Suddenly, Duchamps arched back, flung the toss, and

looped his racquet with dislocating speed. The ball exploded across the court, sharp and low.

Webber charged in, racquet poised, but the shot whizzed past at a crazy angle as he swatted madly at the torpid air.

"Fifteen–forty," came the call.

Grim-faced, Webber trudged back to the line. The mosquito dove in, emboldened, so Webber had to slap his own cheek hard to thwart the assault. Smarting, he peered at his adversary. He could sense Duchamps settling down, gaining confidence. *Damned Earl and his superstitious crap.*

Webber shook his head to clear it. He would not think about murdering Earl or his stinging cheek or how badly he ached to beat Roy Duchamps. He would not think about the spooky woman on the bench. Her face was turned his way now, mouth pressed in a grim, stingy line.

Suddenly, Webber heard a crack followed by a grunt from Duchamps. The ball streaked into the service box before he could react.

"Thirty-forty."

Coach Hardeman howled like a stuck beast. "Tune in, Webber. Focus, for the love of Pete!"

Webber tried. He fixed on Roy Duchamps, unblinking. When the next serve came, he was all over it and then some. His return took off as if he'd launched it. He heard Duchamps chuckling as the ball sailed overhead and kept sailing well out of bounds.

"Dang if that ain't a home run," Duchamps drawled.

"Deuce," called the ump.

From there, Webber made a long, slow slide downhill. His timing was off, everything was. Known for his incredible gets, he now failed to reach easy obvious shots. When he did get his racquet on the ball, he either overhit or smashed the return into the net. His limbs felt leaden. Bats of doubt swooped in his mind, broad wings flapping.

Duchamps took full advantage. He battled back stroke by stroke, game after humiliating game. Soon the score was tied, and then Roy claimed the lead. At some point, the crowd arced over into his camp, heaping their collective energy on the swamp rat. Eventually, even the umpire seemed to slide toward Roy's side of the lopsided equation, handing him close calls and encouraging comments.

Webber had all he could do to finish the match. When it was mercifully over, he forced himself to shake Duchamps's damp, calloused hand and trade a brave grimace for the swamp rat's twisted smile. "Good game," Webber mumbled without feeling.

"Was, wasn't it?" Duchamps crowed.

Webber spotted Earl Emerson in the departing crush and rode a burst of fury to catch up with him. His voice quaked with rage. "Goddamnit, Earl. You cost me the match. You broke my stride with that superstitious crap and made me lose."

"Hush, Bobby. Watch out. She'll hear." He tipped his head toward the edge of the straggling crowd, where the dark woman from the bench was lumbering toward the parking lot.

The Beaumont campus had been carved from an old plantation in the French Quarter, hard by the Mississippi. The boys crossed a sprawling green flanked by iron-terraced guest quarters that had been converted to classroom space and the main house, which now held the chapel and administration offices. Earl refused to speak again until they reached the senior dorm, a two-story tomblike building of indeterminate origin, which was rumored to have served as a dungeon and torture chamber for recalcitrant slaves.

Outside Webber's room, Emerson peered up and down the dim corridor. Slipping inside, he double-locked the door. "Wish it was crap, Bobby. Honest."

Webber hopped on the bed with his hands behind his neck. "I'm listening, and it better be good."

Slumped on the desk chair, Earl shook his head miserably. "Can't talk about it. I do, and I'm toast."

"You don't and I'll toast you, Emerson. Now shoot."

Desperation pinched Earl's tone. "Smarter not to say anything. Honest. Never can tell who could be listening. What they might do."

"Maybe not. But you can imagine what I'll do, dickhead. Now, talk!"

Emerson sighed mightily. "All right. I'll say what I can, but you got to promise not to tell anyone you got it from me."

"Shoot, Earl. I mean it. I'm running out of patience fast."

Earl raked through his spiky hay-toned hair. "That old witch calls herself Maman Mechant. Means nasty mother in French, and that's just what she is. She does voodoo. Works these real nasty spells."

Webber snickered. "No problem. I've got a drawer full of kryptonite. Never leave home without some."

"Can't blame you for figuring it's bunk. But trust me, Bobby. Be a shame for you to learn it the hard way. Like me." Emerson rubbed the wormy web of scars between his right thumb and forefinger.

Webber sat and pitched forward. He had been dying for an opening to ask about Earl's deformity. "Are you saying she had something to do with that?"

"Caused it."

"Yeah? How?"

Earl rubbed harder at the scabrous flap of skin. "Back in ninth grade, I was on the team. Not just a gofer like now. Had me a real good serve. Killer lob and a wicked net shot. Gave old Roy a run for his money a time or two. Came precious close to beating him, which Maman Mechant didn't like one bit."

"What's it to her?"

"Way I hear it, she and Roy's folks go way back, used to be neighbors over in Slidell. Lived right on the bayou and got from here to there on those flat-bottom boats called pirogues. One time, Roy's daddy saved Maman's youngest boy from drowning when he fell overboard trying to catch a fish, so she believes she owes Roy. If anyone threatens to get in his way, Maman fixes it so they don't."

"Do you honestly expect me to believe that old woman hurt your hand with some spell?"

"I'm telling you what is. This one day, I had Roy near beat. All sudden like, it started raining something fierce, so the ump said we should pack it up and finish the next morning.

"That night, I went down to dinner. It was still pretty nasty out, so I went to get myself a nice hot mess of gumbo from the crock. I was holding the bowl in one hand and spooning with the other when out of nowhere I get this monster cramp in my gut. Next thing I know I'm flat on the floor and my right hand is burning like crazy, screaming pain. Doc checked me out head to toe, found nothing wrong except the burn. But that was more than enough. Thing wouldn't heal for the longest time, and then it scarred over all weird and knobby, like you see. That was it for me and tennis. Can barely hold a racquet with this ugly mitt." Emerson's chest heaved. "Used to fancy I'd maybe be a tennis star someday. Pretty rich, huh?"

Webber cradled his own right hand protectively. "That sucks, Earl. But what makes you think the old woman had anything to do with it?"

"Maman told me so, that's what. I'm walking after class a couple of weeks after the accident, and she comes up right out of nowhere. *No one goes after my boy,* she tells me. *You stay away from Roy, or I'll tie you up way worse than the belly cramps next time. Worse than you can imagine, boy. You hear?*"

Webber sniffed. "So she found out you had a cramp and she decided to spook you. Doesn't prove a thing, Earl. How gullible can you be?"

"Hear me out, Bobby. I heard tell there were other kids she'd hurt. Back in first grade, there was this boy named Freddy Fenold. Dorky kid with a temper, he was. Anyway, he got into a fight with Duchamps over something or the other. Next day, Freddy trips in a gopher hole and breaks his back. Spent six months in the hospital, strapped to a frame. Poor kid's still all twisted up, I'm told. Can't hardly walk."

"Sounds like a rotten accident, Earl. Nothing more."

"Maybe so, but after that was Stevie Krulwich, who accused Roy of cheating on a spelling test and got a ruptured appendix for his trouble. Then came Pete Cady a couple of years later."

"The deaf kid?"

"Wasn't always," Earl said gravely. "Pete couldn't abide Roy for some reason, picked on him something awful. This one afternoon, he goes into town to buy himself some gum. On the way back, he kicks at a lump of dirt at the side of the road. Turns out to be a live grenade. Nobody knows how it got there, but *Maman* let Pete know he had her to thank. Of course, Pete couldn't hear anymore after that grenade blew up in his face, but he could read her lips, clear as day."

Webber hunched behind hard-crossed arms. "It's nothing but talk, Earl, rumors. Every school has stories like those. I bet that old lady is harmless."

"There've been others, Bobby, plenty more. Kids just don't get sick like that, one after another, sick and hurt."

Webber sniffed. "That's it? That's your whole stupid story?"

Emerson caught his lip behind a fence of chipped, yellowed teeth. "I said way too much already."

"You said plenty of nothing. You've got some major nerve costing me a match over that." Webber rose to leave. He crossed the floor in three long strides before he realized this was his room after all. "Get the hell out of here," he ordered. "Being around you is giving me worse than a cramp."

The chair squealed as Earl got to his feet. "That's fine, Bobby. You go on and be mad as you please. Just be careful is all I'm asking. Craig Sichel wouldn't listen. And now . . ." Earl's voice sank to a mournful plaint as he headed out the door. "If only he'd taken it serious, like I begged him to."

"What are you talking about, Earl? Who's Craig Sichel? What happened to him? Get back here and tell me!"

The door thwacked shut, and Emerson's flat footsteps slapped away down the hall. Webber thought to follow and wring the story out of Earl's chicken neck, but he had a better idea. If you wanted to know the facts about anything around here, there was only one place to go.

Darwin Fassberg, a wiry, weasel-faced boy, lived one floor up at the end of the hall. His room was triple the size of Webber's and boasted a pond view, kitchenette, and private bath. Normally, the prime space was assigned to a resident dorm counselor or faculty member, but Fassberg was a very special case.

Darwin was a bona fide genius whose chosen field of intellectual endeavor was the care and acquisition of wealth. Early on, he'd shown prodigious aptitude for investing, parlaying his allowance, birthday, and bar mitzvah gifts into a portfolio rumored to be worth a megabuck or more. While other parents bragged about little Johnny's A in arithmetic, Fassberg's folks proudly reported that their Darwin, at the tender age of eight, had talked them into buying one thousand shares of Cisco, which, after splits, had swelled to a tidy $12 million.

Naturally, numerous schools had vied for Fassberg's attendance. Beaumont Academy snagged him with a full scholarship, a self-guided curriculum, and the novel promise that he would be the first student in academy history to hold a voting seat on the board of directors. In assuming that post, Fassberg's first official act had been to engineer the modification of the school's charter, allowing him to declare his dorm room a fully autonomous sovereign state. Next, he helped reinvest Beaumont's endowment fund, increasing it by 58 percent in a year.

Webber read the long list of rules and prohibitions on Fassberg's door. As prescribed, he tapped his initials on the wall-mounted keypad, pressed his thumb to the fingerprint scanner, and then waited. Several minutes later, a buzzer sounded, which meant he was free to enter.

Then, not free exactly.

Fassberg perched on a throne-sized leather chair beside a gunmetal strongbox. Clustered behind him were gilt-framed portraits of his heroes: Bill Gates, Donald Trump, the sultan of Brunei, and the James brothers. He wore a T-shirt embroidered with his guiding principle: *A buck for anything and anything for a buck.*

"Hey, Darwin. Got a minute? I need to ask you something."

"You have entered Darwinia, Mr. Webber. Before we proceed, you're required to pay the border tax. For a short midweek stay, that will be fifty Fassbergmas."

"What's that?"

"Coin of the realm. If you happen to be financially embarrassed at the moment, our bank can arrange a loan for 22 percent, compounded daily."

"I've got a Visa card."

"Sorry, we do not accept credit or debit cards. But we can take U.S. currency. Of course, there is a commission and handling charge." Rising, he tapped some calculations into the laptop computer on his desk. "Unfortunately, the dollar is way down against the Fassbergma. At the current exchange rate, that will be twenty-two dollars and fifty cents."

Webber emptied his pockets on the chrome and glass coffee table. Fassberg eyed the money with adoration. "Now then, what is the nature of your inquiry?"

Webber perched on one of the low, stern wooden guest chairs. "I heard a rumor about kids here getting hurt by voodoo spells, Darwin. Some creepy old woman who hangs around the tennis courts supposedly does them. You know about this?"

"Certainly. It's common knowledge."

"But it's not true, just nonsense. Right?"

Fassberg shrugged. "For as long as I've been here, the woman known as Maman Mechant has taken credit for a series of serious mishaps involving Beaumont students. Of course, no one can say as a certainty whether her spells are causative or simply coincidental."

"What do you think? You're the genius."

Fassberg stroked his pointy chin. "Quite honestly, I try not to think about her at all. But then, given that I'm not a tennis player or any threat whatsoever to Roy Duchamps, I don't need to worry about it, thank the Lord."

"You're scared of her? I didn't think you were scared of anything but inflation and margin calls."

"Scared is an overstatement, Mr. Webber. I'm simply suggesting that it can't hurt to be vigilant. Presume the worst and take sensible precautions. I rarely counsel defensive behavior, but in this case, I see it as the only rational tactic."

Webber had expected cool reassurance, nothing like this. "I don't get it. Why didn't anyone warn me about that old witch before I came here?"

"That's obvious, isn't it? The last thing Beaumont Academy needs is for a thing like that to get out. As you can imagine, it would not exactly elevate the school's desirability or standing. The administration keeps waiting and hoping for the old lady to die or for Roy Duchamps to graduate, which he will, one way or the other, at the end of the year."

"But why can't they just get rid of her, bar her from the campus?"

"That's obvious, too. Banishing her would be tantamount to acknowledging her powers, admitting that she has caused all the misery and death."

"Somebody died?"

Fassberg shuddered. "Appalling incident. Happened about a year ago. A junior named Craig Sichel was one point away from taking Duchamps's crown. Suddenly, he clutched his chest and keeled over, foaming at the mouth. He turned this awful shade of gray, twitching and heaving. I'll never forget the sight. It's positively emblazoned in my memory. Almost as tragic and shocking as when they broke up Microsoft."

Webber nipped his cuticle hard and tasted blood. "He could have had a heart condition or something. Kids do."

"Certainly he could have, but signs point to the cause of death as highly unnatural. The autopsy report was circulated at a board meeting. Sichel's heart ruptured, exploded like a tossed tomato, unheard of in a strapping, healthy kid like Craig. Furthermore, he had been through a comprehensive physical only two weeks before, including an EKG and thoracic ultrasound. His heart was fine until that voodoo woman worked her grotesque spell."

Picturing Sichel's exploding heart, Webber went woozy. "What should I do?"

"If you want my honest opinion, the only fail-safe response would be to leave school. Back in New York you would not be forced to compete against Roy Duchamps. Maman Mechant would have no incentive to harm you."

"I can't do that, Fassberg. My parents are the best. They've sacrificed so much for me. If I left now, they'd lose all that tuition money."

"Better than losing their son. Is it not?"

Webber shook his head with terrified resolve. "There has to be some other way."

Fassberg frowned. "Nothing nearly as foolproof, to be sure. But as a minimum precaution, you must make absolutely sure she doesn't get her hands on any strings or anything stringlike that belongs to you. Apparently, she requires a person's strings to work her spells. Weaves them into her knitting and then—"

Webber remembered Emerson grabbing for the shoelace. Who knows what hideous agony had been averted. "Sure. I can do that."

Fassberg looked doubtful. "That old woman is very devious, Mr. Webber. You must never underestimate the power of such evil determination."

"I won't, Darwin. Thanks for your time."

Fassberg pressed the button beside his high-backed chair, releasing the electronic door lock. "I hope you enjoyed your visit to Darwinia. Travel safely, and remember: No strings."

No strings.

Those words looped incessantly through Webber's mind. He picked at his dinner and found it impossible to study for the pop quiz Mr. Larson gave every Thursday in chemistry. He spent hours going over and over everything in his room, locking anything that resembled a string in his closet.

Sleep hurled him into a cauldron of hideous imaginings. He dreamed he was trapped in a giant web, massive living strings enfolding him, squeezing out his breath. Escaping that, he was thrust into a dense, suffocating forest, unable to move without razor thorns raking at his flesh, drawing bloody strings along his limbs. Several times, he wrenched awake with his heart stampeding and his sheets drenched with nervous sweat.

In the morning he felt wretched and dull. He brushed and flossed and showered in a fog. He nearly fell asleep in class and drew a total blank on the chemistry quiz. Lunch revived him somewhat, but he anticipated the afternoon's practice with cold metal dread. He and Alex Caden were scheduled to play doubles against Roy Duchamps and Brian Beck. Normally, he would relish the challenge, but there was nothing normal about any of this.

He thought of pleading sick, which was hardly a lie, but Hardeman did not accept excuses short of death or dismemberment. The coach was not what anyone would call easygoing. If a player disappointed him, he'd rip out the kid's ego and stomp it to dust. Falling into that man's disfavor terrified Webber almost as much as Maman Mechant and her evil spells.

In the boy's room, Webber caught a glimpse of himself and scowled. Dusky circles rimmed his eyes and his skin had the sickly cast of wet cement. He turned the tap on full and splashed his cheeks with cold water. The shock jarred a few of his brain cells, stirring a useful idea. All he had to do was lose. Unless he threatened Duchamps's crown, the old woman would have no reason to target him for an injury or worse. Staying in second place at Beaumont would not be the end of him. Webber could still go on to play in college and work his way into national competition from there.

Beck, Duchamps, and Caden were warming up on court one when Webber arrived. A few spectators were scattered in the bleachers, but fortunately, there was no sign of Maman Mechant. Coach Hardeman finished up a sophomore practice, and then strode over to their court.

Cords bulged in the coach's neck as Hardeman unleashed his mighty temper at Alex Caden. "I got my eye on you, you lazy little slug. You show me something, or I'll show you the door. Win this practice, or you can kiss your scholarship goodbye. There is no free lunch here. You read me?"

"Yes, sir. I won't let you down, sir. You'll see."

"Yes I will, Caden. I see everything. Now get to it!"

Roy Duchamps served the first game, fast and clean, scoring two aces followed by a neat crosscourt rally return and a dazzling line shot. Next up, Webber botched the first two points with double faults, but a look at Hardeman's face convinced him to change his tactics. He directed his next serve at Duchamps's monster forehand. Roy countered with a wicked smash to Caden's flabby backhand, but somehow Alex shot back a perfect zinger out of Beck's desperate reach.

Hardeman scratched his close-cropped head. "Not bad, Caden," he said grudgingly. "Let's see more like that. Maybe inspire your partner to move his lazy butt, too."

To Webber's horror, Caden rose to the challenge. He played better than he ever had, better than was reasonable by far. Whenever Webber missed a shot, there was Alex, dashing out of nowhere to back him up. Caden's first-serve percentage was nearly perfect, and he covered the court like a plague. On the other side Duchamps and Beck traded angry asides and looks of sour disbelief as they slogged toward a certain defeat.

Webber and Caden were winning, which was no good at all. Webber's desperation grew as he spotted the voodoo lady ambling toward the bleachers. Heavily, she sat down the row from Earl Emerson and drew her knitting from the canvas bag. As she started working the needles, a glossy white string snaked up into the row of blood-red stitches. Webber's hand flew to his mouth as he remembered dropping his dental floss into the trashcan in the dormitory bathroom.

No strings.

Suddenly a hot spike of pain shot through Webber's temple. Reeling, he watched Beck's net shot spin past him as he stood paralyzed by the ferocious hurt and fear. Hardeman hollered something, but Webber couldn't hear past the howling agony in his ears. He could not see past the hellish ache. His head was on fire, stomach lurching up to put it out.

He awoke to a blur of muted voices and fuzzy lights. Everything swirled in dim, hazy currents, including the kindly, bespectacled face that loomed over him.

"There you are, Bobby. Nice to have you back. I'm Dr. Seplowitz. Are you feeling better now? Can you sit up?"

Webber's mouth was a swamp, and he felt as if someone had bubble-wrapped his brain. Slowly, he sat and waited for the walls to stop shimmying. "What happened? Where am I?"

"You're in the school infirmary, son. Have been since early this afternoon. As to what happened, I honestly can't say for sure. Let me help you up to your feet now. Slowly, good. Hold out your finger, and then bring it to your nose. That's good. Now I want you to close your eyes and balance on one foot."

Webber went along with the prodding and poking until the doctor finished his exam.

"What's wrong with me, Doctor? Am I going to be all right?"

"Absolutely. Nothing to worry about."

"I don't have a brain tumor?"

"Of course not. My guess is you got too much sun. Or maybe not enough to drink. You passed out. It happens. Think of it as the body's way of demanding you get a rest."

Webber touched his head gingerly, recalling the scorching pain. "I feel okay now."

"Glad to hear it. I'm going to sign you out. You go on and have yourself a nice dinner and a good night's sleep. I bet you'll be good as new in the morning. Soon as I reach your folks, I'm going to tell them that exactly."

"Don't call my parents, please. They're big worriers. My mom, especially. They'll get all upset for nothing."

The doctor smiled. "You're a considerate young man, Bobby. I admire that. Tell you what: If you promise to come back and check in with me next week, I suppose that call won't be necessary."

"Thanks, Dr. Seplowitz." Webber hesitated, but he decided he could trust the man. "Can I ask you a stupid question?"

"There are no stupid questions, son. Only stupid answers."

"Do you believe in spells, Doc? Voodoo and stuff like that?"

"No, I certainly don't. I'm a man of science, Bobby, trained to believe what can be tested and proven."

"But what about all those kids getting hurt by evil spells? Killed even. Doesn't that prove anything?"

Seplowitz set an avuncular hand on Webber's shoulder. "That's only talk, son. Words. You're too smart to fall for such hogwash."

"You don't believe it's true?"

"No, I do not. And neither should you. Boys who spread such rumors are just playing with you, trying to get your goat. You just go about your business and forget that foolishness."

"But what about Pete Cady and Craig Sichel and all the others?"

"Bad things happen, Bobby. That's a fact of life some folks can't accept. They find it easier to blame someone or something. Like that voodoo silliness."

Webber dearly wanted to believe him. But as soon as he joined the cafeteria line at dinner, Earl Emerson turned up, jumpy as a flea.

"Jeez, Bobby. You okay? I couldn't make it to practice today. Heard you took sick."

"It was nothing. Doc said I probably just had too much sun."

"Got to be more to it than that," Earl whispered. "First you, then Caden."

"What happened to Alex?"

"Hush. Not here." Earl drew him out of the bustling hall and around back between the trash Dumpsters. The air was thick with honeysuckle and the rhythmic thrum of cicadas. "After they took you off the court, Caden hit the showers," Earl said. "He's washing up like always, minding his own business, and real suddenlike, his hair comes falling out in clumps. Kid got flat-out hysterical, screaming so hard and crazy the coach had to slap his face to calm him down. Way I hear it he's bald as a light bulb now. Won't leave his room, he's so ashamed."

"That's crap, Earl. You're just making it up to try and get my goat."

Earl huffed. "Go see for yourself. Coach asked me to bring Alex some dinner. You can do it just the same."

Webber's hands shook as he balanced the tray on his hip to knock on Alex Caden's door. "Hey, Caden. It's room service. Open up."

"Leave it outside," came a tremulous voice.

"No can do. The dean's dog will be all over it in a heartbeat. If I let Sparky eat this poison junk and he croaks, I'll get in big trouble. Now, open the damned door."

"Promise not to laugh?"

"I promise. Now come on. The slop gets any colder, it'll stiffen up."

Webber didn't laugh, he gasped. Caden's dark eyes sat like coal lumps in his pale, naked face. Not only was Alex bald, but he had also lost his eyebrows, lashes, even the faint line of whiskers that ran like a dirty smudge above his lip.

"My god, Caden. What the hell happened?"

"You can see. First you passed out on the court, then this. It's got to be that old witch who's always hanging around. She does voodoo you know."

"I heard. Could she have gotten something of yours, Caden? Some kind of string?" Webber asked.

Frowning, Caden resembled a bowling ball in pain. "The string is missing from the hood of my sweatshirt, why?"

"I heard she needs strings to do her spells. You have to lock up anything that has a string in it: tennis racquets, yo-yos, clothing, shoes, even dental floss. I'm pretty sure that's how she got to me. Duchamps must have fished my used dental floss out of the bathroom trashcan and given it to her."

"I heard something about strings, but I didn't pay attention. Honestly, it never occurred to me that all that voodoo talk could be true." Poor bald Alex stroked his gleaming skull. "What am I going to do, Bobby? You think it'll grow back?"

Webber forced a smile. "Sure. It's bound to."

"What if it doesn't?"

"Don't think like that, Alex. You just go ahead and lock up those strings and everything will be fine."

The next day, Webber drew a bye on the practice ladder. Grateful for the break, he settled in the stands to watch Tommy Madison play Roy Duchamps. Madison was a wiry, high-strung kid with a serious consistency problem, but when he managed to rein in his nerves, he could be a fierce competitor.

Strangely, Tommy seemed in cool command this afternoon. Talk about poor bald Alex had run like wildfire through the locker room, spreading a pox of jitters that infected the entire Beaumont tennis team. Everyone was wary of Duchamps and terrified of the voodoo lady, wondering who might next incur her vengeful wrath, imagining what horrific form her boundless malevolence might take. Word had also spread about Maman Mechant needing strings to work her spells. All the boys had locked away anything they thought she might use against them.

Still, Tommy Madison's game was strong and clean. He matched Duchamps stroke for stroke, serve for serve, and point for point. The lead bounced from court to court in the tightest set Webber could remember. His gaze kept darting down the row toward the voodoo lady. Her expression never changed, but each time Madison pulled ahead of Roy, the needles clicked more sharply in her cruel, determined hands.

Webber couldn't believe Madison's nerve. What could he be thinking? Crazy kid had to be suicidal.

In the end the match was tied and Hardeman called for sudden death overtime. Webber went woozy with sympathetic fear as Madison took the first point. From the corner of his eye, he spotted Maman Mechant hunched lower over the tote bag, pulling up a ragged white strand.

He wanted to warn Madison, but the words caught like a bone in Webber's throat. Tommy was asking for it, arranging his own funeral, and Webber would be nuts to risk his own neck by getting involved. He bit his tongue as Duchamps served the next point, driving home a stunning ace.

Tommy blew his first serve, and Webber dared to hope that

the kid had come to his senses. But he burned in a risky full-out second serve that left Duchamps swinging at the breeze.

Roy countered with another ace, sending Madison back to the line. As Tommy prepared to serve again, Webber spotted another white thread snaking up onto Maman Mechant's needle.

Sweating now, Webber pulled his eyes away as Tommy hit the ball. Swinging through, he lost his balance. His ankle twisted, and he came down hard, howling. Hardeman checked the injury, frowning, and helped Tommy hobble off the court.

"What's the deal, Coach? We call a forfeit?" asked Duchamps.

"No such thing in my vocabulary," Hardeman said. "Let's see which of you lucky ducks gets to finish out this match. Round and round she goes, and where she stops nobody knows."

Webber's blood froze as Hardeman's trailing finger pointed his way.

"You're it, Webber. Get your butt out here and finish up."

Webber heard clicking needles, and he felt Maman Mechant's smoldering gaze. "I can't, Coach," he stammered. "Please. I'm—I'm not up to it."

"Get up to it. Now! No excuses. And don't let me catch you playing less than all-out."

"This ain't fair at all, Coach," whined Duchamps. "I'm supposed to play Tommy Madison, not him."

"You play who I tell you to play, Duchamps. I say he's Tommy Madison until this match is done. Now, get to it."

Approaching the court, Webber set his mind. All he had to do was lose two points. Two lousy points, and Duchamps would win. He could do this.

Ready, steady.

He made a good show of going for Duchamps's first serve. Carefully, he swung through on the return so the ball hit the net with convincing determination.

His own first serve nicked the tape, triggering a let call. The next went wide.

"Serve the damned ball, Webber," Hardeman demanded. "Don't you dare let me see another cream puff like that."

The coach's eyes were on him, and so were Maman Mechant's. Webber approached the baseline like a condemned man. He looked across the court at Roy Duchamps, willing him to make a brilliant return.

He tossed the ball and brought his racquet down and watched the serve shoot toward the service box. Duchamps raced for it and caught the shot inches from the ground. He brought his racquet up and the ball looped in a teasing arc toward the net. Turning away, Webber exhaled like a blown tire in relief.

"Point to you, Webber," Hardeman said.

Heartsick, he saw that Roy's return had dribbled down the net on his own side of the court. Worse, Duchamps's first serve went wild and out of bounds. Roy pulled back too far on his second try, and the ball failed to reach Webber's court.

"That's a match," called the coach. "Congratulations, Webber. You have helped Madison uncrown the king. Too bad, Duchamps. This puts Tommy Madison at top seed and makes you number two. Guess you'll have to try harder."

"No fair!" cried Duchamps. "You can't do that, Coach. He took me for a couple of points, not the match."

"Cry on your own time, number two. Right now, you'd do better to work on that serve."

Webber stood rooted in terror, expecting some dread malady to strike. But nothing happened. Then it occurred to him that Maman Mechant had no way to work a spell against him. He had been too careful to lock up all his strings.

Giddy, he left the court and traded high fives with several teammates. Fassberg, the genius, was right. All he had to do was make sure she had no strings.

Webber made it nearly to the dorm before Earl Emerson came running up behind. "Hold up, Bobby. You left your bag."

Emerson was flame-cheeked, huffing hard. He held Webber's gym bag in his wormy, scarred hand. The zipper gaped open.

"Thanks for bringing this, Earl, but you didn't need to snoop in my stuff."

"I did no such thing. It was open like that when I found it."

"That can't be. I know I left it shut." Webber seized the bag and pawed through it wildly, searching for trouble. No strings had been taken from his spare racquet, and the string in his gym shorts was intact. He checked his extra socks and tennis shirt, but he did not spot any telltale pulls in the fabric where Duchamps or his voodoo lady might have stolen a thread.

"What's up, Bobby? Something wrong?" Emerson asked.

"I don't think so." He was at the bottom of the bag now. All that remained was his toiletry kit, which had also been left unzipped. Fortunately, it did not include any dental floss. But with a sick, sinking feeling, Webber remembered that it did contain his hairbrush. He pulled out the brush by its wooden handle and erupted in a hot rash of fear.

The brush had been picked clean. The dense mass of hair in the bristles was gone. Maman Mechant had enough strands to destroy every organ in his body.

"Did you see her, Earl? The voodoo lady? Was she still at the courts when you picked up the bag?"

"Matter of fact, she was. I heard her talking to Roy, telling him not to worry, that Maman was going to see to everything. Make things right again." Emerson shuddered. "Gave me the creeps, Bobby. I got to tell you."

Webber's head started to throb, and his vision went cloudy. On lead feet, he went to his room, unlocked his closet door, and packed his things.

Hearing the anguish in his voice, his parents asked few questions.

"All that matters is that you be happy, Bobby," said his dad. "I'll call the travel agent and arrange to have a ticket for you on the next plane out."

"But I feel so bad about you losing the tuition money."

"Forget about it, honey," his mom said. "We'll be delighted to have you home again. You just calm down and travel safely. Remember, things happen for the best."

Fassberg offered a lift to the airport in his BMW. "Sorry to see you go, Webber. You were one of the few kids I could have an actual conversation with in this godforsaken place."

Webber hauled his overstuffed duffel bags from the trunk. "Thanks for the ride. And thanks for the advice, Darwin. You saved my hide."

"Here's another piece of free advice for the road. Keep an eye on the semiconductor sector. There's going to be a giant pop at the beginning of the next quarter."

"Thanks, Fassberg. I'll tell my dad. Maybe he can make back some of the money he's forfeiting on my tuition."

"If he plays it right, he can make all of it back. Tell him I said to buy big and take the profits early."

"I will. Thanks." Webber slipped inside the cool terminal. Despite his misgivings, he was glad to be headed home. Maybe his mother was right, and everything did happen for the best. Maybe there was a good side to bad things like Maman Mechant's spells.

•   •   •

Fassberg watched until Webber disappeared out of sight toward the departure gates. Satisfied, he drove back to the dorm, calling ahead on his cell phone to arrange a meeting.

He found the others awaiting him outside the border checkpoint to Darwinia. Fassberg strode in first and settled comfortably on his throne before admitting each boy in turn and extracting the required fees. Lovingly, he regarded the growing pile of currency on his coffee table.

"Fine work, team. Bobby Webber is in the air by now, winging back toward JFK. Mission accomplished," Fassberg said.

"Sure do hope that's the last one we got to handle," drawled Earl Emerson. "This routine is getting a mite old."

"I suspect Webber is the last, unless the coach insists on bringing someone in midyear," Fassberg said.

"If he does, we'll take care of him like always," said Tommy Madison.

"Fine. But this time someone else gets to shave his head and all. Plucking those lashes hurts like hell," said Alex Caden.

"Wearing these fake scars is no picnic either," Emerson declared. He winced as he tugged at the rubbery mass glued between his thumb and index finger.

Fassberg raised his hands for silence. "Gentlemen, please. Keep in mind that all these little sacrifices will pay off major dividends when Roy Duchamps becomes the hottest name in tennis. Think six-figure purses. Think seven-figure product endorsements. Think a franchised string of Roy Duchamps tennis academies nationwide. Make that worldwide. Sky's the limit."

"Sounds real good to me," said Duchamps.

"It's good for all of us. Members of the Fassberg Sports Management team representing the Duchamps tennis franchise will each be in for one percent of net profits. We're talking big numbers, gentlemen. Huge."

"How big, Darwin?" Duchamps asked. "You never say exactly."

Fassberg chuckled. "That's because there is no way to compute the exact sum in advance. We can project going out the length of your expected career and beyond, but there are so many unknown factors. For instance, if that old lady stops hanging around at courtside all the time, we'll have to hire an actor to take the role."

"About how big, then?" Duchamps persisted.

Fassberg's weasel eyes narrowed. "Big enough. Of course anyone who's not satisfied can bow out any time. No one is irreplaceable, Roy, including you. I've got most of the school begging for a piece of the action."

There was a rumble of general assent, but then Roy Duchamps got to his feet.

"This is my hard work you're talking about, Fassberg. My sweat, my name, my future. I want to know what I end up with. I want to know what piece of the action you fix to take."

Fassberg snickered. "Don't you worry your pointy head about it, Roy. You just keep on swatting that little ball over the net and leave the rest to me."

"Hell with that, Darwin. I ain't some dumb cracker."

"Is that so?" Fassberg unlocked the large metal strongbox

beside his chair. He extracted stacks of neatly tied stock certificates and ten-dollar bills. Underneath was the ironclad agreement Duchamps had signed on his eighteenth birthday. "Here's your John Hancock, Duchamps. By signing this, you agreed to pay twenty percent of future gross earnings plus expenses to Fassberg Sports Management, in other words—me."

Fassberg chuckled. "*Expenses.* Such an interesting term. So difficult to define precisely. So in answer to your question, you end up with exactly as much as I decide you get. My advice is to begin sucking up to me and to continue to do so, early and often."

"You said that was a standard management agreement I was signing."

Fassberg wagged his finger. "I said it was *my* standard agreement. Anyhow, if you weren't a dumb cracker, you'd know better than to sign anything you haven't read. That's the first law of business. Survival 101. Too bad."

"Fassberg's right, Roy," Earl Emerson said eagerly. "Tough luck."

"I agree," said Caden, and the others quickly massed on Fassberg's side.

"Good show, gentlemen. I say this calls for celebration," Fassberg declared. He went to the kitchenette and extracted a half-gallon jug of Pagan Pink Ripple from the fridge. Darwin would not touch the rotgut himself, but these Dixie dopes would swallow almost anything.

While the others clamored around, joking and drinking, sucking up to Fassberg, Roy Duchamps hung back near Darwin's leather chair. When nobody was looking, he reached down, untied a packet of bills, and pocketed the string.

Later that night, he passed the string to his longtime friend and mentor, Maman Mechant. After all she had done for him over the years, he hated to be asking for yet another favor. But she listened with a knowing smile and patted his hand before she tucked the string into her tote bag.

"Maman will see to that bad, greedy boy, my son. Don't you fret yourself one snip."

"You're so good to me."

"Good as you deserve, sweet baby. And you deserve the very best. Come here to Maman."

Duchamps yielded to her warm, engulfing hug. The night was rich with jasmine and the soothing beat of cicadas. He shut his eyes and let his anger drift away. No snake-tongued, wrong-headed northern boy was going to tie him up. His career was in the very best of hands.

A KILLER OVERHEAD

ROBERT LEUCI

The reason I said sure, whatever you want, to Lester—he'd always taken good care of me, looked out for me, even when I cracked up, started doing coke, got weird and crazed, blew all my cash, ended up sharing a crash pad with a couple of lesbian cowgirls from the rodeo. Lester pulled me out of all that and gave me work. I mean, when you hit the pit, somebody reaches down and pulls you out, gives you that new lease, you owe him, owe him big-time. So when Lester tells me, "I think my only child, Laura, is being abused, humiliated, by this character she worships." He says, "I hear that this tennis-playing half-a-hump gets a sadistic thrill out of degrading my little girl." Lester tells me, he's lost weight, can't sleep, the joy has left his life. "I'm asking a favor," he says, "a little help. Go check this bum out. See what's happening, then do what you have to do."

You see, I believe in the philosophy of looking out for your friends. You know, "Like a bridge over troubled waters, I will ease your mind." I mean, you cannot pick your family, we all know that. It's your friends that you choose. Anybody with a half a brain knows that. So, I'm thinking, what's there to think about. You owe this man your life.

See, for thirty years I'm a half-assed connected guy out of South Brooklyn. I do a little bit of this and a little bit of that. I'm not saying that this is necessarily a good life, just that it was my life. Ey, we do what we do. Anyway, time goes by and the next thing you know, you're a highly regarded guy with all that baggage. It's no longer a thing you do, it's who you are. You get a tremendous rep and you play that, work at it. Give the people around you a little Robert DeNiro action and before you know it, they all want to hand you a bit of work, everybody's your pal. It's not very tough, it's a matter of style. Don't believe me? go rent *Godfather Two* and *Goodfellas*, you'll see what I mean.

I had a good year, made two or three major scores and packed it in. I'd been throwing rocks for years, enough already. I'm hanging out and enjoying myself, some Atlantic City, some Vegas, Saratoga in August, Florida in the winter. I'd earned it, I was happy. Every once in a while I'd get bored, then I'd run into some of the fellas, they'd moan and groan about the new breed, the young ones, the fresh ones out in the street. I'm thinking, I'm glad I'm out of it, glad I'm done. Then, ba-bing, Lester calls and I'm off to Newport, Rhode Island.

Talk about being out of my element; I'm sitting on a folding chair, on the grass, at the home to the legends of tennis, the International Tennis Hall of Fame.

A cozy stadium, I mean, you're literally yards from the players. They call it the Tennis Casino, I'm checking the joint out, thinking casino, looking for a crap game, maybe a little blackjack. Nothing happening, is how I would describe this place. It's strange: lots of old-timers in wide straw hats, a few good-looking broads that run the gamut from old as baseball to young as yesterday. I'm sitting next to some gap-toothed New England patriarch who's wearing a cream-colored suit, red bow tie and a pair of white tennis shoes. He's eating a tomato and lettuce on white bread sandwich, watching the tennis match, his mouth sagging in delight. I'm in my blue on blue Adidas sporting outfit. So you understand, I have four or five Armanis, but I wear this outfit to sporting events and see no reason to make an exception for Newport. Being by nature and profession a tight-lipped person, me and mister bow tie have no conversation.

Playing right out in front of me is Lester's future son-in-law, Rudi Bass. A tall guy, nice build, long hair, looks about twenty-nine, thirty. He's good. I'm no expert, but the guy's winning, easy. Any time his opponent makes a point, Rudi groans and smashes his racquet off the grass. I'm watching the kid play, and man, this guy can go in the air like a soul brother and he crushes these killer overheads.

Coming up, I had handball, stickball, slapball, stoopball, no tennis. You kidding, in my neighborhood you walk around with a tennis racquet, people figure it's a weapon and stay away from you.

So, I got my head down like I'm reading the program but I'm really checking Laura out through a pair of sunglasses. She's sitting a row in front of me, wearing a kind of sundress, a blue one, expensive, a big hat and sandals. An expression on her face like the Madonna on Valium, adjusting and readjusting her hat.

Suddenly, it was over and the crowd's applauding.

Rudi comes off the grass court, strutting his stuff like he'd just copped the middleweight crown. He waves to the crowd, strips off his shirt, then drops heavily into his chair while his trainer quickly goes to work massaging his legs, his thighs. The trainer, a young and strong-looking guy, worked quickly, never said a word, and he had this funny look on his face, like he wasn't very happy. Rudi took a plastic bottle of water and drained it, then crushed the bottle in his right hand. Right away I pick up on the fact that this is a strong kid. He grabs another bottle and drinks that, too; I figured he'd been out on the court a good two hours, he looked exhausted and sore. He's maybe ten feet from me and I could hear him complain that Alex, his Spanish opponent, lived on the baseline and would not challenge him at the net. He says the little sneak hit moon balls and looping, bullshit women's shots trying to keep him out there, running him sideline to sideline, causing him to cramp and nearly stole the match from him. Not only that, he said, a group of "Spanish creeps" kept shouting "Olé!" whenever he lost a point and I can hear him bitch to his trainer about the grass here, how it can't compare to Wimbledon, and that Alex loved the clay, and couldn't serve and volley to save his ass.

People are up and moving around, Laura is standing, arms folded across her chest, I move in behind her. "Atta boy, Rudi," I say, "atta boy." I tap her shoulder. "Geeze, this guy is good, you wouldn't know what his ranking is?"

"He's number thirteen in the world," she says, "he's on the rise." She was smiling, a sweet sort of smile.

"He could beat the top guys," I say, a little too much like a sports announcer. "He's probably a spoiled brat, these tennis stars, a self-centered bunch."

"Not all of them," she says, ruffled.

"I mean, all these athletes nowadays. What I mean is, they have it made, even the average ones getting treated like superstars."

"Do you have any idea how much training it takes, how much work and commitment, how tough it is?"

"Got no idea," I say. "I mean, they gave some baseball player, a shortstop, a hundred and twenty million dollars. What's more to say, yeah, he's good, but a hundred and twenty million, nobody's that good."

Her tone softens a little. "When it comes to professional sports, nothing makes much sense anymore," she says.

"See that guy out there," I say. "Don't think, look; he comes out here and plays a game, they pay him a box full of money, he plays a game for a living. And, I think, you know, teachers, firefighters, even cops. I mean, it don't make any sense. Look at those two sisters, black girls, they lift weights, got muscles way bigger than mine, they're an enterprise, a corporation molded by their father, everything is wacky." I say, "Tell me something, ten rounds, twelve-ounce gloves, Venus Williams and John McEnroe, who's left standing?"

She laughed at that.

I had this peculiar feeling that Laura was looking at me as if she knew me. "Where are you from?" she asked.

"The city."

"Your face is so familiar. What city?"

"New York, Brooklyn, New York. Bath Beach."

"I was born and raised on Ocean Parkway," a real big smile. "It really is a small world."

"Sure is."

"Do you know the Town and Country Club on Flatbush Avenue?"

"Famous place, of course I know it."

"My father owns it. You know," she says, "you remind me of my father, you look like him. He hates tennis. As a matter of fact, the only athlete he ever liked was Rocky Marciano." When she smiled there was this row of strong, white teeth, a good wide smile.

On the one hand she wasn't beautiful, on the other hand she had what I'd call, a look. A thin face, round black eyes and one of those Sophia Loren noses, like something off a Roman coin. When she laughed she'd cover her mouth with her hand like she was embarrassed. This was a sweet woman, and I know all about women, I'd had my share of relationships, ten meaningful ones. I could tell, the way she looked at me when she laughed, I'm talking about sweet and vulnerable.

She turned her head and scanned the stadium, then suddenly looked at me with those black eyes. "Would you like to meet Rudi Bass?"

"Sure, do you know him?"

She touched my arm and whispered, "He's my fiancé."

"He's a rising star," I say. "I'd certainly like to meet a rising star." That was true.

Rudi walked over and told her to quit bullshitting and hurry up, he wanted to get going. He said bullshitting and I thought, I don't like you. He moved his head from side to side, a little exercise, and pretended to study the stadium, looking around like he was going to paint the joint. "Rudi," she said, "come meet this nice man, he's from Brooklyn, my old neighborhood."

Rudi turned his head sharply and whispered something to her; Laura's face went red. Oh, yeah, perfect, I thought, just perfect. He looked at me, I mean, he really looked at me, it wasn't a nice, friendly look. "Pleased to meet you," Rudi said, and leaning past Laura he shook my hand. "Laura," he said, "whadaya say?"

Lester had clued me in, telling me the tennis player didn't go for spit, wouldn't spend a dime, and he loved seafood. When I asked him, how is that going to help me? he said, "One never knows. But better to have too much information than less."

He was right, Lester is a very smart man.

"I'm ready," Laura told Rudi, "all set to go."

"You're terrific," I say. "Rudi, you're some tennis player."

He exhaled noisily, then turned away. I'm thinking, good, good, that's good.

I told them I knew of a place, a restaurant where we could have a wonderful dinner. I would like them to be my guests. It wasn't fancy and wasn't anything really special but that it had great seafood. That guy, the Piano Man, Billy Joel, he eats there. And let me tell ya, Billy Joel knows seafood.

Laura held my hand and said that was very kind of me. Then she told me that Rudi usually slept for about three or four hours after a match.

Rudi only eats fish and vegetables. He says he thinks Agassi is a vegetarian, an entertainer who has captured the imagination of the public, he says Agassi is no mystery. He asks if the seafood around here is really fresh?

I say that this is the Ocean State, nothing around here but the sea, and in the sea are fish.

"For whatever it's worth, you got my word, you'll never have fresher fish then you'll get right here."

Already I'm annoyed with Rudi's mealy-mouthed bullshit. I knew I had a grabber here, a tightwad. One of those short-armed guys that never picks up a check. The kinda guy that would steal a stove and go back for the smoke.

"How about it," I said, "let me take you two to dinner. I'll pick you up at seven." I grabbed his hand while he was still trying to decide.

"Okay," he said. "Sure, why not." Then he asked if I thought the mob killed Marilyn Monroe as a favor for Jack Kennedy. I told him fantasy always had a lot more jazz than truth.

Rudi and I drank Bacardi Superior and tonic and ate a Portuguese dish, Lestert cod and potatoes. Laura drank champagne and ate clams steamed in white wine. He told me he was born in Costa Rica, but his family were Volga Poles and he'd come here at an early age. His parents were doctors, emigrated from Europe in the fifties. He was pleased that I liked tennis, he hated New York but loved Florida (yeah). He went to school at the University of Miami on a soccer and tennis scholarship. He ran five miles a day, loved scuba diving and he could play the guitar like a pro (yawn). And it was like I figured, Laura barely spoke a word, she looked like a woman that was waiting to be rescued, like a woman that couldn't really hang with the guys. When Rudi left the table I asked Laura if she was happy, nobody's happy, she said, they may think so, but they're not. I told her that Rudi talks about himself a whole lot. "He's a professional athlete. He takes himself very seriously, superstars aren't known for being selfless. It's me, me, me. Plus he is an only child, so what do you expect?"

I pay the check, with cash of course, and leave a heavy tip. This guy Rudi looks impressed, and I figure, that he figures, that we hit it off. Things were going so well, in fact, he invites me to sit in the friends box for the finals. On the way back to their hotel he tells me he is the kind of player the ATP is looking for, a player with charisma. I tell him he has an unbelievable serve. His secret, he says, is that before he serves, he bounces the ball three times. And he has this ritual before each match, he runs a mile while listening to Beatles songs. He tells me that Pete Sampras was a great champion, but that he could beat him.

The thing you should know about me is that I was a pretty good athlete. I played a great game of handball. Or rather, I used to before the knee went, and then the elbow and a touch of the gout ruined my court speed. I finally had to give the game up for good. When I played, I played hard, like Rudi, none of that drop shot, get everything back jazz, hit the ball with all you got, go for the shot, hit winners, screw keeping the ball in, go for it, a big serve and come in, go for the kill. I don't know that much about tennis, but even I know Pete Sampras would kick Rudi's ass.

In the finals Rudi played a newcomer from California, a black guy named Bobby Paul. Rudi crushed him, one and one. When it was over, Bobby told Rudi he'd sprained his ankle in the first set. Rudi told him that life was unfair, but that's the way it was.

Rudi gave me a signed photograph, a tennis racquet and some balls, I gave him and Laura a matching pair of Mont Blanc pens. Standing on Belvue Avenue out in front of the Tennis Casino, Rudi tells an interviewer his goal is to build up computer points with the power of his game, instead of major titles. Since he goes for it in every match, he can't be consistent, sometimes he'll lose the major event, but when he does, he goes down swinging. I drive them to the airport, we promise to stay in touch. Laura takes my hand and holds it, her face is pale, she bites her lip, she seems sad and looks much older than her twenty-five years. Rudi tells me she had a bad night, it was probably something she ate.

I drive back to New York, I don't fly, I hate airplanes.

Lester, my friend and Laura's father, asks how I'm doing, how's it going? I tell him, fine. How long, he asks, how long before you straighten this guy out? I tell him that he should know that these things take time. Lester is pissed at me and tells me that it's his daughter we're talking about. For twenty-five years he's treated Laura like a princess, and this character is treating her like a rag doll. Lester tells me I should hurry up, get it over with. I work at my own speed, I tell him.

I lie awake at night and think of Rudi and Laura, how much and how little I know about them. How frightened and sad Laura looked. I think of the Mont Blanc pens I gave them.

I have this fat bastard cousin, Arthur, who, when he was an FBI agent, sold me twenty-five Mont Blancs. The pens cost me five thousand big ones, each one has a transmitter built in. I told Arthur he was a shit for shaking down his own cousin. "That's not a very nice thing to say, and shows a real lack of gratitude," is what Arthur told me.

Laura and Rudi rent this Brooklyn Heights brownstone. The back of the building faces out onto the Promenade. A magnificent location, with great views of Manhattan and a ten-minute ride from my apartment in Red Hook.

I live above a Korean grocery store on Court Street off Union. The grocery store is not Korean, just the people who own the store. Lester told me not to shop there. Lester hates Koreans and Chinese, too. He'd been in the Korean War, and he says it was the Chinese and the Koreans that taught him all he needed to know about man's inhumanity to man.

Lester lost two toes to frostbite, one from each foot, and now he plays hell trying to find a pair of loafers that fit correctly. I didn't tell Lester that I figured he hated the Koreans and the Chinese because he couldn't wear Bruno Maglis. Him being a major clotheshorse and shoe freak.

It's dark when I get to the Promenade, this Rudi has put the flow back in my step, I feel loose, right on my game. A perfect night, with a light, cool breeze coming in off the harbor, the sky lit with about a billion stars. I really luck out and find a bench directly behind Laura and Rudi's building. My heart's leaping with the pure pleasure of what it is that I do. The service I render. Then that ol' doubt creeps in, I have this unconscious thought, well, not unconscious enough. Lester could be dead wrong. A pair of Koreans walk by with earphones listening to Walkmans. I can almost make out the music and wonder if it's the Piano Man.

Look, look, I tell myself, Lester wants you to check this guy out, see if Rudi really is abusing his daughter, then you gotta do what you gotta do. Maybe, just maybe, the tennis player is all mouth. If that's what it is, just mouth, then you have a talk with Lester and a talk with the kid, pull Rudi's coat, tell him to cool his role.

These guys, these bigshots like Lester, they're always running off half-cocked. Their imagination making it worse than it is. Most times when you check it out, you say to yourself, it's not so bad as they thought. Your partner's not robbing you, and although it may seem that way, your wife's not putting her feet in the air for the insurance man. And, no, your mistress ain't an undercover cop. I worry that I'll make a mistake, do something that will give me nightmares. So I take my time, pay attention, something in me takes over. Listen, you're either good at what you do or you're not. You either take your time and do the right thing or you don't. You're either a professional or some lump off the street. Knowing is what makes the difference. Taking somebody out is a very personal thing. I wouldn't do work for some Colombian drug dealer, those guys blow holes in people because they don't like their ties. I'm one of a kind. You come to me, present your problem. I make the final decision. That's how I work. I make the decision if it's a go or no go. I watch the mark, I follow him, know his routine, try to speak to him, get in a conversation and try to get to know him. Give him a Mont Blanc if I can.

When I'm into my work, I'm there, my whole world comes down to that mark. I blank out everything else, and the mark becomes the essence of my life. It's like having sex, to do it right requires complete and total concentration. And, when I'm done, when it's over, I never talk about it like some people do, wanting to go over it, wanting to hear some applause. For me when it's over, it's done, it's history. Next.

I turned my back to the brownstone, looking across the river to Manhattan. I put on my own earphones and tuned my Walkman. There was the sound of cars from the Gowanus Expressway bouncing up under my feet. The Promenade was like the deck of a ship, couples strolling arm in arm. From my Walkman, the sound of Mozart. My first reaction was to take off my earphones, more confused than angry, I examined them, then put them back on. I played with the Walkman tuner, more Mozart. I could identify classical music like nobody's business. Eighteen months at Greenhaven Prison, my cellmate, a classical music nut. Mozart, Brahms, Tchaikovsky, Liszt, Beethoven's *Fur Elise*, my favorite. You name it, I heard it, over and over, my cellmate always talking his ass off about it. Talk, talk, talk, the little nut was doing a seven-and-a-half-to-fifteen-year bit for manslaughter. The guy was a music teacher, he took out his ol' lady for banging one of his students. Crazy little bastard used a tomahawk.

See, my Walkman's a receiver for the Mont Blanc transmitter. The FM stations cleared between 98.7 and 110, you tune right in there and pick up all the conversation within ten feet of those pens. I thought of Rudi and Laura sitting in their apartment, staring out across the harbor, listening to a Mozart sonata for violins. Nice. I breathe out and relax a bit, listening to the earphones.

I sat waiting.

"Eating again," said Rudi, "do you ever stop feeding your face?" Then: "For Chrissake, don't you care at all?"

"I haven't eaten since lunch," said Laura, in her shy voice. "I'm not you, I can't go without eating, I get a headache."

"It's not how often you eat, it's what you eat," Rudi saying in his needling voice. The background music died, I heard footsteps. The transmitter doing its job. Then I heard a crash, another exhalation. Rudi had thrown a dish into the sink. Then Laura again: "Why are you so angry? It was only a turkey sandwich."

Rudi, loud now, "You're a meat-eating pig. I swear, you disgust me."

I could see Laura in my mind's eye, see her getting up off a chair, hear her rise, hear her say, "What am I doing with you?" Some kind of movement I couldn't make out. "Cow," said Rudi. Then I heard a slap. "Bitch," a Rudi shout, then I heard him hit Laura, listened as she lost her wind in a long, sorry gasp. Heard her collapse onto a chair, a sofa, something. Heard her whimper. "I'm leaving," she moaned, "I'm going home."

"*Pleeze*," Rudi said. "You . . . are . . . not . . . going . . . anywhere. I'm going out. When I get back, you f'n a well better be sitting right there." Silence for a few seconds, then a door slammed.

I could see him zipping up that blue and white jacket with the French Open decals he wears. I see him running his hands through his hair, going down the stairs, moving neatly, quickly, like an athlete. I can see these things very precisely, very exactly. It's one of the gifts I have. I don't try to understand these talents; I do sometimes wonder about them. I could hear the traffic building on the expressway, humming like bees.

I spotted him walking along Willow Street, heading for Montague. There's a tennis club there. He had his bag slung over his shoulder, the kind of bag you and me pay big bucks for. For him, for Rudi, the rising star, it was a gift from Nike. Rudi didn't pay for anything, Rudi didn't go for spit.

I stopped the car when I saw him coming to the street corner, opened the window and called to him. He leaned into the window, "Well, look who's here," he said smiling.

I drive this black Mercedes ragtop, it has absolutely no room in the backseat. Point of fact: People that own this kind of car could care less about the backseat. I mean, all that money for this car, you'd have to have a brain the size of a pea to worry about a backseat.

Rudi looked at me. It wasn't that smartass look. It was a look of joy and genuine surprise. He shoved his bag into the backseat, telling me he had some great news. "I want to share it with someone. I guess I can share it with you."

He looked at me, looked into the backseat and laughed, revealing those perfect teeth. He said, "Wow, what did you pay for this car?" I told him. He said, "Wow, for all that money, you'd think you'd have a backseat."

I smiled. A trunk, yes, a trunk is important, the size of the trunk counts. At least for me it does, and this car has a huge trunk. In addition to its size and the various nuances of a top-of-the-line vehicle, it takes little expertise to line that trunk with plastic. I like the good thick kind, you know, industrial grade. See, a guy like me, I don't need fancy clothes, or expensive shoes, or jewelry, I don't go to a shrink or a periodontist, I have absolutely no angst. You give me a great car, and a chance to do a little gambling, watch some horses run, toss a little craps, get a little tail once in a while, and every so often straighten out a no-good punk, I'm one happy guy. I don't get nightmares or stomach pains. It never happens.

"Hey, man," he said, "you mind if I drive?" I handed him the keys. "Wow, thanks," he said.

"Have a party," I said, "enjoy yourself."

How that sweet thing Laura ever got involved with this snake is a mystery to me. During the two days we spent together, I could see that she had given up completely. For a good-looking guy, to hang around sports stars with the personalities of squid, to be mistreated, insulted and demoralized while on trips to Australia, Italy, France and England. See, I did a little research, I know about "the tour."

Well, Laura is not the world's first fool, and she certainly won't be the last. I spied those groupies in Newport, the way they gathered around Rudi like a bunch of hummingbirds, the way they gawked at his perfect tan and impeccable white teeth. I can understand what must have happened to the little lady, see how she got drawn in. Like a girl, she is a girl. Maybe he was a terrific lover, put the girl in a trance. Ey, I can't worry about such things. I promised Lester a favor, I owe him. Payback time.

We toss his bag in the back and go for a ride, off to have us a great seafood dinner in Sheepshead Bay. His big hands around the steering wheel. He drives the Mercedes down Atlantic Avenue, up onto the BQE, through South Brooklyn, past Ocean Parkway, Bay Ridge, Bensonhurst, and finally out toward Coney Island. We had the windows and the top down, I could smell the sea. And suddenly the Verrazano loomed off to the right, the bridge was like an illustration in a guidebook of New York. We passed ballparks and playing fields and public tennis courts without nets.

He lets go of the steering wheel and throws his arms in the air. "This car can drive itself," he says. His head-full of hair blowing in the breeze.

"You want to hear my great news?" he says.

"Why not?"

"I just signed a four-million-dollar deal with Nike." He put those big hands back around the steering wheel and said, "Four . . . fucking . . . million . . . dollars; I'm golden."

"Laura must be proud of you," I say, making a decision now, coming to that decision and telling myself, it's going to be a long night. I could feel a little anxiousness coming on, but I fought it off.

"Laura," he says, "yeah, Laura. Wow," he says, "this car can boogie, I'm going to get me one."

He pulls off at Emmons Avenue and makes for the shore, Lundy's restaurant, all aglow and waiting. No place to park, the place was jumping. He tooled down the main drag, past the restaurant, past a construction site, with these huge, blue Dempsey Dumpsters and a bright yellow bulldozer. I could see the ocean and day-trip fishing boats. I could see the lights of Manhattan Beach across the bay. The salty smell of the ocean hit me and I sneezed. I wiped it on my sleeve, saying, "There, over there, behind the Dumpster, park there."

He took his bag from the backseat. He got out of the car and walked around to the trunk. "Ya know," he said, "I think this is the best day of my life." Now, could I refute that, I mean, a four-million-dollar deal from Nike? I looked at him and he smiled, he looked good, I'm thinking a handsome guy, this guy. I'm thinking what guy doesn't look good on the best day of his life. I opened the trunk.

"Geeze," he said, "this trunk is huge." He did not look toward me, he dropped the bag in the trunk and pushed it to the rear, it slid well along the plastic. He was leaning over when, with one hand, I removed my pistol, pushed it up against his skin and popped him behind the right ear. I kept it simple, it wasn't a big hole, not too bad. He slumped and I grabbed him and shoved him into the trunk. No sound, he did not make a sound. I mean, I'm good. You have to take it slow and know what you're doing. You have to make that first shot do it all. And in this age of steel-jacketed bullets and quiet guns, it's very simple.

Anyhow, I closed the trunk and checked the street, not a soul around. I walked two blocks to Lundy's, put my name on the waiting list and made a call. I telephoned my other fat bastard cousin, Paulie. Paulie owns a junkyard out in Canarsie. Our family comes from there, out near Flatlands Avenue and Avenue L. As a matter of fact, our grandfather used to make his living fishing the oysterbeds out in Jamaica Bay. I went to Canarsie High School.

Oysters, I love oysters, I especially love chicken and oyster stifle. You make it in a casserole, chicken and cream and oysters, it takes a while to make, an hour, more or less. Well, good, I thought, I have time. And it was like I figured, it took two hours for Paulie and this Russian guy to do their thing. Two hours later, my car was back in its spot, all cleaned up and ready to go. That oyster stifle, it was magnificent.

The following day I get a call and show up at Lester's place, and there is Lester sitting in a booth, a Dewars and water in his hand, a cigar in his mouth. I barely slide into a seat opposite him when he says, "Are you completely insane?" Lester giving me this sardonic glare.

"What's the problem?" I said. "You seem a bit uneasy."

"Uneasy? Why should I be uneasy?"

He put down his cigar, took a drink and I could see that his breathing was quick, irritated, and barely under control. There was the slightest pause before he said, "You whacked the kid. This boy who just signed a four-million-dollar Nike deal."

"Excuse me?"

"You heard me."

"You told me to straighten him out. I did just that."

"I told you to check him out, then see what you gotta do."

I waited for him to go on.

"You know, my daughter, my Laura, she loved this guy."

"Getting abused, getting humiliated."

He took another drink. "She could handle him, she was learning how." He paused, looking for the right word. "High-strung," he said finally. "That Rudi Bass was high-strung."

"Yeah, I'm sure he was."

"Ey," he said, putting down his drink alongside his cell phone, "sometimes you've got to take a little to get a lot. You have to learn how."

"It depends on what you call learning," I said, moving around in my seat.

He ran his hand through his hair. "I wanna know how you, on your own, make a decision to go and do what you do."

"You don't know?"

He paused. "Do you?"

"Lester," I said, "do you know the story of the scorpion and the crow?"

"Whadaya talking about?"

"There's this scorpion, he wants to get across this pond. He needs to get to the other side. So, he asks this crow to give him a lift. Please, he says to the crow, fly me across, my family is on the other side. The crow tells him, you're a scorpion, you'll sting me, I'll die. The scorpion says, why would I do that? I need to get over the water. So the crow tells him, okay, get on my back, I'll fly you across. Halfway across the pond the scorpion stings the crow in the neck. You killed me, the crow says, what is wrong with you, you gave me your word. Ey, the scorpion says, what can I say, I can't help myself. I'm a scorpion."

He thought for a moment. "Yeah, I've heard that story before." He shrugged. "What are you telling me, you can't help yourself?"

"I take my time, Lester, check things out. When I make a decision, I stay with it. I thought you liked how I work," I said.

"I used to."

"So it's the money?"

"Four million is a lot of wood." He paused for a moment, looking around. "Laura was learning to handle him," he said again. "What does that tell you?"

I figured it was best not to tell him what I thought, so I said nothing.

"I'll tell you what it tells you, it tells you these two were going to work it out."

Right about then his cell phone rang. He sighed, then picked up the phone. He held the phone close to his ear and leaned forward on the table as if he were having trouble hearing. "Marion," he said, "what the fuck are you talking about? Do you know what you're talking about? I mean, how stupid are you? Do . . . you . . . *ever* . . . listen . . . to . . . me?"

My stomach was growling, you know, growling. My stomach talks to me, my stomach tells me a lot of things. All I need to know sometimes.

He put down the cellular.

"Ya know," he said, "I got nothing around me but lames and zips and zeros. This woman, this Marion, my wife, this stupid bitch that I married. This woman makes me crazy."

Sometimes I know things, I don't know I know yet. Lester was looking at me curiously.

"Pally," he said, "I have got to tell you, you're no scorpion, you're just stupid."

"I'm sorry that you feel that way."

I have always been interested in how these things come to me, these decisions I make.

"I'm thinking, I trusted you. I did, you know, I trusted you and you let me down. Now I got this feeling that I don't want to see you anymore." His voice had something new in it. A threat.

"Listen," I said, "this Rudi Bass was a bad actor. Real bad."

"I want you to go, I don't want to see you again." He sounded worried and that confused me.

I saw him looking at my hands, at the fountain pen I was holding in my hand. "What are you going to do," he said, "write me a note?"

"No," I said, "this was a gift to me, it's a valuable pen, I treasure it."

"Let me have it."

I nodded. Exactly what I thought he'd say. I scare myself sometimes. I swear to God, I scare myself.

I handed him the Mont Blanc, he put it in his pocket and took a drink, wiping his lips with the tips of his fingers. He had pretty hands, clean nails.

Needle Match

Peter Lovesey

Murder was done on Court Eleven on the third day of Wimbledon, 1981. Fortunately for the All England Club, it wasn't anything obvious like a strangling or a shooting, but the result was the same for the victim, except that he suffered longer. It took three days for him to die. I can tell you exactly how it happened, because I was one of the ball boys for the match.

When I was thirteen I was taught to be invisible. But before you decide this isn't your kind of story let me promise you it isn't about magic. There's nothing spooky about me. And there was nothing spooky about my instructor, Brigadier Romilly. He was flesh and blood all right, and so were the terrified kids who sat at his feet.

"You'll be invisible, every one of you, before I've finished with you," he said in his parade-ground voice, and we believed him, we third-years from Merton Comprehensive.

A purple scar like a saber cut stretched downward from the edge of the Brigadier's left eye, over his mouth to the point of his chin. He'd grown a bristly ginger mustache over part of it, but we could easily see where the two ends joined. Rumor had it that his face had been slashed by a Mau Mau warrior's machete in the Kenyan terrorist war of the fifties. We didn't know anything about the Mau Mau, except that the terrorist must have been crazy to tangle with the Brigadier—who grabbed him by the throat and strangled him.

"Don't ever get the idea that you're doing this to be seen. You'll be there, on court with Mr. McEnroe and Mr. Borg—if I think you're good enough—and no one will notice you, no one. When the game is in play you'll be as still as the net post, and as uninteresting. For Rule Two of the Laws of tennis states that the court has certain permanent fixtures like the net and the net posts and the umpire's chair. And the list of permanent fixtures includes you, the ball boys, in your respective places. So you can tell your mothers and fathers and your favorite aunties not to bother to watch. If you're doing your job they won't even notice you."

To think we'd volunteered for this. By a happy accident of geography ours was one of the schools chosen to provide the ball boys and ball girls for the Championships. "It's a huge honor," our headmaster had told us. "You do it for the prestige of the school. You're on television. You meet the stars, hand them their towels, supply them with the balls, pour their drinks. You can be proud."

The Brigadier disabused us of all that. "If any of you are looking for glory, leave at once. Go back to your stuffy classrooms. I don't want your sort in my squad. The people I want are functionaries, not glory seekers. Do you understand? You will do your job, brilliantly, the way I show you. It's all about timing, self-control and, above all, being invisible."

•   •   •

The victim was poisoned. Once the poison was in his system there was no antidote. Death was inevitable, and lingering.

 •   •   •

So in the next three months we learned to be invisible. And it was damned hard work, I can tell you. I had no idea what it would lead to. You're thinking we murdered the Brigadier? No, he's a survivor. So far as I know, he's still alive and terrifying the staff in a retirement home.

I'm going to tell it as it happened, and we start on the November afternoon in 1980 when my best friend Eddie Pringle and I were on an hour's detention for writing something obscene on Blind Pugh's blackboard. Mr. Pugh, poor soul, was our chemistry master. He wasn't really blind, but his sight wasn't the best. He wore thick glasses with prism lenses, and we little monsters took full advantage. Sometimes Nemesis arrived, in the shape of our headmaster, Mr. Neames, breezing into the lab, supposedly for a word with Blind Pugh, but in reality to catch us red-handed playing poker behind bits of apparatus or rolling mercury along the bench tops. Those who escaped with a detention were the lucky ones.

"I've had enough of this crap," Eddie told me in the detention room. "I'm up for a job as ball boy."

"What do you mean—Wimbledon?" I said. "That's not till next June."

"They train you. It's every afternoon off school for six months—and legal. No more detentions. All you do is trot around the court picking up balls and chucking them to the players and you get to meet McEnroe and Connors and all those guys. Want to join me?"

It seemed the ideal escape plan, but of course we had to get permission from Nemesis to do it. Eddie and I turned ourselves into model pupils for the rest of term. No messing about. No detentions. Every homework task completed.

"In view of this improvement," Nemesis informed us, "I have decided to let you go on the training course."

But when we met the Brigadier we found we'd tunneled out of one prison into another. He terrified us. The regime was pitiless, the orders unrelenting.

"First you must learn how to be a permanent fixture. Stand straight, chest out, shoulders back, thumbs linked behind your back. Now hold it for five minutes. If anyone moves, I put the stopwatch back to zero again."

Suddenly he threw a ball hard at Eddie and of course he ducked.

"Right," the Brigadier announced, "Pringle moved. The hand goes back to zero. You have to learn to be still, Pringle. Last year one of my boys was hit on the ear by a serve from Roscoe Tanner, over a hundred miles per hour, and he didn't flinch."

We had a full week learning to be permanent fixtures, first standing at the rear of the court and then crouching like petrified sprinters at the sideline, easy targets for the Brigadier to shy at. A couple of the kids dropped out. We all had bruises.

"This is worse than school," I told Eddie. "We've got no freedom at all."

"Right, he's a tyrant. Don't let him grind you down," Eddie said.

In the second and third weeks we practiced retrieving the balls, scampering back to the sidelines and rolling them along the ground to our colleagues or throwing them with one bounce to the Brigadier.

• • •

This was to be one of the great years of Wimbledon, with Borg, Connors and McEnroe at the peaks of their careers, challenging for the title. The rivalry would produce one match, a semifinal, that will be remembered for as long as tennis is played. And on an outside court, another, fiercer rivalry would be played out, with a fatal result. The players were not well known, but their backgrounds ensured a clash of ideologies. Jozsef Stanski, from Poland, was to meet Igor Voronin, a Soviet Russian, on Court Eleven, on the third day of the Championships.

Being an ignorant schoolboy at the time, I didn't appreciate how volatile it was, this match between two players from Eastern Europe. In the previous summer, 1980, the strike in the Gdansk shipyard, followed by widespread strikes throughout Poland, had forced the Communist government to allow independent trade unions. Solidarity—the trade union movement led by Lech Walesa—became a powerful, vocal organization getting massive international attention. The Polish tennis star, Jozsef Stanski, was an outspoken supporter of Solidarity who criticized the state regime whenever he was interviewed.

The luck of the draw, as they say, had matched Stanski with Voronin, a diehard Soviet Communist, almost certainly a KGB agent. Later, it was alleged that Voronin was a state assassin.

• • •

Before all this, the training of the ball boys went on, a totalitarian regime of its own, always efficient, performed to numbers and timed on the stopwatch. There was usually a slogan to sum up whichever phase of ball boy lore we were mastering.

"Show before you throw, Richards, show before you throw, lad."

No one dared to defy the Brigadier.

The early weeks were on indoor courts. In April, we got outside. We learned everything a ball boy could possibly need to know, how to hold three balls at once, collect a towel, offer a cold drink and dispose of the cup afterward, stand in front of a player between games without making eye contact. The training didn't miss a trick. At the end of the month we "stood" for a club tournament at Queen's. It went well, I thought, until the Brigadier debriefed us. Debriefed? He tore strips off us for over an hour. We'd learned nothing, he said. The Championships would be a disaster if we got within a mile of them. We were slow, we fumbled, stumbled and forgot to show before the throw. Worse, he saw a couple of us (Eddie and me, to be honest) exchange some words as we crouched either side of the net.

"If any ball boy under my direction so much as moves his lips ever again in the course of a match, I will come onto the court and seal his revolting mouth with packing tape."

We believed him.

And we persevered. Miraculously the months went by and June arrived, and with it the Championships.

The Brigadier addressed us on the eve of the first day's play and to my amazement, he didn't put the fear of God into me. By his standards, it was a vote of confidence. "You boys and girls have given me problems enough this year, but you're as ready as you ever will be, and I want you to know I have total confidence in you. When this great tournament is over and the best of you line up on Centre Court to be presented to Her Royal Highness before she meets the champion, my pulse will beat faster and my heart will swell with pride, as will each of yours. And one of you, of course, will get a special award as best ball boy—or girl. That's the Championship that counts, you know. Never mind Mr. Borg and Miss Navratilova. The real winner will be one of you. The decision will be mine, and you all start tomorrow as equals. In the second week I will draw up a short list. The pick of you, my elite squad, will stand in the finals. I will nominate the winner only when the tournament is over."

I suppose it had been the severity of the buildup; to me those words were as thrilling and inspiring as King Henry's before the Battle of Agincourt. I wanted to be on Centre Court on that final day I was fated to be best ball boy. I could see that all the others felt like me, and had the same gleam in their eyes.

I've never felt so nervous as I did at noon that first day, approaching the tall, creeper-covered walls of the All England Club, and passing inside and finding it was already busy with people on the terraces and promenades chatting loudly in accents that would have got you past any security guard in the world. Wimbledon twenty years ago was part of the social season, a blazer and tie occasion, entirely alien to a kid like me from a working-class family.

My first match was on an outside court, thanks be to the Brigadier. Men's singles, between a tall Californian and a wiry Frenchman. I marched on court with the other five ball boys and mysteriously my nerves ended the moment the umpire called "Play." We were so well-drilled that the training took over. My concentration was absolute. I knew precisely what I had to do. I was a small, invisible part of a well-oiled, perfectly tuned machine, the Rolls Royce of tennis tournaments. Six-three, 6–3, 6–3 to the Californian, and we lined up and marched off again.

I stood in two more matches that first day, and they were equally straightforward in spite of some racquet abuse by one unhappy player whose service wouldn't go in. A ball boy is above all that. At home, exhausted, I slept better than I had for a week.

Day Two was Ladies' Day, when most of the women's first-round matches were played. At the end of my second match I lined up for an ice cream and heard a familiar voice, "Got over-heated in that last one, Richards?"

I turned to face the Brigadier, expecting a rollicking. I wasn't sure if ball boys in uniform were allowed to consume ice cream.

But the scar twitched into a grin. "I watched you at work. You're doing a decent job, lad. Not invisible yet, but getting there. Keep it up and you might make Centre Court."

·   ·   ·

I can tell you exactly what happened in the Stanski-Voronin match because I was one of the ball boys and my buddy Eddie Pringle was another, and has recently reminded me of it. Neither player was seeded. Stanski had won a five-setter in the first round against a little-known Englishman, and Voronin had been lucky enough to get a bye.

Court Eleven is hardly one of the show courts, and these two weren't well-known players, but we still had plenty of swiveling heads following the action.

I'm sure some of the crowd understood that the players were at opposite extremes politically, but I doubt if anyone foresaw the terrible outcome of this clash. They may have noticed the coolness between the players, but that's one of the conventions of sport, particularly in a Grand Slam tournament. You shake hands at the end, but you psych yourself up to beat hell out of your rival first.

• • •

Back to the tennis. The first set went narrowly to Voronin, 7–5. I was so absorbed in my ball boy duties that the score almost passed me by. I retrieved the balls and passed them to the players when they needed them. Between games, I helped them to drinks and waited on them, just as we were programmed to do. I rather liked Stanski. His English wasn't up to much, but he made up for it with the occasional nod and even a hint of a smile.

Stanski won the next two sets, 6–4, 6–3.

Half the time I was at Voronin's end. Being strictly neutral, I treated him with the same courtesy I gave his opponent, but I can't say he was as appreciative. You can tell a lot about players from the way they grab the towel from you or discard a ball they don't fancy serving. The Russian was a hard man, with vicious thoughts in his head. He secured the next set in a tiebreak and took the match to a fifth. The crowd was growing. People from other courts had heard something special was happening. Several long, exciting rallies drew gasps and shrieks.

Voronin had extraordinary eyes like wet pebbles, the irises as black as the pupils. I was drilled to look at him each time I offered him a ball, and his expression never changed. Once or twice when Stanski had some luck with a ball that bounced on the net, Voronin eyeballed him. Terrifying.

The final set exceeded everyone's expectations. Voronin

broke Stanski's service in the first game with some amazing passing shots and then held his own in game two. In the third, Stanski served three double faults and missed a simple volley.

"Game to Voronin. Voronin leads by three games to love. Final set."

When I offered Stanski the water he poured it over his head and covered his face with the towel.

Voronin started game four with an ace. Stanski blocked the next serve and it nicked the cord and just dropped over. He was treated to another eyeballing for that piece of impertinence. Voronin walked slowly back to the line, turned, glared and fired a big serve that was called out. The second was softer and Stanski risked a blinder, a mighty forehand, and succeeded—the first winner he'd made in the set. Fifteen-thirty. Voronin nodded toward my friend Eddie for balls, scowled at one and chucked it aside. Eddie gave him another. He served long. Then foot-faulted. This time the line judge received the eyeballing. Fifteen-forty.

Stanski jigged on his toes. He would never have a better opportunity of breaking back.

The serve from Voronin was cautious. The spin deceived Stanski and the ball flew high. Voronin stood under, waiting to pick it out of the sun and kill it. He connected, but heroically Stanski got the racquet in place at the far end and almost fell into the crowd doing it. The return looked a sitter for the Russian and he steered it crosscourt with nonchalance. Somehow Stanski dashed to the right place again. The crowd roared its appreciation.

Voronin chipped the return with a dinky shot that barely cleared the net and brought Stanski sprinting from the back to launch himself into a dive. The ball had bounced and risen through another arc and was inches from the turf when Stanski's racquet slid under it. Miraculously he found enough lift to sneak it over at a near-impossible angle. Voronin netted. Game to Stanski.

Now there was an anxious moment. Stanski's dive had taken him sliding out of court and heavily into the net post, just a yard from where I was crouching in my set position. He was rubbing his right forearm, green from the skid across the grass, and everyone feared he'd broken a bone. After a delay of a few seconds the umpire asked if he needed medical attention. He shook his head.

Play resumed at three games to one, and it felt as if they'd played a full set already. The fascination of the game of tennis is that a single shot can turn a match. That diving winner of Stanski's was a prime example. He won the next game to love, serving brilliantly, though clearly anxious about his sore arm, which he massaged at every opportunity. Between games the umpire again asked if he needed assistance, but he shook his head.

Voronin was still a break up, and when play resumed after the change of ends he was first on court. He beckoned to me aggressively with his right hand, white with resin. I let him see he wouldn't intimidate me. I was a credit to the Brigadier, showing and throwing with the single bounce, straight to the player.

Stanski marched to the receiving end, twirling his racquet. Voronin hit the first serve too deep. The second spun in, shaved the line and was allowed. Fifteen-love. Stanski took the next two points with fine, looping returns. Then Voronin met a return of serve with a volley that failed to clear the net. Fifteen-forty. The mind-game was being won by Stanski. A feeble serve from the Russian allowed him to close the game. Three all.

The critical moment was past. Stanski's confidence was high. He wiped his forehead with his wristband, tossed the ball up and served an ace that Bjorn Borg himself would have been incapable of reaching. From that moment, Voronin was doomed. Stanski was nerveless, accurate, domineering. He took the game to love. He dropped only one point in winning the next two. It was over. The crowd was in ecstasy. Voronin walked to the side without shaking hands, slung his racquets into his bag and left the court without waiting for his opponent—which is always regarded as bad form at Wimbledon. Some of the crowd booed him.

Stanski seemed to be taking longer than usual in packing up. He lingered by the net post looking down, repeatedly dragging his foot across the worn patch of turf and raising dust. Then he bent and picked something up that to me looked like one of the needles my mother used on her sewing machine. After staring at it for some time he showed it to the umpire, who had descended from his chair. At the same time he pointed to a scratch on his forearm. The umpire nodded indulgently and I heard him promise to speak to the groundsman.

I learned next day that Stanski was ill and had withdrawn from the tournament. It was a disappointment to everyone, because he had seemed to be on a roll and might have put out one of the seeds in a later round.

Two days after, the world of tennis was shocked to learn that Jozsef Stanski had died. He'd been admitted to St. Thomas's complaining of weakness, vomiting and a high temperature. His pulse rate was abnormally high and his lymph glands were swollen. There was an area of hardening under the scratch on his right forearm. In the night, his pulse rose to almost two hundred a minute and his temperature fell sharply. He was taken into intensive care and treated for septicemia. Tests showed an exceptionally high count of white blood cells. Blood was appearing in his vomit and he was having difficulty in passing water, suggesting damage to the kidneys.

The next day an electrocardiogram indicated further critical problems, this time with the heart. Attempts were made to fit a pacemaker, but he died while under the anesthetic. It was announced that a postmortem would be held the following day.

I'm bound to admit that these medical details only came to my attention years later, through my interest in the case. At the time it happened, I was wholly taken up with my duties at Wimbledon, programmed by the Brigadier to let nothing distract me. We were soon into the second week and the crowds grew steadily, with most interest on the show courts.

Eddie and I were picked for the men's semifinals and I had my first experience of the Centre Court in the greatest match ever played at Wimbledon, between Bjorn Borg, the champion for the previous five years, and Jimmy Connors. Borg came back from two sets down, love–6 and 4–6, to win with a display of skill and guts that finally wore down the seemingly unstoppable Connors. I will go to my grave proud that I had a minor role in that epic.

I'm proud, also, that I was one of the ball boys in the final, though the match lacked passion and didn't quite live up to its promise. John McEnroe deserved his Championship, but we all felt Borg had fired his best shots in the semi.

Like Borg, I was forced to choke back some disappointment that afternoon. I'd secretly hoped to be named best ball boy, but a kid from another school was picked by the Brigadier. My pal Eddie (who wasn't on court for the final) put an arm around my shoulder when it was over. We told each other that the kid had to be a brown-nose and the Brigadier's nephew as well.

I may have heard something later on radio or television about the postmortem on poor Jozsef Stanski. They concluded he died from blood poisoning. Samples were sent for further analysis, but the lab couldn't trace the source. At the inquest, a pathologist mentioned the scratch on the arm and said some sharp point had dug quite deep into the flesh. The match umpire gave evidence and spoke of the needle Stanski had picked up. He described the small eye close to the point. Unfortunately the needle had not been seen since the day of the match. In summing up, the coroner said it would not be helpful to speculate about the needle. The match had been played in full view of a large crowd and there was no evidence of anyone attempting to cause Stanski's death.

Huge controversy surrounded the verdict. The international press made a lot of the incident, pointing out that as recently as 1978 a Bulgarian writer, Georgi Markov, a rebel against his Communist government, had been executed in a London street by a tiny poison pellet forced into his thigh, apparently by the tip of an umbrella. The poison used was ricin, a protein derived from the castor-oil seed, deadly and in those days almost undetectable in the human bloodstream. He took four days to die, protesting that he was the victim of political assassination. Nobody except his wife took him seriously until after he died. The presence of the poison was discovered only because the pellet was still embedded in a piece of Markov's flesh sent for analysis. If ricin could be injected in a public street using an umbrella, was it so fanciful to suggest Jozsef Stanski was targeted by the KGB and poisoned at Wimbledon two years later?

In Poland, the first months of 1981 had been extremely tense. A new prime minister, General Jaruzelski, had taken over and a permanent committee was set up to liaise with Solidarity. Moscow was incensed by this outbreak of liberalism and summoned Jaruzelski and his team to the Kremlin. The Politburo made its anger known. Repression followed. Many trade union activists were beaten up.

The papers noted that Stanski's opponent Voronin had quit Britain by an Aeroflot plane the same evening he had lost. He was unavailable for comment, in spite of strenuous efforts by reporters. The Soviet crackdown on Solidarity was mentioned. It was widely suspected that the KGB had been monitoring Stanski for over a year. He was believed to be acting as a conduit to the free world for Walesa and his organization. At the end of the year, martial law was imposed in Poland and the leaders of Solidarity were detained and union activity suspended.

Although nothing was announced officially, the press claimed Scotland Yard investigated the assassination theory and kept the file open.

Since the Cold War ended and the Soviet bloc disintegrated, it is hard to think oneself back into the oppression of those days, harder still to believe orders may have been given for one tennis player to execute another at the world's top tournament. In the years since, I kept an open mind about the incident, troubled to think murder may have happened so close to me. In my mind's eye I can still see Stanski rubbing his arm and reaching for the water I poured.

Then, last April, I had a phone call from Eddie Pringle. I hadn't seen him in almost twenty years. He was coming my way on a trip and wondered if we might meet for a drink.

To be truthful, I wasn't all that keen. I couldn't imagine we had much in common these days. Eddie seemed to sense my reluctance, because he went on to say, "I wouldn't take up your time if it wasn't important—well, important to me, if not to you. I'm not on the cadge, by the way. I'm asking no favors except for one half-hour of your time."

How could I refuse?

We arranged to meet in the bar of a local hotel. I told him I have a beard these days and what I would wear, just in case we didn't recognize each other.

I certainly wouldn't have known Eddie if he hadn't come up to me and spoken my name. He was gaunt, hairless and on two sticks.

"Sorry," he said. "Chemo. Didn't like to tell you on the phone in case I put you off."

"I'm the one who should be sorry," I said. "Is the treatment doing any good?"

"Not really. I'll be lucky to see the year out. But I'm allowed to drink in moderation. What's yours?"

We found a table. He asked what line of work I'd gone into and I told him I was a journalist.

"Sport?"

"No. Showbiz. I know why you asked," I said. "That stint we did as ball boys would have been a useful grounding. No one ever believes I was on court with McEnroe and Borg, so I rarely mention it."

"I made a big effort to forget," Eddie said. "The treatment we got from that Brigadier fellow was shameful."

"No worse than any military training."

"Yes, but we were young kids barely into our teens. At that age it amounted to brainwashing."

"That's a bit strong, Eddie."

"Think about it," he said. "He had us totally under his control. Destroyed any individuality we had. We thought about nothing else but chasing after tennis balls and handing them over in the approved style. It was the peak of everyone's ambition to be the best ball boy. You were as fixated as I was. Don't deny it."

"True. It became my main ambition."

"Obsession."

"Okay. Have it your way. Obsession." I smiled, wanting to lighten the mood a bit.

"You were the hotshot ball boy," he said. "You deserved to win."

"I doubt it. Anyway, I was too absorbed in it all to see how the other kids shaped up."

"Believe me, you were the best. I couldn't match you for speed or stillness. The need to be invisible he was always on about."

"I remember that."

"I believed I was as good as anyone, except you." Eddie took a long sip of beer and was silent for some time.

I waited. It was obvious some boyhood memory was troubling him.

He cleared his throat nervously. "Something has been on my mind all these years. It's a burden I can't take with me when I go. I don't have long, and I want to clear my conscience. You remember the match between the Russian and the Pole?"

"Voronin and, er . . . ?"

"Stanski—the one who died. It should never have happened. You're the one who should have died."

Staring at him, I played the last statement over in my head.

He said, "You've got to remember the mental state we were in, totally committed to being best boy. It was crazy, but nothing else in the world mattered. I could tell you were better than I was, and you told me yourself that the Brigadier spoke to you after one of your matches on Ladies' Day."

"Did I?" I said, amazed he still had such a clear recollection.

"He didn't say anything to me. It was obvious you were booked for the final. While you were on the squad, I stood no chance. It sounds like lunacy now, but I was so fired up I had to stop you."

"How?"

"With poison."

"Now come on, Eddie. You're not serious."

But his tone insisted he was. "If you remember, when we were in the first year, there was a sensational story in the papers about a man, a Bulgarian, who was murdered in London by a pellet the size of a pinhead that contained an almost unknown poison called ricin."

"Georgi Markov."

"Yes. We talked about it in chemistry with Blind Pugh. Remember?"

"Vaguely."

"He said a gram of the stuff was enough to kill thirty-six thousand people and it attacked the red blood cells. It was obtained from the seeds or beans of the castor-oil plant, *Ricinus communis*. They had to be ground up in a pestle and mortar because otherwise the hard seed coat prevented absorption. Just a few seeds would be enough. Old Pugh told us all this in the belief that castor-oil plants are tropical, but he was wrong. They've been grown in this country as border plants ever since Tudor times."

"You're saying you got hold of some?"

"From a local seedsman, and no health warning. I'm sorry if all this sounds callous. I felt driven at the time. I plotted how to do it, using this."

Eddie spread his palm and a small piece of metal lay across it. "I picked it out of a litter bin after Stanski threw it away. This is the sewing machine needle he found. My murder weapon."

I said with distaste, "You were responsible for that?"

"It came from my mother's machine. I ground the needle to a really fine point and made a gelatine capsule containing the poison and filled the eye of the needle with it."

"What were you going to do with it—stick it into my arm?"

"No. Remember how we were drilled to return to the same spot just behind the tramlines beside the umpire's chair? If you watch tennis, that place gets as worn as the serving area at the back of the court. The ball boys always return to the same spot. My plan was simple. Stick the needle into the turf with the sharp point upward and you would kneel on it and inject the ricin into your bloodstream. I'm telling you this because I want the truth to come out before I die. I meant to kill you and it went wrong. Stanski dived at a difficult ball and his arm went straight down on the needle."

"But he went on to win the match."

"The effects take days to kick in, but there's no antidote. Even if I'd confessed at the time, they couldn't have saved him. It was unforgivable. I was obsessed and it's preyed on my mind ever since."

"So all that stuff in the papers about Voronin being an assassin . . ."

"Was rubbish. It was me. If you want to go to the police,"

he said, "I don't mind confessing everything I've told you. I just want the truth to be known before I go. I'm told I have six months at most."

I was silent, reflecting on what I'd heard, the conflicting motives that had driven a young boy to kill and a dying man to confess twenty years later.

"Or you could wait until after I've gone. You say you're a journalist. You could write it up and tell it in your own way."

He left me to make up my own mind.

Eddie died in November.

And you are the first after me to get the full story.

The Rematch

Mike Lupica

He sat down near the court in the temporary bleachers they'd put up along the first fairway at Westchester Country Club, waiting to see for himself if the prick had changed now that he'd finally agreed to play on the has-been circuit.

How long had it been? Could it have been nine years already? It was, nine going on ten, since the semifinals of the Open that time, in what Ted Carlyle had always thought of as Louis Armstrong Stadium at the National Tennis Center. The prick—Tony Douglass—was making his last run at an Open title that year, what would have been his third, unseeded after taking most of the year off, even skipping Wimbledon for the first time since he was a teenager while he supposedly rehabbed a knee injury, though Ted had always suspected Douglass might have been rehabbing the booze again, though no one could ever prove it. But he got well by the time he got to New York in September, upsetting seeds in the first round and Round of 16, finally knocking out Andre Agassi in the quarters, a five-setter they still talked about as some kind of classic. And the idiot New York crowds, filled with people who'd always forgiven Douglass everything even though he was a Brit, came back to him bigger and louder than they ever had.

The tennis writers, of course, sensing a Big Story, sniffing around it like dogs in heat, immediately developed fucking amnesia about the way Douglass had always treated them, which meant the same way he had treated umpires and linesmen and lineswomen and ball boys and ball girls and, if the tabloids were right—please, God, let them be right—a topless dancer one time.

Somehow everybody forgot all the times when a call would go against Tony Douglass and he would pitch such a fit you thought someone had set the sonofabitch on fire.

All they cared about was that he might win again. Winning had always made everything all right with Douglass, from the beginning. Ted Carlyle had always wanted tennis to be different from the other sports, better, more dignified, more *old-school.* But when it came to keeping score, it was exactly the same as everything else; all that mattered was the bottom line, everybody acting as if winning could even cure cancer.

So this is what you always heard about Tony Douglass:

He just acts out this way because he wants to win so badly.

He's just a perfectionist, is all, the way any high-strung artist would be.

And besides, isn't the kid great box office, the way Nastase and Connors and McEnroe, the other bad boys, were before him?

Ted Carlyle, who'd followed tennis his whole life—for whom tennis was the one enduring love of his life—knew it was all bullshit. He saw that from that first year at the French when Douglass came out of nowhere to make the finals at the age of seventeen. And what Ted who came out of the fifties, who grew up watching Laver and Rosewall and Hoad and Gonzales, mostly saw, what he *knew*, was that this kid was just a nasty fuck who had been blessed by the gods with gifts of touch and spin and the best and hardest and most accurate serve Ted had ever seen.

They said he had a genius for tennis.

He did, only a fool would dispute that.

But Ted Carlyle, who'd seen them all come and go, knew Tony Douglass had an even greater genius for something else:

Meanness.

He'd hit one of his huge right-handed serves and the ball would be called out. Only Douglass would think it was in. And that was all it took for the day or night to suddenly go terribly, hatefully wrong, no matter where the match was being played, no matter what the stakes. No matter how many innocent bystanders, calling the lines, sitting in the umpire's chair, would be hurt before he was through. Suddenly there would be that madness in his eyes, in the whole way he carried himself, and he would be walking toward another chair umpire, pointing with his Wilson racket, saying, "Okay, now it's my turn."

That was his trademark line.

My turn. . . .

It turned out Douglass didn't make it past the semis of the Open that year, didn't get his fourth Open title. He finally ran into a nineteen-year-old phenom named Ken Lockhart, one for whom that particular U.S. Open would be a coming-out party, Lockhart going on from winning that

Open to rule men's tennis for the next ten years. Somehow he would do that as a complete gentleman, this left-hander from Armpit, Florida, who somehow evoked memories of Laver, as much for the way he carried himself as the way he played the game.

Lockhart beat Douglass 6–4, 6–4, 6–4 that Saturday night, the feature match of what they used to call Super Saturday at the Open, never came close to having his service broken. When Douglass would try one of his feathery drop shots, Lockhart would come flying in from the baseline and cover it on young legs. When Douglass tried to stay back and rally with the kid, Lockhart would move him from side to side, making Douglass work harder and harder on older legs, before finally putting him out of his misery and putting another point away.

Even Tony Douglass should have had the grace to accept what was happening; there was no disgrace in losing to a talented kid having this kind of day.

But he could not.

Three games into the third set, with the crowd begging Douglass to come back, to make a match of it, the chair umpire overruled a call by the service linesman, saying Douglass had double-faulted even though the linesman saw his second serve as good. The point gave the game to Ken Lockhart, put him up a service break at two games to one.

Of course Tony Douglass thought the guy in the chair was criminally insane.

It had happened on an odd game, which meant a change of side. Ken Lockhart went to towel off. Douglass stayed right where he was, two steps inside the back line, staring at the chair. Somehow it was as if a fuse had been lit in Louis

Armstrong Stadium. You could hear the ripple of tension, nervous excitement, run through the crowd the way it always did when the people thought Douglass was ready to blow. It had been the same way with Nastase, Ted knew, and Connors, and McEnroe, the whole line of them.

"You saw that ball out?" Douglass snapped.

"I did, Mr. Douglass."

"You thought the call was *egregiously* wrong, that's what you're telling me?"

He was quoting the rules, the umpire was only supposed to overrule in case of an egregious error.

"The ball was clearly out, Mr. Douglass."

The first people, high up in the stands, began to rhythmically clap.

Douglass stood there, glaring still, hands on hips. Finally he said, "Okay, asshole, my turn."

The umpire should have given him a warning right then, for audible profanity, but this was the Open, everyone watching had to know this might be Douglass's last great chance to win the Open. So the umpire gave him some room, hoping only the people close to the court could hear. Douglass wasn't nearly in range of the powerful chair microphone yet.

Even if the umpire knew he was going to be, because now here came Tony Douglass, marching toward the chair.

"The guy on the line said the ball was in," Douglass said, *"you fucking moron!"*

That was it, the whole stadium heard that one. Hell, the home plate umpire at Shea Stadium, across Roosevelt Avenue from where they were, probably heard.

"Warning, Mr. Douglass," the umpire said, having no choice now. "Verbal abuse."

Douglass made a motion with his racquet as if masturbating. An old standby.

"Abuse *this*."

Now they were off to the races.

"Point penalty, Mr. Douglass. Fifteen-love, Mr. Lockhart."

There was an explosion of boos from the crowd. Not for Tony Douglass. For the umpire, who had just given the first point of the next game to Ken Lockhart, doing exactly what the rules said he had to do.

Lockhart had taken his place at the other end, to the umpire's left, bouncing a ball, waiting to serve. Watching, mesmerized, like everyone else.

"Eat me," Douglass snarled, the words somehow sounding worse, as they always did, because of the good-boy Brit accent he'd never lost.

It was all by the book now.

"Game, Mr. Lockhart. He leads 3–1, third set."

The rules in those days were simple enough. Douglass had gone right past his warning, the beginning of the process, and now had two strikes against him. Strike three meant he was defaulted from the match. Semifinal match of the Open.

The ball was officially and irrevocably in Tony Douglass's court. He was the one who had to decide if this was the way he wanted to go out at the United States Open.

"I will not *allow* you to do this to me," Douglass screamed.

"The ball was out," the umpire said.

"*Liar!*" Douglass screamed.

"The rules are fairly straightforward, Mr. Douglass," the umpire said patiently, sitting there in the chair, standing his ground at the same time. "You should know that better than anyone. You are doing this to yourself."

Douglass was right underneath the chair now, staring up, his eyes as hot and bright as sparklers.

"I am Tony Douglass," he said.

The umpire, who'd taken as much as he was going to take, as much as anyone could have been expected to take, put his hand over his mike now and said, "You used to be."

"Fuck you," Douglass said.

"Game, set, match, Mr. Lockhart," the umpire said.

Which is what it should have been.

Which by any sense of justice and fair play is the way the match should have ended, right there. Except that now all holy hell broke loose at Louis Armstrong Stadium. People started throwing programs and seat cushions and soft drink cups. A tennis crowd suddenly acting like one of those hooligan soccer crowds. People running from the cheap seats, or what passed for cheap seats in tennis, down the aisles, trying to get closer to the court, to the action, maybe so they could throw things themselves.

Not at Tony Douglass.

In the direction of the chair.

As if this were somehow the *chair's* fault.

The tournament referee came running out. The whole world saw what happened next, even if no one except the umpire and the referee could hear, the referee apologizing profusely, saying the umpire had done nothing wrong, really did have no choice, but please understand, he, the referee, he was the one who had no choice now, that he was going to have to allow the match to continue, that he was going to have to ask the umpire to step down from the chair.

That he had to do it for the good of the Open.

As if the umpire were the bad guy.

Not the prick.

They cheered Tony Douglass when he went back out, got ready to take the rest of his ass-kicking from the kid. They booed the umpire, kept throwing things in his direction, the ones close to the court even spitting at him, Tony Douglass finally turning everybody lousy, until the umpire mercifully disappeared into the runway between the stadium court and the grandstand.

• • •

Now Tony Douglass was forty-two. He could have tried the new over-forty circuit a couple of years before, but he thought he was too big for that. The exact quote from Douglass, as Ted recalled, was, "I'm too rich and too old for this shit." He had already tried broadcasting for a while, working for TNT at Wimbledon, but had been too lazy off the air to be any good at it, much too mean on the air. There had also been the unfortunate incident his last year on the air, Douglass thinking his mike was dead when he said over a close-up of Princess Anne that she should be pulling the royal carriage instead of sitting in it.

He had produced a couple of movies with some Hollywood friends, gotten divorced again, even written an autobiography, called "What a F———ing Racket," which had spent a couple of months on *The New York Times* best-seller list. Now he had decided he wanted to play tennis again, mostly, Ted had heard from old friends in tennis, because the prick was bored. The people running the over-forty circuit didn't care why he wanted to play, they just wanted him to play, they needed a drawing card, and Tony Douglass had always been that, no matter what.

So now here he was making his debut at Westchester, all the stories leading up to the event talking about how the bad boy of tennis had finally grown up.

Lawrence Semple, Jr., Ted's driver, had said on the way up from the city that there was as much chance of Tony Douglass changing as the goddamn ocean. But Ted wanted to see for himself, see if the stories were just the normal hype and bullshit that had surrounded Douglass during the prime of his career, when he always seemed to be coming back from something, another injury, or one of his famous sabbaticals, which Ted had assumed was another code for rehab, covering a drinking problem that had always been the worst-kept secret in tennis.

Douglass would always talk about a new attitude, a new outlook on his tennis life. Once he said yoga had turned him around. Another time it was Jesus. The year he lost the Lockhart match at the Open, his last year on the regular circuit, he was extolling the virtues of a radical new macrobiotic diet.

The day before the Westchester tournament Douglass had told the woman tennis writer from the *Times,* "I just finally decided that hitting a tennis ball was the only thing I'd ever really loved."

Ted read that one and thought: Where is Jesus when *I* really need Him?

Ted Carlyle: the Laver man. The Rosewall man who'd spent all those hours trying to perfect the same kind of backhand little Muscles had. Ted Carlyle: who'd been a boy in the fifties when tennis was in its last Golden Age, because of the Aussies, and the great Gonzales. Who'd heard the stories about the barnstorming matches between Gonzales and Hoad. Who'd read Gordon Forbes's book, *A Handful of Summers,* a marvelous account of those years from the old South African player, of that golden time in tennis, more than twenty times, because it was a way of going back, of remembering when the players acted the way they were supposed to, when his world would come alive for those two weeks at West Side Tennis Club, on those glorious grass courts, when the Open would come back to town.

Before pricks like Tony Douglass, every one of them, ruined everything. . . .

It happened in the very first set at Westchester.

Douglass was playing Arazi Siddarides, the Greek guy who'd beaten him in the French Open finals when Douglass was seventeen. Ted Carlyle had a front-row seat for that one, too, the way he'd had such a great seat that day for Douglass versus Lockhart. Ted used to love the trip to Stade Roland Garros in May, the elegance and romance and beauty of Paris in the spring, before that was another place Douglass and the rest of them ruined for him.

Now at Westchester, at 4–5 and 30–40 against Douglass on his own serve, he hit what he thought was an ace, a bomb out of his youth, right down the middle.

It was called wide by the woman working the center service line.

"You're kidding, right, lady?" Douglass said.

Ted Carlyle knew the deal with the senior circuit. There was no code of conduct, no rules, no point penalties or game penalties, mostly because the older guys didn't need rules to rein them in, they were just happy to be out there, still making a few dollars playing the game, they were lucky if the matches even made it to Cable America in the middle of the night.

There was another woman, an old friend of Ted's named Helen Kaiser, sitting in the chair.

"The ball was wide, Mr. Douglass," Kaiser said.

"Bullshit!" Douglass said, and now he was walking slowly toward the umpire's chair. "That was a goddamn ace and you know it."

"It's her call," Helen Kaiser said.

"Well, guess what, honey?" Tony Douglass said, his voice loud enough in the small temporary stadium to be heard by everyone. "It's my *turn*," he said.

The idiots, maybe two thousand of them, actually cheered.

"Listen . . ." Helen Kaiser said meekly.

"No, honey," he said, "*you* listen to *me*."

Ted Carlyle watched it like an old nightmare.

"Second service," she said. "Please."

She's negotiating with him, Ted thought.

"You were blind when you were young," Douglass said.

He was right underneath the chair now, pointing at her with his racquet.

Helen Kaiser had been a beauty when she was young, a terrific local doubles player who had actually gotten into the Open a couple of times, then stayed in the game for the simple reason that she loved it, working the lines at the Open in her silly Fila clothes, working her way up through the Eastern Tennis Association until she became president, finally getting the chair for a couple of women's finals after the Open moved over to the National Tennis Center in the late seventies.

Now Ted, right across the court from her, was afraid she might cry.

Maybe the plan started to form then.

He knew he couldn't watch another minute of this. He got out of his seat, walked along the front row of the bleachers, made his way to the parking lot, to where Lawrence Semple, Jr., said he'd be waiting.

Lawrence Semple, Jr., had said he'd rather listen to the Mets than watch Tony Douglass and his chicken ass play another match, no matter how much he said he'd changed.

"I'm sorry . . ." Helen Kaiser was saying over the sound system.

"No," Tony Douglass said, as though he were talking into the same microphone, "you're a moron . . ."

The idiots cheered again, as though this was what they had come to see, this was what they wanted.

This zoo.

The car was right where Lawrence said it would be, parked near the golf driving range, the motor running, as if Lawrence somehow knew Ted was on his way, the back door already open. Ted got in and told him to drive straight to the country house.

There was so much to do.

• • •

Ted Carlyle had retired five years before after making one last huge score in the market, with the equipment that did the laser eye surgery. The score came after the divorce and, more important, after Rachel remarried; it meant Ted could finally look at something as sheer profit again, after all the years when she got half. Rachel had told him during that time she would remarry when the sky was a different color on this particular planet, but then she met the guy whose coffee shops were outdoing Starbucks now, and all of a sudden she didn't need Ted's money the way she did oxygen.

It was funny, Ted thought, how much he associated Rachel with Tony Douglass, as if there were some sort of weird connection there. Maybe it was because she used to tell him so often that he worried more about some obnoxious tennis player than he did about his own marriage.

Maybe it was because the marriage broke up for good the year of Douglass versus Lockhart at the Open.

"He blew up a tennis match," she said, "not an office building."

"You don't understand," he told her.

"You're right," she said.

He could never decide which was worse, his leaving tennis or his wife leaving him.

He traveled, his schedule not built around the French any longer, or Wimbledon; he really did what divorced men of leisure were supposed to do: tried to see new places, from Jamaica to the Scottish Highlands, even to South Africa, trying to see some of the places his friend Arthur Ashe had seen there.

Ted Carlyle followed the tennis results, all right, tried to learn some of the new names. But he did not watch on television and he missed the Open for the first time since he was ten. He tried baseball for a while, but hated the little boutique ballparks, and the slow games, and the high scores, and the crazy number of home runs being hit. He bought season tickets to the Knicks. He took golf lessons.

He still played tennis himself, his regular games at the Vanderbilt Club, and out at West Side, as sad and forgotten as that place had become, Ted having more and more trouble each year remembering what it was like in the old days when it would be the capital of tennis for those two glorious weeks at the beginning of September.

Then one day, like a smoker deciding it wouldn't hurt to smoke one cigarette, he decided it would be all right to start watching *women's* tennis. But he couldn't keep the Russians straight. He hadn't liked watching the Williams sisters even when they were on top. He loved Jennifer Capriati's heart, not her sledgehammer game. One year he watched two Belgian women play the U.S. Open final, and it was like watching the championship of Middle Earth.

It wasn't long before Ted was watching the men again, especially this kid Roger Federer from Switzerland, as talented and graceful as anybody he had ever seen.

Ted decided that maybe it was time for him to come all the way back. A friend was willing to sell him a box at the new stadium at the Open, named after Ashe. He was even thinking about returning to Wimbledon, went so far as booking his old room at the Connaught.

Then Ted picked up the *Times* and read about Tony Douglass's return to tennis, and how he'd changed, how this was like a second chance for him to do things the right way, to honor his talent and his sport.

Somehow, this was like the last test for Ted, some finish line he had to cross, seeing if it was really safe for him to give his heart back to his sport. So three nights later Lawrence Semple, Jr., a former defensive back from the Giants who had later drifted into tennis officiating himself once, was driving Ted up to Westchester Country Club, so they could both see for themselves.

They saw.

In the car now, the Hutch becoming the Merritt, Ted said, "It shouldn't take more than a couple of weeks to get everything together."

"Then we go pick up the trash," Lawrence Semple, Jr., said, bigger now than when he'd played corner for the Giants, the size of him seeming to take up the whole front seat.

"You go."

"My pleasure," Lawrence Semple, Jr., said.

•   •   •

Ted had a friend at CBS who was able to get some of the tapes he needed. And Lawrence knew some production people at both NBC and ESPN from his football days, so it was easy getting the help they needed there, especially with Ted's amazing memory for dates and places.

"How do you remember some of this shit?" Lawrence Semple, Jr., said.

"Because I do," Ted said, giving him the tournaments they needed, the years.

The people from Circuit City got the room exactly the way he wanted, two huge screens positioned perfectly, what Lawrence called some of that surround sound shit, even speakers, though the Circuit City people didn't see why he would need speakers.

Lawrence said, "Sounds like a goddamn recording studio in here when you amp it up all the way."

"Except that we're out here in the middle of nowhere in Wilton, Connecticut."

"No one around for miles."

Ted said, "Just us."

When he had all the tapes, he edited them himself, in his own little studio, pleased he still had the moves from the days when he was first starting out, cutting tape at Channel 9, before he started making commercials; before the company took off and he got lucky in the market.

A million years ago, when the money made it easy for him to see all the tennis he wanted.

When he watched it all, it wasn't as bad as he remembered, that was the amazing part.

It was much, much worse.

Tony Douglass, when he was young, was even crazier than he remembered.

• • •

"Was easier than I thought it was gonna be," Lawrence Semple, Jr., said when Ted came back from the Wilton Market with supplies.

Lawrence weighed about two-thirty now, maybe thirty pounds over his playing weight, but looked as if he spent more time in the weight room now than he did when he was still in the NFL. Ted knew the bodybuilding started when he did that stretch, out in California somewhere, for income tax evasion, another ex-athlete who took a fall for not reporting the money he was making at autograph and memorabilia shows. Lawrence had just drifted for a few years after that, more ashamed than anything else at what had happened, the football money gone, finally taking a job as a driver for Bermuda Limousine in the city. It turned out he had always loved tennis, all the way back to when he had played on the tennis team in high school in West Palm Beach. He became a dues-paying member of the United States Tennis Association, started playing in a regular game at the National Tennis Center, which the public could basically use when the Open wasn't in town, and decided it would be fun to start working lines at some small local tournaments, eventually working his way up to the Open.

That was where Ted met him.

Ted joked one day, after a Connors match, that all tennis officials should be Lawrence's size, look as menacing as he still could when he'd stare at a player with his arm out.

Lawrence said, "I always wanted to stand up, grab one of 'em by they stringy hair and say, 'Who you callin' a moron, white boy?'"

Ted hired him when the Open was over, as much for the company as for the driving.

Now here they were, in the front hall of the elegant old mansion Ted had bought ten years before—Rachel the fixer-upper's last expensive project—and it was as if Lawrence had a team again, with Ted calling the plays.

Even if they really felt more like partners in crime.

Ted said, "I never doubt you, Lawrence."

They walked back to what the original owners, a couple of New York aristocrats who'd built the place in the twenties, had used as a ballroom for their big, formal Fairfield County parties. The two new screens were positioned to the left and right of the chair, the screen he'd already owned in front, far enough away so you could clearly see the picture. Lawrence, Ted decided, had done a beautiful job of painting what looked like the lines of a real tennis court, even putting the net up.

Tony Douglass would be able to see it later, when they took off his blindfold.

For now, Douglass sat tied to the umpire's chair, duct tape over his mouth, one of Ted's Brioni silk neckties tightly covering his eyes. He was squirming like a fish on a hook, but wasn't going anywhere, Lawrence Semple, Jr., had made sure of that.

The growling noises he was making, Lawrence noted, didn't sound so different from the ones he used to make when a call would go against him. Douglass had an apartment in the city, a beach house out in Amagansett, in the Hamptons. Lawrence Semple, Jr., had grabbed him there, on the solitary stretch of beach, behind some dunes, where Douglass liked to take his morning run.

"His mouth," Ted said.

Lawrence walked over to the chair, just a little shorter than a normal umpire's chair in tennis, reached up, ripped the tape away from Douglass's mouth, causing him to howl with pain.

"What the *fuck?*" Douglass said. "What the bloody fuck is going on here?"

Neither Ted nor Lawrence said anything.

"Who's there?" Douglass said. "How many of you are there, for Chrissakes?"

More silence from Ted and Lawrence Semple, Jr., just the sound of Tony Douglass's voice bouncing around the old ballroom, giving off a faint echo, as if this were an empty stadium.

"You want money, is that it? Well, let me explain something to you cocksuckers: I've got more money than God."

Douglass waited for an answer to that and when he decided one wasn't coming he said, "At least let me see you."

He finally stopped trying to get his hands loose, which was

smart, since Lawrence Semple, Jr., had fastened them all the way up to his elbows.

"*Assholes!*" Douglass hissed.

Lawrence Semple, Jr., walked over to the chair, put one foot on the bottom step, and slapped him hard across the face.

Tony Douglass screamed again.

"What . . . is . . . this . . . about?" he said. "Can you at least tell me that?"

In a quiet voice, a friendly voice, Ted Carlyle said, "Sure. It's your turn in the chair, Tony."

They walked out of the ballroom then, Ted and Lawrence both listening to Tony Douglass yell from an umpire's chair this time, instead of at it.

•   •   •

Lawrence Semple, Jr., took care of feeding him the first couple of days, untying Douglass from the chair when he needed to use the bathroom, Lawrence walking him in there, standing right there next to the toilet. The first time they made the trip, Lawrence let Douglass feel the sap he was carrying, telling him he would use it if Douglass made any kind of move to take the blindfold off.

The second day, Douglass tried to pull away as Lawrence was helping him back into the chair. Lawrence Semple, Jr., grabbed a fistful of blonde hair, still longish, as if this were the old days and Douglass were still young and said, "I told you, boy. I will bitch-slap you."

"Who *are* you?" Tony Douglass said in a raspy whisper, his voice already hoarse from all the yelling he did when he was alone in the ballroom.

Lawrence got close to his ear and said, "Bill Tilden. Give us a kiss."

The third day, they started playing the tapes for him on the big screen.

Ted would throw a switch and the room would go to total darkness and Lawrence would remove the blindfold. Lawrence would walk out a side door and then Ted would begin playing Tony Douglass's worst tantrums, from the U.S. Open and the French and Wimbledon and Davis Cup, all three screens at the same time, the volume turned up to ear-splitting levels.

Douglass got to watch himself throwing his racquet around, busting floral arrangements near the court, grabbing his crotch, standing over linesmen and lineswomen while he berated them, even throwing sawdust in the face of a fan who'd said something smart to him one time at the old indoor tournament in Philadelphia.

But the best moments were always at the umpire's chair, Douglass howling at the top of his lungs in the good-boy accent, face contorted with rage.

Always looking, Ted thought, mad as a fucking hatter.

"I can't listen to this shit anymore," Douglass said late the afternoon of the third day, after the show was over and blindfold was back in place.

"Is anybody still here?" Douglass said.

"I'm begging you to shut this shit off," he said.

Ted Carlyle's voice came over the speakers. "I'm sorry, Tony. What were you saying?"

"I said I can't take listening to this shit anymore."

Ted said, "Imagine how the rest of us used to feel."

"You've had your little fun," Douglass said. "I get it, okay? I was an asshole, okay? I was an official asshole. You've made your point. Just dump me back in the car, drop me by the side of the road someplace, I don't even care who you are anymore."

Silence.

"Do I know you?" Douglass said. "I swear I recognize your voice from somewhere."

"Do you now?" Ted Carlyle said.

"Bloody hell!" Douglass shouted. "Who *are* you?"

"All of them," Ted said.

"Fuck you," Douglass said.

"No," Ted's voice said over the speakers. "That's where you have it wrong, Tony. It was 'fuck you' all those years when you were number one, when you were on top, when you came along and actually made Connors and McEnroe look like choir boys. It was 'fuck you' when you were running the sport, when you were the attraction, when you were the one who could get any appearance money he wanted, because promoters would sell their souls to have you play their tournaments. But that was a long time ago."

There was a pause and then Ted said, "Fuck *me*, Tony? Oh, no. Now it's fuck *you*."

* * *

The fifth day Tony Douglass said, "How long is this going to last? I assume you're not going to keep me here prisoner forever."

Lawrence Semple, Jr., had just come in behind him, the lights off and the afternoon show over, and put the blindfold back on him.

"Not too much longer," Lawrence said. "We comin' to the end soon, on account of my boss wanted to do this chronological."

"I'll figure out who you are eventually," Douglass said. "You know that, right? And when I do, I'm going to come after you, you bastard."

It came out bah-stid in his Brit accent.

Lawrence Semple, Jr., said, "'Course if you still haven't learned manners by the time we fixin' to turn you loose, we may have to extend your engagement here at the Bad Boy Ramada."

"Kiss my English arse," Tony Douglass said, and Lawrence slapped him hard across the face, saying, "Somebody shoulda done that the very first time you smart-mouthed somebody in a junior tournament."

Lawrence left him there, went and found Ted Carlyle sitting and smoking a cigarette in his study.

"You sure you want to show him the big one?"

"Against Lockhart at the Open? Lawrence, it's the grand finale."

"He was sayin' the other day he might recognize your voice."

"You know what, Lawrence? I don't care anymore."

"You're tellin' me you don't give a rat's ass he figures out it was you in the chair that day? You who brung him here?"

"Maybe I want him to know," Ted said. "But not before I yell back."

Ted did that the next afternoon, after they'd played the explosion in that Lockhart match over and over again, Tony Douglass pleading with them after two hours to turn it off before he lost his bloody mind. If Douglass knew it was Ted Carlyle who'd been in the chair that day, Ted Carlyle whom he'd humiliated that way, he didn't say.

Maybe, in the end, they all sounded alike to him.

Ted got right in front of him, right in front of the chair, and said, "So how do you like it?"

"It sucks."

"Doesn't it, though?"

Douglass, somehow managing to shrug, said, "What can I say? The shit got out of hand. Whoever the guy you have with you, he's right. Somebody should've stopped me when I was young. But no one ever did." He shrugged again. "Shit happens."

"So it wasn't your fault, is that it?"

"It's not what I'm saying exactly, but—"

"*Shut up!*"

Ted Carlyle said it with such force it snapped Douglass's head back.

"I was just trying to explain—"

"*Shut the fuck up!*" Ted shouted, louder than before, a foot up on the side of the chair, his mouth practically next to Douglass's ear, the one with the diamond stud in it. "I suppose it was somebody else's fault that you only won those four majors with your talent, is that it?" Ted said.

"I told you, shit happens . . ."

"*Bullshit* shit happens," Ted said, spitting out the words. "You know who the ignorant moron was, Tony? *You* were. Did McEnroe have more talent than you? Did Connors or Borg or Sampras or any of them? You know they didn't. But you finally pissed it all away, didn't you? You were more interested in being some asshole bad-boy character than you were in being the champion you should have been. Isn't that right, Tony? At least McEnroe used to play doubles to keep himself in shape. You were too big even for that, weren't you? There was always another party, wasn't there? Maybe that's why you were so pissed off all the time, it was because you were so fucking hung over."

"I worked," Douglass said in a small voice. "Maybe not as hard as the others . . ."

"*Liar!*" Ted's voice was as loud as gunfire in the ballroom. "Who's the one who can't see now, Tony? Who's the one who's so stinking *blind?*"

Ted Carlyle was out of breath, his chest heaving, sweating as if they were playing a match, both feet back on the ballroom floor, a high heat rising in the back of his neck.

Jesus, he thought, it's finally happened, I'm as crazy as he is.

"I'm the one who's right, aren't I, Tony?" he said.

"No, it was more complicated than that . . ."

"*Yes!*"

"No!"

"The people in the chair, the people calling the lines, you just abused them for sport, didn't you?"

"It wasn't like that. Sometimes, maybe, because it had become part of my act by then, people expected it . . ."

"*Liar!* They weren't even worthy of being on the same court with the great Tony Douglass, were they?"

"I just expected them to do their jobs properly."

"Bullshit!" Ted yelled. "They tried to do their jobs properly, but you wouldn't let them, would you? At least not after the first call that went against you."

"I saw things . . ."

"*You saw what you wanted to see!*" There was only the harsh sound of Ted's breathing in the ballroom. "And then you did exactly what you wanted to do, didn't you?"

"Yes." The word seemed to die a foot in front of Tony Douglass's mouth. "Yes," he said, in a whisper now.

Ted said, "You didn't give a shit about anything or anybody, did you? It was all about you, wasn't it?"

"Yes, goddamnit!" Tony Douglass said. "Yes! Is that what you want to hear? I fucked up myself and I fucked up tennis. Is that what you want to hear? Bloody *Christ!* What else do you want me to say?"

"I'm sorry," Ted said.

"What?"

"Tell me you're sorry."

"I'm sorry!" Douglass screamed from the chair. "I'm sorry, I'm sorry. Jesus, I'm *sorry.* Now please let me go."

At last, Ted thought, at last, it was Tony Douglass who sat in that chair wanting to cry.

"Not yet," Ted said, and left him there. Lawrence Semple, Jr., was waiting on the clay court out back for their afternoon hit.

• • •

Ted and Lawrence Semple, Jr., sat on the back terrace having coffee the next morning.

"Was it enough?" Lawrence said.

"It?"

"Bringing his sorry ass here, makin' him watch the shit, talkin' to him the way you did? Was it enough for what he did to you that time? Hell, what he did to everybody *all* the times?"

"No," Ted said, staring down the long expanse of lawn, stretching all the way to the lake, the tennis court right before it looking beautiful in the morning sun, Lawrence having already rolled it. "But it will have to do. I mean, we can't kill the sonofabitch, can we?"

Lawrence smiled.

They finished their coffee. Lawrence had already taken Douglass to the shower, stripped off his clothes as he did every day, thrown him in there with his hands tied behind him, let the water wash over him, roughly dried him before he helped him on with one of the T-shirts they'd bought for him, underwear, jeans, Nike tennis sneakers.

Then it was back to the chair.

They both walked into the ballroom.

"We're done with you now," Ted said.

Douglass sighed.

"At last," he said. "When do we leave?"

"Not just yet," Ted said.

"What do you *mean* not just yet? I've been here a bloody week? You've *tortured* me for a bloody week. I've learned my lesson, I swear to you! What more can you say to me than you already have? What more can *I* say to convince you? I believe your friend when he says that if I ever act up again, he'll come for me."

"I've said all I wanted to say, Tony," Ted said. "But that doesn't mean everybody has."

"We nearly needed a damn waitin' list," Lawrence Semple, Jr., said.

Lawrence opened the double doors to the ballroom then and Helen Kaiser, the chair umpire from Westchester Country Club, dressed smartly in a beige summer suit, came walking across the shiny hardwood floor, the one painted to look like a tennis court, to where Tony Douglass sat in the chair.

"There's so many who want to talk to you, Tony," Ted Carlyle said.

"My turn," Helen Kaiser said.

They had left the windows open when they left her there with him. Halfway through their first set, Ted and Lawrence could still hear the shrill sound of Helen Kaiser's screaming from up the hill.

CONTINENTAL GRIP

DAVID MORRELL

As much as anyone could tell, the murder weapon was a Prince long-body racquet, the edge of which had been driven into the top of the victim's skull. There was some uncertainty because the victim wore a tennis cap, so the indentation that the edge of the racquet made wasn't as defined as the police would have liked. But by trial and error, it turned out that Wilsons and other racquets didn't fit the groove as much as Princes did, so Prince owners became the initial suspects. That narrowed the list to about 50 percent of the club's membership.

The victim was the club's pro, Rocky Radigan. A tennis player doesn't usually have a boxer's nickname, but it fit. The way a first-rate boxer keeps dancing all the time he's in the ring, that's how Rocky moved on the tennis court, always shifting rhythmically. A beautiful thing to see. He was thirty-seven, tall and lanky, good-looking in a boyish way, with hazel eyes and dark hair, although those last two details were hard to notice because almost nobody ever saw him without his sunglasses and his tennis cap. For several years, he'd been on the pro tour, was ranked as high as 85, made it to the third round at the U.S. Open, and had lots of good stories: the shock of seeing Pete Sampras vomit in the quarterfinals at the U.S. Open, for example, or the reaction of the Wimbledon spectators when a female player went onto the court in a white spandex cat suit. Eventually Rocky had gotten tired of the tour's exhausting schedule and moved to Santa Fe, where he became the pro for the Land of Enchantment tennis club and where, after a successful five years, he was found dead on Court One when the first players showed up at eight on a sunny September morning.

Land of Enchantment. The original owner called the club that because New Mexico uses it on its license plates, and over the years, the club adapted to the name, becoming even more weird and special than Santa Fe likes to think of itself. For starters, there's the club's appearance. At the end of a curved potholed gravel street that the post office constantly has trouble finding, it consists of six courts, three on an upper tier, three below it. They're separated by tall cottonwood trees, and they've got rustic wooden benches with sunshades made of interlaced branches stretched overhead between posts. To the left, there's a swimming pool and changing rooms. In front of the pool is the clubhouse, an adobe-pueblo-style structure that seems constantly in need of maintenance—the porch, for example, the boards of which keep breaking. But somehow the ill repair is part of the charm. Visitors need only one look at the silhouettes of Sun and Moon mountains beyond the club to make them instantly want to join.

The trouble is, zoning restrictions keep the maximum membership to three hundred, so there's a list of people waiting to get in. The membership has an interesting mix. A former New Mexico attorney general. A retired Hollywood casting director (lots of movie people live in Santa Fe). A founding member of a major computer firm. A surgeon who invented one of the standard techniques of repairing hearts. A factory-systems analyst who saved several corporations from bankruptcy. A director of a local museum.

That sample might suggest that the club's stuffy and self-important. Not at all. There are plenty of average members, too. If anything, people want to belong because there aren't any pretensions about the place. Take the way the members dress, for instance. At most clubs, there's a contest about who has the most expensive, stylish whites. But at the Land of Enchantment, members show up in the baggiest, most washed-out, most poorly color-coordinated shorts and tops. To look at some of the players, you'd think that they didn't have a dollar to their name.

The owner, Debbie, bought the place ten years ago with an inheritance from her grandmother. She's a fortyish robust woman who's fond of burning incense and going on purifying fasts. She claims she bought the club because she loves tennis, but the real reason is, she wanted the club so she could have a place for all the cats she's adopted. Somebody once counted fifty of them. White ones. Orange ones. Calico ones. Tailless ones. Earless ones. Everywhere you look: cats. The members aim tennis balls at them to keep them off the courts. At night, owls and coyotes deplete the horde, but it doesn't make much difference because Debbie just goes out and adopts more. When members' children show up to swim, they try to pet the cats and get bitten, so Debbie's always having to prove that her cats have had their rabies shots, and then she has to pay for the doctor's visit to have the bite disinfected. It's a mark of how strongly members like her and the club that nobody's ever complained to the Animal Shelter, but an accountant who belongs to the club wondered how Debbie could be earning any money from the place after paying for all the cat food she needs, plus the vet and doctor bills.

As a matter of fact, the police couldn't tell if it was the cats or a raccoon that ate Rocky's nose while he was lying on Court One all night (the autopsy determined that he'd been killed around sundown the previous evening). He still had his racquet in his hand. Rigor mortis had set in, so the police had a terrible time getting it away from him. One of the investigators, a tennis buff, couldn't help noticing that Rocky held the racquet with his favorite grip: the Continental.

For those unfamiliar with tennis: Basically, there are three ways to hold a racquet. The easiest is the forehand grip, in which your hand is to the right of the center part of the handle (or if you're left-handed, to the left). A little harder is the backhand grip, in which your hand is to the left of the center part of the handle (reverse this if you're left-handed). And then there's the cursed Continental, which involves keeping the web between your thumb and first finger directly at the center of the handle. It's used for close shots at the net, or else for overheads and for serving. It's effective when done properly, but it feels unnatural at first and requires a lot of hand strength. Beginning players sometimes take a year and more to feel comfortable with it. Then it gets to be so automatic that they can't make the shift to a forehand or a backhand. Expletives are unavoidable.

The Continental. Rocky was the tennis equivalent of a religious zealot, constantly preaching about that grip. If he mentioned it once during a lesson, he mentioned it a hundred times. Use the Continental. Use the Continental. Of course, he had a whole slew of other mantras. Keep your eye on the ball. Stay in the moment. Move, move, move. Sideways, keep sideways. Bend those knees. Hit low. Get that racquet back early. He even told Debbie to stock his favorite book in what passed for the club's equipment store: *The Inner Game of Tennis.* But at the top of his all-time instruction list was, Use the Continental, use the Continental.

So there poor Rocky was, sprawled on the service line, with his racquet in his hand, looking as if he'd been about to make a drop shot before he himself got dropped. The mixed doubles group who found him phoned the police. When the ambulance and the cruisers sped into the gravel parking lot, the sirens made Debbie's cats scatter (they didn't come out from bushes and under the porch for the rest of the day). Then two detectives arrived, and with all their questions and the lab crew and the medical examiner, not to mention two policemen using yellow "crime scene, do not pass" tape to cordon off Court One, not much tennis got played that day.

Naturally, the members were shocked that Rocky had been killed. They felt terrible for his sister and his parents. But then it suddenly hit everybody that a *member* was probably Rocky's killer and that whoever had done it might come after *other* members next. For the rest of the week, the club was so deserted that Debbie felt nervous being there alone with just the handyman and her cats. But tennis players being what they are, they couldn't resist. They avoided the lonely hours of the evening and early morning, *especially* the evening because that was when Rocky had been killed. The result was, the courts got so crowded during the middle of the day that, if you wanted to play, you *had* to pick evening and early morning, so after a while the club got back to normal, even though the murderer hadn't been caught.

Not that the police didn't try. Rocky was a wonderful tennis player, but he kept lousy records. His daybook in his office made no mention of the people he'd been teaching that afternoon and evening, which meant that it wasn't immediately evident who'd been the last person to see him alive. Eventually the retired computer executive learned what had happened and told the police that, to the best of his knowledge, he'd been Rocky's last lesson the previous day. The sun had been setting when they'd quit. Since there weren't any lights for playing at night, the other courts had been deserted. Even Debbie and the caretaker had gone home. This raised the obvious question of whether the computer executive was the killer, a promising line of thought that ended when the police learned that, his four-wheel-drive having needed repairs, the executive's wife and two children had picked him up in the family Volvo while Rocky was by himself, tightening the net on Court One. The wife might have lied convincingly, but the two teenagers would have gotten flustered, the police believed.

Back to deuce. The police interviewed and reinterviewed all the members, with special attention to those who owned Prince racquets. Any of them might have been the murder weapon, but there wouldn't be any trace evidence on it (blood and hair, for example) because Rocky's tennis cap had been in the way. The cap might have left fibers on the murder weapon, but unfortunately it was a Land of Enchantment club hat, and many members wore that kind. Fibers from those hats could easily have gotten on the racquets.

The police tried to re-create the crime. Because Rocky had been tall, it made sense to believe that whoever struck the top of his head was tall, which automatically suggested a man. The angle also suggested that the blow came from someone who was right-handed. So for a while the range of suspects was narrowed to a right-handed tall man who owned a Prince racquet and a club hat. But then the detectives noticed that there were several tall women who belonged to the club. More, Rocky had been relentless in telling his students to bend their knees on certain shots, so it could have been that he'd been demonstrating how knees should be bent when he was struck. For that matter, maybe he'd been stooping to tie his shoes, which meant that the killer wasn't necessarily tall or male.

Maybe motive was a way of figuring out who'd done it. As the investigators had been taught, there are basically only two reasons for people to commit murder: because they want something from someone else (sex, money, silence, et cetera), or they want to get even. In a way, though, the two are the same inasmuch as revenge is another way of getting something from somebody: the satisfaction of seeing that person die. The same with serial killers, only there it's random and impersonal, but it's still getting satisfaction from somebody. So a specific example of the theory had to be worked out.

The first motive the investigators considered was money. Had Rocky been killed while being robbed? Unlikely. No serious player, especially Rocky, ever played tennis with a wallet in his pocket. So what about sex? Exactly. Rocky hadn't been married. Had he been shtupping some of the female members and a husband of one of them decided to make him stop? Or maybe one of the women had gotten furious when she discovered that she wasn't the sole object of Rocky's devotion. Or maybe he'd been gay and ... The only trouble with the sex theory was that Rocky had been seeing a woman, not someone at the club, for the past two years and had just gotten engaged to her. As hard as the police tried, they couldn't get a whiff of scandal about him at the club. He'd been a gentleman.

Deuce two. Well, actually it was more like game, set, and match. What seemed like a spontaneous crime of opportunity, which in the carelessness of the moment would normally have left all kinds of inadvertent clues, turned out to be potentially unsolvable, unless somebody got drunk and said more than he or she intended.

In the meantime, Rocky's death left a void that had to be filled. An effective club needs a pro to give lessons, organize club tournaments, and generally provide an example to aim toward. So the word went out, and by November, after interviewing dozens of applicants (Santa Fe's a popular place to move to), Debbie settled on a thirty-seven-year-old pro from Houston. His name was Dan Robertson. Like Rocky, he was tall and lanky. He'd been on the tour, had been ranked at 78, and had plenty of stories to tell (like having seen Jeff Tarango's wife go ballistic against that French referee). Debbie gave a party to welcome him. Dan made appropriate remarks about not being able to fill Rocky's shoes and how he was going to do his best to make everybody better tennis players. Applause.

Winter came. Spring. Or if you're a devoted tennis player, you measure the year according to when the Grand Slams occur: the Australian in January, the French in May, Wimbledon in June, the U.S. Open in September. Right after the Australian, though, in March, the rating clinics occur.

Those clinics are important because, if you want to play in

tournaments, you have to be rated each year. The way the system works, four of you go out on the court for fifteen minutes or so. The person doing the rating, in this case the new pro, Dan, gets a pro from another club to help him and make sure that Dan's opinion isn't prejudiced because he knows you. They tell the players to hit balls back and forth: forehands, backhands, volleys, lobs, serves, whatever. Then they tell the four of you to play doubles for a while. Throughout, they make notes. Finally, they've seen enough, give you a rating, and ask for the next four players.

A rating of two means you don't know one end of the racquet from the other. A two-point-five means that you pretty much suck but have promise. A three means that you don't stink up the court. A three-point-five means that you're not too bad. A four is fairly respectable. A four-point-five: Now you're really getting somewhere. And so on, all the way up to the super-expert-top-player-never-been-anything-like-it category of seven-point-five.

After the March rating clinic, the tournament schedule lasted until the end of June. After that, there was the usual summer confusion until the second week in September, right after the U.S. Open, when the club had its own tournament. There were a couple of surprises. A player who'd gotten used to winning in the three-point-five singles category lost in his new category of four. The same thing happened to a player whose rating had been raised from four to four-point-five. Annoyed by the unaccustomed humiliation, the losers wanted more lessons.

They weren't the only ones, and that was how *Dan* nearly got killed just around the anniversary of when Rocky had been killed. It happened at the end of the day, the same time as with

Rocky. Dan was teaching the factory-systems analyst. Might as well call him what he really was: an efficiency expert.

"Watch your grip," Dan kept saying. "Stay in the moment. Move your feet. Stay sideways. Get that racquet back early. Bend those knees. Watch the ball. Use the Continental."

"The Continental, the Continental, the Continental," the efficiency expert said.

"What?"

"Watch the ball. Bend those knees. Tote that barge. Lift that bale."

"*What?*"

"The Continental, the Continental, the Continental." The efficiency expert leaped over the net. "Watch your grip. Well, *here's* what I think of the fucking Continental. I want you to notice that at this very moment as I speak I'm *using* the Continental." He swung his racquet so hard at Dan's head that Dan barely had a chance to raise his own racquet, deflecting the blow.

It was late, the courts were empty, but Debbie still hadn't gone home, so when she heard the yelling, she ran onto the porch (a board broke under her feet) and saw the efficiency expert chasing Dan around the court, trying to hit him with his racquet, screaming, "The Continental, the effing Continental!"

He was still chasing Dan (they were about two blocks away by then) when the police arrived. It turned out that the efficiency expert had been a four-point-five player when he retired to Santa Fe and joined the club four years earlier. He'd been fanatic about playing, did it every day, took two and sometimes three lessons a week, and for whatever reason (maybe because, without his work to remind him, he'd forgotten how to be efficient), his rating had slipped to a four, a three-point-five, a three, and in the recent rating clinic in March, a two-point-five.

He'd become so terrible that no one would play with him. He'd been forced to watch the club championships from the sidelines. In fact, the only person he could get to play with him was for money—Dan, and earlier Rocky. But no matter how much time and money he put in on lessons, he kept getting worse.

The previous September, he'd shown up at the club after the computer executive had left and demanded that Rocky give him another lesson (he revealed this eventually in a moment of lucidity amidst his babbling). He told Rocky that they were going to play by the light of the sonofabitch silvery moon until the cows came home if they had to, but there was no way Rocky was going to leave the court until he made up for the tens of thousands of dollars the efficiency expert had spent on lessons, until Rocky did his damned job and made him a decent motherloving tennis player again. "A two-point-five, for Christ sake! Why, that's for little kids!"

The two policemen who arrived in response to Debbie's 911 call weren't enough to subdue him. The best they could do was chase him to the club where they cornered him at the concrete backboard. Players use it to practice their shots when they don't have anybody to play with. The efficiency expert had been at the backboard a lot lately, it turned out, hitting and hitting, getting worse and worse. The backboard has two concrete arms on each side, so once he was in there, he couldn't get out, not with the policemen blocking the way. It didn't matter. What he was doing before four other policemen and a psych-ward ambulance arrived was holding his racquet as if it were a banjo. He was strumming it and doing a little dance

("Move those feet!") and singing something about the Continental, that there was nothing like it, that it was different and sexy and that everybody was doing it, doing it, doing it, do the Continental, feet, feet, feet, so in the end the motive for Rocky's murder turned out to be that a tennis player had lost his grip.

CLOSE SHAVE

RIDLEY PEARSON

I t all started late one night, when the chorus of summer cicadas would not allow her a decent night's sleep. They sang mightily and strong that night to the backdrop of earthy celestials—fireflies sparking their way from rhododendron to lilac and back. They worked up a frenzy, in a way Jessie could not remember having heard before, and the fireflies too, their stately illumination beyond anything in recent memory. She lay awake, naked in the heat, unfettered by the slight breeze that lifted the tiny hairs on her skin, her thoughts unusually sensual as she watched him sleep beside her. It would take so little to arouse him, to bring at least part of him awake, to waste ten or twenty minutes of her insomnia on self-indulgence, as she rode him in the sultry bedroom, trying her best to put those cicadas to rest.

She drew the sheet off him and studied his form in the faint light. The workouts served him well, sharpening his chest and flattening his stomach. His chest and arms reflected a body capable of 110-mile-an-hour serves, even in the fifth set. A wild line of dark hair ran down from his navel to the nest where she gently touched him—not lightly like a tickle, nor firmly to where she might awaken him. She wanted to move his dreams, to control him in his sleep, and awaken him with her own warmth and readiness, but only as she joined him.

Thought of this commingling heightened her senses. She touched her chest with her free hand and felt a shiver pass through her. A rapid drumming filled her ears, and her breath drew short as she watched him respond, still fully asleep. At first, she believed the sound she heard was nothing more than self-generated excitement—her own pulse pounding more rapidly, more strongly as she witnessed his reaction to her touch. But it wasn't so. It was something outside. Something foreign that had no place at an hour so late: the sound of one thing striking another. Sharply, and crisp.

Naked, she slipped out of bed, leaving him fully aroused, his flagpole in need of a bugle call.

She caught sight of herself in silhouette in the full length mirror as she crossed to the window. Her body was not simply strong and feminine, but a thing of infinite beauty, as finely tuned a specimen of athletic perfection as could be found any-where, from professional dance to supermodels. The few openly gay women on the tour teased her in the locker room about her wasting herself on men. Her taut legs stretched end-lessly to the full curve of her hips and a tummy as flat and firm as a serving tray, her rib cage bulging slightly as it rose to breasts that remained tight and substantial despite the 4 per-cent body fat. Her large, exceptionally dark nipples received the most comments in the shower because, for whatever rea-son, they remained pointed and sharp, erect around the clock. Even now, at three in the morning, there was no mistaking their condition, halfway across the room from the mirror, and in the dark. Men found them so sexy and titillating that she got lurid fan mail describing solo sex acts as they sat in their recliners watching her matches on network television. One fan went as far as ejaculating onto the note he sent her. That particular note had gone into the "Worth Concern" file that both she and her manager kept in the event anything ever happened to her.

She tugged at the hotel room's internal sheer window covering and wrapped it around herself modestly, being careful not to stand naked even in a dark window, as she looked out in search of the source of that sound. It grew louder now, and more clear. As her eyes peered out at the darkened courts, there was no mistaking this sound—a tennis rally. She threw the lock on the sliding balcony door and hauled the heavy glass open a crack, and the sound became even louder and better defined. *Crack* came the serve, *whoosh*, the return.

And yet the courts stood empty.

She jumped as a male hand reached around and cupped her left breast while another hand arrived lower and eased her legs apart. "Do you hear that?" she asked, her body already responding to him. He could do magic with those hands. Other women on the tour found his boyish looks and his constant joking a put-off, but clearly they had not experienced those hands. Her knees quivered. She thought she might fall.

"I hear you breathing heavily," his Swedish accent replied. He pulled himself against her back and buttocks, forcing her to bend over, and she let go the sheer and it spilled away like a wind. He drew up against her and drove her slowly out onto the balcony.

She giggled at his persistence, for it became immediately clear to her that her efforts in the bed had produced continued results. She pleaded, "Not out here . . ." but lacked the resolve to convince him. His hands had turned her skin electric. Heat pulsed through her. She arched her back and reached for the balcony's warm steel rail, steadying herself. "Someone will see us . . ."

"At three in the morning?"

"It'll end up in the tabloids." But she was through arguing. She lifted her bottom invitingly and held on to that rail. He might help her to find sleep.

He said, "Then we'll make it base enough they can't print it." With that, he hoisted her by her hips and helped himself to her, holding her twitching bare feet off the warm concrete, her fingers white where they gripped the railing.

"Do . . . you . . . hear . . . it?" she gasped hoarsely, unable to think clearly, her senses dreamily confused. Her throat went dry, and her eyes rolled in her head, and suddenly she did not hear it herself, only the gentle, moist slap of their skin, and her quickened pulse singing sweetly in her ears.

● ● ●

"Do you believe in ghosts?" Jessie asked Khol. They occupied the same balcony. But morning now stood a few hours in the sky, and they were adorned in white terry cloth bearing the crest of the luxury hotel chain. The sounds from the courts were real. So was the traffic and the screams of the kids from the pool, directly below. He ate from a giant platter of fresh fruit, and drank chilled celery and carrot juice. She ate granola, a plain bagel with lite cream cheese, a fresh banana and a protein drink. She would play in the third round today; he would not. Her opponent was an aging star who wouldn't put up too much of a fight as long as the first set was close. The trick with her was to tire her out with a competitive first set. Regardless of who won it, if the match went an hour or longer, she wouldn't have the strength to win. The endorsements in the off-season had replaced this woman's commitment to six-hour workouts, and she no longer posed much of a threat as long as you worked her hard early on. Her mental tenacity could win the second set if you didn't beat her down physically in the first.

"Not exactly, no," Khol answered. "But in spirits, yes. You bet-cha!" He'd picked up the expression early on in a career that now stretched seven years on the tour. It sounded strangely Minnesotan. She found it endearing: one of those amusing quirks that lovers come to love.

"Spirits, then," she said between mouthfuls. "Have you ever seen one?"

"No, of course not," he dismissed. "Spirit is not something you *see*."

"Hear?"

"Same answer."

"Then how do you know it's there?"

"Not hear as in ears and brain function and all of that," he answered. "Not something a tape recorder would pick up."

"But *you* could pick it up," she attempted to confirm.

"Your spirit could connect with another spirit, with other spirits," he suggested.

"And you would know this how?" she tested.

He looked across the teak table skeptically. "What's all this about?"

"You'd hear it, or see it, don't you think? Or at least you might convince yourself you had."

"Okay. Point taken. Yes, I suppose so."

"And have you ever heard or seen such a thing?"

He pondered this while he appreciated a slice of kiwi. "Sometimes I dream things and I don't understand them until days later when they seem to come true."

"They either do or don't come true," she pressed.

"Sometimes I'll be thinking about a person I haven't thought of in a very long time, and the phone will ring and it's them." He added, "That has happened quite a bit, actually."

"To me, too," she agreed.

"So," he said, clipping off a strawberry top with his thumbnail and then sucking the fruit into his mouth, "you're hearing things, seeing things? Which is it?"

She wanted those lips on her, and glanced around for a clock to see if they had time for that. She had to hit for at least forty minutes before a match, nearly twice as long as most of the girls on the tour.

"You know what time it is?" she asked.

"No idea. Nine-something, I think." He ate another strawberry in the same provocative way. It wasn't a gimmick with Khol, an act. He was a physical, sensual person who came off as sexy whether he tried or not.

"Hearing," she answered.

"Voices?"

"Tennis balls. Late, late at night. Several nights now."

"That's called anxiety."

"No. I don't think so."

"Listen, firemen hear alarms; cops hear sirens; pilots hear air traffic controllers. You hear tennis balls. It's simple: You're preparing for your match."

"I don't think so," she said, repeating herself. "I don't know," she reconsidered, "maybe that's right."

"You're going to win. I know it. You know it. Personally, I think the whole tournament is yours to lose. And *don't* talk to me about ranking. You missed three weeks to that laser surgery. The computers penalized you for that. Technically, you're number two, not number five."

"Thank you for the vote of confidence," she said. She knew better than to argue against his compliments because it angered him. His temper was nothing to mess with.

"You have been so close for so long. Your time has come. You're just nervous about it."

She thought so, too. She had played them all, some more than others, and had identified chinks in the armor of the top three players—a weak second serve in one; endurance, in another; temper, in the third—but had been waiting for another chance to attempt to exploit their weaknesses. This tournament was that chance, and she knew it.

The room phone rang. It was her room; his was the Hilton down the beach. Technically, they weren't supposed to be "fraternizing" while on tour. But everybody did it: the men with the women; the women with the women; a few men-on-men. If rumor had it right, the thirteen-year-old Romanian wunderkind was sleeping with her thirty-six-year-old German coach, a lech of a man with a potbelly and bad English. Jessie had a pit in her stomach over that one. It hadn't won either of the two any friends on the tour. The women's locker room had nicknamed her Lolly, for Lolita, when her first name actually began with a P and was basically unpronounceable. Every play-by-play announcer called her something different. (The current accepted pronunciation approximated "Fotlana.")

Jessie strode inside to the phone, her athleticism and muscle tone evident even beneath a half-inch of terry cloth. "Hello?"

"You're playing well."

"Thank you." She couldn't identify the voice, and yet she recognized it. She hated it when the hotel operators put through fan calls. Her agent had provided the hotel a list of callers she would accept; the rest were supposed to go to voice mail. The hotels seldom got it right.

"We need to talk. You know who this is, don't you? It's Michael. Michael, from the Open."

"I have nothing to say to you." Her voice trembled. She felt all the blood drain from her head as her face went white and her balance faltered. She glanced out toward the balcony where Khol looked in with concern. She couldn't get much past him. Their relationship was all of three weeks old—a record for her while on tour—but he already knew her too well.

"We have much to catch up on," the voice of Michael disagreed. "I'm in the lobby."

"You're *what*? *Where*?" These people were all nerve, no tact. She feared them as much as she feared anything.

"What room?" the man asked.

"There's nothing to discuss," she said, lowering her voice so Khol couldn't hear. "You made certain promises, remember?" She added, "Including never contacting me again."

"And I wish I could keep them, I really do. But I cannot. You *will* see me. And right away."

"I have a match."

"You'll win it in two sets. Fifty minutes at most. What room number?"

"I have a guest. It's impossible."

"Khol Cedarbach? Ask him where his net game has gone."

"I'm hanging up now."

"Forest Park. Main entrance. Two hours after your press conference. Two hours to the minute." He repeated, "Ask him about his net game. If he went to net more often he'd win more games. He can't let a few passing shots take him out of game. Win some lose some, am I right? But his game is at net, and he has gotten away from that."

"I'm hanging up now." Gently, she dropped the phone into its cradle, not at all sure of her own actions.

"Who was it?" he asked. Did she hear jealousy in his voice?

"No one I wanted to talk to."

"You should have them screen your calls." He added, "I have so much to teach you."

"You're a pompous idiot," she snapped, not wanting any company. Her lust of only moments earlier had evaporated without a trace.

He stared at her blankly.

"You should go," she said.

"Jess!"

"Please go."

He looked hurt. She didn't care.

As she spoke, she disrobed and found pieces of clothing in a dresser drawer, donning them. Her body felt firm and not bloated at all. She had gone off the Pill to time her period to end a week before the tournament, and felt physically perfect as she pulled a jog bra in place. "You've abandoned your net game," she said harshly. "You lose a few points and you back off of it instead of trusting it. If you trusted your own talent more you'd win more matches. It's why you do so well in doubles: You lean on your own confidence in your partner, and you're forced to play more net. Confidence and your net game are the only things standing in your way of winning a Grand Slam event. Everyone says the same thing. It's all anyone says bad about you. You have more natural talent than anyone on the court. More physical ability. It's the head game for you. And your net play. You're the Tower of Power, Khol. That nickname didn't just happen."

His mouth hung open, as did his robe from his turning in his chair to face her. "Since when do you . . . ?"

"Since now," she interrupted. "I have a match to play. I need some alone time. I've got to hit some balls."

"Who the hell was it?" he asked, florid-faced and coming out of the chair.

She pulled on the shorts, slipped on the plain white T, and sat down on the unmade bed to find her way into socks and shoes. There would be press in the lobby. And quite possibly *him.* A shiver ran through her. "I'm going out the back," she informed him. "The kitchen."

"They'll still find you. And when they do, they'll ask why all the subterfuge."

She knew he was right. "So I'll use the lobby, but I won't say anything."

"And neither will I, if that's what you're worried about."

It wasn't what worried her, but she didn't tell him that. "Fine," she said. But she wasn't fine. That call had ruined everything.

• • •

Forest Park, the Central Park of St. Louis, steeped in heat and humidity like a cup of fine tea. One hour and fifty-eight minutes after the close of her press conference that celebrated a win over the aging star, Jessie climbed out of the Town Car instructing the driver to wait in the main parking lot. Her face was not known to everyone, the way a Venus Williams or Martina Hingis might have been, but her carriage and composure attracted attention nonetheless as did that badge of physical beauty she wore. A few heads turned, but fortunately, no autograph seekers.

She paused, looking around for him. Not wanting to see him. Hoping he might not show. She had played revisionist history on the drive over, remembering the events of four years earlier on her own terms. Reinventing the wheel. How easy she found it to challenge the actual facts as she knew them and mold them to suit her needs. Players did this with line calls, so why couldn't she negotiate with the Devil? He put that sound of tennis in her ears late at night, after all. She knew the source of such phenomena. Four years those sounds had been keeping her awake. There were few surprises left in her life.

A wide-faced man in his late thirties, Michael carried a row of hair implants in his forehead, a thick, flat gold chain around his neck, and a wristwatch that probably weighed a pound or more. Brown, unflinching eyes. Confident to the point of alarming. He sat with his legs spread apart, his black-and-white checked shirt stretched at the buttons, his pant cuffs riding to the middle of elastic socks. If his teeth were his, which she doubted, they were bleached to the point of blinding. She kept her sunglasses on, and switched her purse to her other shoulder out of habit—always protecting the racquet arm.

"The television does not do you justice," he said.

"You'll never be Tony Soprano, so don't try so hard."

He pursed his lips, as if ready to spit. "Sit."

"Not on your life."

"It is not my life we are here to discuss."

She said, "Do I look scared?" She delivered this impressively. Inside, she was cowering.

"I am going to stand up and you are going to let me hug you. I am going to put my hands on you in ways and in places you will not like. My apologies. But a person cannot be too careful." He rose then, before she could object. She had half expected this precaution from him, so she merely winced and accepted the embrace that led to hands on her back, on her bottom, her underarms and between her breasts. He pulled it off smoothly, without it looking like he was frisking her for a listening device.

She wanted a shower.

"We will walk," he said.

They walked.

"We had an agreement," she said.

"It is true. I feel badly about this. I am only the messenger."

"Four years and no promotion? I'd talk to my union rep if I were you." She said, "You own the unions, but do you have one for yourselves? The Wise Guy Guild?"

"You are nervous. I can understand that."

"You understand nothing," she said. "What's the point of an agreement if you break it?"

"Half of all marriages end in divorce. Did you know that?"

She said, "That doesn't justify your being here, so don't even try. We had an agreement. That's the end of it." She added, "I *knew* you people would do this."

"Good. Then it's not a surprise." He said, "It is not the end of it."

"You arrogant son of a bitch."

The latest fad, silver scooters from Japan, streamed past

like bullet trains, small kids at the controls. Jessie switched to Michael's other side to avoid a collision.

"Injury," Michael said, "is a player's biggest enemy. Do you agree?"

She caught her breath, a pain where her heart should have been, her lungs locked, like swallowing too much food at once.

"You will reach the semifinals without much competition now," Michael continued. "You will lose the semis in three sets. A tiebreaker adds fifty to the three-fifty that will be deposited into any account you tell us."

"Forget it," she said.

"I wish I could." He said, "Five hundred *and* the deed to a condominium in Naples, if you reach and lose the finals. An extra hun if it goes to a tiebreaker."

"You'll pay me six hundred to lose it?"

"And they'll pay you two-fifty."

"But I win seven-fifty if I win," she said. "And I will win."

Michael shook his head, discouraged. "I will be in a LiveWire chat room tomorrow night, called Common Cents. I will be TheWiseMan. Give me the account information then, and I will know you have agreed. Fail to make that chat room and you take matters into your own hands—for as long as they remain hands, that is." He added, "They will hurt you, Jessie. Or that boyfriend of yours. I do not wish that to happen."

"Oh, fuck off."

Michael did just that. She wanted to call him back, to argue. But he took a path to the right and continued walking at the same lazy pace. Jessie stopped, knowing better than to follow, shivering cold. A bead of sweat dripped coolly down her rib cage.

"I won't do this!" Her protest suffocated by the trees and bushes.

"Of course you will." He said this without looking back. People like Michael never looked back.

.   .   .

"Why the game face on a night you should be celebrating?"

She and Khol sat side by side in the stands. Eighth row. On net. A doubles match, the winners of which Khol might face in a night game the following day. Blistering serves from all players. Net play like gunfire.

"You know that for the women, this is the richest purse on the tour," she said.

"Men, too. Tobacco company, don't forget. *Serious* public relations problems. They've got to do something."

"Seven hundred and fifty thousand dollars," she said.

"One-point-two-five for the woodies." He never took his eye off the play. "It's not an excuse. You can't allow yourself to be intimidated by a purse, Jess. Players, yes. Though not you. Not at this point. You've held your ground with all of them. Do not psych yourself out." He added, "Did you mean that this morning? About my net play?"

"Sort of."

"You either meant it or not."

"I was angry."

"That phone call."

"Yes."

He said, "You still haven't told me."

"No, and I'm not going to."

She stood up on the television time-out.

"Something I said?" he asked, meaning it as a joke.

"The loo. Right back."

Khol grabbed her by the wrist. She wondered if the television cameras would capture this moment. Or the tabloids. Her life was Kodachrome. Fuji. The Internet. Beauty and athleticism could be lethal. It could also be profitable. Until that phone call, winning the tournament had meant not only the astounding purse, but also a lucrative endorsement for an athletic shoe company that her agent had been negotiating for four months. One win here, everything fell into place. She was three games away from that. Except for Michael.

He was four rows back, on the aisle, looking right at her. Sight of him caught her breath. Her knees felt weak.

He meant everything he had said. She had known this all along, but sight of him now cemented that certainty. Two young fans jumped out of their seats. Two more. A security man by the stadium tunnel spotted this onslaught, recognizing her, and moved to intercept.

"Seats everyone." The umpire's voice reverberating.

Jessie fired off four autographs. The security man ushered her into the tunnel. "Terrific game this morning," he said. She turned her head, knowing he had said something to her, but having not caught it, unsure how to respond.

She had lied to Khol: she wasn't returning to her seat. Lied to herself for the last four years. She felt like she had cramps. Her eyes stung and her throat was dry. Everyone seemed to be looking at her. Some of them said things to her, but she wasn't hearing right. To her, all the voices were like the umpire's. "Seats everyone." She lived inside an echo chamber. She tried to smile, to use it as her answer, her response to these approaches. She fended off a few more fans and made it to the women's room, realizing too late she should have gone the extra distance and used the player's locker room.

Inside, two women at the sinks and mirrors looked over and grinned at her, unsure how to act. Forty-year-olds, and they stood there like gum-chewing teens backstage at a rock concert. A stall door swung open and the woman there did a double take, sizing her up and down like a side of beef. Or an imposter. She felt more like the latter.

Over the speaker, *thwack, thwack, thwack,* just like the night before as she lay awake in her bed.

She struggled inside the stall, locked the door. Sat down on the open toilet, her pants still up. Placing her face in her palms, she cried. Softly at first, and then loudly enough to silence even the whispering going on in front of the mirrors.

The tabloids would get this for sure.

• • •

Ignoring the amber blinking light on the hotel telephone that indicated waiting messages, Jessie entered the Internet chat room as she had been advised. She signed on as "Player," searching the chat room's right-hand column for any sign of TheWiseMan, but Michael had not yet joined the chat. A dozen people in attendance online wrote messages back and forth, alone and secure in their anonymity, using nicknames that ranged from bordering on the obscene, "hotlicks," to the absurd, "AG45&~6." The latter was referred to as "Aggie" in the one-line messages that confirmed how meaningless a life could get.

hotlicks:::hi Player. Welcome!
AG45&~6:::Player of what?

Her fingers rested on the keys. A player in trouble. A player in need. A player in over her head. Which way should she answer? Tennis, the truth, never came close to her fingertips.

To her left lay the slip of paper bearing the account number from a bank in Belize. She had not used this account in four years, and yet maintained a balance of nearly ten thousand dollars. She wondered why she had kept this account open all these years. Why hadn't she closed it five or six months after the U.S. Open, after the majority of the quarter-million had been moved to other accounts? What had possessed her? Had she known all along that this day would come? Was she so predictable?

Blink. A name to the right of the screen. TheWiseMan. There, waiting for her. For this account number. The other attendees welcomed him: Hi, WiseMan. Welcome. Aggie asked: How wise?

TheWiseMan:::Looking for a friend.

There were any number of mistakes either of them might have made. But his using the word "friend" proved fatal. Her fingers hesitated, hovering over the number keys, ready to type out the account for him. But then, reading his comment, she clicked the <Log Off> button instead, and the name "Player" disappeared from the chat room's list.

She could feel Michael's anger as she shut down the laptop and closed it. She wondered and worried how that anger might manifest itself. But nothing in the world could will her to reconnect and provide him that account information. Ironically, he already had this account number somewhere in his records. It was her giving it that he wanted: the full weight of her consent. Her participation. Her capitulation. Her compromise. And that wouldn't come. Not tonight. Not any time soon.

She drew herself a hot bath, and attempted to feel clean.

•   •   •

The schedule put her quarterfinal match in front of USA Network's prime-time cameras the following night, so she saw no problem accepting a late-evening dinner with Khol and sleeping in a bit. The Town Car picked them up from the lobby at 8:30, and drove them toward Trattoria Marcella on the hill for a 9:00 reservation.

The driver said, "Paparazzi alert, Ms. Jenkin. They've been with us since the hotel."

Neither she nor Khol turned back to look. There would be a camera aimed at the back window just waiting to catch their faces, or a kiss, or whatever could be captured.

"Can we lose them?" She didn't need this tonight.

"I tried something simple just after the hotel."

"I caught that," Khol said, remembering the odd set of turns.

"I can run a light," the driver said. "But it risks my license. I'd rather not."

"Of course not," Jessie replied. She looked to Khol for guidance.

Khol said to the driver, "Please try a couple turns, run some yellow lights and see what happens. Either way, it is not a problem. It is only dinner." To Jessie he said, "You did not tell me we were having company for dinner." It amused him, this comment.

"When don't we have company?" she asked, her mood

sour. She had hoped time with Khol might remove her from everything, but it only sent her more deeply inside herself.

"They never leave us alone."

"Oh, they will one day, Jess. And we will both wish we had them back."

"Not me."

"Yes, you, too. It is the human condition, I'm afraid."

She took his hand in hers, lacing fingers. Their hands, arms, legs—their bodies—carried their livelihood, their paychecks, their futures. They guarded their health, they worked out to prevent tears and strains. For her, the game was as much about the mind, but lacing fingers with him turned her thoughts to the mortal body and its fragility.

"We need to take a break," she said spontaneously. "You and me."

"You asked me out to dinner to dump me?" He didn't sound hurt in the least.

"It's funny to you?"

"You amuse me. Women, in general. Are you serious?"

She asked, "Would I say something like that if I wasn't serious?"

"I am asking you," he said. "Are you serious? If you are, you are eating alone tonight."

She craned forward, holding on through several turns by the driver. "Are they still back there?" she shouted forward.

"Maybe not," the driver said. "I don't think so," he added.

Khol grabbed her by the arm to win her attention.

"I don't know," she said to him.

"You must decide. Alone, or together? I will live through it. Believe me." He smiled contentedly.

"Together," she answered without hesitation.

He nodded, the smile widening. "Good. That is the end of it, then. We have got that straight." He pulled her hand into his crotch. "Other things, too."

"It turns you on?"

He said, "When you are angry? Yes. Very much. It is your neck, I think. So red like that." Leaning across the backseat and touching her thigh, he added, "Red at other times, too."

"You're completely weird."

"We will deal with that later."

She took her hand back, smiling along with him. For a moment, Michael was nowhere in her thoughts.

But only for a moment.

      • • •

The Town Car awaited around the corner. Their dinner at Trattoria Marcella had stretched to two hours, aided by calamari over flash-fried spinach, polenta, lobster risotto and a bottle of Chianti. At eleven o'clock, Watson Road remained busy.

Perhaps, if either of them had bothered to note the license plate of the earlier Town Car, they might have picked up the deception. But with bellies full, faces flushed, and loins eager, the couple sauntered up to the limousine, tried the rear door, Khol immediately knocking on the window, and listened for the door lock to release. He offered for her to climb in first, in part because he wanted to see her skirt ride up her luxurious legs. Dinner with her had proved tantalizing. He wanted to take her while she was dressed like that, standing, and against the wall in her hotel room. He wanted those legs around his waist.

"I'm in a mood," he said, pulling the door shut.

The car pulled away from the curb, executed a sloppy U-turn, and turned right onto Watson.

With no divider in the Town Car to isolate the driver, Jessie limited her response to an admonishing pursing of her lips, followed with a slight flick of her pink tongue and a suggestive licking of her upper lip. Khol replied with raised eyebrows. He seemed to be daring her. She shook her head "no." Not in the car.

Khol was the first to notice. "Is this the way we came?"

No reply from the driver.

"Excuse me . . ."

The driver turned up the radio. Some hip-hop crap that neither of them liked.

"Turn that down!" said Khol.

"Driver," said Jessie.

"Hey!" said Khol.

A left turn that clearly aimed them away from their Clayton destination.

Jessie reached to unclip her seat belt only to find the mechanism didn't release. Khol, who hadn't bothered with his seat belt, leaned over to try to help her.

"Driver," Khol hollered again.

Jessie abandoned her seat belt efforts and fumbled with the door lock. It too had been sabotaged—a piece unscrewed, leaving her nothing to grab onto.

"Oh, shit," she said. "Khol . . . It's me . . . my fault. I fucked up. The Open. Oh, my God!"

The car stopped sharply, throwing Khol forward. The driver climbed out and came around back, so close to the vehicle that Jessie couldn't see his face. Khol was up and pounding on his door.

"No . . . no!" Jessie said, clumsily slipping out of the fastened seat belt, all knees and snags. "No, Khol!"

But as his door came open, an irate Khol lunged for freedom, to make his objections heard. It happened fast: a knee to his face, his arm pinned half-in, half-out of the car, and then the door slamming hard. The sharp sound of a bone snapping like a small tree limb. His cry, loud and savage. The door slamming again. Khol, on his knees, slipping to the car's leather interior, unconscious, his face pale and ghastly. Drool and vomit. That hip-hop so loud that it rattled the car's trim. The car door sagged open.

Jessie thought she heard a car behind them.

Khol's right arm had a red lump midforearm the size of a softball.

"Somebody help," Jessie said, her voice buried by the radio. "Somebody help," she repeated, more earnestly. *"Help me!"* Then she muttered, "My fault, my fault, my fault," and reached over to attempt to resuscitate Khol.

• • •

She slept alone that night, lock and chain and a chair braced against the hotel room door. The phone unplugged. The police had ruled it a stalking, the Town Car having been rented on a counterfeit credit card that came up valid, but belonged to no one. Ironically, because of the stalker designation, the press was not informed. The two reporters who scanned the radios and had caught on to Jessie's and Khol's celebrity were tricked by officers at the emergency room, allowing Jessie to get out of the hospital unseen.

She understood perfectly well that all that did was delay things. The press had its way. It would make ink at some point.

If she were lucky, the cover story, invented by the cops, would hold: Limo slams on its brakes, Khol snaps his forearm because he wasn't wearing his seat belt. The *Enquirer* headline would read something like: Crash Test Dummy: Tennis Star Double-faults!

She passed on taking a pill in order to sleep. Didn't want to mix it with the wine. Naked, in fresh sheets. Air turned way up to chill the room. She cried, sobered, and cried again. Khol's eyes, unforgiving and wounded right before they drugged him for surgery. A plate and two titanium screws. Six to twelve months. They claimed he'd play again, though she wondered how much was for his spirits, how much the truth. Would he serve 110? Would he ache every time a storm approached? Would he ever talk to her again?

She should have kept her mouth shut. Shouldn't have blurted out that bit about the Open. Maybe he'd been in shock. Maybe he hadn't heard. Those eyes said something different, but she allowed a moment of self-deception while hoping for sleep.

Instead, she heard that sound. *Thwack . . . thwack.* She willed it away. Then she pulled a pillow over her head and she swore it lessened. Five minutes. Ten. It continued inside her head. She climbed out of bed, found a T-shirt in a drawer and pulled it on before heading to the blinds. The T-shirt barely reached her crotch, but the balcony would block her from the waist down, unless some adventuresome photographer had bribed his way onto the hotel roof and was looking down on her from across the hotel's lazy curve of glass and plaster. This thought stopped her. She pulled on a pair of underwear. She made a point of not pulling the blinds, not sending any signals. She slipped inside the blackout curtain, between this and the sheer. Then she parted the sheer, unlocked the sliding door and cracked it open a few inches. The sound was louder. The courts were empty.

• • •

Jessie faced an Australian in the semis, a performance-enhanced woman with big hands, wide shoulders and a kick-ass serve. Her groundstrokes came over the net extremely low, difficult for the eye to pick up, and consistently powerful. One in ten caught the net's tape and lumbered across unpredictably, inevitably a point for her. The players called such net shots Funky Chickens, and this Australian could have opened her own restaurant. Her vulnerability came in a backhand that while extremely powerful, always came down the line. Always. Never a crosscourt. Never even a passing shot. Jessie believed she could rush net and exploit this trait to victory, as long as she could push the woman into the corner and make her take those backhands. But the woman knew her own weaknesses and tended to avoid her backhand as much as possible. When she did take one, she hit cleanly and she hit hard right for the far corner. She could move you out of position with that shot, force you to expose too much of the court, and the power behind it required immediate commitment. Jessie made her move to the baseline corner as the woman wound up for those backhands, thankful just to return them. It was a dominant net game that made that predictable a shot a liability, and it was the net game that Jessie exploited.

"If you're going to lose the semis, you'd better make it three sets."

But she wasn't going to lose the semis. She took the first set in a tiebreaker and sensed victory. She pounded shots into that backhand corner, feeling that her racquet connected with Michael's head each time she clobbered the ball.

At the start of the second set she spotted him in the stands. She lost a break because of that—her nerves getting the better of her. He had the audacity to offer a small wave—catching her looking. But then she broke right back love–40, a humiliating service for her opponent, and what proved to be the final straw. It was the first of three more breaks. A trouncing. She hurried off the court, denying the television commentator an interview, a breach of contract that would cost her ten thousand dollars. She refused an interview in the studio as well, another ten thousand. Michael would be pleased by the victory, of course, and it angered her that she couldn't score any points against him. Not yet, anyway.

· · ·

Jessie watched the night game of the other women's semi from her hotel room. She wore bags of hotel ice taped to both ankles and both knees—a trick she'd practiced for some time now. The ice kept any possible swelling down. After two decades on every kind of tennis court surface, she had the joints of a fifty-year-old. She swallowed two Advils, adjusted her pillows and turned the sound up so she could cover that *other* sound. It had begun about ten minutes earlier: the familiar swoosh and slap of a tennis volley. The problem was that no one was out there playing on the hotel courts at this hour.

She didn't really care whom she faced in the finals, though she slightly favored the number-two-ranked player, the Czech, Sylvia Brazinski, with the big backhand, little legs and average serve. She could tire out Brazinski if she played a good, solid net game, and maybe win a break off that serve, although as a leftie Brazinski proved difficult to return. They had rarely met on the court, and Jessie felt confident of her chances.

The knock on the door to her suite caught her by surprise, and a trill of adrenaline spiked her system as if she'd been slapped from behind. "Busy!" she called out, not wanting to deal with the carefully rigged bags of ice on her joints.

She couldn't make out any of the words of the voice on the other side of the door, through the suite's living room, but its rich Scandinavian timbre gave away Khol, and she felt moved to greet him. She hobbled toward the door, checked the peep hole and threw the locks, admitting him. In a camisole, bikini underwear and taped up with lopsided bags of ice, she imagined herself quite the sight.

His arm was slinged and in a cast. He looked much paler than she'd ever seen him. She wondered how a court tan could fade so quickly. She locked the door behind him, and began crying before she turned around. She hated herself for this show of weakness.

"It's all right, it's all right," he comforted her. "I'm glad it wasn't you. They could have raped you. Killed us. They must have planned to kidnap us, don't you think?" She loved the lilt to his voice, but it made him sound all the more naive as he assessed their assault incorrectly.

"We have to talk."

"I came to watch Brazinski with you," he said, drying her eyes of the tears. "Thought you could use the company."

"We'll watch in a minute." She led him into the suite's living room, and Khol must have known something was up: Jessie was far too great a competitor not to watch every last second of this semifinal match.

"Jess?"

"I have something to tell you. I hope you won't hate me. But even if you do, I've got to tell you."

"Who is he?" Khol said suspiciously, unwilling to be seated.

She burst out laughing, in a nervous volley of release. "I wish!" she said. "Sit," she instructed again, and this time Khol sat down. Jessie turned one of the overstuffed chairs to face him.

"What the hell's going on?"

She said, "I threw the Open. Four years ago. That loss to Crispin?"

"You what?"

"I owed some people a lot of money. Khol, I'm in big trouble."

•   •   •

The most difficult part of their plan was acquiring twenty thousand dollars in cash in less than three hours. Khol turned to his sports agent in Chicago, a man named Stan Feingold, who was instructed come hell or high water he was to deliver the amount in cash to Khol before the end of the second set, as no one could predict if Jessie's match against Brazinski would go the distance and reach a third set.

This part of the plan was never mentioned to the FBI handlers who jumped in on the case following Jessie's call late the night before. They might have thrown her and Khol in jail for even thinking about it, but as it was, the federal agents' full focus remained on obtaining warrants for cellular phone surveillance and establishing perimeter security in the face of four thousand adoring fans, any one of whom could be a mob-hired hit man. Hit *woman,* for that matter.

Jessie had been up until four in the morning; had gotten only four hours' sleep as a result of the interviewing (interrogating was more like it) and the lawyering (her attorney in New

York, Susan Steiger, had obtained representation for her here with a firm specializing in criminal defense). She realized she faced an uphill battle in the match against Brazinski—not that it actually mattered. Even when in top physical shape, Jessie found the southpaw no pushover. They'd met seven times. Jessie had won four. Three of the last five. She held a psychological edge, but the wear and tear of the previous late-night negotiations, while supporting the FBI plan, threatened her own.

The FBI plan called for her to lose a close match, preferably in three sets. Michael would believe she had capitulated to his demands following the violence done to Khol and would pay her off for services rendered. This payoff would be monitored and intercepted and recorded by authorities. At the very least, Michael, and perhaps his associates along with him, would do some serious time.

For agreeing to throw the match, to cooperate, the FBI had offered that her criminal wrongdoing at the Open four years before would be expunged from her interrogation transcripts in return for a fine equal to her tournament winnings and her payoff for throwing the Open, plus interest, plus a one-year hiatus from the sport. For this, she would serve no jail time and the ATA would be led to believe this tournament was the only attempt at extortion and that Jessie had come forward of her own free will following the harm done to Khol.

With each of the concerned parties scheduled to win something from the deal, all Jessie had to do was lose, and walk away from the sport for a year, possibly the best tennis she'd ever played—to throw away everything she had worked toward for her entire life. With a victory here, in a major, she would gain enough points to hold the number-one ranking in the world for at least two weeks—the date of the next scheduled major.

She walked out onto that court amid a roar of applause, captured by live television cameras, a mass of confusion, awaiting a sign from Khol that Stan Feingold and his twenty thousand in cash had reached the stadium. Waiting for a sign they could satisfy the FBI's needs, while satisfying their own as well.

A person couldn't always do the right thing.

• • •

Having only twenty-five minutes to warm up, and under the considerable pressure of not only a finals appearance in a major, but a match of such magnitude in terms of national ranking, Jessie approached the first game cautiously. Her return of serve revealed itself as her most obvious weakness and Brazinski capitalized, pummeling ninety-mile-an-hour SCUDS so close to the service tape that twice Jessie waited for Cyclops to chirp his out-of-bounds alert, only to realize the serve had been good. She hadn't even seen the thing. Forty-love. Brazinski won not only the first game, but a piece of the crowd. As number two in the world, Brazinski had legions of adoring fans. Jessie, at a current ranking of number five wasn't quite as well-loved. (It was only through the mathematics of computer-rated standings, enhanced by the number-one player having lost in the first round in her last two majors, that either Brazinski or Jessie had a shot at the bullet. The number-three player had been ambushed by a random drug testing and had showed positive for a performance enhancer that everyone in the locker room knew she was taking—in point of fact, she'd probably been sandbagged by a player or a player's agent in an

effort to get her off the rankings, which seemed inevitable.)
But Brazinski claimed the crowd early. She wore a very tight
top, which would be soaked through in perspiration in a matter of minutes to the pleasure of all the men attending (she
was famous for this wet T-shirt look, and had twice been cen-
sured by the ATA, but the networks weren't complaining,
given the ratings whenever she played), a white and blue
pleated skirt so short that it rose off her cheeks every time she
lifted to serve. It was the way of women's tennis—part athlet-
ics, part soft porn. The real money came from endorsements,
millions a year to the number-one-ranked player who had a
body worthy of national television and billboard ads. The butt-
faces didn't get nearly the offers that the glamour queens did.
In this day and age it wasn't enough to be coached on your
backhand, your media coach meant the difference between
winning and stardom, and stardom paid for the fractional ownership of a private jet, stretch limos, presidential suites, private
masseuses, personal chefs and the rest of the entourage. Jessie
didn't appreciate losing the crowd so early in the match. Now,
instead of having Brazinski to beat, she could add seven thousand
others to the list.

The two women traded service wins up to a first-set
tiebreaker that Jessie understood represented the match.
Brazinski no doubt knew this as well, but Jessie wasn't allowing herself to think about Brazinski, nor the crowd, nor the
fact that Khol had yet to show himself at the appointed place
to signal the arrival of the cash, and therefore, the start of their
plan. Instead, she took a series of deep breaths and pushed
away the cheering and catcalling, knowing that she had re-
gained a large part of the house with her aggressive play, while
Brazinski, as steady as a workhorse, had disappointed the

crowd by her cautious adoption of minimal net play. Jessie considered this a clinic—she was going to show Brazinski how to win both at the net and in the bleachers. She had always played well under pressure, and surely Brazinski knew this about her as well. Tiebreakers played to Jessie's favor. Warmed up now, she muted the sound on the playback of the crowd and focused entirely on that yellow ball. There was nothing in this world but that yellow ball, and each time it tried to get past her, she smacked it, disciplining it and mandating it return to its corner. If it dared to come back at her, she smacked it again, actually talking to it in her head. "Oh, no you don't." "Back you go, little one." "Not this time." She clocked the damn thing. Smashed it into submission, turning its spherical shape oblong, raising fuzz dust off her racquet and cheers from the stands. Harder and harder she hit it, to where she knew she'd found the zone. That yellow ball was hers now. It wasn't going to obey Brazinski. It didn't dare. Jessie took the tiebreaker and a standing ovation, before an official time-out for a network ad and a court change.

In the third game of the second set, Brazinski broke, following Jessie's identification of Khol at the mouth of exit 7, just below the huge TIMEX sign that posted their scores. Khol made an "E" by extending three fingers, and then flashed his hands to signal "34." Jessie's concentration slipped, she double-faulted due to a shitty overruled call on the part of the dykish umpire, and for four and a half minutes she lost focus. In those four and a half minutes she set herself up to lose the second set. Breaking back would not be easy—Brazinski had a feel now for her own reluctance on return of serve, and she exploited it with two aces in a row. The crowd, so very much in her camp at the end of the tiebreaker, began to slip back toward the more familiar competitor, cheering on those aces and turning up the volume with each convincing point.

Jessie buckled down and prepared for the battle of her career.

She glanced over, ensuring that Khol had reported correctly. There, just below the COPPERTONE ad, Michael sat in seat E-34. He, too, was cheering on the aces that suggested a Brazinski second-set victory.

• • •

Khol received the twenty thousand dollars in an aluminum briefcase. He couldn't tell his agent what he was doing without risking the man's career, and the agent didn't want to know for this very same reason. A look passed between them that conveyed the agent's concern, disappointment and regret at having participated in any of this. That look warned that he hoped Khol knew what he was doing.

That made two of them.

The tennis circuit, like all of pro sports, is filled with wannabes, groupies, hangers-on and the suckerfish that cling to one's belly hoping to eat the scraps. The forbidden vice of gambling is rampant—players gamble all the time (seldom on their own games, which is highly illegal and frowned upon even by the most addicted gamblers), using bagmen to place their bets. Khol was not a gambler. He leaned toward the luxury of the groupies—knowing that he could have sex, any kind of sex at all, at nearly any time of day in any city with no responsibility toward maintaining a relationship. Like many of the men on the tour, he knew fine-looking, willing women in dozens of cities around the globe and kept his Palm Pilot brimming with current phone numbers. That he was now involved with Jessie put much of this into the past for him, but when he needed a bagman to place a bet, it required only a trip up to Todd Seaborn's suite on the fifth floor and a passing of that briefcase, one hand to the next. Within minutes, a twenty-thousand-dollar bet was placed on the outcome of the finals match taking place on the court below and currently airing on a national television network. A fee of two thousand dollars was to be paid for special delivery, if the bet paid out. It was placed for Jessie to win the match in three sets. The odds were four to one in favor of Brazinski given a three-set final. As Khol walked out of that suite, that briefcase was suddenly either eighty thousand dollars fat, or dead empty. Only Jessie could control the outcome.

• • •

She never recovered the break. Brazinski won the second set 6–4 to thunderous applause, and the match headed into the third set. To see the look on Michael's face, one might have mistaken him for a cheerleader. He left his seat early in the third set. Jessie wondered if he was gone for good, or to the men's room, or to check in with his bosses over the cell phone. If the last, the FBI was likely listening in at this very moment, and Michael was on his way to exposing his employers. Files would be created. Transcripts of the conversations would be generated. The U.S. attorney's office would be on the way to building a case worth prosecuting.

Jessie returned to her earlier success, punishing the ball in regular strokes with a focus and concentration unmatched in any of the contests leading up to this final. Seeing Khol's signal and knowing their plan was under way allowed her a freedom of thought, a peace of mind, overcoming her anxieties, and permitting her to dedicate herself to the task at hand—defeating Brazinski and upsetting the FBI's sting. She met the ball with the full force of her body; nothing felt quite as good to her as a perfectly executed groundstroke, not even sex, if truth be known. Everything paled by comparison. That one perfect stroke, the ball launched a quarter-inch above the net, the fuzz practically peeled off, trained into the exact spot on the court that the mind intended as if she talked it down through a perfect landing. She sprang back into position, a light bounce to her step, not an ounce of fatigue in her joints or muscles, the racquet already preparing itself—a mind of its own—setting up for another devastating power shot that sprang from her strings like a bullet.

God, but she loved this game.

No one, nothing, was going to take it from her life. Especially Sylvia Brazinski.

· · ·

The first "Ditti" (Digital Telephone Intercept) recorded by the FBI techs at the corporate headquarters of the Global Wireless Corporation intercepted a call from one Michael Raphael to an AT&T wireless owned by Sebastian Califoni, aka "Sid" Califoni, a known racketeer, bookie and gambler who was believed to be tied to the Umbrizi family, a Vegas-based coalition of mobbed-up accounting firms that connected six of the biggest casinos. This call set into motion the possibility of raiding Sid Califoni's residence, which in turn presented the hope that some connection to the Umbrizis might be found. If so, the house of cards would come tumbling down.

Anthony Meta, the St. Louis Field Office's SAC, monitored events from the fairways of the Ladue Country Club by cell phone, wanting to be kept apprised of events but not daring to pass up an invitation to one of the area's premiere courses. His next in command, Donna Fabiano, a woman he'd wanted to bone since she'd been assigned to him, but a woman he would never touch for fear of losing his coveted job, kept tabs on operation Close Shave and reported to her SAC at regular intervals. By the time Tony Meta was informed the chain of command might lead to the Umbrizis his golf game had gone to shit as his concentration waned, and he learned a painful lesson: It's far better to opt out on a golf game at this level than duff through the back nine looking like a kid learning the game.

Donna Fabiano felt giddy with excitement. Sid Califoni. It made sense he'd be corrupting players to shave points and throw games in support of his gambling connections. No doubt a Brazinski win would put tens, maybe even hundreds, of thousands into his pockets. She quickly notified the federal prosecutors to go after the necessary warrants for her to monitor all incoming and outgoing calls to Sid Califoni's home, car and cell phone. The nice thing about the federal court system was that it could move quickly. She sat back, notifying her technicians to begin the necessary work to wiretap Califoni, absolutely convinced those warrants would be in place in a matter of minutes. Now, with a Brazinski win, all was set for the upset of the decade—and that upset had nothing to do with tennis. Thank God, she thought, that Jessie had come to them and was now going to throw the game. When Califoni's winnings came in, they would have an airtight case against him.

Watching the television monitor installed into the Global Wireless Corporation's tech center, one of Fabiano's aides said,

"She's sure trying awfully hard for a person who's supposed to lose."

It was the first bit of queasiness Fabiano experienced. She turned her attention to the television.

It wouldn't be her last.

• • •

At the height of the third set, Jessie no longer felt her body. Somewhere along the way she had merged with the tennis racquet, had *become* the tennis racquet, and now every twitch of muscle, every drip of sweat was aimed at the ball. The ball was everything. She even lost score for a while—something that seldom happened to her—as she focused only on winning each point, not how those points added up. She took the third, fourth and fifth games in nine minutes, a period of time that reporters would later refer to as "perfect tennis." Clips from those three games would run for years on television, as Jessie made her mark not merely as a player, but as *the* player. It was nine minutes of women's tennis no one had ever seen before. Jessie had attained Knighthood, win or lose.

Losing seemed out of the question. The racquet wouldn't let her, Khol wouldn't let her, and finally the crowd wouldn't let her. Brazinski was the last to understand the preordained nature of their competition. It simply wasn't in the cards. Jessie briefly attained the stature of a tennis god, and poor Brazinski found herself on the other side of the same net, giving it her absolute best, and finding it largely insufficient. No matter what she threw at Jessie, the ball came back lower, faster and more perfectly placed. When Brazinski broke her racquet in frustration in the ninth game of the third set, when Jessie delivered a heat-seeking overhead slam to lead 5–4, the television color commentator called the game. "It's over," she said. "Mark my word, Jessie is going to break for match. This one's already over."

• • •

Khol worked the needles out of the fingers of his broken arm as he looked on from a hidden vantage point as Michael Raphael began checking around himself in the stands for any faces he might recognize. With his job to "bring in" Jessie now in question, Michael Raphael had to wonder if his boss had already dispatched the knee-cappers to teach him a lesson about crossing the mob. Khol reveled in the moment and prepared to act out his own risky role in their plot. Raphael, no doubt, still clung to the belief that Jessie would throw what could be the final game, tying the match and inching it toward a 6–6 tiebreaker. But if he was watching the same match as the other seven thousand spectators he knew differently, and hence his increasing concern. Jessie did not have the look of a woman about to lose the final. She was on fire. The crowd could barely contain itself. This match was already over.

Khol placed a call to Todd Seaborn and said but one word, "Go." He hung up. Over the course of the next ten minutes every bookie in this town—and more important, a few in Las Vegas—would hear that Michael Raphael had placed a twenty-thousand-dollar bet on Jessie *to win*. The bookie who had handled the bet would be mentioned by name. Khol couldn't allow all the information to be passed along, not without the setup being spotted for what it was, so he left the rest of it up to greed and malice. The people for whom Raphael worked would already be disconcerted by Jessie's sensational performance. When word came that their own bagman had placed twenty large on a *victory* by the woman who was supposed to shave points, the shit would hit the racquet. Khol's only concern now was that he manage to pull off placing himself squarely in the middle of the chaos that seemed certain to ensue. Anything short of that, and their efforts would fail.

· · ·

Jessie no longer saw herself as a backboard. All these years, and she realized that she'd been imagining herself as a backboard to the other player's serves. *Get in the way of the ball,* and at least it got back over. Suddenly, right there on "center court" of the finals, she found herself attacking Brazinski's serves, winding up and pounding them back down the pipe so that they seemed to return faster than they'd arrived. She caught Brazinski flat-footed and looking on in complete disbelief. The old Jessie was gone. One serve, a single stroke, and everything was different. Jessie was no longer a weak returner. A matter of attitude was all. Jessie took the game 40–love, the set, 6–4, the match 2 sets to 1. Invincible. The crowd erupted in adoration. Jessie searched the stands for any sign of Khol, and prepared herself for the acting role of a lifetime.

The color commentator hurried across the court with a camera crew. Every eye in the place was trained on her, as she shook both Brazinski's and the referee's hands and then collapsed into the chairs alongside her racquet bag.

"What's it feel like to be number one in the world?" the commentator shouted loudly over the roar of the fans.

Jessie bent over, threw a towel over her head, and cried.

· · ·

Khol had been in the stands of tennis matches his whole life and could judge their movement like a fly fisherman can judge a river's current. Michael Raphael, a relative newcomer, hadn't a clue. With his attention on the people surrounding him, now more than ever afraid the Baseball Bat Brigade would fall into lockstep somewhere behind him, Raphael misjudged which exit tunnel to push toward and got caught in the mother lode of all logjams.

Khol mastered his own entry into that throng so that Raphael could not miss seeing him (what with all the fans spotting Khol and demanding his attention) but could not reach him either. Khol made sure that their eyes met and that he smiled in a way that would both frustrate and anger Raphael. He wanted the man pissed off and raving mad. He scored on both counts.

The chase began. Raphael could punish Jessie through Khol—if he could only catch him.

The challenge would prove to be the parking lot. Again Khol knew this better than the thug who now pursued him. For this reason, Khol had a Town Car waiting *outside* any of the dozen parking garages that surrounded the downtown sports facility, parked waiting out on the street by the players' entrance to the facility. He needed Raphael to be able to follow him in the Town Car—and he needed it to seem believable that in all this mess two cars could find each other. He would make it appear that he, Khol, was waiting for Jessie. Michael Raphael was certain to check the players' entrance.

If all went well, the worm was on the hook and the hook was about to sink into the lip. He made one final call, making sure the other money they'd spent had been spent well. Only time would tell. Everything, everyone was now in place.

• • •

Jessie's interview on live television was followed by a presentation of the two trophies. Brazinski spoke eloquently and graciously about the loss, surprising everyone. "The way Jessie played today, no one on the tour could have beaten her." Jessie held up a fake check the size of a desk and paraded it around the pavilion to the cheers of many—money confirmed her the victor. She found this showy moment the most difficult of all. Did CEOs parade their checks around the stockholder meetings? Finally, the ordeal wrapped up with photos and handshakes and air kisses—two sweaty, smelly women pretending to enjoy the exchange of sticky lips on each other's cheeks. The things the ATA put you through!

Jessie watched Brazinski head for the locker rooms as quickly as allowed. She followed a few moments later under the escort of security. The bodyguards stopped at the door to the women's dressing room, which fortunately was out of bounds for press. Jessie was allowed exactly five minutes to pee, towel off and make it to the press room for a press conference. The next thirty minutes were carefully choreographed, giving the national sports press nearly unlimited access to her.

Brazinski was heading into the press conference right as Jessie showed up to use the toilet and fix her face in the mirror. "You smoked me today," Brazinski said. "It won't happen next time." No love lost.

More than anything, Jessie wanted air. She eyed the EXIT

that led down a back hall to the players' entrance. She checked the locker room's wall clock: perfect timing.

• • •

Khol told the driver to wait another couple of minutes. He eyed the dashboard clock and asked the driver twice how accurate it was. As if on cue, a dark Pontiac with a wide grille swept around the corner, Michael Raphael behind the wheel.

"I think we'll be leaving about now," Khol said to the driver. "Remember: Let him come out of the car. We *make* him get out of that car."

Raphael pulled a U-turn and came up behind the Town Car. Khol rubbed the cast on his painful, broken arm, hoping he wasn't about to earn another.

The door at the players' entrance swung open. Autograph seekers had collected here already. A dozen or more teenage girls, some with their mothers, all prepared to wait an hour or more for the stars.

As the door opened, Jessie staggered out, bent and clutching her waist. Khol looked more closely. Her hands were covered in red. Blood everywhere. He threw open the door to the Town Car, shouted, "I'm calling nine-one-one!" and punched the number into his cell phone.

At that moment, only feet away from a fallen Jessie, Khol caught sight of Michael Raphael coming out from behind the driver's seat. A siren. Loud. Close by.

An ambulance screamed around the corner.

A step toward the front of his car, Raphael hesitated. Khol appraised the situation as well. He dove back into the Town Car. "Hit it!" he shouted to his driver, the car ripping away from the curb, while Khol struggled to pull the door shut behind him. He watched as the two EMTs hurried from the ambulance toward the fallen Jessie.

Michael Raphael's black Pontiac left twin black lanes of rubber as the car screamed off in pursuit of the Town Car.

Behind them, the small crowd parted, as the bloodied EMTs raced Jessie onto a gurney and toward the waiting ambulance.

• • •

By the time the Town Car reached the Freeview Motel off I-70, two miles from the airport, Khol's driver had nearly lost the Pontiac twice, and had a good enough lead that Khol wondered if he could make it into the rendezvous room in time. He hurried from the car, crossed through parked cars to room 108 and knocked loudly, his eyes scanning the parking lot for any occupied cars that didn't have their engines running.

Raphael skidded into the motel parking lot in time to catch the door to 108 closing, and in too great a hurry to see the car following him, as Khol was able to.

The empty Town Car sped off.

Michael Raphael parked, climbed out, and actually took a second to brush down his black clothes and inspect himself. He'd seen Khol enter that motel room.

Now, he had a job to do.

• • •

Michael Raphael grabbed a Bosnian house cleaner, working on room 210, and paid her fifty bucks to key open 108, which she did with no attempt at conversation. He thanked her and made sure she was heading back upstairs before he opened the door.

He stepped inside and closed the door. "What's this?" he said to the sturdy man he didn't recognize. The guy looked like a professional wrestler.

The bodybuilder clarified Raphael's identity. "Michael Raphael?"

"Who's asking?"

The brute opened a wheeled airline overnight bag, revealing a suitcase filled with stacks of hundred-dollar bills. "Eighty thousand dollars."

"What the fuck?"

"You wanted your winnings delivered here, pal, not me."

"What winnings?"

Califoni's goons came through the door, taking the door-jamb with it. All six men now filled the small motel room.

"Don't fucking move a muscle, Raphael," the leader of the barbershop instructed, brandishing a Glock. He was short and square and needed a change of diet.

"What we got here?" the tenor of the group asked, indicating the suitcase. "Betting against the house, Raphael?"

"Jimmy, Danny," Raphael pleaded to the leader, "this is bullshit."

"Hey," the deliveryman said, "my job is done here."

"I'd say everyone's done here," said the leader of the four, directing this to Raphael. "Go on," he told the deliveryman, "get the fuck out of here." To Raphael the man said, "This here is a no-no. A serious no-no."

One of the two others got the door basically shut behind the exit of the deliveryman.

The first blow came from Jimmy, the lean tenor. He kicked Raphael in the knee, dislocating it backward in a single stroke. Michael Raphael went down hard.

"Fifty-fucking-love, or however the fuck you say it," said Jimmy the Weasel. "Say good night, Mikey. Time for another swerve."

"Serve, you asshole," said Danny Divine, "not 'swerve.'"

"My game's bowling. What can I tell you?" With that, he dropped his shoe onto the other of Raphael's knees. Then the biggest of the four hoisted Raphael to standing, putting all his weight on both knees. He looked a Halloween scarecrow three weeks after the festivities.

His looks didn't improve from there on out.

• • •

The white paddle wheeler, which really wasn't a paddle wheeler at all, but a floating casino and cruise ship made to look like one, steamed lazily down the mighty Mississippi. The boat's largest stateroom was occupied by two people, a man and a woman who had not showed their faces to anyone but room service for the duration of the trip. Nor would they.

Jessie rolled over, naked in bed, talking into the phone. Khol teased her, his one good hand working points south, while she attempted to carry on the conversation. She clamped her legs around his hand, attempting to stop him.

"I see," she said.

"Said the blind man," Khol whispered, still trying to interrupt.

"I see," she repeated.

"You're going to see God in a minute," Khol told her.

"You're sure?" she asked into the phone. She sat up on the edge of the bed then, her back to Khol. "No. I'm fine with that. We're both fine." She made some pleasantries and hung up the cell phone. She pressed its warmth against her cheek. She asked Khol, "How did you know they'd buy that?"

"The Feds will buy anything that makes them look good and gets them the bad guys. They're much more flexible than they're given credit for being. My citizenship went the same way. You pay enough taxes, they listen to you." He hesitated and asked, "Did we get it?"

"The ATA will report that I'm healing from my stabbing and won't return to the circuit for six to seven months. I keep my winnings and my ranking holds until the next tournament."

He hugged her from behind: This had been all they'd wanted. They'd risked everything to win it.

"Michael Raphael?" he asked.

"Alive. Brutally beaten. Won't be skateboarding any time soon. He turned state's witness, as did the four others they rounded up at the motel. He rolled on Califoni. No word on whether that gets back to Umbrizi or not. They—the Feds, I'm talking about—apparently asked about the ambulance. Who had arranged for it to pick me up."

"Don't look at me."

"We—Jan, my attorney, I'm talking about—denied any knowledge of the ambulance. The Feds were pissed we did this to them, but as you said all along, with the warrants in place, and the arrests, they put the best spin possible on the situation and never mentioned the ulterior plan. As far as everyone knows, this was their plan all along. I was never supposed to lose."

"Would it were so."

"We're in the clear, Khol. You did it."

"We did it."

She entwined her fingers in his and squeezed, holding him to her breast. "We got away with it."

"You're number one. Congratulations, Best Woman Tennis Player in the World."

"For two weeks."

"For Two Weeks," he added to her title.

They made love and ordered room service, and for the first time in five years she ate whatever she wanted to eat. She wouldn't allow herself to fall out of shape, and she knew he wouldn't either. There was a lot of tennis yet to play.

That night she awakened with a jolt around 2:00 a.m. Sat up in bed, half in a dream, half in the present. She tossed the covers off both of them in the process, and Khol came mildly awake.

"Those sounds again?" he asked, knowing how they had plagued her.

"That's it," she mumbled out, groggy and still unable to think clearly. "That's it exactly."

"They'll go away," he told her. "Just pretend they aren't there. They'll go away."

He didn't understand. She slipped out of bed and left him to fall back to sleep. She crossed to the set of French doors that led to the suite's small balcony, and she cracked open that door, allowing the river's cool air to spill across her and raise the delicate hairs that covered her, a ripple of gooseflesh coursing across her arms and legs.

The rumble of the boat. The swish of the river water sliced by the flat-bottomed hull. The dull beat of music from one of the floating casino's all-night lounges. She strained her ears, listening for the return of that haunting sound of tennis balls in the dead of night. That sound was nowhere to be found. That sound did not exist.

She glanced back at Khol, once again fast asleep. Six luscious months of persona non grata, the only requirement to give a deposition, and at the city of her choosing. She would not be required to testify. Her next public appearance would be on court in a tennis dress, the unbelievable recovery from a stabbing that could have killed her had it not been a bag of theatrical blood purchased by her lover.

She closed the door, suspiciously still listening for that sound that had denied her sleep for the past four years. Only the hum of the boat, and now his gentle snoring.

She stayed up another hour, just to savor those sounds.

LOVE MATCH

LISA SCOTTOLINE

Assistant District Attorney Tom Moran had barely gotten back to the office when the telephone started ringing, and he sprinted down the hall to catch it. His secretary was long gone; it was after business hours, which to her meant 5:01. *Ring!* Tom reached his office, leaned over his desk, and grabbed the phone. "Babe?" he said, breathless, into the receiver.

"Who's this? Moran, that you? Moran! You hear me? Answer me!"

Tom dropped his briefcase in shock. "Sir?" he stammered. It wasn't Marie. It was Bill Masterson himself; the district attorney of Philadelphia, echoing like the Wizard of Oz on a cell phone. At least it sounded like Masterson. Tom had never spoken to his boss and recognized his booming voice only from the TV news. "I hear you perfectly, sir."

"I been calling you all day. Where the hell were you?"

"Calling *me?*" Tom couldn't imagine why Masterson was calling him. Tom had only been two years on the job, one of 125 fungible assistant district attorneys. Why would Masterson be calling *him?* "I was on trial, in an ag assault case. Didn't my secretary—"

"I don't care. You think I care? I said I need you, Moran. Now."

Now? Tom thought, but was smart enough not to say. He checked his watch. 6:15. What was he going to do? He had promised to take Marie out to dinner tonight, a meager payback for her forbearance during the two-week-long Simmons trial. She'd been taking care of the twins by herself, and they had double ear infections. Two three-month-olds; four clogged Eustachian tubes. Tom couldn't cancel dinner. He'd been trying to be a Better Husband.

"Moran? You there?"

"Of course, sir. Yes, sir. Sorry, sir. How can I help you, sir?"

"Not on the phone. Here. Now. You hear me?"

There? Now? It was going from bad to worse. Tom broke a sweat. He had no choice. He'd have to call Marie and tell her he'd be late. Ask her to delay the reservation; beg the sitter to hang around. He wouldn't be too long, maybe ten minutes. None of the assistants got much face time with Masterson. Last week the boss had fired somebody in three minutes. *What?* Tom swallowed hard. Maybe he was getting fired. He was getting fired! And he'd been trying to be a Better District Attorney.

"Moran! I said I need you. Why are you there when I need you here?"

"I'm on my way, sir."

"I said *now!*"

"Gotcha. Sure. Not a problem." Tom rifled through the clutter on his desk, shoving aside phone messages, draft briefs, and photocopied cases, in layers thick as the earth's strata. He needed to clutch something while he got fired, like a security legal pad. In a minute he spotted a yellow one, embedded in the correspondence like a vein of gold, and unearthed it. "Ready to roll, sir. I'll be in your office right away."

"Not in my office!"

"You're coming to *my* office?"

"Don't be ridiculous." Masterson burst into a *ha-ha-ha* that fired like a semiautomatic. "What's the matter with you?"

Tom couldn't think of the right answer. *Nothing? Everything?* "Where am I going, sir?" he asked, and winced at how dumb he sounded.

"Wistar Plateau."

"Wistar Plateau?"

"Don't cross-examine me, Moran."

"No, sir." Tom didn't get it. *Outside?* Wistar Plateau was a bad section of Fairmount Park, which was the huge, forested park that lay along the city limits. Fairmount was allegedly the largest city park in America, and though much of it retained its Victorian grace and gardens, some, like Wistar Plateau, had gone downhill with the neighborhoods surrounding it. There was nothing at Wistar Plateau but an abandoned playground. Why would Masterson fire him there? *No witnesses.*

"You like your job, Moran?"

Oh, oh, here it comes. Tom prayed it was rhetorical. In fact, he had never stopped to think if he liked his job. All he knew was that it paid the bills. *Twin* bills. He needed his job. Wasn't that the same thing? "I love my job, sir. I really love my—"

"You wanna keep it?"

Gulp. "Yes, sir."

"Then get your ass over here! Now!"

"Yes, sir!" Tom exhaled with relief, his thoughts racing ahead. *What was going on?* So Masterson wasn't summoning him to Wistar Plateau to fire him. Then why Wistar Plateau? That part of the park was close to the city, but it wasn't safe there after dark. You could get killed. Then Tom put it together. Maybe there was a case, a new murder case! A body must have been found in the park! And Masterson wanted Tom to handle the case. It could be Tom's big break. Wowee! "I'll be right there, sir! I'll grab a cab."

"No! Moran! The car's downstairs!"

"Car?"

"The squad car. Go!"

Tom's mouth dropped open. They'd sent a squad car for him. The VIP treatment. It must be a *huge* case. And it was *his*. He had been waiting for this. His first murder case. A real dead body! The cops called them stiffs, and Tom made a mental note to say "stiff." He didn't want to sound like a total rookie.

"Moran? You still on the phone? What, you need an invitation? What's the matter? Go! *Now!*"

"I'm going. I'm coming. I'm there." Tom started to put down the phone but Masterson was still talking. The receiver yo-yoed up and down.

"One more thing! Moran!"

"Sir?"

"Don't tell anybody!" he barked, and hung up.

Tom hung up a split second later, tucked the legal pad under his arm, grabbed his briefcase, and sprinted for the door. There was no time to lose. Masterson had sent a car for him! It had to be a "red ball," as the detectives called it, a murder so high-profile the uniforms turned on their sirens. And Masterson had picked him! Tom raced down the empty corridors to the elevator bank and punched the bottom. He was grateful that no one was in; he couldn't hide his excitement. Tom was realistic enough to know that he probably wouldn't get to try the case himself, if it was a red ball, but at least he'd be second chair to Masterson. He was on his way up!

The elevator cab going down arrived, and Tom jumped in and hit the button for the lobby. He tapped his foot as the cab door closed, his mind reeling. Masterson must have heard about Tom's victory today; the boss knew everything that went on in the office. The man was legend: ace prosecutor, mover, shaker, and close personal friend of the mayor, the governor, and Alan Iverson of the Sixers. And Masterson was up for re-election, a shoo-in, and even rumored to be the next pick for the state supreme court. Tom felt a warm rush of goodwill for the man. The two would become fast friends. The elevator doors rattled open.

Tom scooted into the lobby, ran past the startled receptionist, and shoved out the revolving door to the busy sidewalk. It was dark outside, but parked in a pool of light from a streetlamp in front of the building was a brilliant white squad car, waiting for him. *Just like a limo!* Its engine was running and a plume of exhaust billowed in the November chill. Tom flushed with surprise as he threaded his way through the foot traffic to the squad car.

But the second he touched the door handle, the squad car's siren blared suddenly to life. Tom jumped as if he'd been electrocuted, flung open the door, and leaped into the car. People on the street pivoted and stared. A SEPTA bus halted as it pulled away from the curb. Embarrassed, Tom slammed the door behind him. "What's this about?" he shouted to the uniformed cop in the driver's seat.

"Dunno!" the cop yelled back, and hit the gas. "Hold on, I'm under orders."

The squad car rocketed forward, its siren screaming, and Tom grabbed the cage divider to avoid whiplash. Rush hour traffic parted instantly, a tangle of red brake lights and chalky exhaust. Everyone made way. Tom's embarrassment ebbed, replaced by elation. He was rushing to the scene of the crime. It was such a charge, he was almost high. Then he remembered.

Marie.

Tom felt a stab of guilt. He had to call her. The squad car screamed around the curve of Logan Circle, and he leaned over to reach the Star-Tac attached to his belt. Maybe he wouldn't be that long at the crime scene. Even with a red ball, there wouldn't be all that much to do the night of the murder, right? Meet with the detectives. Take some notes. Supervise the techs. The medical examiner would wait until morning for the autopsy, wouldn't he? It was hard to think, over the blare of the siren and the crackle of the police radio. The police dispatcher didn't mention Wistar Plateau at all; Masterson must have been keeping it hush-hush. Very smart of the boss. What a guy!

The squad car sped to West River Drive, tearing past the art museum. Traffic parted like the Red Sea. It saved a lot of time. Tom could still make dinner, just a little late. He figured he would finish at 7:15, maybe 7:30. Then he'd be a Better Husband *and* a Better District Attorney! Tom flipped open his cell phone and punched number one on the speed dial. WIFEY flashed onto the phone's tiny lighted screen, then CALLING, but Tom couldn't hear if Marie had picked up because of the siren and the radio.

"Babe? You there? Can you hear me?" Tom yelled into the phone, as the huge oak trees that lined the West River Drive whizzed by. Their leaves had all but fallen and those scattered on the West River Drive flew in the wake of the squad car, like

the Batmobile. Traffic fled to the curb, parting for the speeding superheroes. They were entering the park. Five minutes
from Wistar Plateau. Beyond it was gang turf; so many gangs
Tom couldn't keep track of the color codes. And he still
couldn't hear a damn thing on the cell phone. "Marie? Marie?"

The uniformed cop caught Tom's eye in the rearview. "Tell
her I said hi!" he hollered.

Tom decided to settle for one-way communication. In the
circumstances, maybe it was a blessing. He shouted into the
phone, "Marie? I'll be late, but I'll be there! Masterson needs
me! It's a red ball! A stiff in the park! A gang thing! I'll call
when I can! Love you!" Tom pushed the END button to hang
up, but sensed uneasily that Marie had pushed the END button
first.

Ten minutes later, the squad car was streaking to the highest point of Wistar Plateau, and Tom couldn't help but gasp.
He had never seen so many squad cars in his life. There had to
be fifteen of them, all lined up in a row, their white paint and
gold stripes standing out in the dark. Who the hell had gotten
killed? A drug kingpin? An entire cartel? The cruiser sped to
the end of the squad car line, rumbled onto the grass, and skidded to a stop.

Two uniformed cops came running in the dark toward the
car, and Tom had barely opened the door when they wrenched
him out and hurried him beyond the line of squad cars and up
a hill strewn with old newspapers and litter. It was too dark to
see anything but the line of squad cars, whose headlights
shone against a battered cyclone fence. Tom hurried ahead,
crack vials crunching under his wingtips.

"Where's the stiff?" Tom asked, as gruffly as he could, as
the cops huffed and puffed up the hill.

"Masterson's this way."

Tom figured they'd misheard him, although Masterson *was* a little on the stiff side. When he and Tom got to be friends, Tom might let him know as much. It would help his relationships with the uniformed personnel. Everybody needs a sounding board. Even the boss.

The cops hustled him onto a plateau and in the dark he could see that the cyclone fence, broken and bent, had been intended to enclose an urban tennis court. The cops must have found the body—*the stiff*—on the tennis court. The lights from the line of squad cars illuminated the court, and Masterson stood at the middle line, behind the dilapidated wire net. "There he is," said one of the uniforms, propelling Tom alone onto the concrete court.

"Thanks." Tom walked onto the court, then froze at the roar of a zillion car engines, igniting all at the same moment. Suddenly headlights blinked to brightness, almost blinding him on all sides. *What gives?* Tom shielded his eyes instinctively and squinted around in bewilderment. There weren't only fifteen squad cars, there were at least fifty, and they surrounded the tennis court on four sides. All ran their huge engines, and their headlights blasted pools of light on the tennis court's pitted surface. Tom blinked at the large silhouette of Bill Masterson, in a dark topcoat at the net. Was this standard procedure?

"Moran! Get over here!" Masterson barked.

Tom obeyed, advancing with trepidation. Masterson stood six foot four, maybe 220 pounds, an immense and still-fit figure. His ruddy face, with its big, coarse features, had gone red in the cold. His steely hair flew in the brisk wind, and his wiry eyebrows swooped upward. His silhouette was framed by exhaust from the fleet of squad cars, billowing like smoke and hellfire. Masterson had morphed from the Wizard of Oz to Satan himself, and Tom felt an unaccountable tingle of fear. Something strange was going on. "Sir?"

"You Moran?" Masterson fixed Tom with a fierce blue-eyed gaze. His large mouth formed a grim line.

"Uh, yes."

"You play tennis."

Tom didn't get it. Was it more police lingo? It could be so confusing. Once Tom had called a detective a dick and gotten hit for it. He decided to answer his boss's question, straight up. "Yes, I play tennis," he said slowly.

"You have to think about it? You said you did. You play or not? Do you? Or was it bullshit?"

"No. I mean, yes. I play tennis," Tom answered, as quickly as possible. Still he didn't know what Masterson was talking about. He hadn't told his boss he played tennis. He'd never even spoken to the man. It was time to get to the bottom of this. "I never said I played—"

"You said you used to teach it," Masterson fired back. "On your résumé. My girl found it in personnel. Or was that crap? Like that altar boy shit?"

"No, it wasn't crap. I taught tennis, at a camp, for three summers in a row. I didn't lie on my résumé."

"I'm no altar boy. I did. I said I like classical music but I hate it. Who the hell likes classical music?"

Tom did, but he knew enough not to say so. "I really was an altar boy, too," he added, instead.

"I can tell by lookin' at you. That's why I trust you with this." Suddenly Masterson reached under his topcoat and emerged with a large metal object. Tom glimpsed its aluminum gleam in the headlights from the squad cars. A rifle! The murder weapon? Tom looked again. It was a tennis racquet, a graphite HEAD. A white price tag fluttered from its handle. Masterson thrust the racquet at Tom's stomach. "Teach me, altar boy," he ordered.

Tom took the racquet in confusion. "What about the murder? Shouldn't we investigate?"

"What murder?" Masterson was withdrawing another racquet from his topcoat, a matching HEAD with a price tag that he ripped off. "Steinmetz?" he called out, turning toward the darkness at the court entrance. "Gimme the balls, Steinmetz! Shit, it's too dark. Steinmetz, it's dark! I don't have time for this! Turn on the effin' lights!"

Suddenly, the squad cars switched on their high beams as one, lighting up the tennis court like an operating room. Tom reeled in the brightness until his eyes adjusted, and he took in the ratty wire net, the pitted court surface, and the peeling white baselines. A uniform cop was scurrying over, and he handed Masterson a clear plastic container of fluorescent green tennis balls, then hurried to the end of the net, where he crouched like a ball boy. Another uniform ran onto the court and squatted at the other side of the net. Tom couldn't believe his eyes. It was Wimbledon, with municipal employees.

Masterson yanked the pull-top lid off the tennis ball container, and Tom heard the familiar *pfft* as the vacuum seal was broken. He even remembered the rubbery smell. He had always loved tennis. But was he really called here to play it? With his boss? "I don't understand," Tom blurted out, but Masterson tossed him a tennis ball.

"What's not to understand? The governor's having a tennis party. Round robin, buncha crap. I told him I play but I don't. I gotta learn. I gotta play like a pro. You gotta teach me."

"In one night?"

"Of course not."

"Thank God." Tom sighed with relief.

"In one hour."

"*What?*"

"The party's at eight, Moran. At an indoor tennis pavilion, whatever that is. This is the closest court I could find. Nobody uses it." Masterson's eyes bored into Tom's, blazing even brighter than the high beams. "And you tell nobody about this, understand, Moran? You breathe a word, *one single word,* and I fire you. You're *fired!* On the spot. Understand?"

Tom shuddered. "Understood."

"If I hear back about tonight in any way at all, even ten years from now, if it comes back to me, you're fired. I'll hunt you down like the dog you are and fire you dead. Got it?"

"Got it." Then Tom remembered. The police radio hadn't mentioned Wistar Plateau at all, probably to prevent the press from picking it up on the scanners. Masterson had gone to great lengths to keep this secret, for obvious reasons. If it got out, the boss could lose the election *and* his friendship with Iverson.

"You keep your mouth shut. Don't tell anybody. All these cops, they owe me. And they all swore to secrecy." Masterson paused. "You married, right? It said on the résumé you were married."

"Yes."

"Don't tell her. Kids?"

"Twins."

"Don't tell them. Kids yap at 'show and tell.' I know. Mine did. Only they call it 'circle time' now. Mine gave away the friggin' store, every Wednesday morning. I never did that. I was a good kid. I kept my trap shut."

"My kids are three months old—"

"Don't tell them, Moran!" Masterson shouted. "Don't make me ruin you! Don't make me. Don't make me leave your family in the lurch. You want your wife to go begging? Your kids? Do you know how many important people I know in this town?"

Tom nodded. *Enough to stage a taxpayer-funded tennis lesson?* "I won't say anything, I swear."

"It's my ass if the press finds out. This is just the kind of nitpicky shit they love." Masterson held up the tennis racquet. "Now how do I hold this thing?"

Tom looked around. Was this really happening? Heat simmered from the high beams, warming the court. The police ball boys crouched in readiness at the net, their handcuffs swinging in the breeze. If Tom was teaching tennis for only one hour, at least he could make dinner with Marie. *Oh, what the hell.* He took his racquet and wrapped his fingers around the leather grip, still covered with cellophane. He hadn't taught in years, but it was coming back to him. "Shake hands with the racquet, Mr. Masterson."

"You don't have to call me Mr. Masterson," he said as he gripped his racquet. "Call me Chief."

"Okay, Chief."

"How's zat?" Masterson brandished his racquet like a happy schoolkid, and Tom couldn't help but smile.

"Nice grip, Chief. Let's hit a few."

"Great! Great!" Masterson said, elated. "Whaddo I do?"

So Tom sent his boss down to the baseline to practice a few swings, *Keep your racquet face perpendicular to the ground, don't break your wrist,* and in no time Masterson was returning a few shots. The Chief did surprisingly well, hustling to meet the ball on the first bounce, his black topcoat and tie flying behind him, silhouetted in the squad car headlights. The ball cops scrambled constantly, since Tom had only three balls to work with instead of the usual basketful, and the Chief kept hitting them out of the crummy court, which required an assist from the entire Third District. Other than that, Tom began having fun.

Suddenly one of the police sirens screamed to life, and a uniformed cop from the Fifth sprinted onto the court, waving his arms. "Chief, it's Action News! Hartwell picked up the newsvan on the Drive!"

Masterson blanched, as Tom's volley whizzed past him. "Ticket him, for Christ's sake! He hadda be speeding! They speed all the time! They're Action effin' News!"

"He did that already, that's how he knows. Somehow they found out what's going on up here. They're on the way! They got cameramen!"

Tom halted, stricken, at the net. *Oh, no.* The press was on the way. They'd find out. It would be all over the papers. The TV. What would Masterson do? How would it make him look? And what would happen to Tom? Would he lose his job? *No!* Tom heard his tennis racquet clatter to the ground.

"Moran! Let's go!" Masterson shouted, dropping his racquet, and they both sprinted for the court exit, which was when all hell broke loose. Steinmetz and the other ball police sprinted for their cars. All of the squad cars around the court were reversing out of line and taking off. It was every municipal employee for himself. Masterson and Tom reached the cyclone fence, panting raggedly.

"Chief, they're leaving!" Tom said, panicky. "Can they leave?"

"They're outta district. They don't want to get caught."

Tom looked at his boss in dismay. "But where are your people? Don't you have people?"

"They're at the governor's party, stalling for me." Masterson squinted over his shoulder in the darkness, and Tom followed his gaze. Wistar Plateau was an exodus of squad cars. At the bottom of the hill, Tom could see a bright white newsvan, and on top was a tall microwave transmitter. The newsvan! It was blocked by the squad cars, but after a minute, it bounded onto the grass and headed straight for the tennis court.

"They got us!" Tom said, hearing the fear in his voice.

"Screw 'em! We'll make a run for it!" Masterson shot back, and took off into the darkness. The district attorney's topcoat flew behind him like Superman's cape.

"Run for it?" Tom said, running after Masterson in disbelief He couldn't believe this was happening. Was he really running for it? *"Run for it, Chief? Is that the plan? Is that the best we can do for a plan?"*

"You got another idea?" Masterson snorted, as he puffed ahead. They left the gravel path, Tom sprinting right behind his boss, and plunged into the woods of the park, where Tom felt a craziness rising in his chest.

"I sure do, Chief." Tom's breath came in ragged bursts. "How about *run faster?*"

He started laughing, and the Chief laughed, too, but it vanished when they picked up the pace over a rocky ridge. It grew pitch black as the woods filled in, and the lawyers ran downhill, powered by momentum and fear. As they ran they raised their arms to shield their faces from the low branches. Their wingtips churned through the underbrush. Behind them came the slamming of the van's doors, *one, two, three, four.*

"Uh-oh," Tom said as he ran, and Masterson put on the afterburners impressively. Tom remembered the boss had played Big Five ball. Maybe they really could run away. He felt suddenly free. "We're movin', Chief!"

"DISTRICT ATTORNEY MASTERSON!" boomed a megaphone behind the lawyers. "ARE YOU THERE? WE KNOW YOU'RE THERE!"

"Holy shit!" Tom said, but Masterson only chuckled. "Must be the big game!"

"DISTRICT ATTORNEY MASTERSON!" Another flashlight came on, then a third. "WE KNOW YOU'RE HERE! HAVING A *TENNIS LESSON!*"

Tom glanced over his shoulder as he ran. A circle of flashlight jitterbugged through the bare branches, casting around for the lawyers. "Chief, they're right behind us!"

"Moran! Keep up!" Masterson tore down the slope, his breath labored. "Those pansy-asses haven't got a chance! I'm a *city boy!* I *necked* on Wistar Plateau! I know this park like the back of *my effin' hand!*" Masterson leaped into the air, expertly hurdling a fallen log, but Tom didn't see it in the dark.

"Oh, no!" Tom wailed. He tripped on the obstacle, lost his balance, and flew face first onto the wooded path, hitting the ground with his chest. His nose landed in a pile of scratchy leaves. His ankle felt sprained. *No!* "My ankle! Shit!"

"Moran?" Masterson stopped on the path and came rushing though the underbrush back up the hill. "You okay? Moran!"

"My ankle is killing me! You'd better go ahead! I'll slow you up!"

"No! Get up, Moran!" Masterson commanded. He grabbed

Tom by his shoulders and tried to drag him to his feet, but Tom's ankle throbbed.

"Go, Chief! They'll hang you!" Tom felt in the darkness to see if his ankle was broken. He reached the log and his hand fell on something soft, like cloth. It wasn't rough like wood, and Tom bent over, squinting in the darkness. He blinked twice. It wasn't a fallen log on the path. *Jesus, Mary, and Joseph!* Tom found himself eye level with the wide-open eyes of another man.

"DISTRICT ATTORNEY MASTERSON!" boomed the reporter, the sound closer. The megaphone and the flashlights hurried down the ravine. "GIVE IT UP! WE KNOW ALL ABOUT IT! IT'S OVER!"

"Get up, Moran!" Masterson pulled at Tom. "What's the matter with you?"

Tom's breath remained lodged in his throat. He was too horrified to speak. The whites of the man's eyes bugged out and they stared at Tom in the darkness. Unmoving, as if they were dead. Were they, dead? Dead! "Chief!" Tom squeaked. "Chief!"

"MASTERSON!" Suddenly a set of TV klieg lights came on, whisking the woods with hot white light, searching for the lawyers. "ALL WE WANT IS A COMMENT! WHAT DO YOU SAY TO THE VOTERS ABOUT THIS FLAGRANT ABUSE OF POWER?"

"Moran, let's go!" Masterson said, finally yanking him upright, but Tom's knees had gone weak from shock. Between Jell-O knees and a swollen ankle, he almost fell down again.

"Chief, it's a . . . a . . . *stiff!*" Tom blurted out. He couldn't wrap his mind around it. He had never seen a freshly dead body before. "Right here!"

Masterson yanked again. "What's a stiff?"

"A dead body!" Tom whispered, horrified. He could see the corpse clearly now. The man, a large man, was dressed in a heavy coat. A hunting knife protruded from his chest. His pallor was chalk. "It's a dead man! Right here! In the woods! I tripped over the body!"

"A body?" Masterson grabbed Tom's shoulders. "Did you say, a *body?*"

"Yes. A *murdered* body."

"You're shittin' me!" Masterson said, and leaned over. Tom couldn't place the sudden note of glee in his boss's voice, but he almost fainted as Masterson straightened up and slapped him five. "All right!"

"MR. DISTRICT ATTORNEY!" the megaphone blared. Suddenly the TV klieg light found Bill Masterson and the body with its spotlight, and Tom watched in amazement as the scene unfolded before him.

Masterson stood protectively over the corpse, raising his arms. "No cameras!" he boomed, almost as loud as the megaphone.

"OH, MY GOD!" The reporter was a stunned shadow in front of the klieg light. He lowered the megaphone. "Is there a *body* there?"

"Of course! What do you think we're doing here?" Masterson scowled for effect. "I said, no cameras! Next of kin haven't been notified! I don't permit cameras on a murder victim before next of kin have been notified! And *kill those lights!*"

The TV lights went suddenly black. But not so black that Tom couldn't see his boss's smile. Tom felt a mixture of admiration and revulsion for the man. He whistled softly. "Jeez, Chief."

"Lemme do the talking, altar boy," Masterson said, with a chuckle that vanished as soon as the reporter approached.

• • •

Tom and Marie sat at the best table in the main dining room, before a roaring fire that wasn't even gas-powered. Fresh white roses adorned each covered table, and the rack of lamb had been pink and perfectly juicy at the center. When the coffee arrived after dinner, it was just hot enough, and Tom had tasted crème brûlée for the first and last time in his life. His dessert loyalties would stay with apple pie and vanilla ice cream, but this restaurant didn't offer that. It was a classy restaurant. Much classier than Tom could have afforded before he tripped over a dead body.

He poured Marie another glass of champagne, from a chilled bottle that stood in one of those freestanding ice buckets beside the table, then rewrapped the bottle in its thick cotton napkin and returned it with a flourish. "Pretty good for a kid from East Falls, huh?"

"Very good."

They were celebrating. Tom had been only an hour late to dinner. He'd bribed the sitter to stay. He'd upgraded the restaurant. Plus he'd been assigned to try the body-in-the-park case by himself, and a promotion to the Homicide Unit was automatic. Even his ankle felt better. Life could be good, when death intervened. Tom watched as Marie's pretty face disappeared behind her champagne flute, then reappeared when she set it. down. "Happy?" he asked.

"Extremely," Marie purred. "You?"

"Absolutely."

"Champagne is fun."

"So are you." Marie was smiling at Tom. She hadn't stopped smiling at him all night. She had balanced his dinner conversation of defensive wounds and fingernail scrapings with chatter of stuffy noses and baby droppers, and somewhere inside it struck Tom that he needed his wife more certainly than he needed oxygen.

"I love you," he told her, when the thickness in his throat went away.

"I love you, too, and I'm very, very proud of you. I think it's wonderful that Masterson picked you for this new case. I told you he'd see, in time, how great a prosecutor you were."

"Oh, I don't know." Tom managed a modest smile. He didn't feel great about lying to Marie. He hadn't lied to her before, except once when she was nine months pregnant and had asked him if she looked fat. She'd been bigger than a courthouse, but of course he wasn't going to say so.

Tom was an altar boy, but he wasn't crazy.

A Peach of a Shot

Daniel Stashower

They have to turn back after two blocks because Jane has forgotten to hit the switch for the dog door. This has happened twice in the past three weeks. Franklin wants to keep going. "So he does his business on the linoleum," he says. "It's not the end of the world." In the end she wears him down, as she always does, and he turns the car around.

He stands in the kitchen doorway with his arms folded. "Why do we need a dog door that has to be turned on and off, anyway? They don't even have the simple decency to call it a dog door. A 'canine entry system,' if you please. Jesus. Like he needs a retinal scan or something to do his business in the yard."

Franklin starts jingling his car keys while Jane freshens the water bowl and arranges the chew toys in a half-circle. "Is sweetums gonna miss Mommy?" she wants to know, straightening the dog's collar. "Is sweetums gonna miss his mommy-kins?"

"Enough," Franklin says, tapping the crystal of his watch. "You treat that mutt as if—"

Her look freezes him. He lets his hands drop. "I just meant that you treat him better than me. Can we get moving, please? Jarrett said eleven."

Jane takes her leave of the dog and they climb back into the Taurus. Franklin drives hunched forward, with grim purpose. "Remember what I told you," he says.

"The divorce isn't final. I know. I'm not supposed to ask questions about the cupcake."

"Kaylie. She's a nice girl. Smart."

"I'm sure she is. I have no doubt. In fact, that's just what Alice was saying on the phone the other night, you know, when she finished crying her eyes out. Everything's fine, she said. It's twenty-three years of my life down the tubes, but it's all right because the cupcake is a very nice girl."

Franklin's hands tighten on the wheel. "Please. These memberships don't come up every day. You know how often these memberships come up? Never. This is a one-in-a-million chance. A real dipsy-doodle, Jarrett says."

"No kidding? A dipsy-doodle? That's so vivid! He's partner material for sure!"

He doesn't answer, and neither of them speaks again until they reach the front gates. Franklin, still trying to make up time, takes the first speed bump too fast. He hears something smack on the undercarriage and curses under his breath. Jane's hands go out to brace herself against the dashboard. "Take it easy," she says. "We wouldn't be late in the first place if you hadn't spent all morning in the bathroom. With that goop."

He sets his jaw and guides the car over a second bump.

"I don't know why you use that stuff, anyway. You're not fooling anyone."

"It's called making a strong first impression. Putting my best foot forward."

"What first impression? You see Jarrett every day. The cupcake, too, for that matter."

He is trying to be reasonable. "Look, this is like an audition. A test drive, if you will. There are certain to be other members hanging around. Jarrett will introduce us. At the next membership council they'll talk about us. About our suitability."

"That Franklin Walbert seems to be a decent fellow. If only his temples weren't so gray."

His eyes go to the rearview mirror. "It projects a sense of strength and vigor. They want fresh blood." He glances at her as he swings the Taurus into an empty spot. She is wearing her hair in schoolgirl braids, with bows of red yarn. She asked him once, years ago, if the style was too young on her.

"Just don't mention the situation," he says, flipping the door locks. "About the divorce. Let sleeping dogs lie."

"All *right*," she says. "You've only told me about fifty times."

Franklin pops the trunk and grabs the racquet bags. He turns and heads for the reception doors in a rolling, forward-canted walk, as if moving across the deck of a wind-blasted ship. Jane has to trot to keep up. "Hey," she calls after him. "Slow down. You're killing me with all the strength and vigor."

Jarrett and Kaylie are waiting in the lobby. Kaylie is seated on a lime-colored banquette with her legs crossed, tugging at a white ankle sock. Jarrett is leaning against the far wall, which is papered in a dark tartan meant to suggest Turnberry or St. Andrew's. Jarrett's eyes dart to the clock over the door. The clock's face shows a whimsical sketch of a drunken swell in a top hat

and monocle, tripping over a sign that reads "Tee Many Mar-
toonies."

"Sorry," Franklin says, shifting the tennis bags to extend his
hand. "A thousand pardons." He rolls his eyes at Jane, following several paces behind. "Had to check on the dog. I've told
her a million times—"

"No problem," Jarrett answers, with a note of forced ge-
niality. "We'd better get right onto the court, though. They
won't hold it for us. Club rules."

"Right," Franklin says. "Of course." He nods at Kaylie. She
is cool, slim and elegant in a sleeveless knit dress with navy accents. Her bare arms are tan from a beach holiday. She smells
of coconut. Franklin introduces Jane with a detached, apolo-
getic air, as though she is a last-minute replacement for someone more suitable.

"So nice that you could join us," Kaylie says, as Jarrett leads
the way out onto the court. "I hope you'll have time for a drink
afterward. They have one called a Tanqueray Topspin. You really must try it."

"I have tried it," Jane says. "Many times."

"Have you? But I thought you weren't—"

"With Alice."

Franklin, walking behind with the bags, narrows his eyes
and presses his lips together, the equivalent of a swift kick
under the table.

"Oh," Kaylie says carelessly, "then you know all about it."

They are less than ten minutes late getting onto the court,
but the delay gives a sense of hurry to the first few minutes of
play. Jarrett suggests that they skip the warmup volley, though
Franklin can tell that he's already loosened up at the practice
wall.

Franklin and Jane drop the first two games without scoring a point. Kaylie is quick at the net and has a long reach; Jarrett has a solid forehand but not much else. Her speed complements his power, but there is a curious formality in their play. They are at pains not to run into each other.

As the set progresses, Franklin and Jane begin to pick up their game. Franklin is a strong player, and made varsity in college. He hasn't played much since, but he can still send a thunderbolt up the line when he gets his feet planted. Jane is sluggish and heavy-footed; she doesn't address the ball so much as deflect it, as though trying to swat away a bothersome insect.

Franklin doesn't mind losing, but he doesn't want to look bad doing it. He begins coaching Jane from the baseline, in a voice loud enough for the others to hear. He wants to sound cheery and supportive, to show what a good sport he is, even when saddled with an inferior partner. He keeps telling Jane to cover her clay. "Watch it, honey," he says. "Don't forget to cover your clay." He has an idea of how people are supposed to talk at a tennis club, and it seems to involve the use of phrases cribbed from Wimbledon announcers of the Rod Laver era. "Bravo!" he cries at one stage, as Jarrett sends a winner across the forecourt. "Peach of a shot!"

"Why are you talking like that?" Jane asks him, as they switch sides after the first set. Franklin and Jane have taken only one game, and her composure is fraying.

"Like what?" he asks, wiping the handle of his racquet. He is watching Kaylie as she takes a long swallow of some bottled iced tea drink with a dancing elf on the label. Tangerine-Raspberry Glee.

"Like what?" he asks again.

"Oh, I say, chaps! Spot of bother with Jerry over Saulier. The Archies are pounding the hell out of the air."

"That's not what I sound like," he says, but he keeps quiet through the next three games.

By the fourth game Franklin has found his serve and it keeps the set competitive. It pleases him to feel the ball thundering off his racquet, and he takes a secret pleasure in watching Jarrett flailing after an ace, wrong-footed and off-balance. He imagines that Kaylie will see him in a whole new light. Perhaps she will talk about it at the office. "You should see this guy on the court. He's got a cannon in that arm!"

The set is tied at three games when Franklin begins crowding Jane at the net. He keeps riding her heels, reaching around to stab at the drop shots. "Stay back," she says, after their racquets tangle on a return. "You're all over me."

"Sorry," he says, in his carrying voice. "Try to cover your clay."

"If you say that one more time, I will kill you," she says. "I swear to God."

Jarrett and Kaylie take the second set, and the game turns in the third. Franklin's arm is tired and Jane has grown timid and fretful after catching a ball on the shoulder. Jarrett is impatient to finish. He says something about clearing the court for fresh players. Earlier he had been taking something off the balls he hit to Jane, now he smacks them straight up the gut. She can do little more than get out of the way.

They're down a break when Jarrett sends a two-handed smash up the middle. Jane can't move in time. The ball catches her on the side of the head, right at the jawline below her ear. Her racquet clatters to the ground and her hands fly to her face. Kaylie is around the net in a heartbeat; Jarrett runs off the court for a towel and some ice. Two players from the next court run over to see if she's all right. Jane is embarrassed by the fuss. She works her jaw muscle and says she's fine. She was just startled, is all.

Franklin has been strangely quiet during all of this. He doesn't know quite what to do or say, and he recognizes that Jarrett's remorse over the incident has given him an edge. Now, as Jane smiles and declares herself fit to play, he gathers himself to be magnanimous. "Don't worry about it," he says to Jarrett. "These things will happen." Turning to Jane, he says, "Next time, cover your clay."

She picks up her racquet and slams it against his head with every ounce of strength she can muster. It is a peach of a shot. A real dipsy-doodle. Franklin is dimly aware of the red clay rushing toward him, of the voices raised in alarm, of the expression of mute horror on his wife's face. He perceives these things as if from the window of a passing car.

For the first time in many years, he feels as if he has all the time in the world. His mind is lit up from within, calling forth moods and mementos long since lost to the clutter of shopping lists and spreadsheets and canine entry systems. He sees his mother in a long calico dress, glancing backward over her shoulder as she reaches to hang a piñata. He hears his father's steps heavy on the wooden porch, indignant over the discovery of a broken taillight. He tastes the coppery bite of a new retainer as he presses his lips against those of his seventh-grade girlfriend, huddled behind the splicing table in the audio-visual room. He fingers the three dollars in his pocket as he stands outside the house, waiting for a ride to the hobby shop. He feels his grandfather squeeze his hand goodbye that last time.

His thoughts take a bad bounce and he finds himself at the beginning of that terrible year. He sees it all—the doctor moving slowly toward him along the corridor, the grim face, the shake of the head, the pink balloon slipping from his fingers and floating lazily to the ceiling. He recognizes this for what it is, the moment when the game turned. He swats it aside. No point in arguing a bad call.

Franklin's head strikes the ground and there is now a great deal of blood coming from somewhere. He is aware of this but it does not interest him much. For him, it is a winter day in Columbus. He is in his dorm room, sophomore year. There is a poster over his head, Picasso's Don Quixote, and the gooseneck lamp on his desk has a large jagged chip in the plastic shade. He has just walked Jane back from the library, but she is already on the phone, telling him that she misses him.

There is a Browns game on. Nick Skorich's last year and Brian Sipe's first. Franklin is trying to listen through an earpiece without letting Jane know that he is listening. "What did you say?" he asks.

"I'm just saying that it's going to be great. Thanksgiving."

"Of course it'll be great. Why wouldn't it be?"

"Oh, you know. You meeting my parents. That whole *parent* thing. But it'll be good. Great. I have no clams whatever."

Franklin reaches for the transistor and spins down the volume. "What?"

"I said I have no qualms about it. You and my father will get along great."

"That's not what you said. You said clams. You said you have no clams whatever."

"I did not."

"Yes, you did. Clams."

She giggles. "I didn't."

"You did. You said you have no clams whatever." He swings his feet onto the desk. "Why don't you have any clams? This worries me, I have to admit. What if I want clams? Will we be able to get them if we need them for some reason?"

Jane is laughing now. "Stop it. That's not what I said, I said qualms."

"Have it your way. I'll just qualm up."

Phipps hands off to Pruitt and Pruitt fumbles, but Franklin does not care. A beautiful girl is on the other end of the phone laughing at his wry manner and telling him that she misses him. If he were to press the phone closer to his ear, he would hear a certain strident tremolo in her voice that might alarm him, but he is not listening for that now. He adjusts his earpiece and turns the radio back up.

He has no clams whatever.

CPSIA information can be obtained
at www.ICGtesting.com
Printed in the USA
LVOW07s2240190817
545632LV00001B/85/P